T0311983

AN UNTOLD TALE

There is something about me, ain't there? You noticed the moment your eyes grew used to the dingy light of the tavern. And you came here, like everyone who struts these worn boards, for tattle of Anne Bonny and pirates. Buy me a dram, tread closer, and my tale will make your eyeballs roll. Do you remember that scoundrel Calico Jack? Well it all started way way way before his day. But what may surprise you is that I myself roved among them—the unsung miscreant—the one that slipped through their net. I see you are tongue-tied and burning to ask how we lived like sows? Rutted like pigs? Killed like boars? I'll explain, good as I can, but you won't like my answers, I'm telling you now, mister. There's no glamour . . . no quest . . . no founding of colonies . . . just the tugging of the moon against fate. Who am I, you finally think to ask. You may as well know—I was Blackbeard's thirteenth wife—and very unlucky for him.

FIRE ON DARK WATER

WENDY K. PERRIMAN

BERKLEY BOOKS, NEW YORK

THE BERKLEY PUBLISHING GROUP
Published by the Penguin Group
Penguin Group (USA) Inc.
375 Hudson Street, New York, New York 10014, USA
Penguin Group (Canada), 90 Eglinton Avenue East, Suite 700, Toronto, Ontario M4P 2Y3, Canada
(a division of Pearson Penguin Canada Inc.)
Penguin Books Ltd., 80 Strand, London WC2R 0RL, England
Penguin Group Ireland, 25 St. Stephen's Green, Dublin 2, Ireland (a division of Penguin Books Ltd.)
Penguin Group (Australia), 250 Camberwell Road, Camberwell, Victoria 3124, Australia
(a division of Pearson Australia Group Pty. Ltd.)
Penguin Books India Pvt. Ltd., 11 Community Centre, Panchsheel Park, New Delhi—110 017, India
Penguin Group (NZ), 67 Apollo Drive, Rosedale, Auckland 0632, New Zealand
(a division of Pearson New Zealand Ltd.)
Penguin Books (South Africa) (Pty.) Ltd., 24 Sturdee Avenue, Rosebank, Johannesburg 2196,
South Africa

Penguin Books Ltd., Registered Offices: 80 Strand, London WC2R 0RL, England

This is an original publication of The Berkley Publishing Group.

PRINTING HISTORY
Berkley trade paperback edition / June 2011

Library of Congress Cataloging-in-Publication Data

Perriman, Wendy K.
   Fire on dark water / Wendy K. Perriman.
      p. cm.
   ISBN 978-0-425-24104-2 (pbk.)
   1. Romanies—Fiction.   2. Teach, Edward, d. 1718—Fiction.   3. Pirates—Caribbean
Area—Fiction.   4. Queen Anne's Revenge (Sailing vessel)—Fiction.   5. Domestic
fiction.   I. Title.
   PS3616.E78F57   2011
   813'.6—dc22

                                                                        2010054243

147204767

For Steve
near and far—always and ever

What fates impose, that men must needs abide;
It boots not to resist both wind and tide.

WILLIAM SHAKESPEARE

January 5, 1719

The severed head bobbed afore the mast of the pirate sloop like a grisly lantern exactly as rumor predicted. But the black eyes now only flickered intermittently when glazed by shafts of sunlight, and the septic snarl was set against further cursing. The trophy——tied by its long gory mane to the bowsprit——twisted on air like licking vipers, conjuring life where it had long since ceased to writhe. Shock had frozen the face in a roar of defiance, and confusion lay trapped in the hazy whites of his eyes. A swollen tongue protruded from the black matted beard while the nose, still screwed up for battle, lay lost in the purpling wax of decaying flesh. The decapitated prize twirled ceremoniously in proof——a public deterrent for fellow buccaneers to witness.

*When the townsfolk of Hampton heard the news, they swarmed to the north shore of the river like a flush of vengeful ducks, huffing and squawking to waddle ahead of the press, anxious for confirmation and to claim their brag in history. Is it him? I ran too——eager to know if the law had finally vanquished the Terror of the Seas. I jostled my way toward the front of the mob, and the impact of that spinning skull knotted the breath in the base of my throat. I could scarcely believe in the prize hung before me——*The infamous Blackbeard is dead!

Now, I know some folks may contend that I am far too enamored of these sea villains, having recently completed an account of The Life and Strange Surprising Adventures of Robinson Crusoe. *But the moment I gazed at the dead captain's eye pits I felt a compelling urge to begin a new book, although* possibly under some pseudonym this time. I have a notion to write a general history of the most notorious pirates, so that their brave and terrible deeds may not fade unrecorded—an idea that came to me as I scanned the crowd surrounding Governor Spotswood and noticed him conferring with some common gypsy wench.

Thinking it strange that the most esteemed gentleman in the colony would be holding court with such a lowly creature, I immediately inquired of a bystander as to who this young slattern might be. I judged she was not yet of age, but even under the youth and grime I could tell she was some gamy thing—all lithe legs and wide, moist eyes. Well, consider my surprise when someone whispered she was Blackbeard's doxy. And then imagine my utter disbelief when I learned that she was the one who had betrayed him!

It is my deepest desire to interview this trollop—for whom better to give me an insight into the outlaw's secret kingdom? But as soon as she had identified the dangling head, she scurried into the crowd and was lost to sight. I have just heard rumor that she may be headed for one of the Carribee islands—which is where I will begin my search as soon as I have the resources. Whatever it takes, I must find this wench. For I believe that my entire future enterprise depends upon it. . . .

Daniel Defoe

1

MURK SUNSET AND FOUL SUNRISE

1702–1712

There is something about me, ain't there? You noticed the moment your eyes grew used to the dingy light of the tavern. And you came here, like everyone who struts these worn boards, for tattle of Anne Bonny and pirates. Buy me a dram, tread closer, and my tale will make your eyeballs roll. Do you remember that scoundrel Calico Jack? Well it all started way way way before his day. But what may surprise you is that I myself roved among them—the unsung miscreant—the one that slipped through their net. I see you are tongue-tied and burning to ask how we lived like sows? Rutted like pigs? Killed like boars? I'll explain, good as I can, but you won't like my answers, I'm telling you now, mister. There's no glamour . . . no quest . . . no founding of colonies . . . just the tugging of the moon against fate. Who am I, you finally think to ask. You may as well know—I was Blackbeard's thirteenth wife—and very unlucky for him.

Folks call me *Lola ... London Lola ... The Gypsy ...* or just plain *Doxy*. It depends on who they are and what they're after. I once claimed to be Cockney but that was to clothe my Romany roots—I wasn't born nowhere near Bow Bells. So, aye, I'm a gypsy and come from a long strand of travelers. Our lives were spent in tents or on carts, roaming round England from crop to new harvest. The men reaped grain when autumn permitted while youngsters picked fruit in the orchards and fields. My uncles sold horses (acquired by dubious means) and kept the cauldron stewing with fresh-poached game. I learnt many neat skills as I tagged along beside the woods and rivers. When the picking season ended, the caravan rested on Battersea Common and the perpetual battle ensued once again against harsh, icy winter and the even colder townsfolk.

Grandma Vadoma was the knowing one. She told fortunes in the markets for our sustenance and campfire stories for our pleasure on the road. Shona, my ma, was a dancer—exotic, mysterious, mesmerizing. But it wasn't her face that snagged farmers and sailors, who were drawn to her sinewy hips that slithered and writhed with forbidden allurement. She would tempt in the squares, fields, streets, and taverns, and sometimes sold her nights to a high-enough bidder. I spent ten years absorbing the feminine divine and owe much of my charm to them.

Do you recall that before the Queen Anne's War there had been a terrible famine? Well, Shona's income became crucial to the tidbits earned from begging. So in town she frequented the docks and alleyways and was more in demand on her back than on her feet. But I ain't been told much of the bastard that sired me—excepting he was an Irish sailor who may (or may not) have been called Paddy. He gave me the tint in my chestnut red hair, the blue eyes that marked me Outsider, and apparently paid for his pleasure with a plundered gold doubloon. I was born, inconveniently, at the height of the picking season in a ditch at the edge of a strawberry field. And so was named Lolomura (for the red berries) but everyone knew me as Lola.

By the fifth harvest I was already earning my keep, charming the gentry with Romany ballads and prancing. And you never saw nothing like me—I was a proper little dazzler. I learned that the ladies paid well for tradition and the gents liked it best when I pouted and swayed. So I watched every lilt, every thrust of Ma's pelvis, and before long my belly worked figures of eight. The nobs would comment on *dexterity* and *timing*, admiring the *artistry* and *rhythm*, but I spotted how men's eyes were fixed on Ma's nipples, and how they drew tighter breath whenever my little arse thrust backward.

Cousin Marko played drum, Stefan fiddled, while Uncle Bo rattled our urgent cup. Then when smog turned to darkness they would pimp my ma and horsy-back me home down potted lanes. But sometimes—when Shona grew sloppy—I had to accompany the punters and sit in the gloom as she slapped and moaned, guarding the payment with full attention so it wouldn't be plucked from her gin-soaked daze. That, however, all stopped the night a jack-tar grew greedy and tried to have me too. As he pinned me beneath his stinking body Ma ripped his ear with the heft of a chair. See, she never married because some country squire spoilt her at fourteen (but she'd grander plans for me). Anyway, we left that john bleeding and screeching, and after that Uncle Yan took up watch. Yet there in the dust motes, there in the creaking, there in the candlelight as I sat and observed, I realized that men could be equally exploited—if you timed it before their throbbing fell limp.

Then around my tenth year came the blast of fate that changed things forever. We were camped for the season just below Chelsea when the snows started coating St. Paul's in whiteness and the Thames froze so hard you could slide right across. Shona had the coughing sickness and was stuck to her bed for ages, so one particular Friday me and the minstrels set off to ply the Wayfarer's Inn in Whitehall. Now, I ain't one to brag—but Ma never danced any better than I did that evening. The discs in my hair caught the flickering light and gilded me bright as a rainbow trout. I twirled with abandon, my newly learned tambourine melding with the drum and fiddle—vigorous—bursting with ripening promise. As the frozen flakes stealthily covered the roadway the cesspools were cleansed in an icy shroud, but no one wanted to venture out in that wilderness so the men began drinking our hard-earned spoils. The gruffness grew louder, then the fiddle struck up again, and this time a discordant chorus spewed forth. The singing grew ever more lively and it soon became apparent that none of us would be leaving until morning, so the landlord finally shut the front door, took his money, then led his scrawny wife upstairs to bed.

The one remaining barmaid—their daughter Nance—beckoned me away from the noise. She asked, "Are you hungry, love?" I nodded. She smiled and whispered, "Come with me then." I hesitated for just the briefest moment, glanced across at my merry brethren, and followed the smart young woman into the kitchen. We subtly looked each other up and down and I reckoned she wasn't no way over nineteen. I saw a tough, perky brunette in a new deck of clothes and she seemed equally delighted with my appearance for she cut me a big chunk of ham and a slice of coarse bread. As I sat washing the supper down with milk she inquired, "What do they call you then, dearie?"

"Lola," I replied.

"You dance well," she flattered. I looked coyly away. "How old are you?" She was still smiling as she ran her hand over my cheek and stopped to admire my adornments.

I thought for a while and said, "Ten."

Nance walked quietly over and closed the kitchen door so we would remain alone. She sat down across the wooden table and looked earnestly into my eyes. Weighing me up. Assessing.

"Are you still a maid?" she asked curtly. I didn't know what she meant. She recognized the confusion and clarified, "Untouched . . . a virgin . . ." She tried, "Zuhno?"

Ahhh! Now I understood. Had I opened my legs for some fat, drunken punter? I blushed and turned my head.

My response seemed to please her for she gave me a lump of cheese and said excitedly, "How would you like to do a special dance for a gentleman friend of mine?"

I had no idea she was procuring me for some dissolute toff to deflower. And so I considered her proposition. "I ain't sure. . . ."

"There's lots of money in it. Pounds and pounds," she promised.

Pounds and pounds? Just for dancing? It all sounded a bit fishy. But just then I heard Uncle Bo call my name so I stood up to excuse myself. As I was leaving she hissed, "If you want to get rich, come back when they're sleeping. Wait for my signal. It's only a short way across town and he'll treat you like a proper little lady." She winked and added, "It'll be worth five quid to you. . . ."

Five pounds? I gasped. That was more than we'd seen all year.

"What about my kin?"

"They'll be snoring like dogs before long."

"But I need music. . . ."

"It's all right, love. He has his own *instrument*. . . ."

I wasn't sure because I'd never danced to a piano before. So I asked, "Can't I just . . ."

But she shook her ringlets and confided, "It's a private party. But don't worry, duckie, I'll be there too—you'll be safe as houses with me." Her friendly smile bathed me in comfort while the vain side of childishness convinced me that I truly was an exceptional dancer. I could make my sick ma proud.

Sometime during the witching hour the tavern fell into a stupor and gradually—one by one—the eyelids closed. Nance appeared at the kitchen door and when she silently motioned me over I picked my way around the sleeping bodies and headed toward the candlelight, carrying my outdoor boots. Only after she had shut the door did I notice a strange man standing by the chimney breast.

"This is Bertie," Nance told me. "He works for the gentleman I mentioned before."

The well-mannered servant removed his hat and feigned a small nod. I felt honored by such charming attention. No one had ever bowed to me before! I didn't see nothing suspicious about him so I replied with a tiny curtsey. He grinned at his accomplice and said, "She'll do fine, Nance—if you're sure she's fresh."

"Fresh as a daisy," the young woman flashed back. "I know how to spot a good mark." The man nodded and held out a thick velvet cloak that I needed little encouragement to wear. I'd just got my boots tied when Nance picked up a tankard that was resting on the table and said, "Here, love. Drink this." It looked like ale, and the milk had made me thirsty, so I readily downed the draught.

"What is it?" I thought to ask after I was nearing the bottom. The sediment tasted gritty and a little sour.

Bertie also showed some concern but Nance waved him back with her hand and confided, "Just a touch of snuff to help her relax." They carefully swaddled me against the cold and together we left through the back door and entered the alley. The streets were so white and empty. We walked awhile toward Westminster, three sets of footprints gradually fizzling to nothingness as they filled up with plump, dewy flakes. Nance chattered encouragement all the way there promising, "No harm will come to you."

We stopped in front of a beautiful house that opened on the third knock. Bertie said to Nance, "She's waiting upstairs. Room Three. I'll meet you outside when you're done." I wasn't really conscious of their prattle because I ain't never seen nothing like this place before. There were ripe velvet drapes tied by ornate gold cords. Fancy tasseled rugs. Pictures. Fine blooms in gilded vases. Wonderfully elegant furniture, and paintings of angels and birds on the ceiling. It might have been Hampton Court itself.

A richly dressed lady appeared from the drawing room with a glass of wine in her hand. She said, "Welcome, my dear. It is so good of you to come. Here, this is for you."

She said quietly to Nance that I looked like I needed a drowse. I was overwhelmed by all the attention so I graciously took the drink. Having never tasted fine wine I didn't know what to expect but immediately my head began to feel queer and my body turned light and floaty. I was worried I might mess up my dancing steps but they urged me to finish the tainted draught and so I did. And then they nudged me upstairs.

"How do you feel?" Nance inquired sympathetically.

"I . . . I'm woozy. . . ."

"Then let's get you seen to," she said. And she led me into Room Three.

I was surprised to see a nurse there, but she looked kind and motioned for me to sit on the ornately carved bed, and so I obliged. She felt my forehead and wrist and announced, "She seems healthy enough. No fever." She removed my wet boots and gently rummaged under my costume. I grew nervous as she prodded and messed, and was alarmed when she started touching my privates, but she told me that she was a midwife and that this was her job and that everything would be fine if I just relaxed. *"Virgo intacta,"* she proclaimed. The lady slipped something to Nance and the nurse then urged me to take another glass of wine. I heard the midwife mutter to the women, "Poor little mite. She's so small, it's really going to hurt her." I guzzled the wine to block out the sounds. She added, "If she's torn, bring her back and I'll patch her up best as I can."

I think that was the moment I finally realized my fate. I struggled to get up from the bed but my eyes swam dizzy and as strange hands grasped under my arms, everything dissolved in a sepia daze. I came round a short time later to find myself being transported in some kind of cab. Nance was stroking my cheek murmuring, "It's all right, duckie. Everyone does it. And better to get rich than give it for free to some vagabond." The wheels and the whispers soothed me back to slumber and the next time I awoke I was back on a strange squashy bed. I struggled to squeeze my eyes into focus, suddenly conscious of a headache that felt like a tar drum pounding and thrumming my skull. I groaned.

Nance appeared out of the gloom and commanded, "Drink this." I tried to refuse but realized I couldn't move. My hands and feet were strapped to the four posts of the bed. I yelled. Loudly. Nance looked down into my face and said, "Go ahead—bawl your lungs out! This house stands in its own grounds and with the thick stone walls and shuttered windows no one can hear you." She lifted my head and made me drink more laudanum. "The servants are at the far end but they wouldn't hear nothing anyway on account of the double carpet and heavy drapes."

I made a cursory study of my body that had been plucked naked and apparently washed clean. "Why . . . Why are you doing this. . . ?" I stuttered.

"Money, duckie. It ain't nothing personal. I get paid half. . . ."

"I . . . I thought you were my friend."

Nance shook her head, smiled vaguely, and said, "We are mates. You do this for me and we'll get along just dandy." Then she warned, "But if you make any trouble you won't get nothing. Understand? So be a good girl and do as he bids." The young woman readied herself to leave. She said, "I've got to get back home now before I'm missed." And I never saw her again.

A few moments later a tall man entered the room cloaked in urgency and shadow. I heard him lock the door and pocket the key before he dropped his robe and stood naked in front of the bed. I stammered, "Sir . . . could . . . could I have another cup?"

He shook his head and lulled, "Not yet, my dear." He stared through fish-dead eyes and said, "I want to hear your screams."

The next thing I remember I came around on top of the chilly bedding. My bonds had been unfastened and the monster was dozing beside me. Every patch of my body felt bruised and itchy, dirty and sore. As quietly as possible I slid to the floor and wended my way to the door. It was still locked. I hurried to the windows. They were all shuttered tight and I realized I was to remain his prisoner. I was about to search for the key when the beast yawned, reentered consciousness, and said, "Come back to bed. You can go a second time now because it is only the first one that counts." I started crying with great heaving sobs. The bloody streaks sticking the tops of my thighs told me I was forever ruined. But the well-spoken man in a patient tone said, "There is no use in crying, my dear. What has been done cannot be undone." I sucked my cheeks together, trying to restrain the tears because my anguish seemed to further excite him, and it was sickeningly apparent he was readying to teach me new horrors. He came toward me but the touch of his flesh was repulsive, and before I knew what was happening I was screaming and clawing like a feral cat, slashing and rending his face. He jumped back. Startled. I snarled and spat and bit and hissed and backed him into a corner. A terrified look turned his face to slate and he began shouting for help that never arrived. The man fended my teeth off with one hand, but the other took hold of my swinging hair and tugged with all his anger until he had me pinned to the floor. The golden ornaments tore free and cartwheeled across the room. Then he knelt on my breastbone until I could barely whimper and began punching my cheeks and chin. Over and over—pounding and smacking—until the rising fog deadened all feeling.

Now, I ain't never understood to this day why a respectable gentleman would want to do what he did to me that night. Was it the sex that excited him? Being my first when I was young and tight and convinced that I might want it? Perhaps a virgin meant less chance of catching the pox? Or maybe he thought that common girls had no right to resist? I've since learned, of course, that men like that can't relate to grown-up women. And I've even heard them blame the lass herself for her own seduction! But I have to say, he showed no conscience or kindness, so I think it was all about power—the thrill—the infliction of will. . . .

*   *   *

The chattering of my teeth brought the harsh awareness I wasn't no longer in that house. I was soaked through so knew it was raining and when I opened a crusted eyelid, I discovered my hair had set in ice beneath the slushy cinders. I'd been dumped in some dank, stinking alleyway. Panic shot through me as I focused on raising my head. The first thing I saw was the half-melted corpse of a dog, his last snarl caught in a ghostly grimace a few inches from my left shoulder. My whole body shuddered. The flimsy costume they'd dumped me in was torn and mushy with dirty snow, and my legs felt cold and broken and achy. I realized my kin would have missed me by now but they'd never know where to find me. I wasn't sure myself—excepting the smell of fish wafted over the sewage so I gauged I must be somewhere near the docks. I had to find shelter. The crowds were about their business best as the weather would permit, a constant thrum of noise throbbing from either end of the jagged alley. But this smoggy passage was dirty and stagnant from the Great Fire of long ago, and was not a good place to be trapped. So I started to crawl away from the steaming horses, through the melting soot toward a decaying door. I rolled my weight against the wood and suddenly tumbled into someone's parlor.

"Well, well, well. And what have we here?" a deep voice crackled through the swelling glow of firelight. Somebody shuffled and coughed. The shape came toward me carrying a hefty club and I slowly absorbed the vision from the slippers up. I was staring up at the widest woman I'd ever ever seen. Her legs were like two oak trunks and she waddled on buoyant hips swaying in swathes of blubber. I noted gold hoops set in a nest of grizzled curls and chestnut cheeks topping the rungs of brown flesh that stepped up in layers from her giant bosom. "And who might you be, dearie?" she asked.

When she realized I was no threat, her voice became more sympathetic and the menacing club transformed into a walking stick. I looked into her bird-dark eyes and whispered, "Help me. I'm lost. . . ."

The woman intuitively took in my plight. She lifted me to my feet and steered me onto a chair by the fire. "You sit here, love. I'll warm some ale."

I gratefully accepted her offer and the bitterness began spilling. As I shared my ordeal she listened wisely, her plump lips betraying very little. When my last hiccup faded she said softly, "You can rest safe with me until you're feeling better. Then we'll sort out what to do with you."

"But I must get back to my folks . . . before they start traveling."

She shook her head and said sadly, "There ain't no going back for you, darling. You do know that, don't you. . . ?"

"No! I . . . I . . ."

The woman took my deathly hand in her warm soft paw and added, "Little chey, the gypsies will treat you like a gorgio now." She stared into my sadness and explained, "Because you are no longer pure."

Ma's life flashed into my mind and I instantly understood. But how did she know our ways? I faltered, "Are . . . Are you . . . ?"

"Romany? Ain't no more, love." She looked away and revealed, "Something like what happened to you once happened to me." She stood up and stoked the fire, then concluded, "But that ain't the only good life, if you know what I mean." She winked and smiled a toothless grin. "There's much to be said for staying in one spot. It gives you a chance to make something of yourself." She looked proudly around the room and my own eyes followed.

They took in a comfortable level of wealth that the decrepit exterior concealed well. This was obviously no vagrant's dwelling. My pupils expanded in wide appreciation and my hostess seemed gratified by such response.

"Your room's lovely," I told her.

"Room?" she cackled. "I own the whole street, duckie!"

I was speechless. A burble of spit came out before I could formulate actual words. Then I muttered, "How . . . How did. . . ?"

She chuckled and said slyly, "You might just find out, darling, if you decide to stick around."

"I can stay?" I asked in genuine astonishment. "Here?"

"In one of the other houses you can. . . ."

Over the next few days my hostess ministered my physical wounds with poultice and herbs until I was able to walk again. She made up a trundle bed by the hearth and had her girls feed me delicacies and keep lively company. The girls—an attractive assortment of vibrant young slatterns—worked in the Big House. From scraps of gossip, I discovered that my patron had progressed from whore to madam, building a powerful empire with her pirate lover, Dandy Dick Brennar. Richard Brennar had sailed with the famous Captain Morgan right up to the Sack of Panama. Now he was *officially* lost at sea—but it was rumored that, being so canny, he was most likely resting quietly and enjoying the fruits of some Carribee island.

Within a week I was up and about. And before I knew what was happening I'd become the newest recruit of Mother Lovel's bridge gang—known to insiders as "Dya's Odji"—and to outsiders as the "Black Guard." Now, I ain't too happy at this point, as you can imagine, but I quickly adapted to circumstance and soon as I'd properly healed I intended making my way back to Battersea before the spring thaw. I couldn't accept being banished from my tribe—it seemed so unfair. But in the meantime, I was learning lots of new tricks so there wasn't no time being wasted. The gang consisted of eleven of us ranging from four to fourteen. We were split into two crews and my lot worked the West Side. Our con went something like this: I was dressed as a street urchin and Dya usually rented some baby or other for me to lug round. Our adult minder picked a suitable mark, then I stared through big bleary eyes and begged for money, claiming I was orphaned and sold matches (pegs, flowers, pins) and owed money for lodgings and didn't know how I was going to afford breakfast. The toff would take in the ratty clothes and dirt, stare guilty from his own silks and lace, and then would fish out some paltry appeasement of conscience. Once we knew where he kept the wonga, the others would come charging round and little Sal would lift his purse and slide it in her bloomers. Poor nobs never knew what had hit them. After a few weeks' training on a coat sewn with bells I could lift a pocketwatch or handkerchief as slick as the rest, and Janky (a pimpled, sandy-haired youth of fourteen who hadn't enough brawn to join the men yet) was unsuccessfully trying to teach me how to pick locks. Whatever valuables we poached were given straight to the minder for Dya to fence, alongside those she'd acquired from her regular source of jack-tars and highwaymen. Mother Lovel was known wide and far, but her patch actually stretched below Cheapside from London Bridge to the Tower. She had been in business some thirty or forty years and had a finger in almost every pie the underworld cooked. And there was never any trouble from the locals because they were all too aware of the muscle at her command.

One day Dya gave me a child that was wan and silent. The

bundle felt cold and the thin lips were turning blue. I gasped and said, "This baby's dead."

She nodded and confided, "Make sure the punters can see its face. They always pay more."

I was horrified at the thought of carrying a corpse around and I panicked. I thrust the burden back at her and stood stammering, "I . . . I . . ."

"Listen," she hissed. "Take the child and do as you're told." Then she added, "I've a mind you should try around Battersea today. What do you think?"

Battersea! She meant I could look for my folks. I took the baby back and awaited further instructions. Dya yelled, "Janky!" The leader of our crew appeared in the doorway. "Do you know your way to Battersea?" The youth nodded confidently. "Right then. Your lot are going there with Dobby. If Lola finds her kin all's well and good. But if they want to buy her back it'll cost two guineas." She turned to me and said, "To pay me back for your keep."

I felt my first jag of concern. Did my folks even have two guineas? And would they want me back since I was ruined? But I knew I must seem grateful so I whispered, "Ta," and hurried after Janky as he left to find Dobby and round up the others.

Now, over the years Dya had given birth to four sons (a motley band of cutthroats and wide-boys), and Dobby was the youngest. He was built like a bulldog, with the speed of a lurcher and the cunning of a wolf, and I ain't kidding when I say he put fear of the devil into most folks. He was to be our minder, which meant he'd dress as a sailor carrying a large ditty bag and would stroll on ahead to choose our mark. Then we'd make our play, quickly passing him the stolen loot in case we got caught. And we always got away with it—because even those who saw the switch thought better of challenging Dobby.

Those of us from London know it's two or three leagues from the tower to Battersea, so we stopped a couple of times to filch a likely score before we crossed over the bridge. I was feeling quite weary by the time we arrived and the baby was starting to stink of sour death, but as we approached the common where I'd left my folks my body drained entirely. Our bender tent was gone. I ran to the patch of worn grass in desperation but all that remained was a pile of muck and a cold campfire long deserted. *No.* I threw my revolting bundle to the mud and hurried from wagon to wagon shouting the names of my folks, but no voice answered. Eventually a worn face peered from a sailcloth tent and stared in my direction. I screamed, "My kin! Do you know where they are?" I pointed at the vacant spot. The creamy eyes followed my arm, then a gnarled thumb flicked the whiskery chin in a gesture that meant they'd done a flit—left for their own private reasons. The face disappeared.

Almost gagging in panic I returned to the emptiness and scrabbled through the garbage searching for clues as to where they might be. It was too early to be on the road yet. Why would they leave? Now, perhaps it was the rotting debris, or perhaps the realization of truth, but the next thing I knew I was vomiting and heaving and choking all over the garbage. The others stood silent at the edge of the grounds, letting me find my own knowledge. I wiped my lips on the hem of my dress and tried to regain some clarity. *Think.* Where would they hide a message? The only other structure was the campfire so I cautiously approached the charred ring of stone, knelt down beside, and carefully began blowing the ash away. And there I saw it.

Hidden beneath the soot lay a large smooth stone with an arrow made of wood pointing west. I ain't never felt so much relief as I did just then because they'd not forgotten me after all. The bile dribbled down my chin and suddenly one of my crew (a rough girl called Polly) stood tentatively stroking the back of my wrist. I allowed her to take my hand and lead me over to the rest of the gang, who smirked, or swallowed hard, or looked away into their own choked memory. Janky said, "Right then, let's be off." I numbly retrieved the dead infant and wiped off as much mud as possible, while Dobby led us back through the rough pasture toward Southwalk.

There were always good pickings to be had around the bridge so Janky suggested we make a few more hits on our way home. I was so drained I didn't care what we did—which I suppose made me look even more pathetic—and perhaps that's why the ever opportunistic Dobby selected a grander target than usual. He singled out a big, fancy wig, who was chuckling with his pretty thing as she delved among a covered stall of velvet and taffeta. I watched from the shadows of a cheese vendor until they stepped out into the open, and then shuffled forward to make my play, scrunching the stinking bundle to my chest. I pleaded, "Good sir! Spare a coin for a poor wench?"

The young lady reached out to move the blanket for a better look at the baby, then automatically recoiled. "Oh, my Lord. . . ." I slipped into role and looked pitifully down at my charge, my round blue eyes popping with pathos. "Is . . . Is this your sister?" she asked sympathetically. I nodded.

The toff peered anxiously, first at the child and then at his mistress and then at me. He inquired, "Where is the mother?"

"Dead, sir" I replied. Then I launched into my monologue

about selling flowers (explaining that there weren't many this time of year) and how I couldn't pay my lodging and couldn't feed the child and I was all alone in the world and could the lovely lady find it in her heart to offer me some charity? The young woman nudged her companion and he dipped in his waistcoat to fish out a silver cob. My now-trained eyes spotted the bulge of a silk handkerchief, the chain of a pocketwatch, and the outline of a snuff box as I waited for the coin. The gang would have rich pickings. And while both heads were focused on his actions I plucked the beautiful gold chain from the lady's wrist and tucked it inside the blanket. Dobby, who stood way behind in the mingling crowd, was urgently signaling me to move so I thanked the couple and scurried by. But before Janky and the others could act, my elbow was grabbed by a half-drunk man, and as I furiously tried to wiggle free, the grip just tightened and tightened.

"Ow!" I complained, looking up at his red-rimmed eyes. "Get off me. . . ."

It suddenly occurred to me this middle-aged man might be one of the City Watch, and when I saw his pole and lantern my heart froze. I wanted to drop the baby and flee but he'd now got an arm around my neck and was pinning me against his bony hip. I frantically looked for Dobby or Janky—to show me what to do, to help me out—but the crew had slickly spirited themselves off and I was apparently alone.

The official shouted to the lady, "Ma'am, I believe you're missing a bracelet."

The young woman instinctively felt for her empty wrist and cried, "Oh!"

"I saw this little crook-thief lift it while she was begging." The man from the Watch turned to me and demanded, "Where is it?" I blushed and clutched the stinking bundle closer to my chin. The gentleman stepped forward and struck me across the cheek with the side of his hand. I recoiled in shock and smarting. He angrily snatched the blanket from my chest and shook the contents to the ground. The dead child rolled at the lady's feet, which made her flinch, step back, and moan as her gold chain tumbled into a crack between the cobblestones and was quickly retrieved by the official. He wiped it on his breeches and passed it back. He then pried the silver cob from my clutched fist and returned that to the toff. The gentleman was huffing and wheezing as if I'd committed some personal slight, while the young lady's eyes were transfixed on the motionless baby sprawled by her boot. The watchman disdainfully picked up the corpse, wrapped it back in the blanket, and thrust it into my unwilling arms. "Would you care to press charges, sir?"

"Most definitely," came the curt reply. I'd obviously bruised his pride and ruined his afternoon jolly. He gave the official his name and address, then put his arm round his mistress's quaking shoulders and steered her into an expensive furrier.

I peered up at the mottled face and asked belligerently, "Can I go now?"

He sneered and roared, "The only place you're going is the roundhouse."

"I . . . I ain't going nowhere with you. . . ." I pushed the bundle at him and tried to run the other way, but before I'd got a couple of steps he'd caught one of my wrists in a thick hemp noose and swiftly tied it to the other behind my back. Then he steered me through the crowd like a fractious donkey, rolling the floppy baby along the street with his feet.

The watchman stopped at a butcher's stall and pointed to the macabre ball, now twisted and covered in mud. "Benny, get rid of this, will you!" he instructed. The butcher looked down in the gutter and nodded. Then I was prodded off toward the constable's cell where I spent the night in the airless, crowded roundhouse with the rest of the careless caught that day.

On the morrow I stood before a justice of the peace and was told I'd be sent for trial because there was *some measure of deceit and cunning* in my failed ruse. So for the next few nights I was one of the small guests at Newgate, where I slid into the wretched shadow and willed myself invisible. Word spread round I was one of Dya's Odji so everyone knew to leave well alone. But my fate at the Old Bailey was a different matter—especially when they realized I was Romany.

See, the gorgios take us for wayward rogues and lump us together with the Jews. Some say we're cannibals or occultists, that we live ungodly lives. Happen they're frightened by our clay-dark cheeks and exotic, secret language, or maybe they're intimidated by strong sensual men and lithe, seductive women? Perhaps they envy the gaiety and freedom, but we ain't no more lazy or unclean than any others—although we do have to poach, beg, and scam sometimes—and we're probably far less promiscuous. Still, they can't get rid of us or make us conform to their government. And every year we come back stronger . . . proud and wild and defiant.

The judge was some pinched-face aristocrat who wanted to scapegoat London's Black Guard and its gypsy gangs in particular. He said, in his most disdainful manner, the fact I'd used a dead baby showed strong evidence of malice, and the expense of the item I filched had put a noose round my neck because incorrigibles over seven years of age could be executed at Her Majesty's pleasure. My blood set solid as I stood, and understood. Then the grim judge added that I might be made useful if retrained for colonial labor and ruled that, "In order to break this gang of rogues it is necessary to transport this child—young as she is—to America for seven years."

I'd got no appeal against servitude in the New World . . . and so that was that.

2

SOGGY SKIES DRIPPED DOWN

SPRING, 1712

The fog was a proper pea-souper that last day in London. I was somewhere up front of our coffle as we marched through the steamy streets from Newgate to Wapping Stairs—first stage in banishment to the New World. At the docks it seemed like hundreds of prisoners were cramped aboard a few sturdy lighters, and the men were made to row down the Thames to a transport ship that would sail northabout through the mouth of Pentland Firth, and then across the Atlantic Ocean to Chesapeake Bay. Punishment had begun.

I was youngest aboard our barge. For most of the passage I sat shackled between an old salt called Charlie (convicted of murder in a drunken brawl)—and a woman I later learned had poisoned her husband. Charlie talked in rhythm with his heaving oar. He nudged my arm with his elbow and whispered, "What're you doing here, love?"

I swallowed hard and looked up into his mottled face. His breath stank of rancid grease but his eyes gazed keenly from beneath haystack brows and he flashed me a tallow-stub grin. I turned to his ear and confided my sin. He nodded and continued pulling on the strain. The river was a floating carnival of mayhem crammed with small ships and boats of every description, each trying to nudge its way in or out of the tidal flow. A jumble of bowsprits, sails, and cargo floated on mist, and leathery voices blasted from every direction. I ain't never been on water before so my stomach tossed and lilted with each dip, until the bile pitched into my throat and I struggled to swallow the acrid taste. My face turned from brown to white to pasty, and globules of sweat stuck my rump to the bench. Charlie looked across and said sagely, "You'll soon find your sea legs, to be sure." Somewhere at the other end of the craft a whip cracked, bit flesh, and was met with a sickening groan. The wielder roared several variants of, "Pull, you lazy, worthless bastards!" until the rowers found harmony and slid us haphazardly into the mainstream. And as we edged through the shrouded city Charlie whispered our position at various spots on that bumpy drag out to sea.

By the time we reached Greenwich the mist had cleared sufficiently to reveal the palace, but I didn't see nothing on account of my head being between my knees the entire time. I swear my cheeks were tinged green, and I'd have given anything to be on land again. So I curled over my knees, hugged my frail stomach, and willed the swaying world to stop tipping and rest. I glanced up past the marshy fringes at Woolwich and saw lighter-men loading wool onto vessels, then I didn't look out again until we arrived on the north bank at Tilbury. Our boats were steered to the fort where we disembarked at the water gate to wait out the changing tide. Women were separated from men, then hurriedly stripped and scrubbed at with the end of a horse-broom dunked in a scummy tub of water. They took our street clothes to burn, refitting the men in slops and shirts, and the women in coarse itchy shifts. My shapeless dress was way too big so I rolled up the sleeves and used a piece of twine as a belt to secure it to my frame. Then we were given a tepid ox soup with biscuit, and a welcomed pint of ale that helped quell my heaving guts. They locked us in the courtyard and instructed us to rest while we could. And by then I was feeling quite dozy so soon fell into slumber.

We were roused by the snapping of thong leather above our skulls before being poked like obstinate cattle back on to the lighters. At Gravesend someone pointed out the church where an Indian princess was supposed to be buried, and then we made ready to rendezvous with the transport ship—the *Argyll*—that was anchored offshore, waiting to tender us aboard in small clutches. We'd be sailing via North Britain because a running ship like ours (sailing without a convoy) sought to avoid the enemy privateers that infested the lower English Channel.

The men were taken off first, so by the time I arrived in the female section belowdecks it was apparent this new wooden realm was some morbid visitation from hell. Now, I thought I'd seen as bad as things got in the days I'd crunched lice with my bare feet on the sewer-soaked flagstones of Newgate—but believe me, you ain't never seen nothing more rotten than this demonic place. There were twenty-odd crewmen for two hundred felons— mostly men—who were stuffed in a hole on ledges like mackerel in a pail. They were shackled in pairs, wrists and ankles, with long chains reeved through the bilboes around their legs that allowed them to wiggle as far as the nearest mess-tub. For feeding and cleaning they were brought up on deck, but for much of the journey they lay on each other in darkness and stench until disease or despair overwhelmed their senses and prompted either a stoic acceptance or some rash and foolhardy vengeance. Those who survived the twelve-week ordeal were destined to sweat as sons of toil on faraway plantations, but that portion of cargo who succumbed to blackness were hastily thrown overboard to feed the waiting jaws. And they were considered the lucky ones.

The thirty or so women were dealt with differently. We were unchained and locked in a separate pen, where we at least could stand and move about—apparently we were to be kept healthy or there wouldn't be no takers. Eventually the seasickness subsided and the nights slipped into an endless routine of sleeping and aching and groaning and sorrow, broken only by cruel dreams and crueler weather. Most mornings we were all brought up on deck to be washed and inspected for illness before being fed our meager rations, then some would be set to cleaning and sewing for the crew, while others found ways to exercise limbs, tongues, and wits. The men were taken back late afternoon, and until the boatswain's bells signaled the end of the first dogwatch the women became the entertainment. I quickly confirmed that (alongside the cabin boy) I was the only other youngster, so it didn't take long to find a way to be granted my run of the ship.

Now, I ain't never been very political, mister—but I have to entreat you historians not to overlook the white slave trade too. Alongside the transported felons, there were thousands of poor Europeans also forced into indentured servitude long before the Africans arrived. You ask the Irish Catholics, or indigent Scottish, or the poor folks of Liverpool—about the deceitful advertisements—the soldiers and press gangs—and the crooked judges who weighed their destinies on plantations in sugar and rice. If and when they finally managed to earn freedom they became a financial nuisance to those casting greedy eyes from state to state. Of course, some folks did make it back to England absolved of debt or past crime—but most stayed enmeshed in familiar drudgery because they were too worn and broken.

The first time we saw daylight must have been three days into the journey once we were way out of sight of land. But down in the belly of the monster, tentative shipmates were already forming. I was adopted by three kindly trollops who'd been caught in the midst of a blackmailing scam—Violet, Maude, and Dollie. They instantly squashed any unfair play made by others on account of my age, and wouldn't allow no bullying. And although they were all in their early twenties, Violet was apparently the ringleader. She was dainty and thin, with straw-colored hair that hung in ringlets down past her waist. Men often mistook her wispy blue eyes as innocent but her mind and frame were supple as a horny cat. Maude was a Yorkshire lass with straight dark locks and a wavy figure, while Dollie had shorter brown curls, apple red cheeks, and the Cockney sense of adventure. Maude and Dollie knew many of the popular tunes and were ever humming and whistling, while Violet pined for the country dances she'd known before landing in Whitechapel. She thought some tar might have brought bagpipes on board, and promised that when she got a chance she'd teach me her fancy footwork (if I showed some of my own moves in return). The three pals tried to stay cheerful—painting the darkness in gallows humor and pretending we weren't all about to be sold—while I asked any who'd answer what they thought would become of us. But none could lie sufficient enough to lend me a brighter truth.

When the morning watch began, we were prodded on deck. The men were chained in strands to ringbolts, but the women were able to meander at will. Most of us stayed hugged on the starboard or port sides, but the few with prior attachments ran the gauntlet of groping hands and eyes to find fathers, partners, brothers, or sons. Barrels of saltwater allowed us to wash before being inspected by the callous surgeon. When it came to my turn he roughly grabbed my face in his bony hand and stared scarily into my eyes. I'd to open my mouth, lift up my arms, and stand patiently while he rummaged in my hair looking for spots, scabs, or fleas. Then we lined up, wooden bowls at the ready, to receive the watery oatmeal and chewy bread. Some of the prisoners were ordered to work and seemed grateful for the diversion, but being left to my own company I instantly set off exploring.

Every view from the creaking ship showed open water. The sea spread out to the edges of forever, gray and crinkled and shiny. I breathed in the chill, fishy air, filling my lungs to eradicate the stink of belowdecks, glad to have finally settled my stomach. The sky was crowded with surly clouds that threatened to keep the sun at bay, but I liked the throb of the wind on my neck as it billowed round my hair in tune with the sails. Then some hardmouthed sailors told us it was time to exercise and they made everyone leap and jump to avoid their brutal whips. I didn't mind, being glad to stretch my muscles, but some of the women were unimpressed and a lot of the men spat curses under their breaths. I caught a quick glance at Charlie stumbling in chains, trying to remember some lively steps. He winked when he saw me, then carried on prancing—it was probably the first time he'd ever tried dancing the hornpipe sober. Those who cooperated and didn't cause no bother were rewarded with chewing tobacco or beer. The wan sun appeared briefly just as the afternoon mess was being served, but the men were taken back below before they could enjoy it. And now that there was much more room to be had the women came out from the shadows, and a few of the coarser slatterns began baiting the jack-tars above on the quarterdeck. I watched in fascination to see what would happen.

One of the sailors brought out a fiddle and as the screeching notes bounced round the bulwarks many of the younger women started swaying. The older dames stood round the edges, clapping, nodding (or expressing their disgust) while most of the crew stood on the platform above and watched from behind the heavily armed wooden barricado. Violet saw me leaning against the foremast and eagerly beckoned me to come join the girls. She showed me some morris dancing, bounding around with enthusiastic skips and jumps, and when Dollie and Maude recognized one of the tunes they got several of the spectators to join in the chorus. For the first time in months I began to relax, losing myself in the scraped, poignant melodies. Then the fiddler began a familiar gypsy ballad and I fell into an old dance I thought I'd forgotten. Now, it ain't easy being elegant in a baggy shift, but as I closed my eyes my spirit swam free with the mermaids, and smoldering hope relit in my soul. This was my own personal freedom.

When the last note floated away on the wake I realized everyone had stopped to watch me. Violet yelled, "Give us another one, Lola," and the fiddle struck up once again. About halfway through this routine the predators descended the steps and began edging in on the women, offering them swigs of rum, and before long, the deck resembled a tavern. Just as I finished twirling, a rough arm grabbed me round the waist and pulled me onto a waiting knee. A clean-shaven man with a powder-burned face had taken a liking and was trying to kiss me, and the more I tried to squirm away the more urgent his slobbers became. Then suddenly Maude appeared and said, "Hello, handsome." She mashed her breasts up against his cheek and lulled, "Wouldn't you rather have a proper woman, darling? I'll show you a real good time." He pushed me away absentmindedly and dragged Maude off under the rigging.

On top of the stairs the quartermaster glowered at the scene from inside his fiery whiskers. He paced back and forth, growling orders at some less than able seaman. I scurried back to Dollie and Violet, at the same time that two eager tars appeared to stake their claims. Violet pushed me behind her back and hissed, "Go hide yourself. Quick!" Then she turned to the drooling crewmen and wiggled provocatively to provide a suitable distraction. I fell to the planks and scooted on all fours behind the water barrel into the shaded part of the deck, where I peered through a tangle of rope and tackle to determine a safe enough spot. The longboats! As cautiously as possible I crept round to the edge of the pile of overturned vessels and wiggled myself underneath the nearest edge.

The interior was black and humid. A stench of tar hung cloyingly in the thick, smarting air. Then I froze—terrified—when my bare foot touched something live and fleshy, and gagged as an eerie voice snapped, "Piss off! This is my spot." I rolled round in the confined chamber and instinctively put my hand out toward the noise. My fingers found a mop of coarse hair and the velvety skin of an unshaved chin. It was the cabin boy.

"What are you doing here?" I asked in amazement.

"Hiding. Same as you."

"Can I share then? There's some big fellow after me!"

The bodiless voice was quiet for a moment and then said, "Yes. I suppose. . . ."

I squeezed his shoulder to express appreciation. After a few moments I asked, "What's your name, then?"

"Bristol," he whispered. Then as an afterthought he asked, "You?"

"Lola."

His breathing echoed round the wooden skin and then formed into the inquiry, "Are you a gypsy?"

My heart stilled for the briefest pause. I replied, "Of course I ain't. I'm Cockney!"

"Good." Then he added, "I bet you cannot guess where I am from. . . ."

I stifled a giggle and said, "I reckon I can!" We shifted ourselves into more comfortable positions before I inquired, "Who's after you then?"

Bristol sniffed and then said quietly, "That bastard surgeon . . . Dr. Simpson."

"What's he want you for?"

The young voice quivered and confided, "Vile things." He paused and added, "You know. . . ." I didn't really, but I said nothing further. Then the four bells boomed in the background and the surrounding deck responded with a swift change of movement. Bristol slithered under the rim and was gone. I peered cautiously out and quickly wormed into the center of a group of women being steered back down the hold. The grate was locked above us and the darkness of another night descended.

The rain began sometime before dawn and saturated those sleeping nearest the grid if they failed to rouse and roll away quick enough. After several persistent hours we were all drenched by the rising puddle that slopped and pitched, sloshing from edge to side and basting us all ankle deep. The crew (now all hands on deck) battled to steer against the torrent to keep the wayward craft stable, and after some jack-tar fell off the ratlines and broke his back on the capstan, the few who responded to our shouts made it pretty obvious we wasn't getting no food until everything returned back to normal. We shivered and voiced our own briny complaints until late midmorning, when the waves became ripples and the clouds eventually stopped shedding. The late sun peeked out, drawing everything steamy, and we were finally finally finally allowed up above. I deliberately chose to sit in a shaded corner right below the quarterdeck so I'd be harder to spot, because much as I love to dance I didn't want no one paying any more undue attention. But before I'd even settled my arse Bristol appeared at my arm and said, "The captain wants to see you."

Up close, I could see Bristol was taller than me and was obviously more well-to-do. He'd a curly halo of bright red hair and keen green eyes that were lost in a starburst of freckles. I'd spent several of the previous wet hours puzzling over his appearance on this ship but at that precise moment my own dilemma was more pressing. "What's he want?" I asked. The boy shrugged his bony shoulders and indicated that I was to follow him past the boatswain to the cabin door. I looked furtively around to signal one of my friends what was happening but all the girls were now otherwise engaged in their own affairs. A gruff voice barked to enter and Bristol nudged me forward, then shut the door. I was alone with Captain James Mack.

I stared down at the hem of my soggy dress because I didn't want to acknowledge such a formidable enemy. I'd no idea what I'd done wrong—but instinctively dreaded the unknown reprisal. The captain's long stare bored into the top of my skull and I started shuddering. He lumbered toward me, lifted my chin so he could study my face, and muttered, "Mmmm . . ." He rotated my neck to observe each profile and added, "So you're our wee dancer, eh?" I didn't utter no sound but stood and let him take in his fill. At last his grip released me and he ordered, "Look at me, lassie." I immediately obeyed and beheld a beefy, squat man with gray curly whiskers, peppery beard, white thinning hair, and flint-specked eyes. He was heavily scarred in the creases across his forehead and over his nose. And he was missing the tips of three fingers from his furry left hand.

"My boy says your name's Lola." I nodded. "What will you drink? Wine? Rum? Ale? Water?" I said nothing. "Milk?" he tried.

I looked at my toes and stuttered, "If . . . If you please, sir."

He strode to the door and sent out instruction, then sat on the tilting bunk and bid me perch alongside. "Address me as Captain," he lulled in his genteel Scottish accent.

When Bristol brought the warm-squeezed milk he was told to balance on the window bench opposite—I assume to make me feel safer—and together we listened to the sailor's oft-spent tale of ascension through the ranks to his command of the profitable *Argyll*. When his monologue finished, his tongue ran on into Bristol's story—revealing how Mack had been sent to sea under Bristol's father (a worthy mentor called Captain Jude Armstrong) and how he owed all of his skills to this fine tutelage. Apparently, Bristol was the youngest of five sons and when his father was lost in battle against the Spanish, Mack felt obliged to recruit him as cabin boy to pass on the family trade. I listened to the mellow words and kindly intent, and gradually my toes uncurled and my fingers stopped clenching. Bristol also seemed relaxed and comfortable now, so I wondered why the ship's surgeon was able to give him so much grief. The captain then turned to me and said, "It'll soon be time for the bells. But come here tomorrow, straight after breakfast, and we'll see if we can find you some dancing clothes." I swallowed hard, wondering how to respond. By the time the clapper rang its final strike I'd already jumped to my feet in time with Bristol's own swift movement for the door and, anxious to be dismissed, bobbed a curtsey at the square-shaped man. Then I joined the other girls to pass on my seeming good fortune.

The pitchy hold was still damp so the women were bickering for space on the dryer planks. I sat back to back against Maude, nestled between Violet and Dollie, who spread out the width of their shifts in a rough kind of sheet to keep off the salty slime. Maude twisted her neck round and asked, "Where did you get to, Lola?" When I'd explained in rapid whispers what had occurred in the captain's cabin Violet muttered something to Dollie I didn't catch, then she squeezed my leg and said, "Best get some sleep, duckie"—so I rested my head on her shoulder and allowed the bouncing waves to rock me to elsewhere.

Next morning began nippy and brisk. When I looked over the netted bulwarks the sea was puckered in peaks like the endless coils of an inky dragon. I tiptoed shyly across the quarterdeck and knocked on the cabin door, dismayed I couldn't see Bristol nowhere about. A voice yelled, "Come you in!" so I timidly entered the carved-out room. Captain Mack was eating breakfast at his small table. He motioned for me to sit on the other chair and passed me a jug of frothy milk to pour for myself. Then he carefully shared some bread and cheese—the most delicious things I'd tasted in weeks—before pointing to an open sea chest. I wiped my mouth on the back of my sleeve and followed his eyes. "Take your pick," he said. Then he settled back to watch my greed. I lifted the lid and saw a dazzling collection of frivolous cloth. There were gossamer sheets that flowed like silk, ribbons of every brightness imaginable, velvets and calicoes and lacy scarves. I wasn't sure what he wanted me to do with them so I stood gawking until he clarified, "For your dancing." I ain't never touched nothing so fine in all my life so I gulped and said "They're lovely," and started pulling the items out, each one more splendid than the last, until I eventually found a silver filigree belt small enough for my waist. I could loop strands of ribbon through the holes and attach a lace-edged scarf to make a skirt—and use a similar piece of brocade work as a bodice. The captain sucked on a lidded clay pipe that he wouldn't ever light belowdecks on account of the fire risk, while I busied myself for my evening performance. A short while later Bristol arrived with the fiddler who'd played that first night, and we talked over some songs we both knew. Then suddenly the lookout spat an urgent alarm and everyone rushed from the cabin. I heard "Sail ho! Starboard fore, Cap'n. . . ." waft in through the open jamb, before the lock snapped behind and realized I was alone in the officer's lair.

I wondered if I dare snoop around—then worried that this diversion might be some elaborate test so decided to focus on dressmaking. There were small rusty shears and some sailcloth needles lodged at the bottom of the chest, and by peeling off thin strips of ribbon-thread I managed to construct a pair of drawers to wear beneath the flimsy gauze. As a finishing touch I plaited several colorful strands into a vibrant headpiece, but when I finally donned my fancy red finery there was no reflective surface to admire my handiwork. Still . . . it was proper grand being out of that smelly, damp stuff so I spent the rest of the time brightly practicing my steps without the slightest idea of the panic ensuing outside.

Now, you've got to imagine the angst of an unknown mast

before you spot its ensign. Is it friend or foe? What size of vessel and how many gun ports? The captain goes aloft with his spyglass, squeezing his eyes to assess the danger. And whatever he spots in the wavering round is usually followed by a pressing desire to slip by, undetected. Meanwhile, the prisoners are locked back down the hatches so every hand can attend his station (the entire drama performed in muted urgency to prevent any sound from reaching alien ears). "Load, but don't run out the starboard guns!" is followed by "All hands make sail, ahoy!" Then the long, eerie silence marked by the gallop of a speeding bow blasting through tacky water. Everyone sucks in air and prays to their deity of choice for the slide to safety. And only when they are alone again on the empty horizon do they finally exhale and dare a return to breathing.

When the door let in light some time later, the captain found me draped in costume asleep on top of his bunk. Bristol was dispatched for victuals while Mack helped himself to a hefty swig of rum from a tapped barrel swinging by a chain from the rafters. He then filled me a small cannikin with instructions to sip it slowly. The syrup burned my tongue but left a sugary afterglow that tingled right to my navel. The cabin boy returned with salted beef and the last of the bread, and the three of us sat round the table munching apples for dessert. While the two sailors chatted familiarly I tried to think of something to say and eventually asked, "Was it another ship out there?"

The captain looked at me and said, "Aye. A French man-o'-war."

I hadn't no idea what that meant so inquired, "That ain't good then?"

Mack turned to his student and signaled with a nod the

chance to show off his schooling. Bristol eagerly explained, "We're at war over the Spanish succession." My face remained blank so he continued, "See, when King Charles II died heirless the Spanish throne was claimed by both Philip of France and by Leopold, the Holy Roman Emperor. England joined the emperor's side against the French and Spanish." Now you'll have to excuse my ignorance but I didn't know nothing about any of this lot.

"Why?" I asked, confused.

The captain interjected, "Those Froggie devils are trying to expand their territories and we need to put a stop to them."

"Oh," I replied. I thought on the information and deducted, "So the French ship would have attacked us because we're English?"

"Or they could happen be privateers. . . ." he added. "Corsairs—with letters of marque."

Again I lacked comprehension, until Bristol explained that privateers are private warships licensed by their monarch to raid enemy vessels in times of war. But my face must have still displayed suitable ignorance for the young boy groped for simpler words I could grasp. He tried, "Like . . . legal pirates." Suddenly I understood. Of course I knew all about pirates—monsters that plague the high seas—villains and cutthroats and demons (except for Dya's lover, the Dandy Dick Brennar). My bottom lip began wavering in aftershock as I pondered our narrow escape.

The captain apparently noted my distress and lightened the mood with, "But enough of this! Display for us your outfit, my bonny. . . ." So I stood a little from the table and sank a sweeping curtsey. "Turn around," he commanded. I happily obeyed. He nodded his approval. Then he walked to the door and barked the following orders, "Mr. Owens—signal the eight bells if you please. And Mr. Kimble—an extra ration of rum for the men and a flagon of brandy for the officers. . . ." He glanced across at Bristol and confided, "Lola is going to entertain us."

Apart from the watch, all the sailors were grouped on deck either hanging over the quarterdeck barricado or propped against the bulwarks, drinking, smoking, engaging in crude conversation. The fiddler stood highlighted up on the forecastle deck and an empty space on the waist—directly between the foremast and mainmast—was to be my stage. The prisoners were locked below, but as soon as the music began I saw Maude and Dollie press their faces against the grid to add their own accompaniment. It was reassuring to feel their support inside that threatening ring of men for I was concerned some tar might molest me. I ain't kidding when I tell you I was scared looking round those lecherous faces, all battered and scabbed and blistered. Some licked pocked lips or scratched their privates yelling offensive suggestions, and soon as I stood center of the deck the circle closed in sniffing for thrills. But then I spotted the frown on the captain's face. He stood at the top of the staircase and I instantly recognized safety—Caesar had apparently claimed me his own. He took up his speaking trumpet and shouted, "Stand off and yap not!" The men reluctantly edged back to the sides of the ship, curtailing their snarled lips and itching for me to commence.

I began with a simple dance consisting of tiny stamps and finger clicks. Maude added depth by singing "Yah, yah, la, la, hup, hup, hup," and before long the audience joined in, banging and clapping in time to the beat. This was a calm, measured opening that allowed my muscles time to stretch and warm. The fiddler then picked up the pace and I exploded into a joyful piece with light sidesteps and little kicks forward. My long chestnut hair bounced in time with the waves and followed my back in a splash of curl. I flashed like the sun, the ribbons bouncing in rainbows of color. Another piece of music struck up. Then another. And I alternated my scarf to form a whisking shawl, airy wings, and a sultry, exotic veil. I went through my entire repertoire, bouncing on toes, crossing ankles, twirling and spinning, faster and slower. I sashayed my hips, and swished my skirt, wiggled and pouted and swayed. At some point an ardent jack-tar sprang forth to partner me in a lively duet. He slapped well-defined legs, flipped lithe heels to wrists, clapping and stomping alongside my movements. His mates egged encouragement but the fiddle suddenly sputtered from discord to silence. . . . The captain had decided that this show was now over.

As I walked back to stern to change my clothes I realized Bristol must still be hiding from the doctor who had propped himself high up on the steps. Captain Mack was already in his cabin by the time I got back and he seemed excited by my performance. I wasn't any concerned when he locked the door behind me because I thought he was gallantly ensuring my privacy. But when he pointed to a linen shirt with a finely laced collar and told me to make it a nightgown I realized I wouldn't be spending no more nights in that stifling hold. And I was glad.

Now, I can tell you there's much advantage in being the captain's favorite. I ain't never had a father—but I imagine that's how one would treat me—gentle and attentive and generous as he trained me to his pleasure. Of course, now I know he was just another dirty buggar who got his jollies preparing young girls, but back then I thought he really liked me. He said that I was special. Two weeks in his bunk taught me to touch and kiss and lick and tease, and four weeks left me no illusion I was truly damned forever—complicit in my own seduction. I danced all manner of command performances and was groomed to satisfy the basest requests. But it kept me safe from the rest of the crew. I got fed well, wore nicer things, and was free until afternoon watch. I was now made to address my lover as Master—and instructed to stay away from the other prisoners (in case I caught something nasty). All I had to do was be his very good girl.

And you ain't never wanting to be crossing Captain James Mack! One time, some old salt pulled a knife on the first mate and the surgeon was ordered to chop off his hand. We all had to watch. If two sailors got fighting it was three duckings each from the yardarm for both offenders, and those caught thieving had their heads shaved, then were tarred with oil and feathers. Anyone falling asleep on watch was flogged, and if someone got drunk and incapable they were tied to the foremast for days. And that's how he dealt with his crew. Now the prisoners were even more brutally used—they were shown absolutely no mercy. Any infraction at all brought a lick from the cat-o'-nine-tails (which leaves a rumpled scar like the knots of a gnarly tree). And as water grew scarcer, that became an added incentive, because I can't never describe how it feels to be really really thirsty but you get to the point where you'd kill for a few drops of fresh. See, at first the liquid goes sweet in the casks. Then thick. Then slimy. And after several weeks it turns stagnant and full of green things. And you can't drink the sea for it makes you sick, so even I ended up supping ale, gradually progressing to wine, rum, and brandy. I have to admit I grew rather partial to brandy—it numbed the pain, dulled the worry, and helped the evening smut roll by much faster.

During the mornings I spent time with Bristol at his chores and picked up some of the trade as he worked his maiden voyage. First, he taught me my way round the ship. He explained that our vessel was commissioned along the lines of a Spanish galleon, and that this was unusual for a British merchantman. We stood together at the top of the quarterdeck steps and he explained, "See the three masts?" I nodded. "The one at the front is the foremast and that holds the foresail. The middle is the mainmast with the mainsail, and behind us is the mizzenmast and mizzen-sail." The front of the ship—fore—is the bow, and the back is the stern or aft. Understand?" My grin indicated that I did. "To the left is port and to the right is starboard," he added.

"And there are four decks," I observed helpfully.

"Yes. To the rear, above the captain's cabin, is the after. We're on the quarterdeck. Below is the waist, and at the front above the galley is the foc's'le or forecastle." I quickly absorbed all the information and smiled my understanding. "Now repeat!" he demanded, and I related what I'd just learned. Later my new friend showed me some rope skills. I observed him make a stopper knot to keep lines from threading through holes, and learned alongside—from the second mate—how to tie bowlines, lightermans, clove hitches, and the fisherman's knot. Any spare moments we'd raced each other in friendly competition until we both became quite proficient. I wasn't allowed to do no dangerous or heavy tasks, though it did amuse the crew when I volunteered to help swab the quarterdeck, and I actually enjoyed learning to mend sails. But I was more than glad not to join Bristol cleaning the prison holds because it made him physically sick, even though I understood why they needed to be done twice a week. While I didn't mind filling up the buckets of sand used to scrub the muck off I wouldn't no way have wanted to empty the mess-tubs or scrape away the crud. Everyone got out of the hold by the time the fire pans were lit for drying, and when the chambers were smoked clean with tar, tobacco, and brimstone even the hardiest sea dog steered clear of the acrid smog.

Bristol circulated around the officers as an assistant steward to learn their various tasks and I often scuttled alongside him. First the sailing master showed how to set the sails (but I got lost in his complex explanation of tacking to beat upwind). Then we spent several hateful days shadowing quartermaster Kimble— who was vicious and harsh and relished the power he spent like a wealthy toff. I didn't learn nothing from him for he made my head wobble with that much dread I couldn't keep nothing inside it. The boatswain taught Bristol to fix ropes and pulleys, while his mate showed me how to club hair in a nautical braid. And the carpenter chirped cheerfully away as he went through his routine checks of the mast and hull. But best of all I enjoyed navigation—complex, artistic, skillful, technical—and always thoroughly engaging. I learned about the rise and set of the sun, the tracks of the moon through the heavens, and stars took on names with increasing importance as I opened my ears and eyes.

Then as the weeks rolled past the first month into the second . . . some of the crew began falling sick. One day the gunner woke up with Cupid's disease and tried to blame it on Maude. She was singled out during the doctor's inspection and roughly hauled before Captain Mack. He turned to the gunner and asked, "Is this the one?"

The sailor spat in her hair and hissed, "Aye, Cap'n. That's the filthy doxy as gave me the Great Pox."

Maude looked horrified and yelled, "He didn't get that from me!" The trembling young woman was instructed to undress in front of the entire crew so the doctor could further examine for pustules, rash, or fever. Unfortunately, Maude had scraped the inside of her thighs a few days earlier when she slipped on the greasy ladder, and in the dingy hold the wound had formed tiny pimples. Despite her protests and explanations, Dr. Simpson determined she was highly infectious and had to be rendered impotent for the rest of the voyage.

The captain nodded, turned to the quartermaster, and said, "Mr. Kimble—approach if you please." The two men determined Maude's fate in wily whispers, then the captain ordered the young woman to kneel at their feet. The quartermaster signaled for the marlinespike a sailor was using at the base of the mizzenmast and, with one ruthless swipe, he ripped open Maude's pretty complexion from right ear to far left cheek. Her sparkling eyes dimmed in disbelief, then the pain struck home and she clutched her gaping face that had split like an overripe plum.

"You're a wee bit less handsome now, lassie," he sneered as he handed back the weapon. The captain looked on with sickening approval and said, "Sew her up, Doctor. She'll not be infecting any more of my men."

I hadn't never seen nothing so cruel, and I cried the grief her damaged face could not. My poor friend had been torn and brutalized and would never find tolerable work again. They'd maimed her a figure of nightmare—for even after the thick stitches healed she was left lopsided and scarred. And I never once heard her sing from that day forth. All her spirit and humor deserted her and she sat in the shadows, marooned on her own black island. That same evening I got bloodied too. The captain expected me jovial and dancing but found me a sniveling nuisance. I made the mistake of questioning his judgment, and got rewarded with a violent blow to the chest that forced me across the cabin, cracked my rib, and made me feel queasy for days.

He was careful, of course, not to damage another face—and to punish me further he put Violet in charge of the entertainment, supposedly until I healed.

I realized that night I never had no real influence over my master at all, and thereafter resolved to keep my thoughts close in my own clotted head. He was in charge of our everything— and that was just that.

3

A FLIMSY SHIFT ON A BUNKER COT

SUMMER, 1712

Now toward the end of our second month at sea the food rations grew fitful. The cow stopped making milk so was butchered and eaten, and all of the chickens had since found their way to the pot. The salted pork was blistered with maggots and the biscuits grew lacy where weevils invaded. Bristol and me tried our hands at fishing but neither of us had any luck. So while the prisoners made do with pottage and dried peas, the crew ate the last of the beef and set up nets to catch turtles or dolphins or whales. But at least there was plenty of booze left.

One afternoon we'd a temporary panic when another ship was spotted, but it turned out to be a friendly vessel on route to England so our captains made eager trade. Their boat had recently repelled an attack from pirates off Bermuda and was running short of powder and shot, which we readily swapped for their salt, goat meat, cheese, oranges, rice, and flour. They also gave over five barrels of water in return for some sailcloth and candles. While all the commotion drew attention I slipped beside the women's hatch and whispered down to Dollie to find out how Maude was doing. Not well. Violet crept over to join our talk and began probing me with strange questions. She breathed, "Where does the captain keep the keys to the shot locker and powder room?"

"I don't know, Vi. Why?"

"Think, lovie. It's important," hissed Dollie.

"What's going on?"

The women mumbled under my hearing and replied, "There's things afoot you need know of, Lola." After a pause Dollie asked, "Can you filch something metal? A spike . . . knife . . . something of the sort?" I answered that I might. "Good. You know that prisoner, name of Charlie?"

"The old salt who killed some tar in a brawl?"

"That's him." They motioned for me to slide closer so I lowered my ear to the grid. "He's been waiting to hear news of pirates abroad because he and his mate reckon that means we're closing in on land. We've been plotting together for weeks and now the time's at hand—we're going to take over the ship!" I stifled the gasp pressing my throat. My skin turned cold and bumpy. I mumbled, "But . . . but . . ."

"Hush up!" Dollie commanded. "It's a full moon two more nights from now. That's when we'll make our move, so you've to get the spike to Charlie tomorrow. Understand?" I nodded, woodenly.

"And, Lola," Violet added, "don't tell the boy." I bubbled something unintelligible and stumbled away to the stern to calm myself down. Everyone was busy loading the supplies, so I slipped up to sit by the stern lantern and stared out at the trailing foam. What should I do?

Of course I wanted to help my mates down below because I was furious with how the men had maimed Maude and all that—but there was only a frail little girl hiding inside of me. I was terribly terribly frightened. What would they do if they caught me plotting? How would we fare if we failed? And if we managed to take the ship would enough men even know how to sail her? Where would we go where we could hide in safety? Might we be hunted the rest of our days? And what would happen to the crew—I didn't want Bristol getting hurt. . . .

The terror ran round the inside of my skull until I thought my eyes would spark. But then a compelling force pulled me on my heels and made me wander the decks in search of something metallic. Of course, being a prison vessel the sailors were well-drilled in keeping things stowed safe against insurrection, but I thought one of the tars might be careless amidst all the hustle and transfer of goods. No such luck. I couldn't find nothing suitable at all. That night I eagerly scanned the cabin in the hope of discovering some tool but then I remembered that even our food was cut by my master's lone knife (which he always kept on his person) and I didn't dare try to steal that—or his keys. After he'd taken his rough pleasure I lay by his snoring carcass staring widely at the rafters. I pined for Janky's flair at lock picking and wished I'd paid more attention when he was showing me. There must be something! I ransacked my thoughts for some half-forgotten memory that lay close by and irritating. And when I finally remembered the small rusted shears now locked in the wooden chest I remained fully conscious the rest of the night, tossing and thinking and scheming.

Next morning, as we broke our fast with the new provisions,

I drew in my courage and said, "Master, I think I'm well enough to dance again." He responded with a bored expression and I worried he was tiring of me. So I lowered my eyelashes and said seductively, "It's a private dance—proper special—just for you."

A flicker of lust flashed the backs of his eyes and he responded, "Aye? Tell me a wee bit more then."

"It's forbidden . . . but I believe the gypsies call it the Dance of Veils."

"Dance of Veils, eh?" he replied thoughtfully. "I've heard tales of the like. . . ."

I decided to push while I had his attention and added, "But I'll need to fix a new outfit."

He finished his drink, rubbed his nose with the nub of his missing fingers, and said, "Aye. I'll open the chest afore I go." Then he asked, "And music?"

"There's a song I can sing for myself."

Captain Mack scratched his thigh and shuffled in his coat for the key to the box. He turned the lock, collected his things, and winked as he left the cabin.

I rummaged through the material to the bottom of the container and quickly found the shears. Each piece of material was seared in my memory so I'd already designed the costume I would create and quickly set about cutting the pieces. Now I'd only ever seen this Dance of Veils once before, when Shona was giving a rival performance at a village fair and I managed to slip from Grandma Vadoma's sight for a few brief moments. I slipped beneath the skin of the men's tent to find out what all the ruckus and hooting was for, and there I saw a scantily clad beauty displaying her charms to a bunch of avid admirers. When the final veil dropped, the place exploded and I ain't never seen so many coins thrown for just one dance. Then Grandma discovered my ankle protruding under the flap and I was dragged away home in disgrace. But I knew the tune she was singing because we children had often repeated the words, oblivious to their meaning. And I went over all the verses as I put together the outfit.

Now, as luck would have it another blustery storm hit the ship that same midmorning so the prisoners were hurriedly chained back down in the hold to wait out the tempest. As the gaiting cabin buckled and dipped I was appreciative not to be facing the carnage belowdecks, which (I'm ashamed to admit) somewhat challenged my loyalty. In the end I reasoned that if I poked the shears through the men's hatch I'd have done my bit to help my mates, and so as soon as the wind returned to normal I carefully plucked my way across the slippery deck. The crew was busy with the sails and Bristol was occupied with navigation—keeping the pegs in place on the traverse board so we wouldn't lose our position. I crossed the waist and intentionally stumbled so as to fall against the wooden grate. In an instant I'd wiggled the shears through a hole and heard them drop with a ping on some unfortunate below who spluttered a surprised curse back up at me. But by the time I returned to the cabin I was shaking—wondering if I'd just made the worst mistake upon ever.

When the winds drew back into the thick, stuffed clouds and trundled away behind us, the skies began to gradually lighten and thin. The sun remained hidden, but after the wetness had melted from the deck the captain decided the crew was too exhausted to exercise the cargo that day, so the prisoner's rations were taken below and dished up down there. And to keep the weary sailors happy an additional keg of rum appeared at the start of the second dogwatch. Just before dusk Mack returned to the cabin to find me ready and anxious. I was worried he'd detect my nervousness so I covered by saying, "I . . . I ain't never done nothing like this before, Master." He nodded a curt understanding, then took off his damp clothes and lay naked across the bunk. Waiting. He ran his good hand across his thinning crown and laid his head back against the wrist in a careless, decadent pose.

I battled to still my quivering voice by humming the first verse before I began any movements, glad for the shimmering veils that disguised my shakes. I stood in the confined space and began the chorus.

> *She sang la la, I beseech thee—listen what I say,*
> *The man who can guess each riddle may claim my virtue as pay.*

Captain Mack's pupils widened in their narrowing eye slits as his breathing turned raspy. I noted his stubby hand tapping time on his thigh as I sang the introduction,

> *The Sultan's gift arrived bejeweled across from dusky lands,*
> *She hid herself in swathes of silk and talked with two fair hands,*
> *Her dance was light as swan-down,*
> *Her voice like a bubbling brook,*
> *She stole the king's heart easily—one glance was all it took.*
> *She sang la la, I beseech thee, listen what I say,*
> *The man who can guess each riddle may claim my virtue as pay.*

Now, if you ain't never heard this song before, it unwraps the woman like a fancy gift. And the riddle's dead easy to guess because each answer relates to the section of body revealed when that particular veil is dropped. For example, the first verse goes,

> *This part of me contains the nod obeying your command,*
> *It also holds the tender lips that pucker to kiss your hand,*

The canvass flushed with blushes,
At the merest sight of you,
Two gems for dazzling my new lord—set in heavenly blue.
She sang la la, I beseech thee, listen what I say,
The man who can guess each riddle may claim my virtue as pay.

I toyed with the first wrap, until the captain finally grinned he knew the answer and pointed to his own face. Then I carefully untied the headpiece and let the silk slide languidly to the floor, all the while swaying in tantalizing circuits. By the time I dropped the final veil I had obviously captivated my audience, and he spent the next spill of the hourglass feasting on his spoils. Eventually, however, Mack slipped a shirt over his head and pushed his face through the door to send Bristol for food. I put on my night robe. But while he dressed in sated contentment I couldn't help wondering what was going on down in the hold.

After we'd partaken of goat meat and rice I set about tidying the valuable cloth scattered around the room. Now, to this day I can't never rightly remember what made him suspicious but all of a sudden the captain marched over to the chest and threw back the lid. He rummaged inside, and then tipped the box upside down so the needles and ribbon scattered like falling leaves and fell tangled against the materials. Then he meticulously began shaking each piece as I scurried to fold and tidy the discards after he'd finished. Finally, he stood up, banged down the lid, looked over the cabin surfaces and roared, "Where's the shears?" I gulped. Then froze. Then gulped again. My tongue was dry and too scratchy to answer, but my body sprang to action and mimed a frantic search around the space. I looked under the blankets, groped round the floor, checked each container, and pretended to be clueless. Unfortunately my show lacked conviction and the next thing I knew he'd grabbed my wrists and bound them tightly with ribbon around the table leg. And when he blustered out of the room, puffing with fury, the ship exploded into chaos about him.

Now, I ain't never been so despondent as in that long blank timelessness curled up in the straining dark, listening to the panic. I found out later what happened. The captain ordered a full crew turnout and organized a thorough search of the prison quarters. Line by line the men were dragged up the ladder through the hatch into the moonlight, where they were stripped naked and inspected by the doctor. Anyone foolish enough to speak was instantly flogged with the cat. Then they were chained to the ringbolts to watch the next line of men being processed. About halfway through emptying the hold, one of the seamen let out a yell, followed by a huge commotion. Several other sailors sprang down, only to discover the unfortunate tar grasping at a pair of shears that had been thrust through the side of his neck. Someone cried out for the doctor, but there was little he could do because the scissors had severed the victim's splaying vein. Meanwhile, the two prisoners who'd freed themselves from their shackles were being mercilessly pummeled by a hoard of angry crewmen—and one of these unfortunates was Charlie. When the escapees were bludgeoned almost unconscious they were hauled up the ladder, stripped naked, and lashed either side of the foremast. The rest of the prisoners were brought up on deck, and even the women were chained up this time. I listened with mounting fear, trying to guess the turn of events. But even in my farthest imagination I couldn't never have conjured up what happened next.

The cabin door flew open and the quartermaster's burning mane lit up the gap. He cut my wrists from the table legs and mangled my arm up my back to propel me outside. Every soul on board was now gathered around the waist deck. Every pair of eyes there to witness my disgrace. I was marched to the top of the steps at the edge of the quarterdeck where Captain Mack stood waiting. He twisted my hair into a rope and viciously pulled my head in place, squashed tight against his chest. I saw the dead sailor laid out on top of the skiff, saw the shears—and realized in a long sticky moment of forever that I had stupidly been caught. This was the one thing they could trace back to me! Hot tears scaled my skin as snot began bubbling at the tip of my nose. And then I saw Charlie lashed to the mast and my involuntary wails echoed round the shadowy ship. Several of the women began crying too and all of us shuddered against the night air, awaiting some terrible retribution.

The gunner fired a pistol in the air and a gradual hush descended. Captain Mack yelled through the speaking trumpet, "Be done with your babble! Listen up." All ears obeyed. He pointed to the crumpled men lashed to the masts and said, "These two scurvy bilge rats have been planning a wee insurrection aided, so it would seem, by this here lassie." All faces turned in my direction. I hung my head, awaiting the blow that would set it rolling. "Witness your eyes how we deal with rebellion, so you won't ever be tempted to such foolhardiness again." He signaled for the quartermaster, who arrived with the most ferocious leather whip I've ever encountered and stood alongside Charlie, awaiting the order. "A hundred lashes!" the captain commanded. And everyone gaped in anticipation. One of the crew lit the scene with a lantern and only then did I notice the gashes on Charlie's wrists where he'd struggled to free himself from the iron shackles. He was barely conscious, and after twenty-some strokes he seemed to slip away on a maelstrom of flying gore.

I heard the quartermaster roar, "Damn my soul if I don't bleed you a death that will make this rabble remember for a century!" When fifty of the blistering cracks had been delivered the body was turned to provide a fresh canvas and Kimble allowed the boatswain to take over. The prisoner's flesh hung in gaping strips like the pith of a peeled banana, and his blood twirled in whirlpools that drained in jagged lines to the deck. I actually saw very little of all this though—on account of the haze and tears—but when I vomited violently down the steps Mack just twisted my hair even tighter in his monstrous grip and made me swallow the after-burn. On the final stroke a roar rang out from the crew and the boatswain passed the slimy crop back to Kimble. And it was obvious even to me—Charlie was dead.

Two sailors came forth and chopped the limp corpse free, then dragged it across the deck through the chains of women amassed on the port side. When they got to the bulwarks they suspended the body between them by armpits and ankles, and started swinging until they'd achieved enough momentum to throw it over the gunwales and into the sea. Charlie landed with a loud *plop* and everyone turned to starboard for the second act.

The captain pointed to the other victim at the mast and announced, "This mangy dog is apparently the ringleader. Ready the ropes for the Spanish torture!" Immediately several crewmen began stretching lines from the mainmast to foremast that ended in two yawning loops. The prisoner—a Geordie called Baker—was then cut free of his upright bondage, only to be laid on his back with his wrists in one loop and his feet through the other. As the crewmen pulled on both ends they tightened and stretched him on their makeshift rack. I thought they intended to pull him asunder, but the captain suddenly ordered, "Bowel him!" and the quartermaster leapt forward with his cutlass at the ready.

Bloodlust queered Kimble's furious face. He cried, "By my soul, I'll carve your gizzards into pound pieces!" He held the blade aloft, then vigorously descended the tip into the soft flesh, slicing from left to right as if through hard-skinned cheese. A morbid fascination gripped the crowd and they pulled on their leashes for a closer taste. The prisoner gave a blunted scream that turned into sharp squeals as he watched his shiny bowels being hoisted into the moonlight on the cusp of the tipsy blade. I think the shock got to him first—because his eyes seemed to flicker in horror before his head lolled round a couple of times, then faded away on a bleat.

I didn't have nothing left in my own guts to throw up but my own twisted stomach tried anyway. I heard myself muttering, "No, no . . . prithee . . . no!" Because I knew my turn came next.

As the body was tossed overboard Captain Mack shouted, "Blame yourself for your own death!" His livid eyes scanned the rest of the prisoners and asked, "Be that lesson plain enough for all?" He turned to the crew and commanded, "Back to your posts!" and watched while the first strand of prisoners was led away. Still holding my hair he twisted me back to the cabin and threw me down on the wooden bunk. "I've a fair mind to thrash you and throw you to the sharks!" he roared. I knew that he wasn't kidding. "But I've too much invested to afford that waste. And there's other wee ways to make use of you." I could tell he wanted to smash me in splinters but wouldn't risk damaging the goods. What a dilemma. I knew enough not to utter a word so I just slumped there awaiting his judgment. Then the captain suddenly pointed to the pile of cloth and said, "Put on the veils." My heart fluttered a pattering hope. He wanted an encore!

I'd just finished dressing when the boatswain's pipes trilled over the quarterdeck to signal the funeral of the murdered sailor.

It felt strange standing with the crew wrapped only in silken sheets as we all watched the body being sewn in a weighted hammock. I cried when the needle's last stitch pierced through the corpse's nose. Then someone said a prayer and the doctor read a psalm from the Bible. The fiddler played a haunting lament as the seaman was gently eased into the waters and I stared until there was nothing more to see. The captain then pushed me up onto the forecastle deck to stand alongside the musician and trumpeted to the solemn audience, "This wee wench gave the rebels the shears that took young Walker's life." A murmur of disapproval ran round the men and some of the grimy mouths spat anger. He continued, "So to recompense her betrayal she's going to entertain us." The fiddler struck up a tune and I knew I had to dance as if my life depended on it. Because it did. Of course, this costume wasn't very sturdy and as soon as I started leaping and skipping the ties began unwinding leaving me half-exposed. At the end of my usual routine I curtsied to the fiddler and bent to collect the items that had fallen. A murky hush descended. Not a soul moved. Then I heard the captain say, "She'll now dance the Seven Veils." No! I was mortified. I couldn't no way strip myself naked in front of these animals.

Wide, wet eyes pleaded to his better nature as my creaking voice cried, "Nay, Master! Don't . . ." But he was already halfway up the stairs on his way back to the cabin. A magnetic spark flashed across the waist and a few young sailors toasted me with their grog while others elbowed closer. The only way I could get through this nightmare was to pretend it wasn't me up there, so I blanked my mind, took a deeper-than-deep breath, and slowly began humming the chorus. As soon as the first veil tumbled my voice was drowned by a barrage of whoops and yells urging me on to the grand finale. But by then the fiddler had picked out the tune and no one was interested in the words. The second sheet fell. Then the third. The fourth. And fifth. By the time the sixth descended my tiny nipples were bare and the instant the seventh veil hit the deck I was swamped by a growling mass of sweaty arms and grabbing fingers. Suddenly I was on my back and someone was trying to push himself inside me. I tried to struggle, but other forearms pinned me to the planks and the fire bit my thighs so intensely it smoked out all sense and drenched me in clammy darkness.

I ain't got no idea how long they left me there—throbbing— bleeding—unconscious—but sometime around dawn I awoke to chattering teeth. At first I had no idea where I was until the previous day tore back through memory and reminded me why I was sleeping outside. Everything that happened after the Dance of Veils still hovered in shadow but when I tried to move there was no feeling below my hips and my cumbersome body refused to obey. Slowly I edged myself to a sitting position. I could hear the ship cracking and spraying on its endless, endless journey, the grunts and snores of the more fortunate sleepers scattered around the deck, and the night whispers of those still abroad or on watch.

Then someone touched my shoulder—I instinctively flinched and squiggled to escape. "Lola, it's me!" I recognized the hissing voice. Bristol put a tankard of ale in my wobbly hands and said, "Drink this."

He helped me down the liquid as I murmured, "What have they done to me? I can't move!"

His face turned away in embarrassment. The first gleam of dawn gilded his cheekbone a lighter gray before he coughed and said, "They took your . . . er . . . costume . . . as booty—I suppose. . . ." He pointed to the piece of tarpaulin draped over my lap and said, "That's all I could find." And then suddenly, in a squeezing roar of sensation, the feeling returned to my crushed body and with it came the pain.

"How do you feel?" Bristol asked.

"Bloody awful . . ."

"Can you stand?" I tried, but collapsed in a shaky pile. Bristol put his hands around my chest and heaved with all his strength but I wasn't no way budging. He mumbled, "Can't do it! I'll have to get the surgeon."

"No!" I didn't want Bristol to go to that man's cabin alone and asking for favors. But he'd already set off toward the stern. I cradled my knees in a ball and lay there rocking and smarting. It was ages and ages and ages before help came. I watched the orange clouds part to let the sun rise, and my spirit melted into the planks every time some sleepy sailor stumbled by to use the head. Then Dr. Simpson appeared, tossed me over his shoulder like a sack of turnips, and carried me back to the only other cabin on board. Bristol was lying naked on his bed, the blanket screwed in a tight knot between his legs and chin. He was staring dumbly at the wall. He never stirred, even when I was dropped on the other bunk beside him, but I couldn't block his whimpers from my ears—not that night nor any of the others. Poor, poor boy. I knew exactly what he was feeling.

And there I stayed for the rest of the voyage, healing. First I had to be stitched up—you know, down *there*—and washed with warm salty water several times a day. After the catgut was removed I was allowed to move, but only round the cabin. Then I was stuffed with plugs of alum to make my insides shrink—and finally I was allowed to sit in the chair and sew. Bristol became Simpson's shadow (under pretext of learning the surgeon's role) and I didn't get a chance to thank him properly because we weren't never left alone now. Each day the air seemed thicker and warmer and I was grateful not to be bundled below with the others. I could only imagine the smell in the sweltering holds. The tears. The fear. The tensions. Then one day the lookout spotted some beautiful islands that tiptoed like stepping stones into the horizon and I perched myself at the tiny window to imagine and absorb their enchantment. Somewhere, out on this vast empty plane, the waters had turned from gray to dusky blue under a puffy white-cloud sky. And way, way out on the port side glimmered a mound of land trimmed with wavering green fronds. I was hoping this was our final destination—until the doctor told me it was called the Isle of Devils and the sailors didn't dare land there. So I sighed as we sailed on by and watched in dismay as the quivering paradise faded to a tiny brown dot.

But not long after came a bout of the bloody flux that showed no regard for rank or situation—crew and prisoners were equally infected (probably from tainted water we'd taken on board). Fortunately, me and Bristol were spared the runs but the putrid smell coming from the holds was enough to make you instantly gag and the groans that drifted from deck to deck were pitifully harrowing. The surgeon—give him his due—worked day and night snatching a few blinks of sleep when the need overwhelmed him. I was kept busy mixing blackberry syrup for the prisoners, and measuring the much more expensive *Doctor Robert James's Famous Fever Powder* for the sailors. When the syrup failed we tried bark tea, then rhubarb elixir and tartar. Bristol assisted with the bloodletting and any able seaman still healthy enough was kept busy cleaning up slop. But several folks succumbed to dehydration and passed away in a delirious fever—their bodies were quietly disposed of under cover of dark. And the only spark keeping things active during that long desolate drag was the knowledge that we were almost *there*.

When it was clear we would make landfall within the week the surgeon's cabin turned into a barbershop and all day long I helped Simpson and his assistant steward get the valuable cargo ready for sale. The ship's rats had bred a fresh batch of fleas so the first thing to be done was a thorough cleaning of the holds, followed by a good dousing with brimstone and vinegar for everyone on board. Then the prisoners came to visit us one at a time. Bristol and me washed and untangled their hair while Simpson checked for obvious signs of illness. Sores were disguised using a lunar caustic or powder. Gray hairs were dyed. The dried-out skin on the arms and legs was softened with palm oil. Nails were clipped and scrubbed, while teeth were brightened using sticks of salt. I'd also to sort through the piles of clothes that the purser sent to find suitable breeches, skirts, shirts, or shifts to fit everyone. And during all this activity Dr. Simpson was the only person allowed to converse with any of the prisoners. When all the men were ready, the women came. I'd saved the very best skirt for Maude—it was the only one with a bit of shape—yet I might have been dressing a scarecrow for the notice she paid. But Violet squeezed my hand every time the surgeon turned away, and Dollie managed a quick secret hug when I helped to put her shift on. As we drew close to the shores of this strange land— America—a tidal tube of mist rolled out to greet us. And when we all knew this was the very last day, I was instructed to clean myself thoroughly under direct orders from Captain Mack.

In the late of the afternoon Dr. Simpson returned to the cabin and threw me a calico dress from the captain himself. I was amazed to find it was exactly my size—and I wondered how many other young girls had traveled this route before me. I looked down at the finery but didn't budge. "Something wrong?" he asked. I remained motionless. He eyed me with an amused expression and said, "We need you looking your best." Then he became impatient and snorted. "Get dressed." So I did.

Now, I wasn't any in the habit of conversing with the surgeon but I couldn't stop my tongue from blurting, "What happens now, sir?"

He stroked his chin and replied in measured tones, "We shall dock in Chesapeake Bay soon. There was thought to be a particular interested in you—but the captain will now have to settle for some other arrangement. . . ."

"Arrangement?" I stuttered. What did that mean?

Some kind of malice blunted the shine of his eyes and he snapped, "We could have placed you nicely if you had known only one master, but now . . ." I blushed in shame and turned away. He cleared his throat and continued, "Well . . . we will just have to take what we can get."

Now, as it happened, I was apparently being groomed to join the Golden Planters Club—and you probably ain't never heard of it on account of it being all secret. It's a society of Southern gentlemen bonded by a mutual predilection for immature females. They've several magistrates and sea captains on their payroll who make constant supply to their twisted demand, often kidnapping babes off the streets and conditioning them for slavery. The girls are then passed from podgy paws to gnarly fingers within their inner circle—until one of the men takes a special liking (and negotiates to take her home) or they all grow bored and start afresh (then they dump her in some brothel). Of course, having been had by most of the crew I was considered well-soiled. And because the captain had a profitable reputation to uphold he decided, instead, to capitalize on my time in the surgeon's cabin. He declared I was now to be sold as a fledgling nurse.

In a flurry of activity and apprehension our battered craft eventually edged into the harbor, but it still took a good day and a half before my feet touched land. The men were taken off first in pairs, knowing full well that regardless of their official sentences the chances of ever seeing any freedom dues were pretty remote. The ones with crafts—smiths or weavers or tailors or carpenters or shoemakers—were most in demand and obviously brought the best prices. The rejects, however, would be weathered outside to toil among the tobacco plants. When all the men were processed the other hold was opened, but the only sorting out here was done by lusty masculine eyes. Women who were deemed appealing would be sent to the whorehouses of towns boasting six men to every woman. Those who were old (or maimed like Maude) would be trained to work in kitchens— their one hope that they could develop some skill that would keep them safe from the fields. Then, when all the other prisoners had gone, the surgeon and his apprentice accompanied me down the gangplank and steered me toward a cluster of wooden-fenced buildings that looked remarkably like a half-moon fort.

The others, I later learned, would be paraded each day in the courtyard until purchased by some wealthy tobacco farm, while the most comely women were destined for another sail to ply their trades in the docklands of Charles Towne. But, to my dismay, I wasn't sent to no hut like the other women. We walked straight past the market and plodded our way through the town of Norfolk until we came to a fancy house. Dr. Simpson rang the bell, gave something to the manservant who answered, and pushed me up the wooden steps onto the porch. He whispered,

"Keep your mouth shut and do as you are bid." The manservant signaled I was to follow him inside.

When sneaking a last glance back at Bristol I saw the surgeon's possessive arm leading him away to the nearby inn. I realized that I was now all alone in this sinister New World—but that, I'm afraid, was that.

4

TEN FATHOMS DEEP
ON THE ROAD TO HELL

1712–1713

I was eventually deposited in a buttery-rich office that boasted several open glass windows. But even with the cross breeze wafting from the gaping sills the heat still basted the cloth to my shoulders, making me fidget uncomfortably. Some toff sat beside his writing desk and didn't take no notice of my arrival for a while, so I'd plenty of time to absorb his glossy brown wig, fine ruffled shirt, rich brocade waistcoat, silk breeches, and bright buckled shoes. The manservant coughed none too discreetly, causing a break in the gentleman's concentration and a crinkle in his brow. When he eventually looked up, his employee announced, "A girl is here from the ship, sir." The servant, waved away with a waft of hand, then quietly trod off toward the rear of the building. A kestrel-sharp pair of eyes scanned me from crown to foot and after a length of awkward silence his shrill voice came forth from between pinched lips stating, "My name is Dr. Arnold." I bobbed a curtsey and kept my face facing the floor. "And you are . . . ?" he inquired.

"Lola, sir." He awaited more information so I added, "Lolomura Blaise."

The corner of his mouth smirked crookedly as he began assessing my value. He contained his amusement long enough to ask, "And how old are you, Miss Blaise?"

"Fourteen, sir," I lied. Well—I felt I'd aged that much—maybe more.

I ain't sure he believed me but he played along with the charade anyway by saying, "And you have some nursing skill, I am told?" My cheeks reddened and I kept my eyes hidden under their lashes. I would be whatever I needed to be. Dr. Arnold scanned the paper in front of him and revealed, "I have a letter here from my good friend Captain Mack claiming you assisted the *Argyll*'s surgeon during a recent outbreak of bloody flux. Is this correct?" I nodded. He continued reading, "And affirmation from Dr. Simpson that you can proficiently mix the necessary ointments and tinctures for such diseases. . . ." He glanced in my direction and said, "I assume that would come from your Romany days?" *O dear Lord! He knows I'm a gypsy.* A jolt of panic ran down my legs and made them feel all at-sea again. I didn't have no idea what to say so I just stood with my knees each knocking against the other. "I believe that you are a gypsy," he said, "but that will not be held against you over here." I exhaled my relief. Gradually my eyes wandered up to his face as he continued, "We cannot afford to be that choosy." He searched through another bundle of papers on his desk until he found the advertisement he was after, then he carefully read over the details, occasionally glancing in my direction. "So you can deal with fever and the runs?" I indicated that I could. "You know how to birth babies, stitch wounds, and tend sores?" I ain't got no idea about that but pretended I did. "It is unlikely you will ever be asked to minister the mercury cure," he mused, adding, "but might you be able to assist a surgeon with bleedings and amputations?"

My stomach heaved at the very thought of it. But I took a very deep fill of air and responded, "What I don't know I can learn, sir."

"Good. That is the spirit." He tapped the paper recently mined and said, "You are going to a very good family in Carolina who recently lost their housekeeper to marsh fever. The folks there are rather isolated and have a profound preoccupation with their personal well-being so wish to have someone with medical knowledge on hand in case of emergencies." He looked directly in my face and added, "It is a precarious life on the plantations—fevers, smallpox, plague, and flux—but you will be treated well if . . ." and a long silence hung in the air before he added, "if you can put aside your criminal tendencies."

So he knew I was a convict then. Of course he did. But I also began to realize that whatever I'd been in my past life might now be left behind. I looked up again and met his gaze before replying, "I reckon I've learnt the error of my ways, sir."

He grinned a chilly smile and added, "That is as well, because if you are caught thieving down South they will chop off your hand, whip you, or hang you." I never doubted for one moment that they would so I nodded my full understanding. The doctor then rang a brass bell on the top of the desk and the housemaid who appeared was instructed to prepare a sack of provisions for a journey I'd apparently be taking at daybreak.

In the peachy gray of morning a merchant pulled his covered wagon into the courtyard and the manservant bundled me aboard. Dr. Arnold appeared with a letter addressed to a William Cormac (Esquire) at the Black River Plantation in Craven

County near Charles Towne, and a pouch of money that he gave to the driver. The doctor said, "You will get the other half when I receive notice from Cormac that Miss Blaise has arrived safely." And then I heard him whisper emphatically, "She has nursing skills . . . and is one of your own. Take good care." The merchant doffed his hat and bent down to snap a leather cuff round my ankle to chain me to the cart.

I flinched at his touch but he said cheerfully, "It'll be just a wee while till we clear the town, missie. Soon as we're on the Virginia Path I'll be taking it off again." I gaped at him with a silent mouth as he continued babbling, "You'll not be wanting to escape in the marshes or woods. Not with the snakes and wild boars and alligators and such." He winked in a jovial fashion, clucked the horses into action, and off we sprang. But it would be two unpleasant days of skirting the Dismal Swamp, in and among a constant flow of clumsy herding cows, before the road turned from pools of stagnant water into anything resembling what I'd call a forest—and even after he eventually unfettered my leg, the thought of leaving the safety of the wagon would never invade my mind.

Being back under canvas was comforting, despite the hardness of the bench and the joggle of wheels in the sloshing earth. I looked back into the cart and spotted the pots and pans that clattered every time we hit a rut, smelled puffs of coffee and tea that wafted from various chests, and marveled at the barrels of gunpowder greasing the boards smooth as they slid up and sideways. There were wrapped bolts of cloth for every occasion, a few pieces of furniture from England, plus several labeled packages to be delivered on our route. As my courage grew I snuck a look at the driver's dark ginger hair that spread in curly whiskers down the sides of his crinkled face. He sounded to me like he was from Ireland and I wondered how he had managed to find his way here. I must have been staring too long because he suddenly turned and said, "How are you doing, Missie Blaise?"

I looked down at the shackles and replied, "The name's Lola."

He though for a moment and said, "Ah, that's grand, so it is. But I'll still be calling you Missie Blaise when we're in company." He flashed a set of startlingly white teeth and added, "So you're a Didikoi too, eh?"

Too? What did he mean? I didn't see nothing in this strange man's face that resembled a member of my own tribe so I stuttered, "Are . . . are you . . . ?"

He grinned, touched the brim of his hat with a thick, tanned palm, and announced, "Shane the Tinker, at your service." To this day I still don't know whether Shane was his first or second name but he exuded the same friendly manner as my uncles and I instantly knew he was a fox, not a wolf.

I returned his smile and, wanting to keep the long path interesting, asked, "How far off is this Charles Towne?"

"The best part of three or four weeks," he answered. "But you're jammy to be bound for the Black River. It's as fine a place as any."

"You know it then?" I asked.

"Aye," he responded. "I've been Willie Cormac's mate for donkeys' years. Soft as shite, so he is. . . ."

"Is he married?"

The tinker chuckled at some private memory and coughed, "He's a bit of a one with the ladies." This was not what I wanted to hear—and concern must have registered on my cheeks because he quickly added, "But you'll be working with the second Mistress Cormac—Mary, the lovely Peg—and they've a wee gal about your own age, so I'd be guessing."

"What do they call the child?"

"Annie, as I believe. Aye—Annie, so it is." And that's the very first time I ever heard of the woman who'd grow into the legend of Anne Bonny.

I avidly absorbed all the information so as not to be making any rash mistakes when I got there. After a pause I probed, "Did you know the first Mistress Cormac then?"

He stifled another smirk and finally decided to let me in on the family drama. Now, I ain't never been one to forget conversations so I think that his tale went almost like this. He answered, "That I didn't." And then went on to explain how, "Willie and me met aboard the ship from Ireland. He'd been a lawyer in County Cork—but then lost his head with their pretty house-maid and was caught rotten when she got pregnant. His wife made a big show, charging them with adultery and fornication, and before long the scandal had all but broke Will's business. Then the wife got even more stroppy, accusing Peg of stealing some spoons and tried to have her arrested. So, not before time, Will and Peg ran off with Annie, bought their passage to the New World, and set up shop in Charles Towne." As I didn't want to interrupt his monologue I listened attentively, nodding in all the appropriate places. He continued, "So Willie became a merchant with the hastily gathered money he'd managed to salvage, and bought a place on Broad Street selling rare and fancy goods. He'd export rice—then import silver, crockery, and plate ware—until he made enough to buy his own plantation. Aye, the canny fellow even grows the rice himself now, that he does!"

I had to admit I was growing increasingly impressed by this land of opportunity. Was it really that easy to reinvent oneself? To strike against the wind and tide? But then I looked across at

Shane and remembered he was still a tinker. I tried (and failed) being subtle when I asked, "How about you then?"

He gave me another glint of teeth and tapped the side of his nose. He whispered, "Ah, the planter life's grand, for them that like it. But there's Romany blood in these here veins. . . ." And he felt no need to elaborate.

After a suitable pause I ventured, "Have you no folks back in Ireland then?"

He answered sadly, "None that'll be missing me any some." He looked across at me and added, "And your own kin?" I bit the inside of my cheeks so I wouldn't start crying and quietly shook my head. The gypsy in him understood. And said nothing further.

After we'd stopped to eat our packed victuals and water the horses Shane took the shackle off my ankle and I began feeling sleepy. He indicated a sack and blanket squeezed in between the cargo and said, "You go on back away and have a wee kip." I slept for a good few hours and when I eventually opened my eyes I lay thoughtfully on the rolling planks listening to Shane's melodic whistling.

So what makes a person willingly give up all that's familiar to sail across dark water to some unknown fate? And what is the lure of this muggy America? Now, from a felon's perspective, anything beats the squalor of Newgate—and happen there ain't much crime here on account that they all seem to live in well-guarded houses or forts—but to freely give up family and friends and set on some bold adventure means they were either looking for treasure (like pirates boast of) or they felt misunderstood, unwanted, and didn't fit in. We Romany folks know all about that—but the whole country can't be formed of banished rogues and gypsies! Still, this place does hold promise and boasts a fresh start. There's plenty of trees to build houses, and far more space than the people to fill it. I guess it's a brand-new land with its own rules and social order. I mean, where else would little Lola be addressed as Missie Blaise? Where else could an untutored girl be taken for a healer without even trying? I might really make something of my nursing experience if given chance to plot my own course. But had I wandered through the pearly gates to paradise . . . or crossed the bubbling Styx on route to Hades?

We trotted down an endless hoof-beaten road under a dappled canopy of shade that was carved out of the eternal spread of trees far as the eye could detect. The trip ended up taking almost a month—on account of some swollen rivers and too-muddy pathways—but I enjoyed the lull of familiar custom and the companionship of the chattering Shane. At Edenton a violent thunderstorm stopped us for two days, so we unhitched the wagon at a wayside inn and waited it out in their barn. This gave the horses a chance to rest and allowed us time to dry out our clothes. And by now we'd reached a Romany understanding—as long as I was treated with the respect accorded skilled workers I wouldn't be causing him no bother. When the ridge had dried sufficiently we trundled beside the sound toward New Bern, and after several numbing weeks we entered Wilmington, a bustling town clustered around a thronging harbor. We passed days of spectacularly colored beaches awash under fiery skies before we plodded into the swampy lowlands and crossed the marshes of Craven County.

When I noticed some perky pink plants growing haphazardly across the countryside I thought to ask Shane what medicinal purpose they might serve, for it occurred to me I needed to learn any magic this strange soil could yield. He scratched his scruffy face and said, "That's indigo, so it is. Some say as it can cure the cough, but it's mainly used for the blue dye made from the leaves."

"You don't think it helps the lungs any, then?"

He shrugged his neck and replied, "There's many a remedy better than that." It was time for us to break again for water, and when he'd tied the horses to a tree he rummaged around in the back for a small wooden box. "Give us a moment and I'll show you. . . ." When Shane carefully removed the lid I saw a row of tear-shaped fruit in various stages of drying. The softest still wore glints of red and yellow skin, while the oldest had cured into sticky brown discs. "These be figs," he explained, "from Florida." I had no idea where Florida was until Shane indicated it was much farther south. He let me hold one as he continued, "They're grand for the cough—when someone can't shit—and for easing childbirth, bad mouths, and boils." I stared at the squishy fruit, awed that something so small could render such bountiful relief. Shane then produced a waxy paper and put several of the cured rounds inside. He folded the package, thrust it toward me, and said, "See if you can't find a wee empty casket back there. You'll be needing to start your own medicine chest, that you will."

I was overwhelmed by this generosity and murmured, "I don't . . . Thank you. . . ."

"Aye, well don't rabbit on about it." He was equally embarrassed.

Now, on this particular journey I didn't never see Charles Towne itself because before we got there we took the right fork at a large crossroads and set off alongside the Black River. Shane stopped to trade with a passing merchant and came back holding some crescent-shaped fruit. "Ever seen one of these beauties?" he asked. I held one of the fibrous moons in my hand and shook my head. "It's a plantain," he explained as he cut off the tip with his knife. I examined the pinkish fruit and noted the wooly texture. Shane indicated I should eat it so I put the entire piece in my mouth. It was sour and felt like I was chewing sawdust. I pulled a face and spat it out. My companion laughed aloud and said, "It's not that bad when it's ripe or well-soaked, and it's a wonderful remedy for stomach upsets." I stared at the remaining stump with new respect. "The leaves are good for the eyes," he revealed. "And the boiled juice is given for back gripes and the worms." He then handed over the other plantains he'd haggled to add to my growing collection. Apparently it wouldn't do for a skilled employee to arrive at her station without tools. I almost felt like a proper apothecary.

Now, one evening as we plodded through twilight, Shane said he wanted to talk to me as a brother and he began explaining what some call *the birds and the bees*. Of course, I knew well enough about that lark yet pretended I was a maiden. I think he suspected I wasn't—but he let me squirm and grimace as he explained the ways of men. Eventually he told how he'd once caught the Great Pox and been given the mercury cure—and how after that his wood wouldn't harden—so as to assure me I was safe from his smutty musings. And then he passed on that intimate knowledge that has helped me from that day to this. "First off," he said, "if you want to grab a man's interest take care to suckle hard on his chest teats." I giggled at the thought, but the earnestness on Shane's face bade me stop and listen more closely. "And second," he added, "to keep from getting ruined when you're older you must pee and then wash yourself clean as soon as ever you're done." I nodded that I'd heard, even though I was skeptical that any such remedy would work.

Of course, throughout the whole trip Shane told me lots of grand stories—some real, some imagined—and the time passed by much quicker than it might have otherwise. And only once did I get myself in a panic, when we were stopped in the road by the strangest creature I'd ever seen. He was a leathery-faced man, with shiny black hair parted in two on either side of his berry-dark eyes that were painted one white and one black. I caught only a glimpse of this weird apparition before Shane pushed me backward over the bench and hissed, "Hide!" So I scurried behind the barrels of gunpowder and dragged the surrounding sacks to cover the gaps. From outside the canvas I heard a grunted command and the wagon instantly pulled to a halt. Muffled conversation drifted to the rear and I tried to breathe as quietly as able. Before long the cart began moving again but I stayed where I was until I heard the words, "How are you faring back there?"

During the rest of that afternoon I learned all about the Indian Massacre the previous year and discovered that the native I'd seen was a Catawba scout requesting information. Whatever Shane told him sent him away—but I could never entirely erase him from my curiosity. Now, according to my companion, the Tuscaroras were a nation who lived peacefully with the first white settlers up north. But when so many others followed (and took over their hunting grounds to build plantations), the natives turned angry and decided to make a stand. It all got messy—scores of Europeans killed—so the Southern whites (with the help of friendly tribes) went to their aid. Since then, several local incidents have threatened the fragile truce that could flare into full-scale warfare at any given moment. So for all the charm of the lush, calm countryside we were passing through—this wasn't no Garden of Eden.

Our passage grew ever more dense and swampy but the marvelous birds and the otherworldly beauty made the night bugs almost worthwhile. Fortunately the mosquitoes didn't seem to like me any but they gave poor Shane the odd nip or two. My favorite bird wore a little red crown that fluttered when he flew past the great white herons posing gracefully on the sandbanks. I spied the most enormous gaily painted butterflies imaginable, and heard strange eerie chirps from alien creatures that clattered like drunken grasshoppers. And the flowers! Huge clusters of red camellias . . . gaping white magnolias . . . I ain't never seen nothing like it. And whenever we caught a view of the river itself it looked like a silver serpent wending its way through a tunnel of cypress and oak trees, all festooned with a feathery plant that Shane called Spanish moss. Best of all though—and it still takes my breath after all these long years—was sight of the rising moon set in a sky of pink and purple velvet. It was absolutely stunning. And then one day, out of the shimmering heat, came my first glimpse of the Black River Plantation that was to be my future home. We entered a distinctive stone gateway and drove the long shaded path to a large white house with a ceramic tiled roof, nestled in front of a cluster of huts, sheds, and barns. The place vibrated like a busy hamlet tucked away in a wasteland of wood and water. For, as I was about to discover, the rice harvest was in full swing.

Now, I didn't know nothing about what a rice plantation would look like but in them early days (when they were still learning how to grow Carolina Gold) the place resembled a small country estate on the banks of a black tidal river. If you ain't never seen rice growing before it looks like swampy fields of rye, cut through with dikes as I'm told they have in the Netherlands. Sweetness hangs in the sultry air. The fields are lush and copious. Then, of course, you find all the other things you'd expect on a farm—cattle and sheep, hogs and chickens, wheat and corn and vegetables. There's an orchard bursting with ripening fruits, with plenty of deer and game lurking in the swamp. The river yields fish and fowl and turtles but—as in every Eden—you've to be wary of the snakes (and on this particular waterway of the log-sized alligators too).

William Cormac had built himself an unusual three-story federal-style home on a raised foundation of stone. The main floor consisted of two large rooms, each with its own fireplace and chimney off a long side hall that contained both front and back doors, entered from three granite steps framed with fancy porches. The upstairs mirrored the lower floor plan, with two huge bedrooms and a smaller guest room that contained a spinning wheel. From the landing a winding staircase led to an airy attic that extended the entire length of the building and was divided comfortably to accommodate all the white servants. The kitchen was located in a separate shed set back from the Big House to reduce the risk of fire, and a selection of scattered structures boasted a meat house, well house, chicken house, barn, stables, winnowing house, and rice mill. There were apparently eight slaves (with the darkest complexions ever) who worked the fields and lived in two wooden shacks set back at the edge of the woods. The white overseer—Mr. Bart Higgins—resided in the largest attic room with Mrs. Joy Higgins, the cook. And, as I was replacing the deceased housekeeper, I was given the smallest space above Miss Anne's bedroom.

Now don't get me wrong—Miss Anne had the most gorgeous chamber imaginable—but for me to have my own space with two tiny windows and a corded bed was unbelievable good fortune. I was ecstatic. After I'd said farewell to Shane (who went off to conduct his business around the plantation with Master William) I was left in the care of Mistress Mary. She was a thin, delicate woman, with long dark hair and vivid green eyes. I could tell she was shy and didn't much like being boss lady, for she always treated folks graciously in the hope they would respond in kind. And generally they did—all excepting her daughter. Now, Annie Cormac was always a spoilt tetchy baggage there's no mistaking. And I couldn't never understand her. She had everything a bonnie girl could dream of—parents, money, social advantage—and yet she was wild as a pit viper. Her father pampered her every whim and the mistress couldn't do nothing to save her. They gave her the finest home this side of Charles Towne, the most elaborate dresses, the costliest horses to ride, a ridiculously fluffy kitten too pampered to catch mice, and a series of tutors who only managed to teach the basics she chose to absorb. Oh, Annie could read and write and count (in fact, she was the one who taught me my letters), but she was far more interested in farming and horses—perhaps because she was trying to be the boy her father always wanted. Anyways, when she was supposed to be learning to be a refined lady she often outwitted the poor scholar assigned and snuck off down to the river to pester the men. So her father eventually gave in again and agreed to groom her to run the plantation. After all—he was much older than his wife—and they had no other heir.

Mistress Mary guided me round the farm and explained her expectations. She and I would take care of the house and any of the folks who fell sickly (so she was pleased to find me young and green and pliable) and when Mrs. Higgins brought over the meals from the kitchen my job was to serve the family and guests, then clear away the dishes. I would eat later with Bart and Joy in the kitchen and then help Bart take food to the black people out in the woods. The men there had no women to look out for them and they were always too exhausted by the end of the day to do much more than eat and sleep. It didn't take me long to realize that being a white servant was one step up from being a slave—these folks had been bought forever and therefore belonged to the Cormacs, body and soul. I, at least, got to work and sleep in the Big House. My tasks were boring and sometimes arduous (making beds, scrubbing floors, beating rugs, polishing and cleaning), but I didn't have to wade chest-deep in murky dangerous waters digging dikes and weeding rice plants. I didn't have to thresh the crops with flail sticks or mill the rice with mortar and pestle. I didn't have to toil in the fierce stinging sun wearing only a coarse long-tail shirt. It's no wonder the master didn't buy women for his fields. I ain't sure they'd ever survive.

First time I laid eyes on Anne was later that day when she came in from steering the flatboat to the winnowing house. She was definitely older, a good head taller, and looked far stronger than either me or her mother. I stood silently by the mistress as the robust girl shot into the parlor shedding stalks and soil across the polished boards. Her mother pointed to the offending boots and watched as her reluctant daughter shucked them off her feet. Then she announced, "Annie—this is Lola, our new person."

Anne looked me up and down with a disdainful sneer. Then she pointed to the dirty footwear and said, "Take those away and clean them." I looked up at the mistress. Her face indicated that I was to obey so I picked up the filthy boots and took them outside to the river's edge. All the pretensions of Nurse Blaise suddenly fell back to being poor little Lola, and at that point I realized this is how things were to be.

I guess if I'm honest I'd secretly hoped, being almost the same age and all, that me and Anne would be mates. I desperately missed my kinfolks at home, the gang back in London, Bristol's cleverness and friendship, and Shane's amusing banter. But Annie was one of them solitary souls who prefer to keep their own company. In many ways she was much older than her years but I saw right enough in her empty stare that there was something hollow inside her that all the sunlight of the Carribee wouldn't never warm. And I still—to this day—ain't got no idea why.

So after my first encounter I disliked the young miss, especially when she took to following me about my chores, critiquing my performance, and making me flinch on the air of her hostile, sharp tongue. She'd do whatever new trick entered her mind to get me into mischief—for example, one time when I'd finished making her bed she slid back into the room and scattered the linens all through the air to create a mass of dust and feathers. Then she told her mother I'd deliberately thrown things about in a temper and I got a good rapping on both knuckles from a wooden spoon. Annie laughed herself sore that evening, chuckling every time she caught sight of my swollen hands. Later, I got to hating the little snake. She was rude and intimidating whenever she came near, and she made three times more mess than the rest of the household put together. I designed my work schedule to intentionally avoid her but within a few weeks I was lusting to bite out her pearly-peach throat. You see, I'd been given a patch of land to raise herbs and a large chest in which to store my collection. This was my only possession and therefore my greatest treasure. One day I went to my room and discovered that the contents had been emptied. I could hear Annie giggling below so I scurried downstairs and knocked on her door, entering before she could speak. And there I discovered my precious medicines slopped into one big pile at the edge of her rug. Everything was mixed up together. All were utterly useless. I gasped and held my words back by clamping my hand across my mouth. Then I rushed down to the parlor where Mistress Mary was sewing. The angst on my face said all. She immediately rose and said to me, "Whatever's the matter, girl?"

I pointed up to Anne's bedroom and then rushed ahead, but when her mother entered, she flashed her most innocent smile and said, "Look, Mama! I have conjured myself a baby!" She had dressed her terrified marmalade cat in doll clothes and bonnet, then bound it tightly in a blanket to prevent any escape. Mary was torn between relief that her tomboy daughter still had some maternal instinct (which she desperately wished to encourage) and anguish at the lost storehouse of medicine (made apparent by the familiar containers scattered about the floor).

"Oh, Annie!" she wailed. "What have you done?"

The manipulative daughter held out her magic child for her mother to examine and said, "I needed the herbs to transform Miss Kitty. . . ." She then abruptly dropped her bundle on the floor so the poor creature could find sanctuary under the bed, and sprang into her mother's flailing arms to proffer a conciliatory hug. The mistress turned to me in the entrance and said sheepishly, "You'd better clean up this mess, Lola. Salvage anything you can." I numbly obeyed.

It took me several months to gather and dry replacement herbs but I'm glad I ain't never thrashed the little wench because—as it happens—all turned out for the best. First, I was given a larger strongbox that closed with a sturdy lock, and from that time on I always wore the key on a leather thong round my neck. And second, Anne was ordered by her father to spend each evening tutoring me so as I could write down all the medicines and their uses. It took most of that winter for my coarse brain to learn, but the whole episode gave me a grudging respect for the intellect hiding beneath that mischievous tumble of strawberry-blond locks. Annie made an effective teacher—being impatient she cut to the core of the lesson, and being vain she basked in full credit for all of my growing success. I think I became like another of her pets—a silenced companion to be toyed with and changed. And of course she had no real idea of the power she was seeding inside of me. I listened to all of the anecdotes for whatever ailments from every loose tongue, and as soon as I'd mastered the quill I wrote them down. An apothecary needed to record and remember. I was also allowed some time late afternoons to roam river and woodlands in search of new ingredients in the hope that my pharmacy might rival the best in Charles Towne. I discovered how white lips favored the use of rosin pills, spirit of turpentine, and castor oil (which could be mixed in numerous ways for various ills), while black tongues swore that life-everlasting could break fevers, artichokes cured stomachaches, and tar could soothe both tooth and ear. I listened, experimented, observed—and wrote everything down in my raw splotchy code. On Sundays we went round the other estates visiting, and that's where I learned how to talk low and act proper in company. We'd always stop at the Mid Town Estate to drop off and collect the week's laundry, carefully cleaned under direction of their Jamaican washerwoman, the formidable Miss Abbie. And there we'd catch up on the local news.

Then one fateful day my mistress caught the marsh fever.

Of course, this was in the early days—before owners realized that plantation air was lethal from May to September—before they built summer homes in the mountains to escape like they do today. Poor Mary took to sweating and shaking, vomiting and moaning, and I tried everything in the chest to help her condition. But the only easement I could manage was to waft my arms stiff, fanning the flies from her waxy face. The master sent to Charles Towne for the surgeon, who duly arrived, flustered about, and prescribed a new remedy called cinchona bark. I brewed the herbal exactly as instructed but unfortunately it was too little too bitter too late, and the dear sweet lady dropped into a dark slumber and never returned. My own first patient had died, and I was beside myself with fear. What would become of me now?

The next dizzy weeks lay jumbled in my confused memory. There was a wake—and Mrs. Higgins ran me ragged plucking chickens and pounding bread. There was a houseful of mourners—offering condolences, needing attention, and poking round the property. There was a funeral—and we buried Mistress Mary under her favorite live oak by the river. And there was the master—so inconsolable in grief that (like the field hands) he fell disinterested and stopped working altogether. The overseer didn't have no heart to whip the desolate slaves so the entire place hung morbid and silent until the last of the visitors left. Annie spent the mornings with her father dealing with the unwanted guests, and then wandered off around the plantation for most of the afternoons. I tended my garden, roamed the woods for hickory nuts, acorns, cane roots, and artichokes, and raided the orchard of its quinces and plums. I sometimes stopped and watched the Africans as they moved about in their own incomprehensible world. Everything seemed disheveled and awry.

In the midst of this confusion I found a reddish-pink rash speckling my body, strange because it spread across hands and feet. I worried I'd caught the marsh fever too—but although I felt sick and aching I'd not enough sweltering heat for undue concern. No, whatever I had was something entirely different, but as I couldn't afford to be ill myself I snuck potions for the headaches, made toddies for the scratchy throat, and put the weight loss down to the extra panic and graft. Whatever it was passed away with time—and never did cause me no more bother.

Then the following week several more folks fell stricken. Four of the black men who shared the same room now tossed and lurched in a feverish sweat, and I spent many long days teaching the healthy slaves ways to alleviate the distress of their roommates. I could understand little of the strange Gullah language, but they were familiar enough with the white tongue and followed my directions without question. One of the men—Gibby—told me he'd had a similar disease himself as a child. He suggested coating the patients in river mud and spent long hours chanting over their prone shapes, wafting smoldering sticks through the air round their faces. And he placed a bag of queer things called jacks at the foot of each groaning pallet. I brewed the rest of the cinchona bark into a huge pot of tea and spoon-fed as much as each parched mouth could tolerate. Then I instructed the others to imitate my actions to keep the patients watered throughout the long night. In the morning there was little change, except I noticed the restless eyes rolled less in their sleep now, although I didn't know if this was a good sign or not. Gibby brought pails and pails of water and doused the muddy bodies to keep them cool, and Mr. Bart appeared with a thin gruel that we managed to minister with struggle and care. This pattern continued for another day. And another. And then one early dawn I entered the humid hut to find it empty. I rushed to the adjoining structure but there was no one in sight. Then I heard an enigmatic chanting wafting across from the fire pit that usually lay dormant (except for Christmas and Sundays), and there I saw a sparking fire and some kind of ceremony taking place. All four patients were alive! And I ain't never been so relieved. But I also felt like an intruder spying on them with their gods . . . so I quietly crept back the way I'd come and left them to it.

Now, I probably shouldn't be telling you this, but Anne had an odd reaction to her mother's passing. She wouldn't go nowhere near the sick mistress for fear she might catch the disease herself, but then right at the very end she stood rigid in the doorway and watched her die. I never heard a single word pass between them (which I thought was strange) but after her mother's last breath I'm sure I saw Annie smile. She locked herself in her room for a night and a day where she grieved alone, away from her father. Then she opened the door, calm and composed as if nothing untoward had happened, and set about arranging the elaborate funeral.

From that moment on, thirteen-year-old Annie Cormac became sole mistress of the Black River Plantation. And that, unfortunately, was that.

5

CHARTINGS UNDOUBT
WHERE A WOMAN HAD BEEN

1713–1714

So you want to know more of Anne Bonny, do you? Well, I ain't going to pretend we ever became best mates or nothing, but I'm guessing I knew her well as anyone. Her father was desperate to make her a lady and match her with one of the elite Charles Towne families and believe me, she could sure play the Southern belle when it pleased. She'd dress herself up in the finest brocade, her strawberry hair tempered in shiny ringlets, all light manners, polite chitchat, and giggles. Now, Annie had inherited her mother's sea-bright eyes, but she flashed them from under hooded lids in an intoxicating manner that men found wildly exciting. If you saw her binding the stubble into sheaves you wouldn't stop to glance twice, but when she swirled her silks like a gold-jeweled copperhead she could make the breath hang in the back of your throat. Anne was too vigorous to be a beauty—too long and firm and sinewy—yet she emitted a rare sexuality—an oozing sensual musk. By the time she was fifteen she'd ripened into her velvet skin and creamy bosom. Aye, she was bright and adventurous and hardy but there was a darker side to Annie Cormac that many lost souls would discover to their peril. She'd a vicious temper when riled and was given to violent shakes of the tail if she ain't never got her own way—but beyond that there was something foreboding that made her callous and selfish. So if you were to ask me what I liked best I'd have to say it was her lust for life. Annie sure knew how to mesmerize, and at one time or another all of us silly critters were lured to her dazzling fire.

See, Anne was of a mind to blow hot, then cold. One wondrous day she'd allow you close—to demonstrate a gypsy snare or trap—giving her undivided attention to the plucking or skinning or gutting or cleaning. Those times you'd feel a connection, like two minds sharing the same bold adventure. Her personality was magnetic and binding so you wanted to serve her, impress her, love her, win her favor. Then another time she'd have no use for folks and couldn't be sparing the time of day. She'd run moody, irritated and crotchety, and nothing you'd do would suit. You'd try to come up with some grand new distraction but she'd rear her regal head and snap you firmly in place so all you could do was crawl away, wounded and hurt and despondent.

Now, although everyone mourned Mary Cormac's passing, by the spring of 1713 the demands of the new rice crop had prompted a return to order and the plantation settled into a familiar routine. Except at the Big House. Mistress Anne made life as miserable as possible with a constant list of chores and demands that never satisfied even when properly completed. If she'd kept the same routine as her mother we'd have been able to muddle through but Anne didn't help out like the old mistress—she acted on impulse without logic or consideration.

Things reached a volatile crescendo one scorching hot day when Anne decided I needed to scrub the walls and floor of the parlor (which I did). Then I'd to wash the windows and beat the drapes and rugs (which I did). And then she ordered me to empty, clean out, and black the fireplace (even though we wouldn't be needing to use it for months yet). I made the mistake of complaining that the soot would mess up the freshly polished floor and Annie took this as a challenge to her authority. Anyway, she struck a fit and smacked me full across the face, making me bite my lip bloody and causing my eye to bruise. So I scattered from the house and ran to the safety of Mrs. Higgins's kitchen. Joy listened patiently to my burbled complaint, soothed my bruise with half an apple, wiped my lip clear of gore, and then told me to go apologize to my mistress. At first I refused. But then, as I listened to the lilting Welsh accent explaining my limited options, I knew I'd to chew down my pride and accept the necessary reprimand. She accompanied me back to the parlor and listened as I made my peace. Annie gave me a broody look, then said, "You think you know better than I? Then do as you please." She came close into my face and hissed, "But if I ever find anything dirty or out of place, I shall have you whipped like one of the *other* slaves." And then she glided out of the house and made toward the stables.

I felt as if the floor had dropped beneath me because there wasn't no way I could keep the whole place running all by myself. I looked into Joy's gray eyes and cried, "What am I to do now?" Hot tears sparkled down my face.

Mrs. Higgins thought for a moment and then said, "Let me have a word with Master William this evening. I think I can persuade him you'll be needing some help." She squeezed my shoulder, then pointed toward the fireplace and added, "Why don't you make a start on the hearth and I'll go fetch an old blanket to cover the boards and keep the rug clean." And from that day on Anne refused any responsibilities round the home in preference to supervising the men on the farm.

It was decided, however, that I couldn't be relied upon by myself, so the master advertised for an experienced housekeeper who arrived a few weeks later. Mrs. Emily Drayton was the unfortunate second wife of Colonel Drayton from the Pee Wee River Plantation. She was recently widowed—middle-aged and childless—but found the entire estate had been willed to the colonel's three sons from his previous marriage. The vindictive heirs immediately forced their stepmother off the land and therefore she now had to earn her own living. Mrs. Drayton was gray and cold and fishlike. But I can't never say she didn't do a good job (even if she was tightly wound and remote). One thing I will add—she was the only one who could handle Miss Annie. She wouldn't stand no nonsense and that's a fact! I don't know how she did it but the two of them came to some taut understanding and generally stayed out of each other's way. And when Mrs. Drayton turned out to be a bit of a worrier regarding her health she and I hit it right off, because whatever new ailment she developed I was always there with a cure (generally mixed in a base of strong brandy). Meanwhile, Master William was away in Charles Towne turning his shop into an elegant home from which to introduce Anne to society when she reached the age of debut.

That summer was humid and brutal, yet I learned to tolerate the heat. But at the start of the fall I spotted certain anomalies that made me feel uneasy. At first, when I saw large flocks of sparrows making for the mountains, I thought migration season had come early and was curious because they seemed headed in the wrong direction. Then I heard squawking flocks of seagulls flooding inland and began to pay closer attention. Was it normal to see so many snakes suddenly leave their burrows by the river and cross the marshes inland? Where had all the bees disappeared to when they should be storing nectar? And why were the boar and deer apparently making for higher ground? I mentioned my concern to Mr. Higgins, but he just shrugged and said that maybe some storm was brewing out at sea. The air seemed to jell even stickier and the horses became unsettled and agitated, but Annie at least had sense enough to lead them from pasture and secure them in the stables on the rise. Then the dogs started shivering and howling, and everything seemed to cower before some impending unseen force.

Now you'll remember the terrible hurricane that September—the one that took out half of Charles Towne and drowned the rice fields in salt? Well, I ain't exaggerating when I tell you I never seen no storm that awful before or after. It stealthily descended one sultry dawn with a full day of building wind that blustered and spread, and when we woke up the following morning the heavens were steamy and dark and threatening. The northeasterly currents whistled louder as they grew in strength and then came torrential rain that pounded fast and persistent. By now everything breathing had found its way to safety, and when the winds started shaking the scanty wood buildings, Mr. Higgins rounded up all of the men and begged Annie's permission to shelter them in the hallway of the Big House. We all crowded together, black and white, mistress and slave, to brave the devastation. The storm growled like a bitch in heat, slapping and banging the sides of the property, trying to break through the shutters and into our space. Trees cracked and fell. Buildings tossed and tore apart over the rising fields. Frightened critters bleated, whined, growled, yelped, and grunted. Slates began tearing away from the roof as water slid from the rafters and under the doorways. The dikes couldn't hold back the sea that burst inland and it rose and rose above the high-water mark and completely swamped the fields. The surge must have reached several feet high to have breeched the three porch steps because it seeped like a persistent puddle, gaining more and more ground along the hall. When the spill from back and front doors joined together we began to climb the stairs and hurriedly formed a human chain to move anything valuable up to the bedrooms. And then an eerie calm descended and the waters suddenly receded from the house.

I thought that the drama had subsided sufficiently to risk wading to the kitchen for a jug of ale to quench our parched thirsts so I pushed my way past the crush of sticky bodies and slopped to the back door. Gibby grunted a warning about the same time that Mr. Higgins shouted something about the eye of the storm, but I was already through to the porch. Everything was shrouded in a thick honey haze. All lay silent and still and foreboding. Then suddenly something fluffy shot between my legs and in a blinding flash I saw Annie's confused cat instantly skid off the steps and into the knee-deep water. The poor creature tried valiantly to swim, its head bobbing up and down in the dappled yellow smog. I leaned over to grasp the scruff of its neck and just as I was hauling the pathetic animal clear a panic-stricken alligator rose from the murk and snapped its jaws around the fur. I let go with a horrified scream, sickened by the bloody bubbles splattering the surface as the predator thrashed and rolled, churning the wetness to sludge. When I turned back to the house I saw Anne standing fixed in the hallway, a jolt of intensity etched on her face as her brain slowly processed the scene she was witnessing. She came round enough to grab me by the hair, yank me inside, and violently kick the door shut. I blubbered, "I'm s . . . sorry. . . ." Her fierce eyes transfixed me in place making my blood turn to mud. She stared deep into my pupils, all the while twisting my mane round her hand, and would likely have scalped me on the spot if Mr. Higgins hadn't soothed her grip away. Joy Higgins, right at his elbow, cast a motherly arm around the distraught young woman and led her to the bedroom. Bart's shoulder pushed me hard against the door and he turned away in disgust as the numerous eyes lining the staircase hardened with bold contempt. Several black lips tutted and sighed recognizably, their alien language condemning my stupidity. And I ain't never felt so shivery as on that particularly long dank day.

Eventually, during the blackness of night, the rain stopped pounding its anger and we realized the house had been spared. The wind shifted direction and with a loud sucking sound the water miraculously sank back to the river. When the dawning sun finally lit the steam the nearest hand cautiously opened the front door to allow us to survey the wreckage. I can't never describe the otherworldliness. It was like finding yourself submerged undersea. Nearly all of the outbuildings were damaged— the winnowing house had collapsed on its stilts and the rice mill lay in ruins. The roof was missing from both slave quarters, several fences had blown clean away, weak trees were completely uprooted and stronger ones lay crippled, split in half. Only the barn and stable survived intact, being tucked away on the elevated field. Dead fish draped languidly over the bushes, a bloated hog floated by, and a young doe was carefully rescued from the fork of a treetop. Barrels and spars bobbed blithely on the river and any semblance of a pathway was washed flat. There was destruction and mayhem everywhere while the sticky sweet smell of rottenness cloyed the air. I'm told that seventy people perished in that tragedy and most of the plantations north of Black River were washed clean away. Annie Cormac sat on the top porch step, hugging her knees and staring at the debris. I ain't never seen her upset like that and thought it best to steer clear. But Mrs. Drayton approached her timidly and asked, "Are you all right, ma'am?"

Anne raised weary eyes that seemed out of focus and shook her head in dismay. She continued to stare blindly down the ragged line of live oaks and asked, "Where's Papa?"

The housekeeper followed the young girl's gaze and said softly, "He's safe enough in Charles Towne, ma'am. I'm sure he'll be home soon as ever he can."

Now, it actually took the master almost a week to get word to Black River—on account of all the trees blocking the paths, the boggy ground, and the washed-away bridges—and by the time the messenger arrived, Mr. Higgins had everything under control. The men had repaired their own quarters, reslated the Big House roof, and salvaged as much of the winter provisions as possible. The livestock had been attended and the house was still drying out before it could be cleaned. There was nothing to be done about the rice fields, though, so whatever had not yet been harvested was lost—but at least all the people were safe—and the tenuous riverbanks shaped by the sweat of so many muscles had survived the waning tides. Annie seemed to hold herself accountable for the catastrophe because it happened on her watch. But then later she decided to blame God instead, which perhaps helps explain her shocking belligerence toward Him in later days.

When the messenger finally arrived Annie was herding sheep to their new, hastily fenced enclosure so it was just before supper when she finally received word her father had been badly injured in the hurricane. Master William was apparently trying to sand-bag his shop front when the weight of the surge had burst down the door and swept him across the room. He hit the stone counter opposite, breaking both legs just above the knees, and spent several hours in the filthy water before being rescued, so he'd unfortunately also contracted pneumonia. As he was too injured to get back to Black River he requested that Annie leave immediately for Charles Towne with the messenger, so that she could be with him. Me and Mrs. Drayton were to carry on maintaining the house and Mr. Higgins would oversee all the plantation work until his return, which would likely be six or eight weeks away. Annie read the letter of instruction twice through before she spoke. Her cheeks had drained to a chalky white as she swallowed the shock with a silent gulp. She asked a few curt questions about the master's condition, all the while considering the answers. Then her skin flushed an angry scarlet hue. The young woman looked in my direction and snapped, "Can you ride?"

Of course I could so I said, "I've been riding since I could walk. . . ."

She eyed me suspiciously to ascertain that I was being truthful and then commanded, "Then get your things together. You are going to Charles Towne."

The messenger—an arrogant young militia officer called Lieutenant Aaron Ellyott—interjected with, "But, Miss Anne . . . your father gave specific instructions I was to fetch you. . . ."

Annie gave him a scathing glare and barked, "Do I look like I am the nurse?"

The flustered gentleman was not going to risk offending the young lady he was hoping to accompany so he replied, "Of course not, ma'am. I am merely clarifying Mr. Cormac's wish . . . to see you. . . ."

"Tell my father that I must stay and attend the fields. There is still a great deal of salvage and repair work to do and I cannot be running off to town to hold his hand at such a critical time. We have the indulgence of our own nurse—so I am sending her in my stead." And with that Annie walked away to clean herself for supper.

Within the hour the lieutenant and I had eaten, fresh horses were saddled (although I was trained bareback), and my medicine trunk had been brought down and tied to the back of my mare with a bundle of clothes rolled up behind. Bart and Joy gave the young master enough supplies to get us both back to town and before I really knew what was happening I was clopping down a moonlit path tied to an irritated officer en route to who knew what. Now, it turns out that young Master Ellyott was the bachelor son of one of Master Cormac's merchant friends, and the last thing he wanted to be doing was collecting some gypsy wench from a godforsaken bogged-down plantation when he had been dreaming of chivalrously attending the lovely Miss Anne. I don't know what incentive his father or Cormac offered—but it was apparent from the pressing pace he set—by the pistol overtly strung across his chest—by the ornate sword dancing on his thigh—and in his utter dismissive silence—that he knew himself as my better. So I kept my gob shut and fell into a canter behind. We only rested to answer calls of nature, to feed and water the horses at stops along the way, and to catch a mean bite ourselves. And I ain't sure which one of us was more relieved when he finally deposited me at the redbrick house on Broad Street.

It seemed silly to me at the time that any young gentleman wanting to woo my mistress would conduct himself like a surly brat. I suppose he believed it didn't matter what I thought of him, but that's really very shortsighted. I mean, I could readily have put in a good word on his behalf if he'd treated me with any shred of decency. And how could he know I wasn't Annie's mate? Was I so objectionable he couldn't never consider that someone like me might have her ear? As he didn't even bother to find out, I suppose he perceived just a worthless wench to be ground in place by his shiny boot. But something about his nose-in-the-air manner really rankled me. Still, I didn't have to wait long to savor the delicious bite back.

The end tip of Charles Towne lay submerged in ponds all the way up to the very edge of Broad Street. We stopped at a four-story house, still in the throes of construction, where the lower shop level had been badly vandalized by forces of nature and smelled like drying bilge water. The third and fourth levels were just empty shells so all current activity was focused on the second floor. Eventually, a thin, nervous man appeared at one of the two black doors, his brown eyes all but lost beneath the bushiest brows imaginable. The lieutenant left me at the door and pushed his way through to speak with Master William as the flustered employee ushered me inside. He said, "I'm Joshua Steiner, Mr. Cormac's associate. And you must be . . ." He knew I wasn't the haughty daughter so his words puttered away even as he spoke them.

I held out my hand as I'd been taught and said, "Lola Blaise, sir. I've been sent to nurse the master."

He gave the tips of my fingers a quick, limp shake as he inquired, "And Mistress Anne?"

I looked down at my dirty knuckles and murmured, "She's . . .

she's too busy harvesting . . . with the hurricane and all. . . ." Mr. Steiner gave an almost imperceptible snort and then told me to unpack my belongings. A few minutes later the lieutenant brushed past us both and went outside to stable the horses.

Master William was in bad shape. He'd got over the fever right enough but his usually ruddy face was darkened and gaunt. His sandy hair clumped in matted snags and his deep, dark eyes had sunk to blackened specks. One of the town's overworked surgeons had improvised broom handles as splints to immobilize the broken limbs, and now he lay in much discomfort in the bedchamber above the shop. Most of the merchandise had been damaged by the waves that left the lower streets in ruins so Joshua, anxious to see what could be salvaged, was only too glad to hand over the invalid to me. The master had also lost his cook in the storm—she'd had to return to help out her own family—but the neighbors gallantly rallied round to provide food for the two stranded men (although no one had thought to change the bedding and neither house nor patient had been cleaned in ages). I immediately set to work, and later that afternoon Joshua showed me how to prepare the tincture of opium left by the surgeon. The master sure enjoyed this particular medicine because he thereafter took the laudanum every day, even when his legs had fully recovered.

The next couple of months I quickly adjusted to city life. Charles Towne resembled the posh end of London, with its ballast-stone streets and tall, packed buildings (except it was wider, newer, brighter, and the people there feigned a more genteel politeness). I was amazed how quickly the folks recovered in the wake of disaster, but as all of the workmen were involved in the cleanup all progress halted above the master's shop. Still, there was plenty enough time to have the third and fourth floors ready by the fall of 1716, in time for Annie's debut. Eventually Joshua would live at the top of the house and the bedrooms would be moved up to the third floor. Then the second floor would be finished as an elegant reception room large enough for dancing or dining, adjoined by a formal parlor and gentleman's study. The kitchen was a large single-story building set behind the house in the walled backyard, and next to that stood the stable. At the current time there wasn't much house to be keeping, so after the patient was shaved and fed he would fall into dizzy slumber and I got a chance to explore this new damp place.

In the evenings me and Joshua would try to muddle together something that was edible. He was a strange fellow, who reminded me of a squirrel, startled and flustered by every loud noise. And the only thing he knew how to cook was soup. But as I'd spent enough afternoons in Joy's kitchen preparing vegetables, we'd often roast a chunk of meat and live on that and greens until there was just enough left for pottage. As he became more accustomed to me, Joshua relaxed a bit, and eventually I discovered he'd had to leave London when his beloved (Elizabeth) fell pregnant—which would have been all right except she was his boss's daughter. So she'd been hurriedly married off to some goldsmith in Covent Garden and had borne a daughter called Sara. Joshua and Elizabeth still kept in touch through secret missives and the young associate was hoping to save enough money for passage so she could someday run off and join him in Charles Towne. Now, I ain't never been much of a romantic but the way he told his tale struck a chord in my heart. And I never did find out whether Elizabeth and Sara made it, but I hope so for all of their sakes.

When Master William was starting to feel better he grew bored and wanted entertaining. At first I had to read to him but I wasn't very good at the strange long words so after a while he gave up asking and we took to playing games instead. Joshua found a water-damaged compendium in the storeroom and managed to repaint the washed-out wooden pieces. Bristol had taught me Nine Man's Morris on the *Argyll* so I was pretty good at that, and I always found checkers and dominoes amusing. Then the master decided to teach me chess—and from then on that's all I really wanted to play until I became proficient. At first my opponent would let me win, but later I think I managed to beat him fair and square. But I couldn't never interest Joshua in any form of pastime because when he wasn't busy restoring items or selling them in the shop he wanted to immerse himself in the faraway world of Elizabeth.

So things slid into a haphazard routine until one awkward day when I was giving Master William a bed bath and spotted his hardened wood. I instantly pulled away, stuttering, and for some silly reason I started apologizing. A strange look glazed the usually jovial face and his eyes had set in stone. His voice turned deeper as he croaked, "Be a good girl and wash me, Lola. And I'll give you a little extra something for your kindness." He grasped my soapy hands and showed me how he wanted the rub.

And that was the day I became his mistress. I'm sure Joshua must have known what was happening on account of the bumping he heard day and night, and the fact that I suddenly had pretty new frocks and could afford to buy myself boots and ribbons. He never said anything untoward but I did sometimes see him glance sadly from the corner of his eye when the cane rapped the floorboards overhead, demanding my instant attention. And I didn't see nothing wrong with being paid for my services when other men would have just taken them anyway. One thing I did delight on, though—money buys folks more freedom. For now, whenever shopping the cobbled streets, I could purchase nice things all on my own account. Toffee and candy and fancy cakes. Lavender water and powder. I spent long sessions in the Ravenell and Haskell Apothecary Shop watching the leeches swimming in a big clear glass jar and observing Dr. Haskell's skill as an apothecary-surgeon. And I'd listen to the stream of customer complaints, watch how a suitable remedy was prepared, then purchase any missing ingredients for my own collection. Mistress Haskell was always ready with a friendly word and she didn't never complain that I was being a bother. She joked one day that her husband should take me on as his apprentice, and everyone in the place roared with laughter at the thought of a female surgeon! But I did eventually learn from her the most valuable treatment of all—the recipe to prevent unwanted babies. Thereafter I made pessaries from beeswax and ground acacia bark, and learnt to syringe a herbal douche of tobacco, lemon juice, vinegar, and seaweed (and there were other ingredients too but I can't never be giving away all of my secrets).

Meanwhile, the Black River Plantation was still struggling to harvest and sell whatever rice could be marketed. Each Friday Lieutenant Ellyott would arrive to collect a letter or package to deliver to Mistress Anne. And each Sunday he would return with her reply, sometimes carrying the requested books or papers or brandy or preserves. Then one breezy Sunday just before Christmas he failed to show up. And shortly, thereafter, all hell broke loose.

In the first gray hours of Monday morning we were roused from our slumber by a furious knocking at the shop door. I knew Joshua wouldn't never be brave enough to answer so I shot out of Willie's bed and slipped a cloak over my lacy shift. I was terrified to see Anne crumpled on the arm of a frantic Mrs. Drayton. Gibby had tied up the reins of the cart and was ferreting around in the back. He slung a large bulky shape over one shoulder and was the first to find his tongue. He said, "Young master's badly hurt. . . ."

The moment I realized he was holding Lieutenant Ellyott I ushered him into the shop alongside the women. Mrs. Drayton finally explained, "He needs a surgeon." She helped Anne to prop herself against the flour sacks and then pointed to where Gibby should deposit his burden. I scuttled to the young man's side. His crown was a huge scab of blood and deep scratches scored his face. Both eyes were hidden in puffy black hollows. His complexion was bruised as an overblown apple but the breath whimpered ragged and furtive.

"What happened?" I asked, as I pulled aside the blanket he was wrapped in. The whole of his torso was covered in muddy hay, and whatever flesh was visible was turning a mixture of purple and blue. His eyes remained swollen shut and lifeless. A trickle of blood from a damaged gum crusted on his chin and I thought that at any moment he might slip on the dew into death.

There was a series of loud bumps, and when I looked over to the bottom of the staircase I saw the master had made it down on his cane, wrapped only in a nightshirt and the shawl from his bed. "What is going on here?" he demanded to know. And then he saw Anne slumped on the floor and hobbled to her side. At sight of her father Annie dissolved into hysteria and none of us could make out a word she gabbled. So she finally lifted the hem of her dress and showed us her torn bloody petticoat. Her father instantly understood. He stumbled over to the unconscious officer, poked apart his floppy legs, and brought the tip of his cane down smartly on the lieutenant's privates. The body elicited a gurgle of pain before sinking back into the flooring. "Take this thing home!" Master Cormac commanded. So Joshua was sent for, and told to direct Gibby and the lieutenant back to the Ellyott Estate somewhere downriver. Mrs. Drayton was given Joshua's room to rest in, while I made up a sickbed for Annie in my room. I had a vague idea what had happened but I was much more worried that someone would notice my lacy nightgown or that I hadn't been sleeping in my own bed. Fortunately, though, Anne was too upset, and it took all of her concentration to let me clean her up, gently administer the syringe, and finally put her to rest.

After things settled down a bit we heard what had taken place. Apparently Lieutenant Ellyott had tried to woo Anne but she didn't want anything to do with him—or any other beau for that matter—until her official debut, for fear she'd ruin her father's carefully laid plans for a society match. But the young militia man was besotted and, hoping to score an early advantage over the rest of the pack, he'd taken to staying longer and longer during his weekly visits. At first Annie was flattered by the attention, but when his passion became more physical she realized she'd have to speak sharply and put him to rights. Well, this particular Sunday morning Ellyott caught Annie in the stables as she came in from her morning ride. He tried seducing her with poetry but when she told him to run along home he suddenly displayed the dark side of his desire. Cut furious by the rejection he pushed Annie back onto the hay bales—and by sheer, brute force and ardor—succeeded in fulfilling his wicked intent. Annie told us she went totally numb (like she was frozen in a winter pond) and that her vision wavered out of her skin and hovered above his thrusting haunches. When he eventually withdrew she felt a flutter on her thigh and stared in disbelief at the blood oozing down her leg. Shaking in fear that he'd hurt her some more she tried to cover herself up. That was when he tried to push something into her mouth and a rush of anger flooded her head to toe. Annie bit wildly at the lump of flesh, eliciting a screech of surprise followed by a sadistic punch to the forehead. The next thing she knew a pistol was pressed to her ear and vicious fingers were groping her breasts. He rolled her over, pressing her face into the dung-stained straw, and made her scream a second time. Finally sated, he left her sobbing in the hay and hurried to make himself decent. But just as he was exiting the stable Annie came up from behind with a wooden spade. She hefted a vengeful blow that knocked the young man to his knees, then she continued hitting and hitting and hitting, roaring like an Indian brave in the throes of ancient battle. Eventually the lieutenant stopped moving and Annie ran to the house to lock herself safe. Mr. Higgins found the injured man a short time later and set the journey in motion that led to our door. The furious father sat with his daughter throughout the next morning until the vigor returned to her body. Annie's first words were, "Did I kill him?"

Her father shook his head and said, "Fortunately not. I think he will survive."

Annie looked deep to the corner of her soul and spat, "More is the pity. . . ."

That very afternoon Master William rode out to the Ellyott Estate to confront the lieutenant's family, and he eventually returned after dark overdoused in whiskey. We were all sat round the kitchen table going over and over the potential outcomes and nervously awaiting the vengeance of a mightier power. Annie had beaten the young heir half to death. So now she risked being ostracized from their set as the wayward slut who'd led him on and then cried wolf. Her reputation would be ruined, and no respectable beau would wish to marry her. And if that foolish man should happen to die from his injuries Annie might even stand trial for murder. We went over the terrible, again and again, preparing ourselves for all consequences. But the master sat down at the table, took off his boots, and called for a bottle of port. Then in a rather husky voice he finally belched and laughed at the alien drama he'd just partaken of. Anne looked at her father and asked, "What happened, Papa?" I took away the boots, returned with glass goblets, and watched the ruby liquid slide into place as Annie poured us all a good tot.

The master winked, squeezed her hand as she passed, and said, "It has all been sorted." Then he raised his stem in a wobbly toast and yelled, "To negotiation!" We didn't have no idea what he meant but we dutifully raised our drinks and swallowed them down.

But what I could never get my head round was the irony of William's righteousness. So it was acceptable for a man—almost four times older—to seduce me each day whenever he chose to— but not for a reputable, marriageable young man to bed his own virgin daughter? Why was her body more precious than mine? I was apparently supposed to feel some kind of fury on behalf of my brutalized mistress, yet it seemed to me that Annie had got the better of her abuser. But then again—given the circumstances— so perhaps had I.

Now, as it turned out, Master George Ellyott was mortified that his son had been overpowered by a mere slip of a wench, for such a disgrace wouldn't do no good for a lieutenant's career if it were to become public knowledge. And having been assured by the surgeon that the patient's wounds would not leave permanent damage Master Ellyott wanted to hush up the incident and forget that it ever happened. So he schmoozed his Irish friend, greased his words with liquor, and offered an affable solution.

He suggested they both deny anything had ever taken place on the grounds that headstrong youngsters often make silly, rash mistakes. Of course, at first Master William was that burning angry his daughter had been violated, but after several tingling drinks he came to see that if no one knew of the event it would be as if it never occurred. No damage—reputation still intact— and Annie would be able to debut as planned. Cormac could not risk losing such an important business connection either, so he ran with Ellyott's oily words, downed as much of his whiskey as was offered, and finally shook his friend's hand. Annie listened to details of their agreement with cotton-stuffed ears that absorbed the added insult in dutiful silence.

She finally rose to ready for bed and gave her father an empty kiss on his glowing, treacherous cheek, as if that was actually that.

6

LOOKING UP AT PARADISE

1714–1716

Anne was in no hurry to return to the plantation, so after we'd all celebrated the New Year together, it was decided that Mrs. Drayton would stay as chaperone, Joshua would continue running the shop, and the master would return with Gibby to replant, restock, and rebuild. I introduced Mrs. Drayton to Mrs. Haskell at the apothecary and the two of them quick became friends. During their long chats together Annie and I would slip off and explore the other shops around the Four Corners, gradually growing bold enough to venture into the market. We were two young women thrown together in circumstantial friendship—yet Annie always pulled away whenever there was a chance to draw closer and I couldn't never understand why she did that. It was frustrating, mean-spirited, and hurtful. One day after Easter, though, fate blew wind from another direction.

We'd been busy haggling with the market vendors for cloth

to furbish Annie's new chamber on the half-finished third floor, when I saw a vaguely familiar figure sliding among the crowded hat stall. I tried to gain a better view but the bonnet bobbed out of sight so I turned to Annie and said, "Let's look over here!" We followed behind the supple body as it wove easily through the thong of sailors playing chuck-farthen against a butcher's wall. Then the woman turned and headed toward the docks. Just for a second she stopped to watch the toss of the coin, and I immediately recognized the profile of my old shipmate Violet. "I know her!" I yelled to Annie, and ran on ahead to catch up. "Violet?" I asked quizzically. The bonnet turned in my direction and the face inside lit up in amazement.

"Is that you, little Lola?" she gasped. I nodded and awkwardly hugged her. "Where have you been? We thought they'd . . ." Then she held me at arm's length and assessed my situation for herself. Quick eyes took in the new boots, clean calico frock, and laced cap. Then they moved over to scan Anne, who had sauntered across and was standing impatiently waiting to be acknowledged.

I finally remembered my manners and introduced them. "Mistress Anne Cormac—may I present my good friend Violet. . . ." They shook hands as I mumbled, "And, Violet, this is the daughter of Master William Cormac of the Black River Plantation."

Violet knew her place. She bobbed a small curtsey and said, "Pleased to meet you, ma'am."

Then she slipped into her familiar English dialect, chattering away so fast that poor Annie's untutored ears couldn't never keep up. In a short span of time I'd told Violet how I chanced to be living in Charles Towne, and she'd given me the outline of coming here on a tobacco ship and being hired by Madam Elsie as a gay girl in the Red House (a brothel attached to the Pink House

Tavern). She then recalled an important appointment she'd to keep so she hurriedly told us how to find her on Bay Street—apparently the stucco buildings were all known by their bright rainbow colors. When she kissed me on the cheek, knowing she wouldn't never be received at Cormac's shop, she whispered, "I've missed you, darling. Come visit me soon." Violet gave Annie another polite curtsey as she hurried away in the direction of the wharves.

From then on we were kept busy decorating the new upstairs chambers. By Christmas of 1714, Joshua had moved his own attic room on the fourth floor and the rest of us graduated upstairs to the completed third level. The master bedroom faced the street, Annie had the large chamber at the rear, and Mrs. Drayton and I shared an airy room on the adjoining side. On the afternoons when we were able to occupy our chaperone elsewhere, me and Anne would slip off down to the docks and meet up with Violet. Looking back now, I think these were among the pleasantest days I ever ever spent. Mrs. Drayton preferred doing house chores without my dubious assistance so she was more than happy to send me off on her errands about town. And me and Annie could go wherever prudent, as long as we were home in time for supper.

The master came back to the shop from Thanksgiving through to Easter and we had jolly evenings by the kitchen fire, telling stories, singing ditties, or playing clever card games. One early morning Anne caught me creeping back from her father's chamber. Her bone-hard stare took in my crumpled nightgown, instantly assessed the situation, and crinkled into a smirk. She raised her eyebrows—*Well, well, well*—and emitted the tiniest grunt of disgust. Then she turned away and never, ever referenced my nocturnal ramblings again.

During those winter months William made fewer demands on my time, but we girls couldn't get away much on account of the business transactions he supervised at the docks. Even though we both knew he traded with privateers we didn't think he'd much approve of our visits to the wharves, so most of that period was spent renovating the now-vacated second floor in preparation for the parties next year. The master's old bedroom was lavishly converted into a gilt and marble great room, its dual fireplaces adequate for grand dinners and intimate dances. Glass doors opened onto a wrought-iron balcony overlooking the street, and on lucky nights the dappled moon would hang in the gap like a lantern. The master imported a wonderful new instrument called a pianoforte, but as it was too cumbersome to bring up the stairs, it had to be hoisted on ropes and pulleys up to the balcony and installed through the large glass doors. Behind the great room was a formal lounge with tapestry sofas and ornate tables—and under my chamber was the master's study, where the men would retire to partake of pipes and brandy. And before we knew it, there were only six months left until the debut season was to open.

Now, in those early days there wasn't no organized debutant cotillion like they have back in England. All eligible ladies between the ages of fourteen and eighteen were invited to attend as part of the Circuit, alongside any bachelor gentlemen. The debutants took afternoon teas at each person's home, followed by an informal dinner party and dancing. And after this flurry of coming-out events (where potential partners were flirted with, tested, and assessed), the participants were expected to marry. Annie had hired her own Italian dressmaker to produce a stunning array of gowns and petticoats. And she also employed the services of a French dancing master to teach her sufficient grace to gild her more-obvious charms. Of course, I found the lessons enchanting and wished it was me being led on the divine tunes wafting from out of that musical box. But unfortunately Annie didn't have no discipline, so after a frightful hour with Monsieur Lafayette and his surly pianist, she'd spend the rest of the morning swinging me roughly about the ballroom floor, trying to work off her embarrassment and frustration. One day Anne asked me what other dances I knew so I gave her a sample of my old repertoire (minus the Dance of Veils). She looked at me through wider pupils from then on, finally aware of my talent. And once she realized I might have something worth learning she actually let me teach her the formal steps.

Meanwhile, I'd managed to see Violet (with and without Annie) at least once a week. She showed me around the docks, pointing out where it was safe to tread and where a young girl should never venture alone. As we dotted about the wharves, men would grin, tip their hats, or shout to Violet, and she always answered in kind with a smile, small bow, or witty retort. She was obviously very popular. And I was proud to be her friend and to bask in their general approval. One fateful day the pair of us stopped for a sup of ale on Bay Street—and that's when I first laid eyes on the dashing James Bonny. Violet stood chatting to the barman while I blended into the wood and quietly surveyed the scene. It was very much like an English pub, except nearly all of the patrons were buccaneers, which I recognized straight off from the sooty crosses etched in their skin and the evidence of past plunder: gold rings, ear hoops, jeweled buckles, and fancy chains. Most wore recognizable sailor's kit—petticoat breeches or Monmouth caps—but their traditional gear had also acquired the telltale silk sashes and velvet waistcoats. First off, I was terrified to be among this band of thieves, but Violet assured me I'd be perfectly safe, and later she showed me the dagger hid inside her boot. As I watched I became increasingly mesmerized by the banter and merrymaking, having never seen so much fun since my gypsy days. Rum and ale flowed freely as air, and every so often a fight would break out to a stomp of cheers. And I couldn't tear my eyes from that handsome rascal in the corner, Jim Bonny. He was twenty years old. A pirate. The first bloke to ever break my heart.

James Bonny was from Liverpool so he spoke with a funny tongue, but you'd forgive him that just to hear him up close because he was so cheeky and charming. As he sat staring moodily into his tankard I got the chance to take in his wheat-colored hair and elegant features, but when he raised his head and stared at me with metallic eyes I felt the quicksilver drowning my senses. The moment I thought he flashed me a grin I grew flustered and anxiously turned to Violet for a cue. But she was engrossed in some deal or other so I stared at the floor and tried to appear disinterested. Next thing I knew he was making his way across to the bar in his cocked hat and had placed an arm around Violet's waist. She turned to acknowledge him and my heart felt leaden because I could see that she liked him too. He nodded to me and said, "Hey up, Vi. And who's your friend here?"

"Jim—this is my mate Lola. But she's only fourteen and off-limits." I was embarrassed to be treated as a child in such company and subtly kicked Violet on the ankle. Meantime, the young sailor had removed his hat and was performing an elaborate bow to the words, "James Bonny, at your service."

I giggled and replied, "Lola Blaise, pleased to make your acquaintance, sir."

Violet shrugged her shoulders and turned back to complete her transaction at the bar. James asked for another drink and then decided to amuse himself at my expense by winningly drawing my moth to his flame. Before we left that day he'd discovered that I worked for William Cormac and assured me most sincerely that he'd be in here every afternoon until he found a new cruise, and that I'd always be welcome to keep him company. Looking back, I suppose it wasn't no hard task to impress me. And I'd been truly fiercely plundered.

Now Romany women have prospered for hundreds of years by studying human nature. We observe and learn. Who can be trusted for fairness? What type of person makes a good mark? Which words elicit the greatest reward? So it ain't no surprise that I took to studying pirates. Now, I'm sure you think, like I used to, that they're all just a bunch of bloodthirsty rogues but I soon discovered that there are many different types of buccaneer. Take James Bonny, for example. He'd been born in Liverpool to a carpenter who had the misfortune to be press-ganged for the navy at the start of the Queen Anne's War. It's said the frigate got sunk near Flanders, but his headstrong son joined up soon as possible to try to find his lost father. James worked as a powder-monkey (running gunpowder and shot to the sailors manning the warship's cannons) until he'd learned enough to become an ordinary seaman. By sixteen he'd made able seaman, but when the war ended in 1713 he found himself unemployed. A couple of years later he signed up with Captain George Lowther, a small-time pirate operating along the Carolina coast. Their *Happy Delivery* would follow a suitable merchantman until out of sight from safe harbor, then ram into the prize so the men could board and loot it. But when Lowther set sail for the West India Islands Jim decided to wait out the winter in Charles Towne because—as it turns out—he was seeking a richer treasure.

Of course, I'm old enough now to know all this mushy love

stuff is just one big fairy tale that I think men invented to keep women stupid and dependent. But try telling that to a star-struck young heart out on its first adventure! I was besotted. All I could think about was my James, Jim, Jimmy. What should I wear to entice him? What could I say to impress him? What might I do to win his affection? Each afternoon I'd find some errand that meant I could swing by Bay Street. Sometimes Violet would be sat chatting with him—and then I was torn between pleasure and dismay—but usually I'd join him alone at the table and let him buy me a tankard. Jim was ever a gentleman, and although he was warm and welcoming he never made any move. I couldn't never understand what was going on. I flirted with my wickedest looks, danced beautifully when anyone struck up the accordion, suggested remedies for every ailment he mentioned, and hinted that I had experience enough to pleasure him. But while other men pined for my lithe, thin body, or envisaged my rich wavy ringlets billowing over their pillows, he treated me like a sibling or shipmate, never giving more than a wink and a kiss on the cheek. Weeks of frustration went by.

One still afternoon in October the tavern was much more crowded than usual on account of the increase in townfolks readying for the debut season. I pushed my way to the usual spot but was stunned to find James nowhere in sight. Violet beckoned me to join her table where a group of raucous wenches from the brothel were making merry, so I squished myself on the edge of their bench beside them. The young men around were boasting which parties they were attending and then I spotted an unwelcome face in the crowd. Lieutenant Aaron Ellyott stood in the corner surrounded by a large fence of drunken young gentlemen. Several other patrons sported various uniforms—and I suddenly realized why the prostitutes were out—and why the pirates had gone into hiding. Lascivious banter flew across the sawdust until, one by one, the ladies at the table left to ply their trade. I kept a watchful eye on Ellyott, confident he wouldn't never remember me. A couple of hopeful suitors tried to engage Violet but she cleverly put them off without offending, and then I heard the lieutenant's voice rising over the swell. When his friend mentioned Annie's name I picked up both tankards and edged toward the overworked barmaid on the pretext of acquiring refills. Ellyott was talking excitedly to a young planter who was yelling, "I hear that William Cormac has imported a piano-forte for his daughter's ball!"

"Really?" Ellyott replied. "And what have the Middletons arranged for Martha?"

"Her father has engaged an Austrian quartet, so I am told."

"Will you be at both parties?" the lieutenant asked.

"No, I am afraid not. Middleton will not let Martha attend anything at the Cormac home."

"And pray, sir, why not?" Ellyott shouted.

"Well, it seems he does not approve of Cormac's trading with privateers and pirates. . . ." his comrade said.

"But every merchant prefers to bypass those damned English custom duties . . . it means cheaper goods for everyone."

"That is as may be, my friend. But Middleton does not want his daughter mixing in such company." The young man caught the barmaid's arm and indicated she was to refill all the mugs in their circle too.

Then another youth in their crowd said, "Pity you will not be there, Pinckney. I hear Mistress Anne is quite the beauty."

Flushed by alcohol and unpleasant vengeance Lieutenant Ellyot said pointedly, "She is quite the buxom slattern and no mistaking. Arse like a firm ripe peach!"

His companions gasped at his intoxicated inference and someone muttered, "You have not . . . ?"

Elliott winked lewdly and added, "She decided to come out
early—just for me!"

As the gang exploded into scandalized whoops the blood set
to flame in my veins.

I told Violet I was off, and ran from the tavern as fast as my
boots would carry me home.

Annie had been selecting evening wear and when I burst
into the room I saw a crop of brocade stomachers were scattered
about the floor amidst a splash of taffeta gowns. She could tell
from my face something dreadful had happened and I shuddered
under pressure of bearing the message of duplicity and doom. But
I couldn't never do it! It meant the ruin of all their expensive plans—
that Annie was now not eligible—that no one would come to their
parties and teas—humiliation—embarrassment—disgrace.

Anne discarded the silk petticoat she was holding and stood
waiting, but my out-of-breath gasps turned to panic-filled sobs
and I couldn't get no sense out. The mistress marched over and
shook my arm as if violence would spill forth the terrible news.

"What is it?" she cried. "What on earth has happened?"

Bubbles of spittle popped from my terrified lips but I wanted
to be in denial as long as I could so I murmured, "No . . . I . . .
I can't. . . ."

Annie, now at the limit of her precarious patience, slapped
me across the cheek.

I writhed from her grip still unable to disclose. Then, before
I had chance to even rub my face, she had picked up the shears
used to unwrap her treasures and held the points against my
neck. "Speak up!" she commanded. "Or I shall rip the words
from your mangy throat. . . ."

I was stuck on the tips of her blade, petrified, so I stuttered out a garbled version of the lieutenant's public boast. It took several strained seconds for the implication to prick Annie's aspirations before she turned from me in dismay, and before my mind could register what was happening she had swung back—full force—and stabbed the blades of the shears into my shoulder just above the left breast. Her face was screwed up in rage screaming, "Nooo . . . !"

Looking back now, it all happened like a slow, drunken memory. I saw a sail of strawberry hair flash across space, and then felt a burning plunge bite deep in my flesh. I stared, still as a woodblock, looking at the protruding handles vibrating from the force and vaguely noting the froth of blood fizzing around the metal. I instinctively made to pull the shears free, then remembered that they were corking the wound and it was best to leave them in place. My body went icy cold and then grew lighter and lighter until I thought I was going to float away. I crumpled to my knees whimpering in pain. I looked up into Annie's eyes—and the light that I saw there terrified. Her whole face was shining in strange fascination. She looked ecstatic and somehow sated. She made no attempt to catch me, but backed far enough away to take in the glow of her act. And that scared me far more than the blades sticking out from my chest so I started screaming with all of the wind I could muster, and then Annie was moaning too in a lost voice that sounded like wolf howl.

The commotion brought Joshua up from the shop. He took one look at the scissor handles and ran to find the master, but by the time her father appeared Annie had collapsed on the floor and was curled up in a tight ball, bawling great angry curses between hiccups and sobs. Mrs. Drayton was called to take me to the apothecary so I could be properly attended. And Annie was left to break the news that her debut had been maliciously cancelled.

Dr. Haskell did a neat job fixing the wound that would eventually heal to a wiggly scar. Years later I had this here anchor tattoo done to cover it—see, mister? Anyway, next day when things had calmed down a bit Annie came and gave me the third degree. I was still feeling woozy on account of the opium administered for the stitching so I answered vaguely without guile or caution. Her voice was pounding somewhere between my ears and eyes asking where had I seen Ellyott? Did I recognize who he was with? Might he be there again this evening? And before she'd even considered the consequences—or perhaps because she didn't have nothing left to lose—she'd marched me off with grim-set lips to seek out and confront him.

Now, as it happened, the herd of young hopefuls was otherwise engaged that day so when we got to the tavern the sea robbers were back there in force. I immediately turned to take Annie home because I was still feeling very sore, but she was mesmerized by the lip-tingling scene before us and insisted that as we'd come all this way we may as well stop for a drink. By now I'd become friendly with a few of the locals so I reckoned we'd be safe enough from any wandering eyes (and I also knew Bobby the barman kept a loaded musket handy). As we walked in the den the crowd opened up to let us pass, whistling and hooting at the new beauty in their midst. I ignored all shouts of "Who's your mate, Lola?" and "Aren't you going to introduce me?" and steered us to a bench close enough to the door to scat if necessary. Annie's eyes were large as cartwheels as she took in the motley swaggers and taunts. We slowly sipped our ale but when I turned to check out who was there I couldn't see nothing for the throng of suitors clamoring for her attention.

One bird-bent hand reached over the table and wobbled before Anne's bodice as if to fondle her breast, but just as the blackened nails touched lace, there was a scuffle and the wandering arm was roughly yanked aside. I heard Jim's voice yell, "Bail out, matey. Don't you know how to treat a lady?" The manhandled sailor swore back and the table tipped over in the ensuing brawl. I grabbed Annie's arm and pulled us both outside, but instead of beating a safe retreat, my mistress insisted we stay and watch the fray. We couldn't see much through the thick, murky windows, yet we got an occasional glimpse of the mayhem when we dared peer in the doorway. Numerous bodies dived into the fight, some trying to relieve their pent frustrations and others valiantly aiming to part the opponents before anyone got stabbed or shot. Eventually the bawdy suitor was restrained by a pair of regulars and the barrel of Bobby's musket, and Jim was persuaded to turn away in favor of a free mug of ale. The landlord righted the table and the room returned to its regular josh and tipple. Annie stood outside in the street and asked, "Who was the sailor that rescued me?"

I said boldly, "That'd be my mate, James Bonny."

A bright curiosity came into the young woman's eyes and she said, "Introduce me. I wish to thank my champion." So I trotted back with Annie in tow and did as I was bid. Jim was none the worse for wear—if anything the tussled hair and swollen lip made him look even more striking.

As I uttered the formalities Jim lifted Annie's white hand to his kiss and murmured, "James Bonny at your service, ma'am."

But this time when I stared across at his silver-gray eyes I saw they were glowing with molten lust. I'd waited many long weeks to see such desire but unfortunately it wasn't intended for me.

In an instant he and Annie had fused. And I'd lost them both. Forever.

During that same dreadful day Master William had again ridden to the Ellyott Estate to vent his fury and this time there'd be no appeasing him with liquor or veiled economic threats. William was out for blood. Now, there ain't no telling exactly what happened between the two masters but when I finally got Annie back to the shop that damp evening we sat awaiting his return with great trepidation. My shoulder was hurting something terrible so I asked to be excused to go to bed, but Anne wouldn't hear of it and insisted I stay with her to learn the verdict. Joshua kindly slipped me another draught of the master's laudanum and that made the throbbing tolerable, but by the time William appeared I could barely keep my lids wedged open. I remember that it had rained heavily—because his clothes started steaming as he stood near the fire—and his face was red to bursting wanting to spill the news. After the usual greetings and settling in he looked at his anxious daughter and said, "Well, my dear, it has all been set to rights."

Annie gave him a dubious stare and asked, "How so?"

"Lieutenant Ellyott has agreed to wed you."

"What?" Annie stood up, shaking in disbelief. "What did you say, Father?"

"I said—Aaron Ellyott is to be your husband."

"No." Anne looked at him and screamed louder, "No!"

Master William took hold on his daughter's shoulder and guided her back to sitting. Then, calmly as possible, he added, "The arrangement has been made. You will be married at Black River the Saturday of Christmas."

"But . . . I . . . I cannot believe . . . that . . . after . . ." The young girl was submerged by incomprehension. "H . . . how could you do this to me, Father?" Two large eyes stared directly into his chapped face.

William flinched slightly and said, "It is in the best interest of all concerned, given the circumstances. . . ."

"Circumstances?" Annie echoed. "What circumstances?"

Her father evaded her angry glare and muttered, "Everybody is aware that you gave yourself to him. . . ."

"I did not *give* myself—he forced me. You know that!"

"I do, my dear. But no one is going to believe that of the young lieutenant, are they?"

The reality hit home and Anne realized her tenuous rung on the social ladder. She stared into blackness and calmed her inner turmoil sufficiently to add, "You do not know what such a match will cost me, Father."

"I do," he replied sagely. "The entire Black River Plantation."

So, just like that, William Cormac had sold his daughter to the only bidder and thrown in the rice farm as her dowry. He'd apparently decided that once his daughter left home he'd retire to the house in Charles Towne where there was ample enough profit to live out his days in comfort. Black River was to be handed over lock, stock, barrel, and slaves, with Cormac removing only his most personal items. William had agreed to this additional travesty on the assumption that George Ellyott would give the place back to the newlywed bride as her home (but in fact the wily planter had other plans for such a bountiful estate).

Now, all the time her father was gabbling, explaining the merits of such a deal, Annie was retreating further and further away from the impending sentence. I could tell she'd decided to smile and play nice but she wasn't fooling me none for an instant. Quite understandably, Anne didn't want to be in town for the rest of the debut season so by the end of the week she'd persuaded her father to take her back to the plantation on the pretext that they'd a wedding to prepare. Joshua was told he could hire another housekeeper to replace Mrs. Drayton, and with many strained hugs and formal handshakes we all bid him our farewells. The master hired four extra wagons and crew to wheel everything back, yet it still took twice as long to get home as when I'd ridden here after the storm.

I'd been away from Black River so long that my breath again slipped inward when I caught sight of the graceful dripping oaks. Everything looked crisp and new (except for the Big House, which was in want of clean rugs and some fresh coats of paint). Bart and Joy Higgins were overjoyed to see us, and while I was thrilled to find my old room the same as I'd left it, the master began making more frequent demands again so my solitude lost much of its sanctuary. It seemed that we'd about ten weeks left to get everything shipshaped for the coming nuptials so the place would soon be swarming with folks and preparation. Annie, meanwhile, had decided upon a particular wedding gown that could only be made by her Italian seamstress in Charles Towne, which gave us the excuse she needed to stay overnight twice a week. But other than that she showed little interest and couldn't be prodded to favor any particular flowers, cake, food, or whatnots. So Mrs. Higgins took over planning the big event and was truly in her element.

I'm sure it would have been the grandest celebration this side of Boston . . . except that it never took place. For during our soirees to town Anne and James shared wild secret kisses and were soon protesting their love. I had to watch from the sidelines like a reject—the gooseberry—the one who was never quite good enough for anyone wholesome. Those nights brought me many bitter tears as I raged against the unfairness of the world, cursing the driving need that was growing inside me. When we'd meet in the tavern the lovers would sit in their own realm far removed from the rest of us mortals, and Violet would try to tug me to life at the bar. One night I'd a bit too much rum in me and obviously wasn't hiding my contempt well enough. Violet pinched my arm with her long pointed nails and hissed, "What the hell's up with you, Lola? Are you trying to get yourself done in?"

I gave her an unfocused glare and said, "It ain't fair, Vi. I saw him first. . . ."

She followed my covetous pupils to the lovers in the corner and hissed, "Jim Bonny ain't worth the bother. Believe me—I know. . . ."

I thought she was just trying to cheer me up so I said, "Thanks, but it still hurts to watch them together." I swallowed the remainder of my drink and hiccupped. "What's he see in her anyway?"

Violet grinned and replied, "She's his treasure chest, that's what she is." Treasure chest? Was she suggesting that men were more inclined to Annie's full, rounded figure instead of my barely bumped flatness? I stared at my blossoming bosom, desperately trying to remember if there was some remedy I might brew to enhance my chances. But then Violet winked and whispered, "He's only after her money." I opened my puckered mouth to argue but a meaty burp came out instead. My friend looked into my panic-stricken stare and said, "She'll find out herself soon enough." And with that she left on the elbow of a fresh-landed sailor, leaving me to bat off the dregs in the festering night. But it turned out we were both of us wrong. Jim wasn't just after what he could get (either physically or financially). He wanted to settle down with Miss Cormac and raise himself a family. And my face must have made a proper good laugh on the day I finally found out.

See, two weeks before Christmas the wedding dress was completed and I went to Signora Cassava's shop for the final fitting. The signora presented the bride in all her splendor and I have to admit that Annie looked just like an angel dropped from the ether—not that I was particularly bothered one way or another (except I secretly hoped Jim might turn to me once Annie was off the market). The dark blue taffeta gown over pale blue silk petticoat shimmered like running water and the stomacher was delightfully etched with a pink and green sprig pattern. There were matching silk gloves, a gorgeous lace bonnet, and a pair of kid-skin boots to complete the ensemble. When I finally found my tongue I murmured, "It fits perfect, ma'am. You'll do your father proud."

A weird look washed over Anne's face as she whispered, "Do you think *he* will approve?" I imagined any man would be thoroughly delighted but before I could ascertain which *he* was meant she snapped, "Hush up!" She turned to the seamstress and smiled, saying, "It has turned out quite exquisite. Thank you." Then instead of taking the dress back to Black River Annie left it upstairs in her room on Broad Street. And she never told her father when the outfit was ready—otherwise there'd be no excuse to still be coming to town.

The week before the big day the Ellyotts and their son arrived at the plantation for dinner. Annie greeted them warmly and chattered away as if she really couldn't wait to marry the man she would rather have killed. She was most careful not to be left alone with Aaron, but you'd never have guessed from her performance what was really going on in her devious thoughts. I'm sure that by the time her future in-laws left they were singing the virtues of the lovely young lady and musing on the good fortune she'd be bringing their way. The lieutenant was all charm and attention, but how much of him was an act was too hard for even me to read. Nevertheless, in front of the parents he was a proper gentleman, and even Master William seemed at peace with the match. Annie spent the rest of the week packing her trousseau, for the newlywed couple was to honeymoon at the Ellyotts' other home in New York. Now, if the master noticed that his deceased wife's jewelry and plate suddenly went missing he never voiced no objection, and so the one travel-chest Annie favored above all others grew plumper each day with increasing weight.

Two days before the wedding I awoke in the dead of night feeling prickly and uneasy. Was the master in my room again? No. But the roaring outside set my hairs on edge. The pitch of darkness flickered with a russet glow and I realized something was on fire. Flustered horses snorted and neighed. Black voices were urgently shouting and answering. I heard foot stomps and clamor and chaos. Dressing as quickly as possible I ran downstairs but the open bedroom doors told me I was the last soul to vacate this empty building. The master had organized a bucket chain from the well to the stable where the blaze was rapidly spreading and in danger of reaching the barn. Someone had released the horses and they were galloping toward familiar pasture—but some of the cows were still trapped and needed guiding to safety. Bart Higgins was inside trying to untie the stalls and one of the slaves was herding the terrified creatures as they emerged like shadows through the smoke. I quickly realized the best way for me to help was by quenching the growing thirsts of the crew closest to the flames, so I carried pail upon pail of water along the line and stopped so each mouth could ladle its fill. We thought we'd got the better of the fire when someone yelled and pointed toward the kitchen. Thick black bellows were coiling from the doors and it suddenly occurred to us all—simultaneously—that arson was afoot. Joy Higgins tried to rush in the structure but something popped with a very loud flash and the men wisely pulled her back and held on tight to her waist. We watched in dismay as the roof sank inward and all we could do was temper the surrounding soil to stop the flames from reaching the Big House.

Sometime around dawn our will won out and the tongues of destruction finally sank down to ash, but not before a good portion of the plantation was destroyed. Everyone was exhausted. I was covered in ash from hair to ankle, sweaty, smoky, and slightly singed. The master called everyone to the porch and broke out a keg of brandy. Joy brought some cheese from the well house and found some smoked fish to distribute among the workers. William stood on the steps and thanked his people for the valiant effort made and was trying to ease the calamity by highlighting individual acts of bravery when he suddenly stopped midsentence and queried, "Where is my daughter?" We looked around the smeary faces and as soon as we realized Anne was not among us feet scampered off in all directions to locate her, but at that point no one thought to check if a horse was missing. I ran past William and into the house calling her name as I charged up the stairs. Then I darted into her bedroom and immediately realized what had happened. Annie's best chest was missing—along with her coat, riding boots, and some of her favorite trinkets. I saw her jewelry casket was opened and rifled and that no one had slept in her bed. The mistress had vanished in the inferno. And I knew sure as hell where she was headed.

When I think back on that night I ain't got no idea why I

did what I did. I mean, I didn't owe Annie Cormac nothing, and yet she drew this strange loyalty from me that many times almost got me killed. Without hesitation I stuffed the remaining chains back in their box, ruffled the bed so the lines crumpled, and made the chamber look as would be expected. I was trying to buy her enough time to make it to Charles Towne, and then she was on her own. The master was waiting news on the porch and when I returned there I told him the house was vacant so he organized a methodical search of the entire estate, but of course she wasn't nowhere to be found, and her favorite gelding couldn't be located either. Everyone was given the rest of the day to recover and I knew Bart Higgins would have more than his hands full trying to console Joy's heartfelt loss. When I entered the parlor Mrs. Drayton was in a near state of collapse. The smoke and tension were all too much for her frail disposition, so I persuaded her to rest there in the chair and gave her several tonics. I was able to brew tea on the arm over the fireplace and thought I could probably muster up some pottage for supper. As the plantation settled to smoggy calmness Master William stomped about from place to ruin trying to find some trace of his lost daughter. There were no human remains in the burnt ruins so she was obviously not dead. No one had found her wounded or trapped so she was likely unhurt. She wasn't the type to fluster if the wedding had to be postponed. . . . And then the truth hit him harder than a swinging boom. Annie had got cold feet and had run away into hiding. The furious patriarch ran up to his daughter's room and shouted that I was to join him there. I slowly pushed open the door and shuddered before the inevitable wrath of this god.

It took William only a few seconds to see through my cover-up. He turned to me and yelled, "Where is she, Lola?"

I ain't never seen the master so furious so I mumbled, "I . . . I don't know, sir."

He didn't believe my lies and grasped my wrist in a vicious grip. "I want to know where she has gone!"

I quickly estimated enough time had passed to give her the lead so I sheepishly replied, "I think she's gone to town, sir."

"Do you know where?" he roared. I nodded. "To the house?"

That seemed the safest explanation so I told him, "Probably." Then I remembered, "She . . . she left her wedding dress there. Perhaps she's gone to collect it. . . ?" But my quibble lacked any real conviction. Master William knew me well enough to suspect some involvement so he asked, "Did you know she was leaving?"

"No, sir."

"She told you nothing?" I shook my head. William considered this information for a moment and said, "Is she coming back?" I froze. I really couldn't confirm yea or nay but my gut told me she was gone for good. My hesitation answered his question. He pushed me onto the bed and strode to lock both doors.

The master rummaged through Annie's things until he found suitable material to make restraints, then he lifted my skirt over my head and pushed my struggling face down into the quilt. Before I realized what was happening he'd tied my hands to the bedpost so I was bent with my naked buttocks exposed on the counterpane. He slowly removed his belt and brought his arm down hard in an angry swipe. I felt the leather slash my skin and screamed into the feathers.

"Where is she?" he demanded. He hit me again. "Where is she?"

I counted three—four—five—six—and then I couldn't be doing with no more so I cried, "She's with Jim!"

The belt smacked hard again. "Jim who?"

"Please, Master. Don't . . . I'll . . . I'll tell!"

"Jim who?" Another strike.

"Bonny. James Bonny . . . a sailor!"

Shock stopped the arm in midair. William dropped the belt, untied the bonds, and turned me around to face him. I couldn't sit right on my aching bottom so I knelt at his feet to answer his black booming questions. I snuffled and wept as I revealed Annie's secrets. The master listened with a face like a wooden figurehead that absorbed and eventually accepted my truth. He said quietly, "So she does not plan to marry Lieutenant Ellyott tomorrow?" I mumbled that it was unlikely. "And you knew about this all the time?" I shook my head. Then another wave of infuriation gripped the ruined father and he started punching and kicking at me in sickening waves until I slumped on the floor and pretended to be silenced. He turned back the key, stomped next door, and rummaged around for his opium bliss.

I lay without moving. I breathed still as possible, pretending I was unconscious, squeezing my cramped muscles, and resisted the urge to rub my sore arse. I listened until his snoring fell into a regular rhythm, then slowly pushed myself to my feet to assess the final damage. I crept to push shut the adjoining door and locked it. Then I washed myself thoroughly at Annie's toilet stand and dressed myself in her unwanted clothes. When I'd mustered sufficient courage, I limped to the other door and let myself out through Mrs. Drayton's room into the hallway. I slipped upstairs to collect my boots, cloak, medicine chest, and valuables, then made my way across the burnt fields to the horses out at pasture. It took me longer than anticipated to soothe a strawberry roan into cooperation, but I'd come prepared to sling the chest across my back and soon was trotting toward Charles

Towne. My rump was far too sore to have tolerated a saddle but the cool flesh of the horse's flank provided some soothing relief. I didn't have no idea what I'd do when I found Annie. But I feverishly hoped that Violet would.

It was deep into evening when I arrived, and my first stop was the house on Broad Street to see if the lovers were hiding there. Joshua eventually answered my persistent shouts and knocks (once I'd convinced him it was me outside), but he assured me he hadn't seen Annie for days. I slipped the chest from my back and climbed up to her chamber to see for myself—and there was the dazzling bridal outfit still hung up and waiting. By now I was absolutely exhausted and my rear end felt like it was burning so I let Joshua stable the horse and after I'd filled him in on the drama over supper I flopped on my old bed and fell into an even more fitful nightmare.

I was awoken by a familiar raised voice and made my way to the top of the landing, careful to keep out of sight. The master was downstairs shouting at Joshua for all he was worth. Quick as lightning, I pulled on my boots, picked up the cloak and chest, and tiptoed out of the right-hand door as William slammed the left-hand one in the shop. I scuttled to Bay Street among the early risers setting up for the day and knocked on the rear door of the Red House. Some disheveled slattern opened the door and muttered, "What do you want, eh?" I asked to see Violet and was begrudgingly taken up the staircase to a room with a peeling gilt frame. My hostess rapped hard and yelled, "Visitor for you, Vi."

Her sleepy head peeped round the wood and whispered, "Lola? What's up?"

"I need help."

As it turned out she knew all about my trouble and said,

"Wait next door. I'll be there soon as I can." I gave her my chest to hide in her room and, realizing she'd have to get rid of her punter, I quietly let myself out.

A short while later, Violet came into the tavern and stood with me at the bar. The place was dead that early in the morning and Bobby was busy unloading the barrels out back. I got straight down to business and asked, "Have you see Annie?"

Violet's blue eyes gazed sadly into my soul and said, "You've not heard then?"

"Heard what?" I asked. My ears were already closing against the news.

"Jim and Annie got hitched last night." My eyes shut tight so they wouldn't give nothing away.

"Where?" I managed to mumble.

"Here."

"Is that legal?" I asked.

Violet gave a knowing snort and replied, "There's a certain priest will accommodate the odd clandestine marriage for a barrel of rum. Of course, it's a wedding without license or banns—but a contract nevertheless."

My heart dropped into my stomach and was ground up by my intestines. I thought I was going to be sick. But before I could find out any more unwelcome information, the scurry of hooves foretold of a wealthy patron and I had a pretty good clue as to whom that might be. "Master Cormac!" I gasped, looking for some escape. Violet pulled me behind the bar and lifted the trapdoor that slid to the cellar. I scooted down the ladder and lay in the moldy dark, listening with every nerve on edge. There was a good deal of stomping and scraping and muffled voices, and at one point I heard William wail, "No!" Then there was some loud thudding and the door slammed and my ears were ringing and everything started vibrating. As soon as it was safe, the trapdoor lifted and I was hoisted back into the bar.

"Was that Master Cormac?" I inquired, even though I thought I knew the answer. Bobby and Violet whispered affirmation. "So he knows about Annie then?" Bobby's sleeve was wiping a fresh cut on his brow that came courtesy of William's riding crop. He cursed him and muttered something about the whole thing not being worth his bother.

Violet took my sweaty palm in her hand and said, "He knows."

"Did he say anything about me?"

The young woman nodded and said, "Blames you for everything . . . or at least for not warning him. You can't go back there."

"Then what am I to do?" I wailed. "Do you think he'll come after me?"

"Only for revenge—he won't trust you further." Violet thought momentarily and asked, "Would you like to work with me at the Red House?"

No. I couldn't stay here. So, at the risk of offending my only mate I mumbled, "Thanks . . . but I want to be with Annie." Meaning Jim.

Violet squeezed my hand even tighter and sighed, "Well, they sailed this morning for Nassau."

"Where's that?" I asked. She told me it was on one of the West India Islands and that if I wanted to disappear there was no finer spot than on Providence. "How much will it cost?" I panicked. My funds were rather limited.

But Violet cupped my cheeks in her hands and said, "Never you mind. I'll arrange our crossing."

"*Our* crossing?" I repeated.

"Well, of course. You don't think I'll let you go off there alone, do you?" She gave me a nudge with her elbow and confided,

"I could do with some sunshine myself. And I'm fed up of working for that bitch Elsie."

"But won't they come after the both of us?" I asked.

"I don't think there'll be that much fuss made on our account. As long as we steer clear of Charles Towne in future we're hardly worth their bother."

And by the middle of the week Violet had everything sorted, so that—amazingly—was that.

7

—◦∿◦—

LIKE BREAK OF DAY
IN A BOOZING KEN

SPRING, 1717

We ran into calm, balmy weather aboard the *Sea Nymph* so it took almost ten days to reach the West India Islands. A brand-new year! Violet had a regular client—Dick Tookerman— who smuggled goods back and forth for the pirates on Providence. He financed the smart sloop we were sailing on that was captained by an odd sort of rogue known as Fayrer Hall. Tookerman agreed to spirit us off in exchange for the entire purse of gratuities Violet had managed to squirrel away in her time at the Red House, a weighty price for our flight. We'd no choice but to agree, and of course we'd then to find some suitable disguise. So Violet was traveling as Mrs. Hall (fulfilling all the bedchamber obligations of a captain's wife) and I was passed off as a cabin boy by the name of Jake Jones (because I knew something of sailing from the *Argyll*). Actually I looked quite the part once my hair was clubbed, although I'd to be careful to lower my voice and avoid any giggling. The crew knew we were runaways but they believed I was Violet's young brother, and they never messed with the paying customers. Violet did a good job keeping Fayrer Hall happy so we'd a pleasant enough trip compared to last time, and I was allowed to eat at the captain's table after spending most of the day with the sailing master—Sam Clark—who happened to be quite the sea artist.

Sam told me one day how he was from a ship-building family in Hull. His father was an educated merchant who imported timber, hemp, pitch, and flax, which he used to craft sturdy vessels to his own design. But Sam was the eighth child of ten, and as soon as he was literate, any further education was considered a waste. This was a great pity because the young man had quite the mind. He was curious about everything and absorbed whatever he'd been told like a mop. Sam had grown up on the banks of the Humber and was eager to be on the sea instead of in the shipyard so, much to his father's dismay, he started sailing with the local fishermen as soon as he was big enough to haul in nets. And they said he always brought good luck because he had such uncanny instincts. Sam finally met an old salt who could teach him the necessary river discipline and he'd soon advanced his skills into a scientific quest. Now you ask any sea dog and they'll tell you same as me—a good navigator is born, not bred. They're often considered the most important sailor on board and they have to possess many abilities. Not only must they read, write, and reckon, they've to interpret the positions of sun and stars and be accurate remembering waterways. In fact I used to joke it'd help to be part Romany because they're also supposed to predict the weather.

This sailing master was a little more refined than the other hardened crewmen and mostly kept his own company, yet he seemed pleased enough to have my assistance, and I think he must have missed the folks back home because he treated me like a brother. And as it turned out, I was quite good at this navigating lark myself. Now, some days the sea burned a blinding sheet of fire and other times it spread before us like a stunning white-hot shroud, but if you were near land you could *mark one eyeball* and use the natural features to plot a rough course. Once out at sea, though, it all became much trickier. Then you'd to rely on the layout of the heavens and do some pretty clever *dead reckoning* to determine your speed and position before recording it on the traverse board, which was often one of my jobs. I learned a bit more of what the night sky foretold—something of the layout of the islands we were heading for—and how to magnetize the needle of a compass with lodestone.

The time passed quickly, and the only thing I'd a problem with was trying to pee overboard like the men. Violet came up with a good solution when she gave me an old boar's tusk she'd charmed from the cook. I hollowed it out to make a funnel so as I could use it like a cock to secure the deception. Thereafter I always kept it in my pocket. And each evening I'd get to spend some time alone with Violet as the captain made his final rounds or took a turn navigating, and we eagerly shared any gossip we'd managed to glean from the sailors. Now, Captain Hall was quite porky for his age and his nose disappeared between hefty cheeks. He treated Violet right, though, I'll give him that, and he was jovial enough to me with a shameless supply of ribald quips. And he certainly had the respect of his men for there was rarely a time he'd to lash out with anything but his tongue. I guess the crew had all been together long enough to know each other's characters. And there must have been sufficient remuneration for a smuggling job well executed. Of course, later on there was all that scandal when Hall tried to sue Tookerman over something or other (and if I ain't mistaken he was awarded the vessel by the court). But this was long before all that nonsense. Back then he seemed a decent enough kind of rogue.

Violet asked Captain Hall how he came to command the *Sea Nymph* and was given a little of his background. He was actually born in Carolina but his parents had both been Welsh servants. When they'd worked off their dues to a planter in Raleigh they were finally free but unable to earn a living. Hall discovered the urgent need for sailors so he signed on with various privateers who plied the Spanish Main. He worked his way up to quartermaster and then persuaded Dick Tookerman to let him command the new operation he was planning. Hall soon found smuggling steadier and reasonably profitable, and was delighted his parents were able to shift as much contraband as he could secretly acquire on his own account. And as long as he had the backing of the respectable Mr. Tookerman no one asked any awkward questions, excepting the British Royal Navy of course.

Some folks say that there's honor among outlaws but that ain't always true about pirates. See, as Sam explained it to me, for hundreds of years captains could sail with official letters of marque from the English Crown, licensing ships to attack enemy vessels without fear of punishment—so long as the monarch got a share of the prize. But after the Queen Anne's War thousands of sea dogs found themselves without gainful employment so it took little incentive for them to go a-pirating instead. Since they took to plundering anything of worth they couldn't no longer be trusted to attack only foreign ships, which meant even fellow villains tried to avoid their bloody flags. Now, if I remember rightly it was on this very boat that I first heard tell of Edward Teach, although no one knew him as Blackbeard yet because he was still just one of Ben Hornigold's mob—but as we drew close to Providence the watch was doubled, all throats stayed sober, and nervous eyes peered keenly abroad, hoping to avoid the masts of a Vane or Jennings or Bellamy or Burgess. One of the mates on the *Sea Nymph*—Potter—had formerly been on a rumrunner raided by Hornigold and was often prompted to relate the story, even though each time it was told with added embellishments. Potter claims there was one pirate in this crew as huge as a mountain who had a beard that reached all the way up his cheeks, and if you dared to look into his fierce dark eyes it was like staring at living death. He carried six pistols about his neck, had a sword in each hand, and he gutted men like a butcher. Potter apparently could swim (which was something I immediately vowed to learn) so when he was grazed by a lucky shot he fell overboard and made his way out of sight under the bowsprit. The remaining crew were given no quarter and ended up reddening the sea alongside him. The pirates stole everything useful, then left the ransacked boat adrift, its sails a mass of tatters. Potter managed to scramble up a hanging rope back on deck and then floated aimlessly for several days until the *Sea Nymph* rescued him and scuttled the wreck. The lone survivor felt indebted to Hall thereafter. I listened to such fascinating tales and found them strangely exciting, for at that time I foolishly thought that all pirates were simply misunderstood rebels just like my dashing James Bonny.

Now, I know you're wondering why I was still besotted with Jimmy, especially after he'd just run off and got married. But you see I blamed Anne for that because I thought she was using him as her excuse to flee the Ellyotts. I couldn't never believe she had fallen in love with Jim—and not because he was beneath her station for he claimed to be heir to his own family's purse—but because I know she wasn't capable of feeling nothing beyond her own immediate thrills. It must have come as a shock when Annie discovered her spouse was a penniless trickster, and a catastrophe to James when word came that William Cormac had disinherited his heiress daughter. For now there was no turning back from the gambit . . . they'd to see their game through to its grand finale. But all I could recall was the way Jimmy made my skin tingle, the warmth of his beery breath joking in my ear, his bone-hard profile that lied of nobleness, and the danger he wore like a luminous cloak. My cheek burned whenever I recalled his casual touch and I'd go over and over our past conversations in my silly, muddled head. But whenever I thought of him with Annie—lying with her under his pulsing hips—I struggled to suck in enough breath to ward off dizziness and my eyes would fill with a stab of pain. I didn't know then this was girlish infatuation. To me it was real. It was raw. And of course, I thought it was love.

Somewhere out in the middle of nowhere the sea turned a beautiful deeper blue. Sculptures appeared to be carved from cloud and were tinged by the sun in impressive relief. The air grew warmer. The fish grew larger. And no other flags emerged to mar our view. And then came the glorious cry of "Land! Land!" and I looked from the stern through the fluttering sails at the island I'd soon call home. Providence seemed an incredibly apt name. I was eager enough now to shed off the alien Jake, for Lola to emerge and see her beloved again. But as we approached the palm-tinged sandy harbor of Nassau, Violet grew edgy and grabbed my wrist. "Don't say aught to no one, do you hear me?" I nodded. She loosened her grip and whispered, "Just follow my lead and do as I do." When the gangplank was lowered the captain escorted Violet on shore just as if she really was his wife. I followed mutely and kept my head down. But I noticed several of the crew had surrounded us like we were royalty, and that their chapped hands were on the nubs of their swords. As soon as the natives caught sight of Violet I realized why—she had to contend with a barrage of drunken renegades openly leering at her, making vile but obvious sexual gesticulations, and trying to push through the guarding chests for a free grope of her body. We were maneuvered up the beach and hastily taken upstairs to meet the landlady of the Silk Ship Inn. Captain Hall bowed graciously, said farewell, and we were finally on our own.

Now, back in 1717, Providence had become the choice place of outlaws since Ben Hornigold and Tom Barrow proclaimed the sparsely populated island a pirate republic. It was ideally situated on the lucrative trade routes, yet close enough to sell goods to the American colonists. And if you ain't had chance to explore yet, mister, it's a beautiful place full of sunshine and natural splendor, with crisp, sandy shores and sparkling waters (until you get to the parts besmirched by dirty sailors). The small island protects our harbor entrance and creates two approaches—a dual escape route for outlaw vessels—and both mouths have hidden sandbars that large warships cannot cross. There are numerous caves and coves and inlets away from prying eyes, and the hills behind provide a lookout over many a nautical mile. Providence boasts plenty of food and resources, and the chance to rest in safety while enjoying ill-gotten goods. Not surprisingly, it attracts a society dedicated to shifting stolen loot, whether to smugglers, merchants, passing sailors, or in payment for rum and women. And some still say when a pirate dies he'd rather rest in Providence than go to heaven!

At first the place was little more than a shantytown with a long row of wooden structures forming Bay Street. Then some

incongruous businesses popped out of the filth, but the majority of dives are still taverns and brothels where the few working
girls ply their wares, and the men come to purchase a smudgy
moment of love. The Silk Ship Inn is no exception. As you can
see, it consists of one large dirt-floor tavern lined at the far end
with the bar, but boasts a rare kitchen and storage room off
back, and has one creaky staircase leading upstairs to three bedrooms off a dark, bare landing. Dotted here and there about
town, a thriving blacksmith or shipwright services the needs of
captains, a coffeehouse caters for those mocking their betters,
a dressmaker keeps the well-worn women seeming moderately
attractive, and all manner of sideshow entertainments detract
the men from recklessly fighting. Back then, though, the sailors
camped freely on the beach in a hodgepodge settlement formed
of makeshift sail tents and driftwood shacks. They'd spend all
their booty enjoying a high time, then immediately sign up for
another cruise. And if you asked them their expectations, most
replied a short—but merry—life.

Of course, I was used to living down-and-dirty but how on
earth Anne was going to cope was quite beyond me. Now, Jim
couldn't be taking his lady wife to no festering brothel (he was
still trying to keep up appearances), so he arranged with the local
dressmaker to rent a quiet room above the shop. The owner—an
effeminate man called Monsieur Bouspeut—was known to the
locals as Pierre the Pansy because many a sailor found it amusing that he designed and sewed clothing for a living. But Pierre
was a very shrewd businessman who also owned the coffeehouse,
hair salon, and Silk Ship Inn—the very place where Captain
Hall had delivered us. We didn't have no money left but once I'd
slipped into my feminine attire again the landlady recognized
our potential and took Violet to the dress shop to negotiate a

deal. Now, it turns out that sultry Monsieur Bouspeut was a sodomite who'd been caught in Paris with his trousers around the wrong ankles. Declaring him a menace to public order, his neighbors were intent on handing him over to the police as a deviant. Fortunately, Pierre was tipped off by another neighbor, who probably just wanted to get rid of him, and therefore he had chance to escape under cover of night. He hurriedly packed his valuables and took a ship to New York, where he hoped to be reunited with his lover. But the lover never came. So when Pierre heard of a paradise where no legal governor reigned, he bribed his passage on a schooner to Nassau and was canny enough to trade and prosper and flourish. The few women on the island liked to work with him because he never made fumbling demands, and the men either enjoyed or tolerated his eccentricities because this was, after all, divine Providence.

So the three of us reached an amicable agreement whereby I would dance each evening to drum up customers, with the option to sleep with the punters or not, and anything me and Violet made was ours to keep. In return for our beds and a steady supply of patrons we'd give Pierre one piece of eight each per week—a very fair price in that particular market—and he then paid his landlady. Of course I could have probably earned more if I'd set myself up as an apothecary, but I chose not to be dealing with chopped-up limbs and pox-ridden cocks, or the chance of being taken at any time without being paid (although Violet did mention my nursing and herbal skills to Pierre, which pleased me because I didn't want him thinking I was just another common whore). We soon settled into the pattern of working from sunset to midnight or so, sleeping late mornings, and wandering the island on hazy afternoons absorbing our glorious freedom. We were safe enough on Bay Street, but when we decided to venture beyond, we soon learned the value of securing adequate protection.

The first frightful day we tried exploring the beach we'd to turn back for fear of being brutalized by those who could no longer afford us. My skirt got ripped by some grubby salt who'd tried pawing my arse and Violet had been half-eaten by a slobbery jaw that forced itself onto her low-cut bosom. She'd had to whisk the dagger from her boot and tease the lusty face away from her chest at knifepoint. Then we'd to parry through a cluster of limbs, spitting and cursing our retreat back to safety. That night we both charged a pistol in return for our favors, which we thereafter carried everywhere in full view. I'd watched Annie shoot on a number of occasions but didn't really know how to load myself, so we found a former marine on the dregs of his funds and paid him to teach us both. I didn't seem to have no knack for hitting any great distance but Violet had a steady hand and an eye determined to stick. And so, before we knew it, we'd crept inside our bizarre new lives.

Mrs. Anne Bonny, however, arrived in a rowdy storm of outrageous attention. Whereas I'd spent my time at sea learning navigation, it appears Annie had striven to shed her genteel manners. She arrived in Nassau as far removed from a Southern lady as you'd imagine—unfettered, uncouth—with a mouth like a bilge pump. As soon as she set foot on land a one-eared sailor grabbed her elbow and yelled, "How much for an hour with you, darling?"

Annie pushed him off while calmly removing the flintlock wedged in his belt and then backed three paces from him. She lifted the pistol in one hand, aimed skillfully, and tugged the trigger. The loud puff of powder cleared slowly to reveal the mortified suitor bent clutching his gory head. She'd blown off

the pirate's *other* ear! This splendid act made the Bonnys toast of
the town. Within a day everyone knew of the handsome newcomers, and word spread quickly not to mess with this particular
wench. The newlyweds immediately set to work capitalizing on
the interest they engendered and while Annie ingratiated herself
with Pierre, Jim was scouring the taverns hoping to score a place
on the next rich cruise.

Now, being among the few women in town, it didn't take
long for everyone to know who Violet and me were either, nor
for us to establish our own rules of conduct. We were able to
do this because we'd something the men wanted badly that they
couldn't get easily on this island. So we decreed that all business was to be conducted at the Silk Ship Inn (which meant we
were safe from pawing hands on the street or beach), payment
for services was made up front (so we didn't get taken by some
mangy villain), we had the right to decline anyone we chose not
to accommodate (there were plenty of sick, scabby dogs who
wouldn't entice you for a gold doubloon), and there was no
sleeping overnight in our rooms. Once this was understood by
all we were able to walk around the port with relative ease. Of
course there was always plenty of banter when we mingled on
the beaches, but it was now lighthearted and amiable because no
one in this strange democracy was expecting—or getting—any
special favors.

One late morning we wended our way through the shacks and
tents to examine the shells on the shoreline. Three young men
were splashing about at the waters edge naked and unabashed.
They waved when they caught sight of us and one of them hol-
lered, "Ahoy, ladies! Come join us." Violet apparently recognized
them so she turned to see if I might be interested too. I nodded.
We tucked up our skirts so they wouldn't get wet and waded

through the frothy surf. The three sailors had just about spent their riches and were making the best of the free entertainment. One of them—Paul Skinner—swam in the cut-glass water like a sleek, oiled fish. I watched in admiration as he dived and sank, then pulled on his arms and cut through the sea with ease.

When he eventually glided back to the sand I gasped, "Can you teach me to do that?"

The young salt slipped a wide smile and asked, "Mean you to swim then, Miss Lola?"

I was taken aback he'd the advantage of knowing my name but then Violet came to my rescue and whispered, "Skinner, I think."

So I beamed and replied, "Aye, Mr. Skinner. I've a mind to learn if you'd be so good as instruct me."

He stood knee-deep in the water and held out his hands indicating I was to join him offshore. His two friends seemed miffed that he was getting all the attention and they started shouting comments such as, "Stand by, lassie—Sharkey will bite you!"

"Who's Sharkey?" I asked my new friend.

"'Tis I." He laughed. "A nickname—"

"But you won't really bite?" I asked playfully.

"Nay," he quipped. Then he added, "Though you do, indeed, look tasty. . . ."

I giggled at his flirtation but then asked in a more serious voice, "Do your friends not swim?"

He shook his head. "They claim the sea is too great an adversary so if they chance to fall overboard they intend to surrender peacefully."

"Not me!" I shuddered. I took his hands and asked, "What must I do?" By now I was waist-deep too and as the weight of my saturated dress was dragging me down I slipped off the outer layers and threw them to Violet for safekeeping. I stood translucent in blouse and bloomers. The other sailors began whistling coarsely and they invited Violet to join their jovial party. She kindly collected my wet clothes from the breakers, spread them on a rock to dry, then settled down to watch me drown in foolishness.

Sharkey placed both hands on my hips and tipped my body so that I was lying faceup flat on top of the water. I balanced firmly on two supporting hands and surrendered to the weightlessness. Above, overstuffed clouds glided swiftly across the skies so I knew a wind was building on the horizon. I closed my eyes and floated with the current. Then the hands abruptly dropped and I sank under a spray of salty water and came up spluttering for air. I scrambled until my feet touched bottom, not very comfortable with the current sucking at my legs. Sharkey was staring at my breasts, and to my horror I saw the material was completely sheer and sticking to my nipples. He pointed out my dilemma to his shipmates, who responded with a cry of whoops. Now I understood why my mentor was so keen to assist me, but I ignored my embarrassment, sank on my knees so my chest dropped below the waterline and asked, "What now?"

This time my teacher took both of my hands and pulled me off balance toward him. I drifted like a log gliding through the mass. "Kick your legs!" he ordered. I thrashed around clumsily, causing a burst of chaos. "Up and down," he explained. "As if you're running . . ."

Then he let go of my hands and I immediately sank like a stinging wreck. "I can't do it," I wailed.

"Try again," he commanded. And the exercise was repeated over and over.

I went through a whole battery of emotion—excitement—fear—embarrassment—determination—and finally I managed to keep my head up as I clawed the waves like a frantic dog. Violet cheered encouragement from the shore. And suddenly I realized I'd actually swum on my own for the very first time. Now, I ain't claiming to be the most elegant body in the water—I just didn't never want to be the dead one. So I persisted in dunking again and again until I'd mastered the arm strokes and had some sense of when to catch breath. By the end of the afternoon I was cold, disheveled, thoroughly exhausted, and burned by the sun, but when we waded back to the sand I gave Violet the biggest smile and screamed, "I did it!"

"Well you certainly did something, darling," said one of the sailors, grinning. And they both laughed at the sight of Sharkey's swollen wood as he followed me out of the sea.

Nearly every day thereafter I went back to the beach to master my lessons. Sharkey was a good instructor, not only because he was endlessly patient but because he could read my struggle and knew when to be sympathetic and when to push me beyond pure laziness or fear. As my confidence improved he had me treading water and floating on my own, both prone and supine. And of course he frequented the Silk Ship each evening sniffing for due reward. Now, don't get me wrong—I liked the young man—he was kind and funny and decent. But he was developing feelings for me I couldn't no way return. It was one thing giving him a quickie after I'd finished dancing, but quite another when he wanted to stay and talk and woo me. Time was money and I couldn't be giving it for free (or swim lessons) but I didn't want to hurt his pride. So I'd mumble and bluster and feign politeness when I should have just told him to haul up anchor. But whenever I looked into his sad green eyes I was snagged by his unbearable earnestness. Poor sap. He'd got it bad.

Meanwhile, as me and Violet were settling in so were Jim and

Annie. Two nights after our arrival we all met again this side of adventure on a sickly somewhat-surreal night I won't never be forgetting. See, Pierre generally hired whoever was in port to provide musical accompaniment for his tavern, so I'd been merrily dancing to a loud and battered accordion. At the end of my performance, as I collected the cobs my more ardent admirers had tossed, I looked up from the sawdust into Annie's smoldering eyes. James stood beside her, his arm linked possessively through his wife's.

"Well, well, well . . . look what the cat dragged in," Anne sneered.

"Annie, don't!" Jim warned. "Leave it." The wife disengaged herself from her husband and roughly jostled in front of him.

The testy audience loved a good fight and the air was singed with excitement at promise of a feline fray. I pushed the coins into my pocket and stood mutely on the spot.

"What are you doing here, wench?" she demanded.

I mumbled something she couldn't hear. By now Violet had disengaged herself from the group of hopeful suitors and had elbowed her way through the restless crowd to observe what was going on. As soon as she saw the Bonnys she wedged herself between us and spat into Annie's face, "Leave her alone, Anne."

"Anne, is it now?" the new bride mused. "You'll do well to address me as Mrs. Bonny."

Now even the crowd laughed along with Violet as she roared, "Happen I'll be calling you Mrs. Trollop. You be no better than me now, wench!"

Anne blushed in horror at the public humiliation. Then she rose inside to her full height and swayed from side to side savoring the coming strike. The hot, pretty face held everyone spellbound so she turned and appealed for justice, hissing, "This girl belongs to my father! She's my servant. . . ."

Violet was unabashed and said, "Lola belongs to no one. She's free as anyone else here."

The heads in the audience nodded and drooled. Then a finely dressed pirate came forward and proffered a low bow to Mrs. Bonny. "Perhaps I can be of some assistance, ma'am," he offered. I could tell Annie wasn't sure if he was fooling with her or not but she swept a long, long stare over his attire, then held out her hand for the proper acknowledgment. "Captain Harry Jennings, at your service," he murmured with lips hovering over her ring.

"Charmed, I'm sure," Anne responded. Then she launched into a diatribe of every sin I'd ever committed, painting me darker than Satan himself. I was certain, any moment, someone was going to clap me in chains as Anne explained I was little more than the thieving gypsy slattern who'd killed her mother. I shot her withering husband a plea to intercede on my behalf, but Jim was shrinking farther away from the venom spewing forth from his wife's alien lips. This was obviously an Annie not loosed on him before, but he'd sure be seeing a lot more of her in future. Captain Jennings listened patiently, still holding on to Annie's extended hand. He showed no intent to release his grip as he looked at Violet and me, turned to the crowd, then shrugged his shoulders in a patronizing manner. I didn't see no joke—but the rest of the tavern burst into laughter. The captain waited for the air to hush, then he turned to Anne and said clearly, "Dear Mrs. Bonny—it would appear you have arrived at the wrong location." Anne looked puzzled as she waited to hear what came next. "This is Nassau . . . not Nantucket!" More cackles of amusement rang out and her blush flushed a deeper than deep hue. "But please, allow me to explain how things work around here." And he skillfully led her off to his table at the rear. James was about to follow them when Pierre tapped him on the shoulder and gave him a warning wag of the finger. There was some understanding needed sorting that apparently didn't involve her husband none. As we watched their retreat, Violet whispered in my ear, "You've got to stand up for yourself, Lola. I'll not always be here saving your arse." Then she turned to a gaggle of potential customers, flashed her best lecherous smile, and drew them back into the mob. I went over to James and led him by the elbow to a shadowy spot where he could sit and observe his wife without attracting trouble. Within the hour the captain had provided enough drink for Anne to be senseless and to Jim's alarm she now sat on his knee, laughing raucously, and wearing the pirate's feathered hat. I ain't never seen this Harry Jennings before so I used my vantage place to form a quick opinion—and, as what I saw there froze my marrow, it must have petrified the quaking James Bonny.

Captain Henry Jennings was the self-proclaimed governor of the island who spoke with a cultured Welsh lilt. It's rumored he became a privateer to help restore the dispossessed Stuart family to the English throne. But it's also whispered he joined up for adventure, having a fearsome thirst for violence. I estimated he was in his late twenties, and he seeped a sticky sort of charm being witty, well-kempt, and wealthy. Now, two years past, a cargo of Spanish treasure sank in a hurricane off the coast of Florida so Jennings took three ships to salvage the booty. He reputedly drove off sixty soldiers who were guarding the hoard recently brought to the surface, and all of the three hundred tars who sailed with him came back fairy-tale rich. But Jennings, formerly based in Jamaica, was warned that his old home was no longer safe so he founded this new pirate colony on the island of Providence, offering safe haven to fellow buccaneers in exchange for a tribute payment. Everyone was welcome—except his archrival Benjamin Hornigold—and Samuel Bellamy—the friend who betrayed him, stole his goods, and then joined up with Hornigold.

Captain Jennings had a clean-shaven face that was all but hidden by an enviable cascade of springy natural brown curls, and many might call him attractive were it not for the overlong nose that drew most attention. But there was something sharp about this man that quivered of mortal danger, and that was what drew Annie. She had finally found a genuine pirate . . . and her two-bit spineless husband paled in comparison. I took a sly glance at Jim as he sat making a similar assessment. His face was drawn in a weird expression I didn't really comprehend back then. And for the first time I noticed how small he was, and how the sunshine reddened his cheeks but never tanned them. Perhaps the past weeks at sea had caused the outbreak of pimples popping his chin, but when I looked down at his chewed, blackened nails, and then across at the elegant hands of the captain, I felt truly sorry for James and what he was about to surrender. He was physically shaking but self-preservation kept him back off the marauder's sword. Jim never uttered a word to me—he just stared—downed his drink—and left the bar with the gait of a beaten puppy.

Now, probably because I'd been swimming each day I suddenly realized how foul the human body smelled. Of course sailors ain't the fussiest washers—but then again neither are gypsies—yet for the first time in my life my stomach heaved from a whiff of vinegar-spiked hair, the gut-rank breath of rotting teeth, eye-watering armpits that hadn't known soap for years, and clothes daubed in piss, stale food, and sour ale. I wanted to wear clean undergarments so took to washing each week now. And I rubbed my hair in various oils to keep it shiny and untangled. Violet laughed and said I was growing vain—but I didn't want to stink like a pig or have the mouth of a maggoty fish. I spent a long time pondering why our bodies turned so ripe and concluded that the stench was actually a weapon to keep other predators away. Unfortunately, though, it didn't seem to work on pirates, who would amuse their passions with anything gamy in a skirt. But some of the more discerning punters preferred my cleaner bed—and those who swore I smelled of sea air were the ones most loyal and generous.

Now, each night thereafter the Bonnys arrived together, James would drink himself legless, Jennings would appear (or not) as the mood took him, and Annie would either leave on his arm or make her way home with Pierre. The newlyweds had only been married three months but now openly disparaged each other—he, because Anne was playing the strumpet—and she, because Jim was no pirate prince. Then one night around Easter, when the festivities were in full swing and I was mumbling farewell to Sharkey, who'd just signed up on an outgoing adventure, Annie and Jennings were holding court in the center of the room. James was so inebriated that Violet hauled him upstairs to pass out on my floor, where at least he'd be reasonably safe. I'd already earned enough that week so I sat trying to cheer up Sharkey, all the while watching the outrageous behavior taking place out the corner of my eye. Anne and the captain were surrounded by a flamboyant bunch of rogues, each trying to better the other to impress the rambunctious lady. The five sailors were trying to teach Anne a card game and the feast of coins center table attested to the seriousness of their enterprise. At the end of each round the winner collected not only the pot but also a *dollop of trollop*—a good chug of rum delivered by Annie's own mouth. She'd take a hefty swig from the bottle and dribble it directly into the pirate's open mouth as he bent his head back over the chair (an enviable position that also afforded a crafty nuzzle from her cleavage). But she must also have swallowed a fair amount herself judging by the flash in her eyes.

Well, this particular night the chattering voices suddenly muted, warning me there was a newcomer in our midst who commanded everyone's interest. I turned to the door to see a small young woman enter in one of Pierre's finest outfits, her pretty blond ringlets glimmering as she walked. She had an envious air of superiority, cutting through the crowd as if she owned the place and wedging herself behind Captain Jennings's chair as if she owned him. He immediately lifted his cheek and persuaded her to kiss him, which she did, her arched eyes all the while staring down Annie. Anne had just finished administering the most recent dollop of rum so she pushed her fire-flecked hair behind one ear and stood to meet the glare. The captain said casually, "Meg—this is Annie. Anne—meet Megan." Neither woman spoke. They stood suspended in uncertainty not wanting to make the first move. I could see Meg's face etched in lantern light and found her stunning. Her only flaw was a slight cross of the front teeth, but even this produced an appealing pout that drew the eye to her lips. Her gaze remained riveted on her rival.

Anne recovered first and said, "Mrs. Jennings, I presume?"

The table wobbled under snorts of laughter until the captain clarified with, "She's my mistress, Annie. Same as you."

Anne was now pinned in Meg's magnetic stare and of all the moves I might have anticipated, what she did next absolutely astounded me. She went over to where Meg was standing, whispered something in her ear, brushed two fingers lightly over the amply-stuffed stomacher, and then kissed her rival full on the mouth. Every man in the room was hypnotized and a hush fell over their companions. I couldn't no way believe what I was seeing! I'd heard of such behavior but never actually witnessed it with my own popping eyes. I waited for Meg to slap her jaw, to recoil in horror or something. But as soon as their faces parted Meg took Annie's head between both hands and returned the lusty kiss. One of the mates at the table groaned and another was feeling himself through the cloth of his breeches. The captain stood up, put an arm around both women, and led them away to his house down the street. "Are you not staying, Harry, to earn back your loot?" asked the winning companion at the table.

The captain gave him a vulgar leer and said, "With these two darlings to plunder, I think I can forfeit the smaller prize."

And the men stared enviously after him, even Sharkey.

I ain't never seen such a guttural response since I snuck in that tent to watch the Dance of Veils. Something primal had just taken place that I didn't understand. So I talked it over with Sharkey and Pierre, and later with Violet and some of my other customers. And this is what I learned. Men are attracted to women having sex together because they find it incredibly interesting. Now I ain't never had no desire to see two blokes at it—so even when Dr. Simpson was debauching Bristol in the same room I always turned away and stuffed up my ears. But I guess to a sea dog who's seen just about everything, the difference—the unknown—is always exciting. I'm told folks like to watch for voyeuristic motives, and I'm willing to concede there's an aesthetic quality seeing pretty women enjoying each other. Of course, men are also fascinated with female lasciviousness and find willing participants achingly sexy. But what I could never understand were the men who think they'll be allowed to join in the action—because unless they're a Captain Jennings they're cordially not invited.

When James roused himself, around bedtime, we sobered him up enough to get home. He sat on the floor rubbing his eyes and asked, "Have they gone yet?" Violet nodded but didn't say what had occurred downstairs. "Can't I stay here the night?" he pleaded. We both shook our heads and were explaining the house rules when Jim's eyes swelled with salt. "I can't go back to the shop. . . ." he mumbled, hurriedly explaining that now Annie's treasures were all sold they'd got no money. Violet ran downstairs just as Pierre was readying to retire. She pleaded on Jim's behalf and the landlord agreed to let him stay the rest of the month until he found a suitable cruise, but only after Violet promised to make up the deficit herself.

We learned the following day that Anne had moved into the captain's house to live with him and Meg. So that, apparently, was that.

8

DRINK AND THE DEVIL

SUMMER, 1717

James Bonny was mine for the taking if I still wanted him. And for some unknown reason I found that I did. So I listened to his slurring tongue as he bemoaned the loss of a wife, gazed longingly as his bleary eyes grubbed for searing revenge, made sympathetic noises to bathe his scalded pride, and responded with enough encouragement to snag his tattered need. Now I ain't no fool—well happen I am—but I honestly felt I could help him get over Annie. Of course, I knew he came to the Silk Ship every night to see if Jennings was there with his women and when the captain did put in a torturous appearance Jim would pickle his anger in enough rum to render it impotent. But most evenings the ménage à trois found other amusements and then James would implode into the sorrowful creature I took to my bosom and bed. Now, after waiting almost a year, you'd think I'd be ecstatic to finally hold my beloved close. But my booty turned out to be an empty chest some outlaw had already looted, for whenever he lay staring in darkness I knew it was Annie's face he was seeking. Looking back, I can see there wasn't really no heart left, just a terrible urge to quench his despair and make someone else feel the cost. But we went through the motions time and again and tried to pretend we were lovers.

Ships came into harbor with old crews and new tales throughout the following weeks as the island's tropical heat exploded into summer, and with them arrived word that Ben Hornigold might be amassing a pirate navy in the waters around Jamaica. Apparently Edward Teach was now his partner (with a six-gun sloop and seventy hands) and his men were calling their new commander—Blackbeard. From snippets of gossip here and there I learned more of this fearsome duo. Hornigold hailed from Norfolk and spoke with the native drawl, but he'd been raiding ships in the West Indies since 1713, graduating from canoes to his heavily armed sloop called the *Ranger*. His star pupil was Blackbeard, who some say came from Bristol and had cut his teeth as a privateer during the Queen Anne's War. In the past few months the two captains had seized several merchant prizes, including one stocked with flour heading for Havana, a sloop from Bermuda stuffed full of spirits, and a Portuguese vessel laden with sweet white wine. Such flagrant acts had quite incensed the local officials, who'd swiftly dispatched a Captain Mathew Munson to capture the scoundrel seamen. Unfortunately, though, Munson's armed merchant vessel was pitifully outgunned and he barely escaped with his life after running aground on Cat Cay. The escaping members of the battered crew whispered that Hornigold's fleet had seemingly increased to three hundred and fifty men in five terrifying vessels. Trouble was brewing out at sea and Captain Jennings was none too happy. So he spread promise of amnesty to each departing jack-tar and decreed there'd be a general Pirate Council—here—at the end of sweltering July.

Now, before we'd even time to worry about conscientious bounty hunters, news came that Black Sam Bellamy had been lost to a storm off Cape Cod in his latest acquisition, a Guineaman called the *Whydah*. They say that as a young sailor Bellamy fell for a Massachusetts girl called Maria Hallett and wanted to prove worthy so he decided to join the sunken Spanish treasure salvage in Florida and was part of the gang who made off with some of Captain Jennings's silver. This easy success convinced him to throw in his lot with the buccaneers, where he soon became another of Hornigold's protégés, eventually deposing his mentor for command of the *Mary Anne*. He then progressed to the *Sultana* and *Whydah*, and was supposedly heading back to his lover when his flagship ran into the fateful storm.

One of the nine survivors arrived on an incoming rumrunner to spread the tale of doom. Of course, you'll already know how six of the partially drowned eventually danced at the end of the hangman's rope—and that Cotton Mather managed to get the two who were pressed into service finally acquitted? Well, the ninth was a Miskito Indian called John Julian who escaped the hunt and finally made it to Providence. And what a commotion he caused, let me tell you. First off, he'd managed to salvage most of a fifty-pound bag of plunder by packing the loot into wraps secured round his arms, legs and torso. It was top-notch booty that helped smooth his way to anonymity. And second, he was such a fine storyteller he kept us all entertained for weeks. John spoke a mix of English peppered with his own native words but his hands and face enacted the drama so every expression was vividly understood. He told us about being kidnapped by a rival tribe somewhere near his home on the Spanish Main, and being sold to the English and shipped to Jamaica. Two years later his owner took him to be overseer of another plantation in Antigua on board a merchantman called the *Bonetta*. Unfortunately this vessel was captured by Sam Bellamy, who took the captives to a deserted island and forced them to help careen the craft, scraping off parasites and caulking the hull to render it seaworthy.

The captain supposedly took a liking to John and urged him join the Brethren of the Coast, which finally assured his freedom. Then Bellamy—that infamous Prince of Pirates—let the other prisoners leave on his old sloop while the swashbucklers sailed off on the bigger prize. Within a few weeks they'd taken the British *Sultana* as it left the Spanish Main with a cargo of logwood. Their captain offered no resistance because he was recovering from a previous wound, so the outlaws, boasting they were Robin Hood's Men, spared their pleading lives. The buccaneers then took the new vessel to a remote inlet and over the Christmas period converted her into a fighter, soon acquiring even more manpower from the scattered remnants of Captain Martel's crew (who'd been hiding on one of the islands after being attacked by the Royal Navy's *Scarborough*). And by the close of February they'd captured one of the most advanced ships ever built—the *Whydah*. John happened to be on board their new galley the night that she made her fatal run up the Atlantic into a violent storm off the coast of Cape Cod.

The survivor told of the sinking with such flair that I probably ain't going to do it no justice, but here's what I can remember. On that horrendous night John was on deck lashing equipment against the violent nor'easter that had risen up out of nowhere. The ship was driven onto a shoal in sixteen feet of water some hour round midnight. Violent winds pummeled the boat aground making it impossible to do anything but bind to the ropes for safety. Huge incoming waves swept the decks, washing away whatever was not strapped firm, and John clung on with his arms gripped tight round the main mast, hoping his body was wedged close enough in to avoid the hurtling cannons ripping through everything in their paths. Another great surge snapped the top of the mast, which miraculously fell the other side of John, but which drew the ship off the bar and into deeper water, capsizing her and forcing the craft below the freezing surf. John couldn't swim but he held on grimly to the length of shattered wood in his grasp and allowed the tide to sweep him inland. He looked back once to see if anyone else had been thrown to safety but all he saw was the sinking stern—and even the terrified screams were drowned by the screeching gale. The ship had perished in sight of land, so the strong Indian willed his legs forward until he washed up amid a pile of debris on the sand. Each pulse of the sea spewed another batch of dead bodies until the whole beach seemed coated in bloated corpses. John lay semiconscious while the breath returned to his lungs, and then he made himself stand up before those notorious wreckers—the Moon Cussers—arrived to plunder among the salvage. One of the chests swept from the hold had breeched against the rocks spilling its treasure to the angry winds. So John rummaged through the heavy bags of gold dust, tore the shirt off a body that wouldn't be needing it any, and set off inland before the first of the scavengers could arrive. He learned later that only nine souls had survived the disaster, and that the other unfortunates captured for trial in all likelihood would be executed. As John's tale passed from tongue to tongue word came from Jennings that this newcomer was to be shown every civility because he brought with him the best of all possible news—that the deceitful Black Sam Bellamy would cheat no one ever again.

Sometime around the middle of June things came to a head with Annie and Jim. I'd just been trying out some new dances to a whiny set of bagpipes when the captain appeared with his women on either arm. The sailors who were sat center table instantly melted to the edges of the room to make way for the entourage, and their king took up the slack. Anne looked ravishing in a gold outfit that flaunted Pierre's finest cross-stitches while Meg made an equally beautiful companion in a red satin dress that flowed to the floor like wine. The captain ordered a flagon of sherry and invited some of the onlookers to join their party.

Now Jim was sat with a young man called Albert Sparks, one of Violet's regular punters pining to become something more. Albert was about the same age as my mate but his years on the water had cured his face to leather. His thinning hair was the color of gingerroot but his eyes were vivid and kind and he made Violet laugh out loud like no one I'd ever known. Well, as Albert was telling some tall story, Jim looked across at the captain publicly fondling his wife and something snapped in his self-control. Next thing I knew he'd blundered up to Annie's table and had grasped her roughly by the arm. Then he roared, "Hey up, hussy! You're coming home with me."

Anne tried to wriggle free of the pasty knuckles as she shouted back, "Get away, Jim, if you know what's good for you. . . ." But the fingers tightened and lifted the woman onto her feet. She shot a glance at the captain to gauge his reaction. Jennings continued to sip solemnly on the sherry with a half-amused smirk twisting the corners of his mouth. "Harry!" she called to her lover. "Make him let go."

With slow deliberation, Jennings pushed back his chair— then quicker than a rattlesnake his dagger was suddenly pricking the back of Jim's angry neck. "Release the lady," he whispered.

"She's my wife!" James protested. "I . . . I have a right. . . ."

Annie wrestled her elbow free and glared in her husband's face. "I'm with the captain now. And he's twice the man of you!" Jim raised his arm as if to strike her when Jennings caught hold of his flying wrist with his free hand, all the while pushing the dagger farther into his neck with his other. Red beads appeared where the blade snagged and Jim's hands flew to the weapon to halt its progress, wiggling and squirming until the tip slipped round under his chin allowing Jennings to press him into Annie's vacated chair. The rejected husband sat in embarrassment, holding the end of his shirt against the dripping wound. Anne stared pitifully, her mouth grim with loathing. Meg remained seated, and poured the captain another drink from the flask on the table as he took up his former place.

Jennings savored the liquid fire, running his tongue round the inside of his mouth before he decided, "You can take her."

"What?" Anne exclaimed in furious disbelief. "What are you saying, Harry?"

The captain replied, "I'm saying, you should go home, Mrs. Bonny."

"You're done with me?" she demanded to know. "Just like that?"

Henry Jennings nodded his head and cast a knowing glance in Meg's direction. The other woman had never spoken a word— but the delight on her face showed most evidently that she didn't much like sharing her man, even though she shrugged a conspiratorial look of compassion in Annie's direction. For once in her life Anne was at a loss for words. She hauled herself to her proudest height, pushed a stray lock of hair behind her right ear, kicked the miserable man in the chair to his feet, then marched briskly out of the bar ahead of James. The eerie silence hanging over the smoke lay suspended in awe for just another few seconds until the captain roared, "Play us a lively jig!" And the bagpipes groaned into action.

That was a sobering encounter for me as well. I realized that it didn't matter none how much I gave to Jim, or how hard I tried to insert myself into his void; he was a one-woman scoundrel who foolishly believed he'd just won back his prize. And I was once again the dross left rudderless and abandoned. At that time I didn't know what had just taken place, but within the week it became evident that something big had occurred. First off, after striking no luck for months Jim was magically given a berth on the first cruise out of port—a vessel bound for Madagascar, which meant he'd be away from his newly won wife for months. Apparently Jennings had decided that if he was no longer bedding Anne, then her husband wouldn't be either. And second, Pierre warned Annie she needed to find another benefactor quickly since she'd now got no money, no protection, and had effectively been thrown to the sharks.

Yet although me and Anne usually avoided each other, I ached to know if Jim had left me a message before his hurried departure. So a couple of days later, when Violet suggested we pay a visit to Pierre's dress shop, I readily agreed to trudge alongside. I'd expected to find the rejected woman pale and shunned and lowly—but imagine my surprise when I discovered her radiant and gleaming, already at work on her next roguish plan. Pierre joked indiscreetly that Annie had now set her sights on the wealthiest man in the entire Carribees—the powerful Chidley Bayard.

As we entered the shop Annie was bent over a piece of cut cloth conversing with the flamboyant Frenchman about a particular design. She looked up from their chatter and sneered a contemptuous huff in our direction saying, "You're too late. He's already gone, and good riddance."

I nodded that I'd heard that news and then mumbled, "We know. How are you doing, Annie?"

"Mrs. Bonny to you," she corrected. "And it's none of your damn business."

Pierre was embarrassed by Anne's rudeness and said pointedly, "But my dear madame—the Mademoiselles Violet and Lola have been taking good care of Monsieur James. . . ." He knew Violet paid the rent.

Annie, however, did not. She raised a sarcastic eyebrow and spat, "Oh, I'm sure that the gypsy jade has greased his mast on many a past night, although what he ever saw in such a miserable doxy is quite beyond my ken. . . ." The irate wife threatened to move toward me, but Pierre touched her arm with sufficient import to hold her back. So instead she turned her scathing tongue on Violet and muttered, "And I'll warrant that you've had him too!"

Violet replied in an even voice, "Aye, Annie. But long before he met with you."

"Then the only one he's not slept with is Pierre I suppose. . . ."

Her male friend blushed, shrugged his shoulders enigmatically, and then confessed, "Well . . ." He winked at the three of us and there was an uncomfortable pause. Then Annie suddenly burst out laughing. I'm not sure if she believed the outrageous statement (or whether we did either) but his comment broke the tension by highlighting the ridiculousness of this cuckolded wife's moral inquisition. So the shrewd dressmaker took advantage of the shift in mood and asked politely, "And how may we assist my dear jeunes filles?"

Violet stepped forward and said bluntly, "We came to see if

Anne was doing all right . . . without Jim around, I mean." The sour edge of Captain Jennings's memory hovered in the momentary silence.

Pierre answered emphatically on his friend's behalf, "The madame is working as my new designer. She has quite the eye!"

"Really?" I asked. I ain't never heard of Annie ever taking up a needle and thread before. But as I edged closer to the garment on the table I recognized the flair for detail she may well have engendered. "It's nice," I offered. The embroidered pearls were exquisite. "Who's it for?"

"Ahhh . . ." Pierre said cryptically. He held his chin in his hand in an infuriating gesture designed to generate more intrigue. "A very special *cliente* . . . the Señorita Vargas."

I suddenly came over chilly for I'd heard of Maria Vargas—the volatile mistress of Chidley Bayard who'd once supposedly decapitated a child for soiling her linen petticoat. But if Anne really did intend to go after Bayard herself then why on earth would she be designing a dress for her rival?

"You two may accompany me," Anne suddenly declared. "If you keep your mouths shut." And why would she want any company tagging along either?

I nudged Violet's elbow to see what she thought. She asked slowly, "What's in it for us then?"

Anne replied, "An introduction to the most powerful man on these islands. Chidley Bayard is hosting the Council of Pirates—and if he likes the looks of us . . . well . . . it might be very rewarding."

"How so?" I ventured.

"We could be invited to entertain his *special* guests—some of the most famous men outside Christendom!"

Violet understood the offer and nodded enthusiastically, her eyes glinting fast as her thoughts. Of course we'd have crashed the ancillary parties anyway—along with every other clamoring skirt—for all our heads had been turned by tales of successful swashbucklers scattering doubloons in their drunken wake.

Pierre stood with his hand on the half-assembled dress and asked, "Well, who's going to finish this beading work then?"

"I will," I volunteered. I knew that I ran a niftier stitch than Violet and that I could certainly pull a needle with more skill than Anne.

And so the three of us women came to a fragile truce—born from circumstance, fueled by ambition, and frosted with greedy gilt.

Later, when we left the shop and headed back to the tavern, I asked Violet what she thought was behind Annie's offer. She gave me a cheeky wink and said, "I'd already heard from Pierre she's going after Bayard so I was seeking some advantage for us."

My shocked voice exclaimed, "You knew she was going to Bayard's house and schemed to be taken along?"

"Aye," my friend replied. "She'll be wanting to fit her own design—and if it were me dealing with Maria Vargas I'd bring protection too!" I stared at Violet with wide admiration. She was always one step beyond.

Now, I've often wondered why authority is such a compelling force to romance—how even the ugliest king has lovers lining up to bed him. And it seems to be all tied up with wealth. For a partner may be dependable—but if he's going to be anything other than a romp in the sack he must also be a provider. Why so? Well, even women like me who are the most independent—who can make their own ways and survive without panderers—would consider a buccaneer captain the grandest of prizes indeed. Perhaps it's the raw excitement of loving so close to the edge, that point where the dare fires the blood with thrill, and the marrow runs clear of conscience. Or perchance it's the muscle and sway and protection against coarse lesser evils abroad. Anyhow—the higher the rank the better the plunder—as all potential queens are well aware.

As we sat in Chidley Bayard's carriage Anne delivered her instructions. No one was to touch Vargas but her. No one was to speak but she. We were to pass and pin and tuck and snip but only at Anne's request. I had to hide a dagger tucked in a garter under my skirt and Violet had a loaded pistol smuggled inside the work basket. We were told that Bayard would appear to approve the outfit and then give us the purse for Pierre. And if he liked whatever else he saw we'd most likely all be invited to the grandest orgy this side of paradise.

Now, as it turned out, Mrs. Bonny was on her finest behavior, all manners and sunshine charm. She deferred to Maria Vargas as if she were royalty, touching her with a servitude I didn't never know she had in her. The dress fit snug as a kid-leather boot and decked the Spanish beauty in ravishing swathes of ivory, magically setting her inky locks against the dramatic cheekbones. The three of us made appreciative noises and convinced her she shone like a pearl, which actually she did. All went well until the master appeared. He certainly admired his mistress as she twirled and flounced her glory, but when he handed over the payment to Anne I noted he smoothed her wrist with his finger and whispered something low and lewd. Annie stifled a giggle. But when she carefully raised her eyes to meet his own he looked into the fire just a moment too long and then the hell gates opened. Maria Vargas said loud and pointedly, "You three may go now."

But it was too late. Chidley Bayard had seen into Annie's soul and found himself pulled in the furnace like all the others. He coughed, turned to Maria, bowed low toward us and announced, "You three beauties must grace our festivities next week." He added coldly, "Maria, make the arrangements." And with that he left us to face her seething wrath. Vargas was very controlled, though, I'll give her that. She curtly told us to be here for the welcoming party on Friday, that we could keep whatever rewards we made, and that we'd need several dresses throughout the week of any color excepting green or ivory. We grinned to each other as she left the room, already planning our revelry.

Now, I was so excited I couldn't hardly sleep but I knew we'd never outmaneuver Annie for the very best pieces of cloth. So instead of vying for glamour I decided to make all my outfits suitable for dancing. Then, when the opportunity arose, I'd be able to leap out above the glittering crowd. I can see you're wondering why we were so anxious to see and be seen? Because they'd already named the celebrities coming aboard. First we heard that the great Charles Vane was approaching on the *Treasure*. Vane had been part of Jennings's gang salvaging the silver off Florida but instead of raiding the storehouse he'd waited for one of the restocked galleons to head home before boldly intercepting. The plunder he stole from it made him a wealthy man, one of the most successful. But whispers told of a darker side that was brutal, deceptive, and cruel—he supposedly liked to torture captives and had often cheated his own crew. And perhaps because he was fickle himself, he didn't trust many a pirate and had left the sloop with a skeleton guard under his newly appointed quarter-master, John Rackham. So that's why I never got to see the man we'd know as Calico Jack, because he'd to stay aboard the *Treasure* while his captain attended to business.

Captain Jennings would also be hosting alongside Chidley

Bayard, but another infamous guest was already on the island—the wily Paulsgrave Williams. This buccaneer had partnered Sam Bellamy as commander of the *Mary Anne* and only serendipity had dragged him to Nassau instead of Davy Jones's Locker. Bellamy and Williams got separated in fog during the *Whydah*'s last cruise so the *Mary Anne* sailed for Maine (as previously arranged) for a rendezvous in May. Bellamy, of course, never arrived—so after waiting two weeks Williams set sail for Providence as he'd heard there was now a ripe price on his own powdered head. He'd paid Jennings well for some tenuous shelter, and then wisely kept out of his way. I'd seen this punter puffing down the street in a startlingly white wig that looked ridiculous on an old sea dog with such a burnished tan, and the way he swaggered around made it obvious he fancied himself a toff. But even I could tell at a glance—all the silver in Spain couldn't never refine this marauder.

Edward Teach, however, was a different breed of man altogether. I immediately noticed him at the opening party because he was a good head taller than anyone else in the room. And I guessed he was the mighty Blackbeard from the legendary whiskers that spread from ears to nipples. But what most surprised me was his demeanor—for he seemed to be a confident, sophisticated man who'd obviously seen both sides of the spinning coin. I knew he was here with Ben Hornigold, but the unlikely partners seemed diverse as sugar from salt. Blackbeard was elegant and well-mannered, and I'd warrant on his finest behavior, while Hornigold was a blustering square-shaped man with a block head and flat plank nose. Everything about Hornigold seemed wooden and blunt, his language splintered and hard. And I noticed right off that the two of them tried unsuccessfully to blend into the crowd without drawing undue attention. There were lots of other captains and crew summoned to the general council but after I'd caught a glimpse of Teach the rest seemed to blur into nothingness.

Unfortunately though, I didn't impress anyone special that week because they were all too drunk by the time I got to dancing. The pirates met formally each noon to divide up the waters between them and argue the best means of defying the authorities, all the while drowning their differences in darker spirits. And then came feasting and finally the music. Now, as it turned out, even though women were scarce, every doxy in town was there clamoring round the celebrity guests like vultures picking at eyeballs. Violet did a pretty good trade, being swift and precise in her ministrations, but neither of us got anywhere close to Vane or Williams or Hornigold or Teach. And it didn't take long for me to realize I'd make most money by following Violet's lead, so after a brief artistic performance each night I moved my hips to a different dance. Only one time did anyone seem to appreciate my talent and that was toward the end of the week when I capered some old gypsy steps to a skilled accordion. I looked up midway through a leap and thought I saw Blackbeard smiling in my direction, but before my feet even landed, some jade had stuffed his head in her bosom and the two of them stumbled off to the shadows. So after all that anticipation the promise just fizzled and faded into one huge disappointment.

Except for Anne Bonny. As always, the scheming wench got what she wanted and this time her reward was the podgy Chidley Bayard. Bayard was an incredibly rich merchant (whose sister had married the brother of the governor of Jamaica). He looked like an overripe cherub, rosy-cheeked and oozing out of his beautifully tailored clothing. I imagine he was probably bald under the perfectly coiffed wig and he reminded me of a piglet stuffed for a royal table. But his manner was very convivial, ever laughing and joking and spreading good cheer, and I have to say he's probably the most generous man I ever did meet. Nothing was spared for his guests. Bayard was quite literally the soul of the party. On the first night he slyly watched Annie's every move as she flirted and spun her magic. The second night he dared and asked her to join his table, much to Maria Vargas's annoyance. In between punters I edged close enough to hear stolen snatches of conversation and toward the end of the evening I could tell it wasn't going too well. Every time Anne opened her lips and her witty quips met with general approval, Vargas would offer some catty retort designed to demean her opponent. And it would likely have worked with any other rival except this one, who had grown up sassy and comfortable among privilege. As the party fell to closure Violet and I picked our way round the fading bodies and went to see if the carriage was still taking guests home. Annie saw us leaving out the corner of her eye and bid us wait for her too, then she gently disengaged Bayard's hand from her arm and skillfully avoided the slobbery kiss he tried to deliver. I glanced back as we exited and was amused to see him recoiling under the spit of Vargas's tongue.

The next night was the one you've likely heard of—and I can still see it in my mind as if it happened but last week. Violet and I had been invited to dine with some of the lesser men from Captain Vane's crew, and halfway through eating Anne made her entrance. She had flagrantly disobeyed instructions and was dressed in a fabulous gown of shimmering green, the exact same shade as the furious hostess. Vargas looked every inch the beauty, but when Annie slid into view, her throbbing sensuality immediately ousted the reigning queen. I gnawed quietly on a chicken leg with eyes as wide as a goldfish, waiting to see how the drama would play. Now Bayard made the mistake of rising to greet her—indicating there was a place at his table—but before Anne could even reach there, Maria Vargas had risen and positioned herself as a buffer. She stopped Anne's progress with a push to the shoulder, tilting her slightly backward on her heels. Then, in front of the whole company, she raised her right hand and slapped Anne full in the face, cursing her in untamed Spanish. Anne did not flinch, nor move, nor feel for her welting cheek. She looked Vargas over from toe to eye with a tiny grin glazed provocatively on her mouth. "And?" she asked cryptically. Then she pushed her way past the irritating vixen, intent on joining Bayard's table so he would have to choose between them—knowing that merchants could always tell when overripe goods had spoilt.

The mellow spectators were whistling appreciatively at this unexpected amusement when a sudden communal roar warned Anne to look back. Vargas had lifted her petticoat and slid an Italian stiletto dagger from inside her boot. She flourished it threateningly in her right hand, balancing the guard on an expert palm. Annie recognized danger, and with no time for deliberation reached instinctively for the sailor's knife one of the pirates had slid across the ground. She slipped her wrist through the leather thong threaded through the hole in the handle, and as the combatants turned to circle each other both seemed to know this was a duel to death.

Vargas lunged first. It was a high downward thrust from above the shoulder but the point was not properly aligned with a moving target and Anne twisted her body, managing to bat away the fatal arc. So Vargas lifted for the face, lusting to maim and disfigure the opposition, but this time Annie grappled her wrist and stopped the blow midstrike. Then—to create some breathing room—Anne pushed her off as she started feinting and slashing the air, forcing her rival to stay back. The dagger flew out in a counterplay as the women danced in delicate circles, each seeking for the lunge spot. The crowd smelt raw civet and, riled up like animals, began egging the combatants forward. Men were already betting on the outcome so the chink of coins resounded on numerous tabletops, while the women whistled and jiggled on knees squirming with heated excitement. Maria Vargas moved sleek like a feline, all teeth and claws and dazzling blade, while Annie was fixed as a serpent, savoring the taste on air and waiting to strike her fangs. Hoping to intimidate her prey, Vargas started hurling abuse in high-pitched gobbets of cuss, but this momentary lapse in concentration afforded Anne the path to her throat, and before the Spanish harridan could fire another word the sailor's knife had slit her neck in a low backhanded slice that spilt the vein. Blood spewed from her throat and gushed all over her darkening dress. The wounded woman sank to her knees and, knowing she couldn't keep all that gore on the inside, threw out one arm in a gesture for help, pleading to her lover. Bayard sat entranced by the primitive scene enacted on his behalf. Meanwhile, Anne stood over the dying body and watched until the pretty blue lips stopped twitching. Then she calmly cleaned the knife on her opponent's sleeve, returned the blade to its owner, and glided over to the head table to take up Vargas's chair. She gave a pointed look at the coins center table and said to the host, "I hope you bet on me."

It was apparent to every eye present that Anne Bonny had just become Chidley Bayard's new mistress. And that was that.

9

STUFF FOR A PLUCKY JADE

EARLY AUTUMN, 1717

Now I know you're itching to hear about Blackbeard so I'll quicken to that part of the tale. Well, shortly after the Council of Pirates the captains scattered to go about business. Edward Teach branched out independent of Benjamin Hornigold, heading north toward Philadelphia while his mentor set sail down the Gulf of Florida for Cuba. Over the next few weeks Blackbeard captured several prizes, among them the *Betty* and *Robert* followed by the *Good Intent* of Dublin. His handpicked crew was sleek and mean, and once they'd acquired enough tobacco and cotton the buccaneers voted to head back to Providence to squander the rewards of their plunder. So the next time I laid eyes on my future husband was the close of September when he slipped into the Silk Ship Inn surrounded by his officers. And a peculiar crew they made too.

Closest in height to Blackbeard was the man from Barbados

they called Caesar. He shadowed his captain's every move, saying little and ignoring everyone else around. Brawn seemed to wrestle from his clothing, and his skin was so black as to almost seem gray, and he'd the most menacing stare I've ever ever seen that halted even the saltiest tar. Their Welsh lieutenant was called Owen Richards. Now, I ain't certain, but I'm guessing he was bald—on account that he always wore the same red scarf tied grimily round his ears—but he must have been dark-haired at one time because an unfashionable mustache draped his lip like a limp, brown slug. The lieutenant was small but lethal. He delighted in provoking tavern brawls so as to pitch his wits against vanity, and even I'll admit he was a damn good hand-to-hand fighter. I liked to hear him sing because he kept a fine tune—except you'd to stay him at arm's length due to his rotten breath. Will Howard was the quartermaster and another Cockney. But I didn't take to him immediately because he'd one eye of blue and one of brown that pierced and seemed colder than steel. He'd a huge scar on his right arm that some quack had mended with twine. The wound had gaped so long that the hair didn't grow back and all the inside flesh had set the color of rancid bread dough. Blackbeard's gunner was a red-headed Scot who clubbed his mane in a braid that fell almost as long as mine. His name was Philip Morton and half his face was covered in curly red whiskers. I couldn't never understand a word that he grunted but I marveled at the carved ink all over his arms and chest, and I'm not sure he ever heard anything I uttered either as the cannons had left him more than slightly deaf. And last of the bunch was the master, Israel Hands. Hands was also from London, and he had that furtive pickpocket look about him that's familiar to those who've shared the same trade. I didn't trust his long ferret face, especially when he grinned and showed his solo blackened front tooth. Even for a sea dog he was ugly—all of which helped to make Teach appear the more handsome. Now, we were well aware that anyone associated with Hornigold was a natural enemy of Captain Jennings so Blackbeard and his men came forth under cover of dark—in force—and spent their winnings liberally about to foster as many comrades as possible.

Shortly after sundown on that fateful day, Edward Teach came in to savor our house specialty (pigeon pie) and after supper he and his gang sat quietly in the corner playing some form of dice. A couple of tars from rival crews began competing with each other on blazing fiddles and before the sides could get to scrapping I encouraged the musicians to play together for me. That night I danced like the wind was lifting my sails, light as air and haughtily free. And all the time I could feel Blackbeard's eyes staring, seeming to lure me closer by hook and crook. Now, at that point I ain't never had the undivided attention of such a famous rogue before so I showed off my grandest moves with delicate precision and verve. The punters kept shouting for more and more so I performed until my toes began to set numb. Finally I collected the coins thrown, bowed a sweet exit, and ran upstairs to change. Violet was just leaving her room with Albert Spokes. I whispered, "Blackbeard's downstairs with his officers!"

My friend's eyes flared at the thought of all that legendary potential so she gave her beau a slap on the behind and pushed him playfully away. "Time to work," she said. Then she turned back to her room to adorn her charms.

By now Teach and his men were well into the rum. Our landlady—Mary Gee—kept them topped up before their tankards could empty, but she was having a rare time trying to attend to the rest of the rowdy throng as well. When she saw me descending the steps she beckoned me over and said, "Be a good lass and help us out, Lola." Then she thrust the rum jug into my hand and pushed me toward Blackbeard's table. I hovered shyly at the elbow of the giant and waited to be given orders, but he was busy whispering to his dark companion, who immediately downed his drink and took up a place by the door.

The rest of the men were chatting amiably while eyeing up the female prospects when the quartermaster suddenly grabbed my sleeve and pointed to Violet who had just rejoined the crowd. "Ho, darling!" he shouted, pulling me closer, "Who's that corn-head over yonder?"

"Violet," I muttered. "She's my mate."

"Are you Cockney?" he asked. I nodded. "I too," he replied. "Will's the name." He held out his scarred arm for me to shake hands. "Go bring her about, will you, love?" I clasped the jug in both hands and scurried to do as bid. When me and Violet returned I nudged Will's shoulder, made the introductions, then refilled the almost empty mugs. And suddenly I was staring eye to eye with the formidable Blackbeard. My wrist began to shake and it was all I could do to keep from slopping booze all over the table. He must have gleaned my trepidation because his eyes seemed to soften and his mouth broke into a healthy white smile. Captain Teach winked at me and then thanked me for pouring his rum. Just as I finished, though, he gently placed his huge hand over mine and made me set the jug on the table. I thought I'd soon be getting into trouble from Mary for not doing a good job but Blackbeard suddenly rose from his seat, took two steps backward, and swept me an honest bow.

I curtsied in response as the big man asked, "And what do they call you, my lovely?"

"Lola, sir," I stuttered. My complexion was red as a glowing ember so I kept my eyes set on the floor.

Blackbeard lifted my face from the chin upward and said, "Captain Edward Teach. Pleased I am to meet you, ma'am." Then he took my flimsy hand and led me to Caesar's vacant chair. I didn't have no idea what was going on, but when I looked across at Will his encouraging expression indicated I should play along as he sat watching the fun with Violet now firmly ensconced on his knee. Blackbeard picked up a ditty bag stuffed under the table and pulled out a beautiful silver chalice, apparently plundered from some passenger on his last cruise. He wiped the edge on his lacy sleeve, then filled it with rum and passed it to me. "Down the cup and you'll keep the cup!" he promised, then laughed loud and raucously along with his friends as I struggled to empty the contents.

The goblet appeared to belong either in a church or on a wealthy Spaniard's table for it had the balanced weight of a hefty sum and sparkled like ice in the lantern light. I could feel the rum worming its way to my stomach and, although I knew it would render me drunk, I was confident in my ability to win the challenge. When the last drop touched the rear of my throat I squeezed my lips together and wiped them on the inside of my wrist. Blackbeard hit the empty chalice upside down on the wood and the rest of the table screeched in approval. I reached a tentative hand out to claim my prize, and as no one stopped me I pulled the cup in close and made it my own. Then before any of the gathering could change the rules I shot from the table, scurried upstairs, and locked my reward in the medicine chest, safe from villainous eyes. Then I tidied my hair, pinched my cheeks even rosier, and scooted back to see what else I could snaffle from the infamous Captain Teach.

A short time later I returned to refill the jug from the bar but Blackbeard put a light touch on my shoulder that urged me to sit back down. Imagine my surprise when the Captain himself stood up, returned with a refill, and then proceeded to wait on me as if I were Queen of England! Will Howard had his hands all over Violet's thighs and without much more of a to-do they rose and groped their way up the creaking stairs. I expected that Blackbeard would make his move on me at any moment but instead he sat searching the depths of my eyes as if mining for something precious. We chatted for ever such a long time and the more he spoke the more relaxed I became. I was actually enjoying his company. "I do think you're the prettiest wench on this island," he murmured, brushing his whiskers against my neck. Of course I was used to such flattery from every hopeful punter but somehow the words seemed more sincere coming from such a mouth. I smiled and tried to look coy. "What age are you, girl?" he asked. And while awaiting my answer he brushed my cheek with the edge of his thumb.

I replied, "Fifteen, sir."

"Mmmm . . ." he mumbled in approval. "My favorite age."

"Really?" I asked. I thought from the previous parties he liked older women with plenty of chest, but it seems that first impressions were deceptive. As he toyed with my ruddy curls like a plug of tobacco between his fingers I plucked sufficient courage to inquire, "Why, sir?"

I couldn't see his face but he whispered in my ear, "The breasts are blossoming beyond doubt but the hips rest flat and slender." This didn't make no sense to me but I was glad that he found me appealing. Then he told me brief snippets of his wayward life in answer to my childish prompts, although he seemed to be more interested in me—and that had never happened before. Then suddenly the black man returned to our table with the ominous news, "Jennings approaches."

Quick as the changing tide the men drank up the dregs and dispersed to various points of shadow. I saw them one by one wend their way unobtrusively past Jennings and his cronies. "Have you a room close by?" Captain Teach hissed.

"Aye," I said. "Come with me." And before enemy eyes had a chance to adjust to the light I'd whisked the infamous renegade upstairs to my chamber. "Why does Captain Jennings hate you?" I asked as soon as my door was bolted.

Blackbeard gave a wry grin and began removing his belts and weapons to drape on my only chair. "None who sail with Ben Hornigold are much welcome in Nassau, and a pity it is."

"I heard tell Hornigold stole some of his Spanish silver. . . ." I ventured. "Is that the cause?" Teach grunted and settled on the bed, propping himself comfortable with his back against the wall. "But how does that affect you?" I pressed. For even if Blackbeard had been part of the turncoat crew, the responsibility for betrayal always fell on the commander.

The pirate patted the quilt, encouraging me to join him on the bed, but when I made to take off my clothes he shook his head and indicated to just sit down. I was even more befuddled. "I'm not welcome for another cause—and small blame either," he confessed. "I once took one of Jennings's women."

"Oh . . ." I replied. I immediately thought on James Bonny and then I understood. "Where is she now?" I asked politely.

There was an ominous pause before Teach responded, "To my sorrow she is no longer with us." I looked into his face for clarification so he added, "She was verily . . . lost at sea." A disturbing look shaded the previously bright eyes and seemed to close the hatches of memory. I didn't want to upset my guest none so I hurriedly changed the subject and began telling him how lucky his mate Will was to be with a splendid girl like

Violet. Then later I listened to the rich, gruff voice explaining why the young Edward Teach had taken to life at sea.

It seems Blackbeard was the son of a prominent scholar who grew up in the thriving port of Bristol where his father spared no pains on his education, hoping he would follow in the family footsteps to Cambridge University. But he was not inclined to academia, so at the ripe age of twenty-one he married the dark-haired daughter of a wealthy merchant and joined their family business. After several years of trying hard he and the missus finally had a son called Eddie. Now, Blackbeard didn't know why their child had blond hair and blue irises (when both parents were dark-eyed) until the day he caught his wife making the beast-with-two-backs in their bedchamber with her dissolute fair-haired cousin. Edward was so enraged that he crippled the cuckold with his own bare hands, and left his screaming wife for the first berth away at sea. He never returned—and claimed they had long since divorced. Teach's passage took him to the West India Islands where he eventually became a privateer operating out of Jamaica during the latter part of the French War. Then he met up with Hornigold, switched to piracy, and now finally commanded his own vessel. But what started as a vengeful escape apparently turned into an ever escalating ride for the thrill. I could tell it was the excitement that brought Blackbeard to life—and the lust for fame that would ward him safe from death.

Now, I know you ain't never going to believe this but throughout that entire evening the dreaded Captain Teach played the role of perfect gentleman. He sat with his arm round my shoulders, lightly conversing until the last sounds of life faded downstairs, then he gave me a solemn kiss on the fingers, pushed a gold coin into my sticky palm, and made his way softly downstairs where

Caesar and Will were waiting. The next day his mast was a small glint on the wavering horizon and I didn't never see him again until several weeks had passed. But I realized I'd finally got over Jim Bonny when all I could think of was that gentle giant who now invaded my thoughts.

What is this transient thing that folks call love? You'll probably say something like positive regard or affection, but how do you know if it's physical desire, emotional fulfillment, or the thrill of adventure instead? We're so sold on dreams of the happy forever that I wonder just how much contentment survives the leaky years. All the men I'd ever known before were driven by sex, which their prey were conditioned to interpret as love (ever thinking themselves something special). We all know that men need to dominate a challenge that surrenders to their prowess— and in return they'll provide for any offspring, in a deal always weighted to their favor. Of course, some woman may lead a parallel life without loss of self, but most love comes at a terrible cost, paid for in milk and blood.

Now, somewhere around that time Violet fell pregnant. At first she kept denying her rounding figure and claimed all the rum was making her fatten, but when she eventually realized she was four months gone she threw furious accusations in my direction, cursing me out that my herbals had failed. After she'd calmed down she tried bargaining, bullying me to help her as it was supposedly all my fault. My once-funny mate sank into a deep despair as she tried to reject femininity, but I saw that if I didn't do something drastic she'd drown in the bile collecting in her stomach. So I reluctantly agreed to aid in her murderous scheme.

"What do you want me to do?" I asked.

"Make me some trade to remove it!" she hissed.

My medicine chest contained tansy, which I ground into powder and administered as tea four times a day. She took the measured doses for over a week, but to no avail. So next I conferred with Mary, who'd once been a madam in York and, on her advice, managed to acquire some opium. But all the laudanum achieved was the worst headache Violet had ever encountered, and not a single stain of blood. Next we tried marjoram mixed with thyme, parsley, and lavender—and then I even got hold of some savin. Nothing, however, would budge the bulge in her belly. In desperation I turned to Pierre, thinking he might know of some remedy, who explained how women in France often sit over boiling pots of steam. But Violet quit that attempt soon as she scalded her intimate parts and was livid I'd asked the counsel of an ignorant man. She begged me to flush her insides with seawater using the metal syringe. I did—but I told her that only worked in the earliest hours when the damage was first done. She tried sleeping in tightened corsets, binding the cords to strangle the life within, but the pressure made her vomit and turn an ashen gray. Then in the middle of the night I heard her shuffling on top of the stairs and was only just able to prevent her from flinging herself to the tavern floor below. And so she made me promise I'd help in her final attempt—she was going to insert a stick and winkle the creature out from its pearly shell. The next afternoon we snuck to her room to perform the crude operation. I gave her a draught of the opium left to help against the pain and then watched in horror as she skewered her insides with a long pointed piece of limb. She screamed as something gave, and gaped in terror at the redness that gushed like mud in a torrent onto her bed.

"What have you done?" I gasped. I'd never seen so much blood as that coating her hands and pooling under her body.

"Can you see it?" she cried. "Is it out yet?" I scanned among the glistening sod looking for a glimpse of skin or bone. "Ahhh!" she screamed. And she grasped her stomach as the first contraction bit like a rabid skunk. I could see her body undulate beneath the soggy material and put my hands either side of the movement to try to ease things along. Violet was sweating fit to melt and her eyes were rolling white with agony.

"Push, Violet . . ." I cried. "Push it out!"

"Ohhh!" She gritted her teeth and bore down with all her waning strength. Another huge clot spewed forth and within the deep was a perfect tiny baby. It was limp. We had stunted its only faint chance.

I gave a sorrowful gulp and whispered, "It's out now. Gone!"

Violet breathed a huge sigh and made a strangled sound with her throat. "Is it . . . Is it dead?" she hushed. I nodded and squeezed her flushed hand.

"I'll get rid," I promised. "You just relax now." But another contraction brought a similar rush and I could see my best mate's vital force ebbing into the quilt. I tried to stem the flow with blankets, but as soon as I'd got the new one in place it was quickly as soiled as the former. I raised her feet to keep the liquid inside but it still found a way to seep between her powder-white thighs. Violet's nails were turning blue and I didn't know what to do.

"Mary!" I screamed. "Mary! Are you home?" There was no response outside the door. So I threw another blanket over the juddering patient and ran out into the street.

My first thought was to find Pierre—he was familiar with all the incoming ships and might know of a surgeon who could help. He looked wisely at the panic on my face, saw the splatter of womanhood that messed up my hands, and instantly guessed what was happening. "It's Violet!" I screamed. "Help us. . . ."

I vaguely saw Annie in the rear of the shop and watched impatiently as he spoke with her. Then he grabbed me by the elbow and steered me down to the largest sloop refitting in the dock. "Ahoy, messieurs! Where is the surgeon?" he cried. But before either of the pirates could reply, Pierre had squeezed my shoulder and warned, "Stay right here." Then yelled, "Permission to board!" and ran up the gangplank following the weathered fingers that pointed aft belowdecks. A few minutes later he emerged with a tall gray-haired man who was carrying a dirty bag. He didn't look much like any doctor I'd ever seen but as beggars can't be choosers we dragged him to the Silk Ship with the promise of an hour with me after he'd patched up my mate.

Violet's room was rank with the stench of salty musk. She lay moaning in a delirious stupor with most of her bed saturated in sticky blood. The surgeon put a hand to her forehead, tested for life at her neck, then lifted her wrist to find a pulse. He removed the sopping blanket at her thigh and stared at the dribbling discharge. Then he rolled up his sleeves and set to work. "Boil water and bring fresh rags," he charged. And I ran off to do as bid.

When I reentered the room he was trying to show the stained stick to Pierre but the dressmaker had just uncovered the tiny corpse I'd left folded in the corner and I could see he was struggling to hold back his grief. "Here's the bowl," I offered. And I began to remove the messy blankets from the bed.

"Is there a cup?" the doctor requested. I found a mug and a jug of water and watched as he mixed some potion from his kit.

"What is that?" I asked, curious as ever to learn.

The surgeon ignored my inquiry and said, "Help her sip this slowly."

"But what is it?" I persisted. I moved to obey his command still awaiting an explanation. The doctor was busy making some kind of poultice to stem the wound and again chose not to answer.

He gave me a contemptuous look and then directed his speech toward Pierre saying, "She has lost too much blood I am afraid."

Pierre nodded and set about piling the dirty linen into a corner. He wrapped the baby back up into a bundle and placed it carefully on top. "Will she live?" the Frenchman asked. But the surgeon shook his head.

"I . . . I tried to help her. . . ." I muttered in my own defense.

"Well you managed to kill the both of them." He sneered. "Stupid doxy . . ."

Then he directed Pierre to take my place feeding water, wiped his smeared hands on a clean bit of cloth, grabbed me by the arse, and hissed, "So where is your room then, hussy?" I realized that he wanted to claim his payment. And I was so confused and numb I led him to my bed and melted into void as he roughly took his pleasure.

After he was done and gone I tiptoed back into Violet's room. It was cold and bleak now that her beautiful spirit had departed. And Pierre and I wept side by side for a moment, sharing her crusted hand. He took the dead child with him to dispose of the shame. And I waited in the growing darkness for Mary to return and show me how to keep breathing.

Of all the times in my life I've ebbed at low tide this was the worst I can ever ever remember. Not only had I lost my dearest companion but I felt myself complicit in her demise. So much guilt gnawed an ugly hole in the tattered remnants of my soul and I knew now, once and ever, that God didn't care a wit for me or mine. After the sparse funeral, Mary and Pierre helped me clear out Violet's room. They divided her money between themselves—Mary claimed she needed to buy a new bed and Pierre demanded enough rent until the room was reoccupied—and I got all her clothing. Then a couple of days later two new girls called Mayee and Pearl arrived from Jamaica, and Mary none-too-tactfully suggested I should leave. I was in a sorry state and no kidding because I just couldn't stop blubbering, and as this was the worst turnoff for business I'd got no income coming in. I couldn't dance. I couldn't tup. And Mary grew so sick of my hangdog face she arranged for me to move into the garret room over the dressmaker's shop. These days Anne Bonny was often away traveling with Chidley Bayard so kind Pierre made me welcome and allowed me to help in his shop. He encouraged me to start an apothecary in the back room where he could protect me, but I didn't have no heart to do anything but sit and sew a mindless needle in line with his instruction. My tears dried up by the end of the week, but the pressing sadness was much harder to lose.

Now, when Blackbeard next returned to Providence I found out quite by chance. Pierre came back from the docks one afternoon with a rolled up parchment that he immediately pinned to the tabletop. I looked down at the puzzling outlines and asked, "What is it?"

Pierre carefully scrutinized the drawing and answered, "A flag for Captain Teach."

"Blackbeard's in port?" I quizzed.

"Oui. He arrived last evening."

"Oh." I was disappointed he hadn't sought me out yet. Then I realized he'd probably not know that I'd moved. I stared at the parchment and tried to interpret the shapes. My first question was "Why such a flag? I thought they all flew the *jolie rouge*—" the bloody red flag warning death.

The Frenchman looked up in my direction and explained, "There are now so many of these pirates they need to distinguish the one from the other." Then he gave me an insight into the design. A white skeleton was set against a black background—the familiar symbol of death found often in graveyards—that much I understood. But this old bones had horns like a demon to imply that Blackbeard was Satan himself, commonly known as Old Roger. The skeleton held an hourglass tilted in one hand, showing the victim that his time was running out, and a spear pointed down in the other to a heart that was dripping with blood. I didn't need no other clarification. This flag meant that if you didn't surrender you'd meet death at the hands of the devil. "Can you cut out the shapes?" he asked and passed me a bolt of white canvas. I nodded that I could work such a design, and was glad of a genuine distraction.

By next noon we'd finished the flag and were rather proud of our effort. Pierre gave his final approval and sent me to deliver the order in person. I was a little wary trotting round the docks without Violet, so I made sure my pistol was loaded and tucked into the waist of my skirt. I was also hesitant to face Captain Teach as he'd never bothered to seek me out. By now he'd probably succumbed to some new trollop like Mayee or Pearl so I willed myself not to expect any special recognition. Pierre had told me how to identify his particular sloop and I found it without any difficulty. As I gingerly walked up the gangplank Will Howard spotted me and cried, "Ha, how's it with you, darling!" He was looking past me to see if I'd brought my companion. "Corn-head's not with you then?" I stepped onto the rocking

deck and carefully made my way over to his side, then disjoint-
edly told him the awful news. Will continued mending the rope
he was working on and muttered, "Mighty sorrowed to hear
that. She . . ."

We were interrupted by a booming shout of, "Ahoy, my
beauty—it be none other than the lovely Miss Lola!" I spun
round and found myself staring at Blackbeard's enormous chest.
He held me at arm's length between his two hands as if to examine
me more closely. "Hearty greeting—to what do we owe this pleasure?" he mused. I held out the package with the flag inside and
awaited his reaction. He unfurled the material and yelled, "Ha,
Will—look at this!" Then he chuckled deep inside to himself.

I noticed that he spoke differently when on-ship but as I
didn't know any other way of talking I asked, "You like it?"

"I like it without doubt!" he cried. "Wait 'til Cap'n Bonnet claps eyes on it." I didn't have no idea who Bonnet was but
waited patiently as he climbed belowdecks with my handiwork.
Will apparently didn't want to talk now, so my eyes swept round
the vessel and studied the *Revenge* in silence.

Blackbeard's sloop had twelve guns and looked like it might
hold seventy men at a squeeze—the more anonymous members
of the crew I assumed were currently ashore spending their loot.
The craft was flush-decked, with no discernible quarterdeck in the
long, open space, although there was a roundhouse in the aft that
I later discovered led to two cabins below. At the rear was lashed
the longboat, and beyond that was the empty staff where my flag
would soon hang. The *Revenge* had a huge single mast just off-
center toward the fore of the vessel, which held the mainsail
and the foresail, and suspended between this and the impossibly
long bowsprit were three triangular jibs. But the mast was singed
and splintered and the sails had obviously seen better days. Two

cargo hatches opened either side of the mast and the pockmarked vessel—designed for both speed and comfort—looked like it had been in the wars. The quartermaster finished up his work at the capstan and stood awkwardly awaiting Blackbeard's return.

I attempted renewed conversation by inquiring, "Who's this Captain Bonnet, Will?"

And Mr. Howard took great delight changing the subject from Violet by telling me all about the gentleman pirate. "Well now, this is his sloop," Will began. "But it's sailed by Blackbeard." I must have looked puzzled because he continued, "Bonnet got seriously wounded on route so Cap'n Teach was kind enough to take command 'til he recovers." I listened with genuine interest.

Now, as it happens, this turned out to be a very strange tale indeed. Major Stede Bonnet was a rich planter from Barbados who was unhappily married to a shrew called Mary Allamby. The story goes that in order to get away from her bickering tongue the major went and *bought* himself a pirate boat and crew! Such a thing was unheard of among the Brethren of the Coast, who usually pillaged and captured whichever craft took their fancy. And every buccaneer knows that if *there's no prey there's no pay*—so to be given a regular wage for marauding was really quite the joke. Bonnet, however, was canny enough to hire Ignatius Pell as his boatswain, which accounts for his early successes, and all was going well until he ran into the Spanish man-o'-war that killed or maimed half his crew and almost took his own leg off. The sloop managed to limp far enough to safety and make essential repairs at sea but was so suffering from a lack of command that when Blackbeard spotted the disorganized vessel he swiftly pulled his own craft alongside. Perhaps because they're both well-read men Bonnet and Teach hit it off, so Blackbeard agreed to command the *Revenge* until Bonnet was sufficiently recovered. They'd made it as far as Nassau and had stopped to repair the sails and take on fresh supplies. But the major didn't want anyone to know he was here because the folks back in Barbados weren't yet aware he'd gone on the account, and Blackbeard was keeping his usual low profile. So I asked who was looking after the injured man and was told that the carpenter had sewn up his wounds as the surgeon had been killed in the fray.

"Don't you have a doctor?" I asked. Will shook his head and said that they hoped to press someone suitable from the next prize.

"Has he a fever?" I inquired.

"Aye," Will said. "But he won't see anyone in port."

"Would he let me look?" I asked.

Will laughed at the thought and said, "Ha, I don't think it's his cock as needs fixing!"

I blushed and said arrogantly, "I've other skills too, you know." Then I remembered Violet and said more quietly, "I know some apothecary remedies. I'm used to nursing . . . and sometimes I can help."

Howard studied my serious demeanor and decided to take up my cause. "So ho, wait about here then," he said, "I'll see what they answer." And with that Will disappeared into the roundhouse.

Not long after, his head emerged on top of the steps and he called, "Lola! Come away aft." I walked over to his voice and climbed down into the gloom.

Blackbeard was stood by the bed of the patient. The major was nowhere near as old as I'd imagined but his face was flushed with delirium.

"You come in a fair breeze, Lola. Might you assist Cap'n Bonnet?" Teach asked.

I nodded and recognized the smell of decay. I gently pulled

back the grubby coverlet to observe the festering wound. It would need to be reopened, cleaned out, and then stitched properly if we were to save the leg. "I'll have to go get my chest," I said. "And he'll need laudanum for the pain." Blackbeard gave Will enough coins to pay Pierre for the flag, and then told his quartermaster to accompany me back to the shop. Caesar was dispatched to find opium and fresh bedding. And Teach would supply enough rum to see us all through the harrowing ordeal.

When everything was in place Teach reckoned we'd enough hours of sun left to complete our surgery so the patient was moved to the wooden table and all the windows were opened to let in as much light as possible. We waited for the opium to dull his senses, then Blackbeard heated his own knife over a candle until the tip glowed white before immediately plunging it into a bucket of water to temper. Bonnet was strapped down with ropes across his chest, and the offending leg secured at both ankle and groin. The sick man was wounded mid-thigh—just above the knee—with a gash as long as my hand. Teach took up the hissing knife and with one brutal swipe sliced through both stitch and flesh to split the wound. A putrid stink wafted up from the injury, heralding the oozing pus that bubbled up alongside the blood. I took some of the purest brandy from my chest, poured it onto a strip of cotton, and set about cleaning the mess. The patient stared with buglike eyes at something on the rafters but he groaned lightly now and then, assuring us he was yet alive. I ain't got no idea how much he could feel but he was sensible enough not to fight against us. Then as I was dabbing the slime away, my cloth snagged something foreign inside the leg so I poked about gently with my small pincers and managed to remove a portion of shot. "Here's the problem. . . ." I muttered.

When the cleaning was done best as able, I used all my weight to pressure the wound shut ready for stitching. But there was too much blood to work with so I whispered to Blackbeard, "Reheat the knife, sir." I realized we'd have to cauterize the gash. Now, I remember seeing Dr. Simpson seal skin together this way— and I wasn't looking forward to the ghastly stench of burning flesh—but I'd never actually done it myself before so my fingers were a tad too shaky.

Teach was about to hand me the knife when he spotted my hesitation and quickly brought down the sizzling blade at the edge of the gash where it needed to meld. He worked swiftly along the hole, ignoring the gurgles coming from Bonnet, until the edges blistered into one bumpy seam and finally congealed together in a blackened line. "Quickly, if you please!" he ordered. "Sew whilst the skin remains numb." So I used one of Pierre's fine-tipped needles threaded with some valuable catgut I'd purchased in Charles Towne soon after Anne Bonny had attacked me. Now, I reckon I did a pretty good job, if I may say myself. I washed the whole thigh with water, daubed the repair with more brandy, bound the leg in fresh linen strips, and showed Will how to give the patient small sips of water while I prepared a clean bed.

After it was all over I sat on deck with the crew who were still aboard waiting for the sun to drop. The captain broke out some fancy wine and everyone threw whatever food they had onto a cloth draped over the top of a hatch. So we feasted on goat meat, fish, and bread, then had cheese and raisins for pudding. Blackbeard draped his heavy arm across my shoulders and asked if I was getting cold. I nuzzled in closer and said I was fine, and then he slowly bent over and kissed the top of my head. "You did grand today and no mistake," he told me. I pinked with pleasure. "Where did you happen to acquire such art?" he asked. So I gave him a potted account of my experiences learning to be an apothecary, and was thrilled that he listened with full attention. Then imagine my confusion when he suddenly kissed my mouth, looked hard into my gaze, and said, "When will you consent to wed with me?"

I caught the swallow in my throat, took a very deep breath, and whispered, "Whenever my master desires it."

And so, before the next full moon crested, I became Mrs. Edward Teach—as splendidly as that.

10

YO-HEAVE-HO!

MID-AUTUMN, 1717

As soon as new sails were in place and the galleys restocked, we cast off by common consent toward Jamaica. The crew had decided to take the *Revenge*, and Blackbeard's original sloop *Adventure*, to some deserted cove where the vessels could be properly cleaned and restored, so my wedding took place at sea that same first night. I wore my very best red stomacher but was outshone by my husband's velvet attire and lacy shirt. As quartermaster, Will Howard conducted the ceremony, which was immediately toasted by the already-drunk crew with a keg of plundered Portuguese wine. Then two musicians (Bob Dilly from Bonnet's craft and Ron Green from Teach's) set the decks rolling with a vigorous medley of tunes that me and the groom used to initiate even more merriment, and I was pleasantly surprised by how elegantly my big man could caper. Then after we'd exhausted the fingers of our players my master threw me over his shoulder and carried me off to his cabin to a bellow of salty catcalls and hoots. When he told me to turn my back I assumed he was going to unlace my bodice but with a sudden flash of silver his knife cut through the cords of my garment and tore it to the floor. He laughed and cried out, "Heigh-ho, wench. I've waited on you long enough now!" Then he thrust me onto the bed and urgently consummated our union.

Now you may wonder why on earth I'd consent to marry a man I hardly knew? Well, let me try telling you, mister. Firstly—you've to imagine what life's like for a whore on an island of pirates. Given the random violence, disease, and disaster, life expectancy is about three years tops, as Violet painfully highlighted, so having the protection of a formidable patron offers a tempting security. Now, I ain't high-class like Annie so I wasn't expecting to attract no Jennings or Bayard—but a rogue such as Teach I felt was within my sphere. And then secondly, imagine the kudos of being Blackbeard's wife! His reputation would give me some standing in this otherwise fragile community. It meant that if ever I'd to solicit again in the future I could demand a celebrity price—I'd attract more custom from the curious (or those with a grudge content to roger me in the stead of my husband)—and none would ever dare abuse me again. And I've also got to admit there's a certain excitement to union with a genuine swashbuckler. My beau was successful and generous and treated me like a captured princess. The glamour was quite overwhelming . . . and the promise of moving up and away.

Of course, I was still mourning my loss at the time so perhaps I was not as sensible as usual but the captain was certainly a pleasant distraction that loosed my hold on sour memory. So when his sweetness dribbled in my ear I believed what I needed to savor—although you'd likely call me gullible and naive, which was probably my appeal to Teach. And in my defense I ain't the first girl to fall for the wicked mystique of a man sticky enough to be treacherous. He was sensual—in a dangerous way—with a hardness carefully molded, and (truth be told) I wanted to feel those edges and run my finger along the snick until it bled. I was flattered that, of all the trollops, Blackbeard had chosen little Lola, because he opened up a flaming expanse of adventure. And I honestly believed that I'd seen a side of Teach few ever witnessed, so thought to change and settle him down. That we'd have a glorious future together—maybe even a normal life.

Now, being used to all manner of men I wasn't too alarmed by the roughness of my lover but when his passion turned into painfulness I quickly employed some of my brothel tricks to speed up his completion. He finally rolled off and stretched with his arms above his head contemplating the roof as I lay beside and pretended to glow.

"Would you like rum?" I asked. I took his grunt as affirmation and poured us both a cup from the cask on the table. He sipped without saying a word. I began to panic that perhaps I hadn't pleased him so I said playfully, "Is there anything else you'd like me to do?" He emptied his mug and pushed it out for a refill. I topped up my drink too, then sat in the crook of his arm, leaning against his damp body. Now, I ain't never been wed before so I didn't have no idea how I was supposed to feel—but I was hoping for something different than the usual tumble and vacant silence so I tried starting a conversation that began, "I truly thank you for stealing me off." He absently kissed the top of my head but I could tell that his mind was elsewhere. "Anne Bonny wouldn't have never given her consent," I explained, knowing full well that indentured servants couldn't wed against their owner's permission and that no one was supposed to marry at my age without parental consent. "But . . . I . . . I don't know if this is all legal . . ." I confessed.

The black-rimmed mouth opened to its widest extent and sputtered a meaty laugh. "Legal?" he echoed. Then he snorted several times, his face wobbling with mirth. "Legal!" And sweat started forming in the depths of his eyes.

I didn't know then the big joke, but apparently it was on me. Only later did I realize it was the innocence of his thirteenth spouse that so tickled the bigamist's humor. Now I discovered soon enough that ships are not authorized for matrimony—that no officer on board has the power to perform weddings (unless they're also a minister or justice of the peace)—and that valid ceremonies can only be conducted by government officials in port. So no wonder Blackbeard was only too happy for me to run away to sea with him. He now had me totally in his power and no one in Nassau to miss me.

After Teach had dozed for a short while he wanted to renew the coupling, seeming anxious to dock every port in my body. And while we were grinding together, the cabin door burst open and two leering strangers shuffled in to watch. I was really embarrassed, having never consciously coupled in public before, but Blackbeard seemed used to such interruption and winked at a man who had only one eye from behind my shoulder. The sailors watched for a time then filled up their tankards from the rum on the table, and the pocked-faced one hiccupped some coarse words of encouragement as they bumbled out the door. As soon as my husband had finished I asked, "Has your cabin no bolt?"

Blackbeard wiped his forehead and armpits on his discarded shirt and replied, "Thing of it is, every hand has equal access so there's no locks anyplace aboard."

"But . . . this is your room. . . ." I uttered in confusion. "You're the captain!"

He settled himself on the bed and explained the differences from a naval or merchant ship. "Aye—but only by vote. And only so long as the prizes are rich." Apparently the Brethren of the Coast adhered to some democratic principle where each man held equal account with all others. The pirates agreed on who'd be their officers, which routes to ply, the crafts they'd attack, how to dispose of prisoners, and the articles of conduct they'd abide by. The captain had use of the cabin—but anyone could enter at any time and take what they needed therein. Now, all this made my head spin for I realized this would be a very different crossing than on the *Argyll* or on the rumrunner.

We awoke next morning to a jarring bump. Blackbeard loped from the cradle, peed fiercely into the empty bottle and then set to dressing. "What's that noise?" I asked sleepily.

"If the *Adventure's* come alongside it means Richards wants a parley, as I'd guess." He buttoned up his breeches and left me to dress alone. I opened the door a crack to try to eavesdrop while I rummaged in my hurriedly packed sack for my cabin-boy ship clothes. It seemed that Lieutenant Richards was now captaining Blackbeard's former boat, while Teach and the wounded major settled themselves on the more comfortable vessel. The two crews had been carefully mingled and spread between both sloops to discourage Bonnet's crew from planning a mutiny, but it seems some of them had issues with me being on board. I stifled my breath and plugged an acute ear in the shadowy door-gap. It was hard to hear the entire conversation over the creaking boards that groaned as the wake slapped against the stern, but I did catch enough to realize I was in danger. Richards shouted up, "Ho, Cap'n, aloft there! Mr. Pell wants a confab with Major Bonnet."

"Yea?" Blackbeard responded. "On what account?"

There was a pause before a new voice interjected with, "It's in my mind to fetch up about the doxy. . . ."

"Mean you my wife?" Blackbeard asked.

"Aye . . . in the manner of plain speaking." The voices grew louder so I assumed that both men had now boarded. "The crew don't like cruising with a woman." There was another gap and then the embarrassing admission, "Some say she'll bring us bad luck."

"What the devil!" the captain exploded. "Superstitious bilge, I'll be damned." I could hear the men pacing the quarterdeck area trying to keep up with the irate Blackbeard. Then Teach apparently turned to Pell and roared, "It's no business of yours if I sail with a comforter!"

The lieutenant was quick to interpret on behalf of his shipmates, cutting in with, "Indeed, Cap'n. I told them they'd all get their turn. . . ." And then he added, "But sight of a slut gets their blood up and sets them to fighting."

"On my soul, it's no way to run a cruise!" Pell put in. Then he thought to add, "Begging your pardon, Cap'n Teach." Then the party moved out of earshot so I'd to wait until they stepped back toward the roundhouse. I think someone described me as "the devil's ballast," then all was quiet until Blackbeard's voice cut through the darkness again.

"I care not a louse what they think! She nursed their cap'n—the major would surely have lost his leg if she hadn't been a gypsy apothecary worthy of ship room. . . ." There were more mutters that gradually increased in volume as the men began descending the stairs to Bonnet's adjacent cabin. I quickly shut the door and sat on the bed with my ears pricked and throbbing. I couldn't hear clearly what went on in the next chamber but I guess Major Bonnet felt well enough to vouch for me because shortly afterward the tars returned to the other sloop and Blackbeard set about organizing his own mob. I stayed a long time shaking on the bed, worrying about my destiny if the men decided to be rid of me. They could throw me overboard—set me adrift in a skiff—maroon me on some desolate sandbar. . . . I realized I needed to become indispensable if I ever wanted to reach Jamaica. And as I didn't want to be the ship's whore I decided then and there to be the best damned doctor they'd ever sailed with.

Now, how the work ever gets done on a buccaneer's craft is still a mystery to me. The men attend to necessary chores as and when they feel the urge—until they spot a likely prize. Only then do they listen to their officers, and only then do they follow commands. Yet somehow or other, the decks got swabbed, the readings were set, men climbed the masts, and they pushed the capstan. We cut through the glittering waters like two boots skating on ice and eventually some lookout sighted a small island that shimmered promisingly vacant. A light wind drew us in to the coast where we came to anchor side by side in the sheltered inlet so the mates could shout across from one deck to the other. Blackbeard took out his speaking horn and asked if anyone recognized this place. But no one did. A longboat was duly lowered and Israel Hands led a heavily armed party to scout the land for hostile natives or Spaniards, and as soon as he declared the place deserted the other small boats were launched to set up camp.

This tiny spot was beautifully located, set far enough away from spiteful eyes. Our sloops bobbed on fathoms as clear as air, and the honey-white sand stretched far as the glass could see. From the edge of the beach loomed a forest sweeping up over the craggy outcrops to the rim of the clouds, and already I'd spotted turtles, fish, fruit, fowl, and a pond of fresh water bubbling from the thicket and pooling by the bay. The carpenter—a chippie called Roberts—declared the timber sound, so we'd everything vital we needed to repair the two sluggish crafts. But what we couldn't detect were the sand fleas lusting to feed on our unsuspecting flesh, and it was only when the itching began that we noticed the cluster of bites forming from ankle to shin. The men didn't pay any account at first, while I gouged my skin raw to bleeding trying to scratch some relief. So my first task became scouring the fringe of the forest for some plant or leaf to make a salve.

Now, if you've spent any time around seafarers, you'll know careening is something that needs doing often to keep vessels nimble and watertight. After the vessels are run ashore the guns and cargo are moved and the topmasts taken down. Then ropes and pulleys are run from the mast to the trees so the sloops can be tipped on their sides to expose the hulls. The men set to scraping the bottoms to dislodge barnacles, seaweed, and the wood-boring worms—caulking and replacing any rotten planks as they progress—then they mix a coat of tallow, oil, and brimstone to protect against the elements. When one side is done the boats are tipped over and the entire process is repeated on the other sides. Lastly, masts and spars and sails are mended, the water-barrels are filled, and fresh supplies are gathered as the pirates make ready to launch another raid. This work is supervised by the carpenter and two boatswains, and I was glad not to have any dealings with Garrat Gibbens, for he was the meanest boatswain I'd ever encountered—he truly relished his role as henchman.

But the unfortunate plague of sand fleas on shore severely hindered progress. Now, you'd to look real carefully to see the chalky pests so most of the crew didn't know they'd been bitten by punkies until the blisters spread to welts. Swashbucklers, of course, are pretty sturdy stock so most of them ignored their reddening flesh, resisting the fatal urge to scratch and allying any discomfort with hard work and rum. Will Howard had encountered these creatures before and showed how to set up traps around our base. We put out a ring of pans full of soapy water. A lantern was shone onto each tin after dark, which magically attracted the fleas, made them jump in, and drown. So after the second night we'd much fewer nips to contend with. I also found out—by trial and error—that the best remedy was to soak the leg in seawater, then rub salt onto each bite to relieve the itch. Some of the men's sores, though, turned into raised-edged ulcers that I'm told resembled volcanoes, and after that came the headaches and chills, the shivering and bloodshot eyes. Several tars swooned into a dangerous fever so we set up their hammocks alongside the major's sickbed inside a makeshift hut next to the fire pit, where I could attend them, but why some folks got sicker than others I'll never know. I guess bodies are made as different as personalities. Blackbeard also developed a rash—but his was a different design. It seemed to begin with a painless sore on his privates that he put down to an unlucky bite, but when it spread to resemble smallpox he joked I'd given him the French disease. Of course I was outraged at such a suggestion—because I knew I didn't have no spots—so I convinced him he was feeling too healthy for that and when the sores faded to nothingness he soon forgot. Luckily none of the contagion passed to others so I nursed them the same as for marsh fever and by the time we left the island all were out of serious danger, although some of the ulcers did leave a grim, pitted scar.

Yet despite the bugs, after my ankles stopped itching I actually had fun on this island. The days consisted of cheerful work, then at sundown we'd eat what Slouchy the cook rustled up before singing, dancing, and drinking round the spitting bonfire. Blackbeard and I shared a hammock far enough back to be shaded in privacy where I'd set up our own traps against the sand fleas, and when the strange rash no longer bothered his desire we were carefully discreet so as not to provoke further jealousies. Whenever I took a break from nursing I'd chat to the cook while assisting his preparations, and over the languid days we became tentative mates.

I never did find out Slouchy's real name but he was hired specifically as the chef on Bonnet's sloop. He was a half-crippled old salt I assumed had been at sea long enough for the damp to have set his bones misshapen. His legs were so bowed he could barely swagger and his fingers curled like wizened claws. So as he could no longer fire a musket or wield a cutlass he'd thrown in his sword for a spoon and retrained himself to be useful. When the hunting party turned up with our roots or meat I'd sit in the shade peeling and chopping what Slouchy couldn't manage, and he'd cheerfully direct the proceedings among flippant jokes he thought suitable for female ears. Then one day he told one of the tallest tales I'd ever heard, swearing blind it was true and had happened to him. But I wasn't sure if I believe him.

See, Slouchy claimed to have been a privateer working the Spanish Main when one day his ship stopped for provisions at the unfamiliar Rio-de-la-Hache. There was a settlement of huts, and hoping to take on water and meat, a crew of fourteen rowed the longboat and skiff over to trade with the villagers. The natives along that coast were reputed to be most fearsome but the sailors were hungry and when they saw only one Indian stalking the beach they caught his attention and asked in Spanish if fresh water could be procured. The native apparently understood enough to nod and beckon them to land with a series of friendly gestures. Now, Slouchy had been in charge of the skiff, and after they'd refilled the twenty water casks in exchange for two kegs of rum he sent the longboat back to the ship while bartering for some livestock. The Indian indicated that their animals were herded in one of the largest huts, but when the six remaining sailors opened the door a piercing whistle signaled the rest of the tribe and the tars found themselves surrounded by dozens of hostiles. Slouchy was knocked down, stripped of all his clothing, bound hand and foot, and secured to the trunk of a large tree guarded by a gang of their strange-faced women. Unfortunately, the second boat was still rowing back and didn't witness the ambush and the crew on deck was too far away to notice. The remaining hostages could speak neither native nor Spanish, yet they understood perfectly the mime show depicting their fate—they were to be roasted alive in the entrails of night and eaten by this tribe. Aye, I know it sounds fantastic, but others have relayed similar tales to me since, so you can take it or leave it as fits.

Anyway, as darkness crept in, the six prisoners were taken to a well-charred spot on the beach and bound back-to-back on three long stakes hammered to secure them in place. Brown limbs came and went piling brushwood in a knotted hedge around them. This was all too much for one of the tars who started screaming at the top of his voice, until the old native rammed a fire-hardened arrow through his voice-box, strangling the terror on air. Now, Slouchy didn't know this yet, but the scream finally alerted their watch that things were amiss—the crew thought their shipmates were partaking of local custom and would be returning with a fully loaded cargo after dawn. The alarm was raised and the captain launched the longboat with a gang of heavily armed men. He dispatched his boatswain because the man spoke a little more Spanish, and they rowed hard as possible toward the beach to determine what was happening. Unfortunately though, the tide had now turned, and the swell of a mighty current so strongly repelled the oarsmen they'd to return to ship to avoid exhaustion. Any attempt at rescue would have to wait until morning.

Meanwhile, the natives were sampling the rum and, not being accustomed to that manner of drink, the men fell silly and rowdy and the women had to relax their vigilance to attend to the ensuing dramas. Some kind of ruckus ended with two of the braves slumped in a death-grip on the blades of each other's axes, and somewhere among the huts tiny voices started wailing. Slouchy said this was the worst of it—for the men were left to reflect on their impending horrible death. A thousand melancholy thoughts tortured the poor sailors' minds and the remaining victims mumbled words of consolation while offering up snippets of prayer. The fighting eventually gave way to heaves of vomit, and then the sluggish snores of the bold young bucks as they succumbed to the weight of inebriation. The natives apparently forgot to light their fire so the five remaining captives shivered through the longest night imaginable until harsh streaks of dawn seared the sky.

The early light revealed the macabre scene to the watchers on the ship so the captain immediately readied the longboat to launch the moment the waters changed. He determined that the

only chance of rescuing his comrades would be through negotiation. They'd have to pay some hefty ransom. The tribe soon
awakened and despite their ill condition they demanded as much
of the rum as the ship had stowed in return for their miserable
hostages. The boatswain was able to make himself understood
and once the deal had been agreed he and the most skilled rowers
battled the tide back with the tribal demands. Now, as it happened, they'd only four barrels of rum left full so when the time
came to trade, the natives would only release four of the men.
The fifth had died from his throat injury. And the sixth man
was poor Slouchy. He'd to watch as his crewmen struggled to
safety, certain now of his own demise. Then some of the tetchy
savages fell into a rage, either because they'd just lost their supper
or because they felt there was too little of this wonderful new
grog, and unanimously decided to tenderize the lone prisoner's
flesh. So one after the other they approached the stake armed
with lengths of wood and pummeled the hapless victim until the
skin hung in shreds from his naked torso. Slouchy claims they
beat him to the last hourglass of his life. His mind sank under
a blanket of blood.

But the sailors back on ship refused to abandon their mate
and they urged the captain to try another tack. So a plot was
hatched to pretend to sail away, when they really dropped
anchor farther along out of sight. The crew found a good spot
to invade, moved quickly to catch a suitable tide, and after giving
the natives enough time to numb their senses with rum, nineteen armed men crept along the shoreline a few leagues down-
wind. Slouchy drifted in and out of sensibility until the chief
had him cut down from the stake and dragged into the shade
to prolong his nightmare. But just as twilight turned the sky
to purple the sailors launched their attack. It was as swift as

any military operation on board ship and before the tribe knew what was happening, two men had Slouchy slung between them while their comrades provided distraction and cover. A volley of muskets rang out, and the men later boasted several mangled bodies were left as recompense. The tars let the current sweep them back to safety and as soon as the boats were stowed, their ship hauled anchor and sailed away. Slouchy was weak from loss of blood, his limbs were numb, and his fingers shattered, and it took several weeks to restore him to some semblance of health. His hair had turned prematurely white and his skin grew back patchy as a mottled quilt. He wouldn't never be the same man again of course—but what shocked me most was when he told me he was not yet thirty years old!

When both our sloops were declared ready we broke camp and turned the bowsprits toward Jamaica. Now, we must have been but a half day at sea when the cry of "Sail ahoy! Starboard bow—three points north!" fired every marauder into action. We'd spotted a likely prize.

Blackbeard studied the quarry, then lowered his spy-glass to petition his crew. "Ha! What say you, gentlemen? Fair game, I'd be thinking. . . ." The scoundrels shouted agreement so their captain commanded, "Give chase, Mr. Hands!" And a string of orders flew round the deck. We trimmed our sails and steered close to the wind as able, intent on approaching from the rear. The battle of seamanship was in play. Our prey was a buxom, heavily laden sloop and, at first sight of trouble, it broke out as much canvas as possible, hoping to outrun our smaller vessels but, unfortunately for them, the air was small and thin and we were able to level with their port. The *Adventure* positioned itself for a broadside attack, unfurled its new Jolly Roger, and fired a warning shot across the bow, while the *Revenge* stayed aft out of range. Seeing they were heavily outnumbered, the crew lowered their own flag in surrender and put their officers into a longboat on first command. The captives rowed over to Blackbeard's deck and were greeted with, "Good day to you, gentlemen. Welcome aboard!" Their captain was first to be brusquely dragged up the ladder. I squatted on the steps of the roundhouse, poking my head out to watch the drama.

Teach held a cutlass to the victim's throat and manhandled him by the scruff of his jacket as he began the inquisition. "'Twere wise of you to have no truck with Satan, you chicken-hearted dog!" he roared. I watched in fascination as Blackbeard hoisted the quivering man off his feet and peered grimly into the terrified face. Meanwhile, Lieutenant Richards had grappled the bulwarks of the prize from the starboard side and was encouraging his men to bring her close enough to board. As soon as she was tied alongside, a ferocious yell burst forth as the pirates scurried over to plunder her belly. The sloop was a merchant vessel from Charles Towne carrying flour, beans, and rice to the Virgin Islands, alongside bolts of cloth, a ton of tar, and some miscellaneous cordage and ironware. She'd been chartered by a consortium of plantation owners wanting to trade their sugar cane, and was named the *Mary Jane*. I realized—with growing concern—this was no enemy craft. She was British. The imprisoned captain had now been joined by his three officers, who all ceremoniously gave up their swords, and as soon as their longboat was raised up they were hauled out onto the deck. Teach's men crowded in and beat the captives to their knees with the blunt sides of their weapons. Then they circled like feisty sharks savoring the stench of fear.

Blackbeard flipped the tip of his cutlass and sliced a slither of flesh from the captain's ear, drawing enough blood to warrant his full attention. "Who be you?" he demanded. "Who and what?"

The petrified man tried to swallow his horror and replied, "Captain Elridge of the *Mary Jane* . . ." And perhaps hoping for clemency he added, "Out of London via Charles Towne."

"Where headed?" Garrat Gibbens demanded to know. He kneed one of the other officers hard in the jaw splitting his lower lip like an overripe pepper for emphasis.

The beaten face looked tentatively toward his attacker as the captain added, "Tortola . . . the plantations."

"What goods aboard?" the one-eyed rogue yelled into his damaged ear.

"Er . . . general provisions," he said. A dagger at the back of his neck caused him to further elucidate so he mumbled, "Flour . . . rice . . . scullery items . . . some tar and cordage . . . a few bales of cloth . . . a little whiskey."

"Any women?" Bob Dilly asked hopefully.

The prisoner shook his head vigorously before proclaiming, "We ain't no Guineaman." Dilly spat a tarry gob onto the top of his hair in disgust.

"How many hands?" Teach quizzed.

"A dozen," came the instant response. "Benson's my second. . . ." and he indicated to the victim left of his back, "And Smith here's my sailing master." Smith was the man about to vomit at his rear. The remaining crew member turned out to be the boatswain—a mangy character with half his face sewn up—who went by the name of Kelly.

"All secure, Cap'n!" Howard cried from below mast of the prize, and when I peered over the side I could see the remaining members of the *Mary Jane* sprawled facedown on the planks.

I was surprised how the vessel had been captured with so little resistance, but that was before I'd been briefed by my wry and cunning husband.

Of course, if you ain't never sailed with freebooters I'll wager you don't understand their natures any better than I did back then. You likely think pirates savor the brimstone and gunpowder—the guts and smoke—the power of wretched, wrenched screams? But what they really want is a quick surrender that don't destroy any booty before they can loot it. And a peaceful fight where none of their own gets hurt. Clever men like Teach understood how the greater concern you instilled in your prey the easier it is to take them down. So he noted the ways his victims responded and learned to manipulate their most harrowing dread. Some folks still consider Blackbeard the most formidable sea villain ever—and as I've thought long and deep on this subject I can finally give you my insight.

A captain must be courageous and brave—unafraid of personal injury or death—and this came easy to Teach, who thrived on the aching excitement of testing his brawn to the limit. The commander must be a skilled tactician who instinctively knew how those on the prize would react to a given situation—and my husband could read in advance any seaman who ever set sail on these dark waters. Blackbeard was, without doubt, an excellent navigator who could maneuver his vessel exactly where it needed to be, always one league ahead with the trick and surprise. And he understood better than most the intoxication of fear—that if you sap the spirit of your opponents you also crush their defiance. My husband was master of intimidation, heavily armed as he roared into battle, a demon in flight to behold. Indeed, Blackbeard wanted folks to believe he was the devil incarnate. But most cleverly of all he let most of his victims live to tell their mortifying stories, thereby promoting his carefully constructed mythology. Dead men tell no tales—but Teach wanted tongues to brag of his deeds and spread afar the terror, so instead of butchering his victims he'd set them loose on some desolate spot where eventually someone would find them.

Once the crew of the *Mary Jane* was secured Blackbeard stood guard while his men pillaged, ransacked, and formed a human chain to move the food stock across to Slouchy's storeroom, and any other valuables to the quartermaster's hold for safekeeping. The prisoners on both decks were stripped to their breeches, then bound hand and foot in awkward sitting positions. They watched in dismay as their clothes were thrown in a heap to be auctioned at the mast to the highest bidder. Someone found the whiskey, and bottle after bottle was passed liberally between the outlaws. Blackbeard encouraged the liquor to take effect before boarding the captured sloop and performing a dramatic speech to his quaking audience.

"I'm the one folks call Blackbeard," he began, "cap'n of the *Adventure* and the *Revenge*." He paused for his name to sink into their panic-pickled brains. "I'm sorry you won't be having your vessel back—for I scorn to do anyone such a mischief—but as it be to our advantage we'll be taking her with us." He shouted to his sailing master, "Mr. Hands! Have you a mind to captain this craft?"

The surprised sailor beamed back, "Aye, Cap'n Teach. I've taken a fancy to her sure enough."

"Does any man raise objection?" Teach asked. No one spoke out against the appointment so he grandly announced, "Let that be her new name then, Cap'n Hands. Hereafter—we'll call her *Fancy*."

Blackbeard's dark eyes then turned on the shrinking victims scattered around his feet as he continued, "Though you're a bunch of sneaking puppies who haven't the courage otherwise to defend yourselves—as are all who submit to be governed by the laws which rich men have made for their own comfort and security—methinks you merely a misguided pack of cowardly whelps acting on the nod of a parcel of hen-hearted numbskulls. They vilify us, the scoundrels do, when there is only this difference—they rob the poor under cover of law, forsooth, and we plunder the rich under the protection of our own courage. Had you not better become one of us than to sneak after these villains for employment?" He paused to focus specifically on each individual victim. "What say you men?" And he hauled them to their feet one by one to answer his personal invitation to join their ranks.

The first sailor grabbed blubbered loudly, "Aye, Cap'n. I'll go on the account with you. . . ." He was then passed back to Israel Hands, who sliced through his hemp bonds, slapped him on the back in welcome, allowed him to collect his old clothing, and ushered him onto the *Adventure*.

The next three sailors also vowed to take the articles, but the fifth man answered a defiant, "Nay. Not I."

"And what, pray, prevents you from following the wise course of your mates?" Blackbeard demanded to know.

"My conscience will not permit me to break the laws of God and man!" he shouted. "And neither should any of yours. . . ." he called to the other tars. Murmuring broke out among the huddled ranks, and two others rejected the path of piracy when it came to be their turn. The rebels now cowered separately from those who'd capitulated but at the end of the round there were only three brave dissenters clinging fiercely to their old faith.

Blackbeard stomped round and round these stubborn tars as

he continued with his lecture. "You have devilish scruples and no doubt." He raised himself to his impressive full length and cried, "But I'm a free prince, and I have as much authority to make war on the whole world as he who has a hundred sail of ships at sea and an army of a hundred-thousand men in the field. And this . . . *my* conscience tells me." The men stared back with stoic faces, and realizing they wouldn't be budged, Teach concluded, "Yet I see there is no arguing with suckling kittens who allow superiors to kick them about the place at their leisure." The captain belched raucously and yelled, "Warm 'em up a bit, gentlemen! And we'll see who still refuses to join after they've done a few laps round the deck."

And so the games began. The three naked men were made to run a gauntlet of striking weapons, round and round the edge of the deck, while the pitiless pirates whipped and lashed at their backs. The more exhausted they became, the slower their evasion, and one by one they crumpled into a battered, snuffling heap. I shot down to the cabin and reappeared with my nursing equipment but before I could cross to the other sloop Blackbeard caught my eye and motioned for me to stay put. Apparently the victims were to be shown no mercy. They were doused with buckets of dirty water, tied up to various cleats, and left to crust in their own secretions. Then one of the tars suggested that, as Blackbeard was now in command of a small navy, he should be promoted to commodore (to avoid confusion with Captains Bonnet, Richards, and Hands). The motion was carried—and Edward Teach smugly accepted the title with enough passing modesty to be almost convincing.

The officers on our sloop had watched the drama across deck with growing trepidation so each face visibly blanched as Blackbeard turned back to deal with them. I ain't kidding when I tell you how scared they appeared. You could see their pupils visibly explode, misting their stares in petrifaction. Master Smith had edged away from his vomit and now was shaking so much his teeth could barely form the words of prayer. He huddled beneath his knotted brow, hoping against hope he would not be the first selected. Teach looked down at the mess splattered across the man's lap and said, "Reckon you'll be needing a clean, laddy." He signaled to Gibbens, who unbuttoned his codpiece and began urinating all over the cowering form. "Aye, that's the job, by cock!" The other pirates jeered as they followed suit dousing the spluttering officers in a blast of acrid pee. Then Blackbeard lifted Captain Elridge's dripping chin with the tip of his boot, forcing him to make eye contact. When Teach ascertained he was ripe enough he bent to his ear and hissed, "Now, Cap'n. What remains?" Elridge offered up a blank visage.

"Where's the booty hid?" Gibbens demanded to know.

"I . . . we . . . there's no . . . nothing more . . ." Elridge gasped. "You have all."

Blackbeard grabbed a hank of hair and ripped back his head, staring wildly into the horrified man's void. "No gold?" The head bobbed, suspended on the twirling strand. "Silver?" Another negative shake. "Damn you to hell!" he cried, and released the locks with such force that the officer sprawled backward and hit his ear on the planking. Blackbeard pounded his cutlass into the deck and savored the vibrating handle as it twanged aloud his frustration. "Apothecary!" he cried. I suddenly realized that meant me and hurried to his side. Amazement dawned on the officers' faces as they caught sight of whom they'd assumed to be merely a pretty cabin boy. "Go search yonder vessel." I was thrilled to be dispatched on such an important mission, thinking it a sign that he trusted me most (although I later realized that as a former thief I'd know the best places to look). I was helped across the sides by an eager forest of hands and diligently began a methodical hunt of Elridge's cabin. Nothing. It took me ages to figure out where they'd store any valuables, and it was only when I spotted something rare on the fore I became suspicious enough to investigate further. See, most sloops use mess-tubs and don't have a head—but the *Fancy* boasted a lead-lined tunnel with an unusual seat of easement. And, sure enough, when I pinched my nose and stuck my hand in the entrance there was the ring to a secret compartment containing a metal box wrapped in a heavily tarred skin.

I took out the box, shook off the muck from my wrists, and triumphantly carried the find back to my husband. Blackbeard was highly amused when he'd heard where the booty was resting. He pried open the lid, pierced the contents on the end of a dagger, and pulled it out into open view. "What ho?" he cried. All eyes were riveted on the stuffed leather pouch he was wafting in the air. He grabbed the purse with his other hand and quickly opened the tie. It contained hundreds of pounds in coin. A satisfied roar rang out from the buccaneers. Blackbeard squeezed my shoulder and whispered, "Well done." Then he pointed the knife at the deflated captain and ordered, "Tie him to the mast, by God. I've a mind to tear off his lying lips and make the bastard eat 'em!" And, good as his word, Teach watched as one of the tars sliced the captive's unwise mouth into two smeary gashes and grinned when Slouchy took the lips to be boiled. The cook returned a short while later with the rubbery flesh diced into bite-sized pieces, but turned greenly away as Gibbens forced the bits into Elridge's mangled mouth and made him swallow. I was torn between weird fascination and abject fear, wondering how much blame was mine for this poor man's fate? But the rest of the crew rode the crests of delight intoxicated as much by the gory victory as by the emptying whiskey. Blackbeard's eyes glowed with manic passion . . . and I got the first chilled inkling of what might happen if I ever dared to cross him.

Will Howard spoke on behalf of the gathering. "How shall we deal with the rest of them, Com'dore?"

"Shark bait!" hooted Gibbens.

"Maroon 'em!" someone else suggested.

"That was my first thought too, gentlemen," Blackbeard announced. He called back across to the *Fancy*, "How far off land, Cap'n Hands?"

The master surveyed the waters and gave his best guess as, "A ways, Cap'n. We'd have to divert some I reckon."

Lieutenant Richards thought for a moment, then shouted, "The *Adventure*'s got a leaky boat. I say cut 'em loose—let 'em take their chances!" This idea met with general approval and when a vote was cast the ayes won out. So the three remaining officers were bundled across to the far sloop as the rest of the pirates ambled to their allocated crafts. The old longboat was set to sea with a jug of fresh water and some useless pieces of sailcloth—and Blackbeard made sure they were still close enough to witness the splash when Captain Elridge was violently flung to the fish.

Later that same night Teach made a grand toast about the good luck I'd brought to this cruise and persuaded the crew, somewhat begrudgingly, to welcome me into their ranks. I'd apparently discredited the old maritime superstition regarding seafaring women—and so that was that.

11

⌇

DEAD AND BE DAMNED
AND THE REST GONE WHIST

LATE FALL, 1717

Jamaica was much more established than Providence but, unfortunately for us, it no longer welcomed swashbucklers. Now Blackbeard had told me many a tale he'd heard as a cabin boy about the wickedest city on earth—Port Royal—that had once been center of the buccaneer's universe, before the earthquake of '92 sucked it to watery oblivion. Port Royal was a pit of iniquity full of cutthroats and whores, and a major center for trade where the townsfolk welcomed the Brethren of the Coast because a bay stuffed with ships discouraged any Spanish or French invasion. But when the stragglers who survived the disaster relocated on the other side of the Kingston Harbour, the British authorities finally decided to make their stand against piracy. So instead of jiggling their purses for the outlaws, the townsfolk now dangled their prison keys and nooses instead.

Kingston lies on the south of the island, so our flotilla

docked north at Ocho Rios by the most spectacular waterfall
I'd ever ever seen that dramatically swept over rocky steps climbing down from the lush vegetation. This bay was an amazing
place—a tawdry town of vessels and huts—where old breeched
ships had been turned into workshops and stalls, and slovenly
merchants hired hordes of runaway slaves. There was a carpenter, shipwright, and goldsmith on one side, and a blacksmith's
fire pit dug close to the waters. On the opposite side were a
string of shacks selling smoked fish, salted pork, nuts, fruits,
and vegetables. And two wooden auction blocks were set back
under a screen of leaves. Soon as we arrived everyone crowded
out to the shoreline to see who we were and what blunt might be
bartered. Our three sloops anchored side by side and the crew
immediately set to moving the goods from hold to shore. Blackbeard and Bonnet sat on barrels in the shade discussing how the
loot should be sold, then Ignatius Pell blew his whistle to sum-
mon the bidders and Will Howard began our trade. After folks
had taken their pick, any remaining items were heaped together
to be hauled back on board the *Revenge*, then the quartermasters
shared out their crew's pay, and the men wandered off to the rickety sheds back in the trees to buy themselves a tryst with some
mulatto doxy, or to drink themselves beyond lust in the grog
huts. One of the merchants asked Blackbeard if he could have a
closer look at our bolts of cloth so I carefully unfurled the par-
cels for his perusal. He was particularly interested in the cloth
of gold but didn't seem willing to pay our hefty asking price. I
raved about the brightness of the silk and the shine of the thread,
extolling its merits for a sumptuous ball gown or waistcoat. The
merchant turned to his minion, whispered something in his ear,
and watched in satisfaction as the man leapt to a waiting horse
and galloped along the shoreline. Then he gave us a doubloon to

secure the bolt in his name until the morrow. I assumed he'd sent for his wife or lover—so imagine my surprise when a handsome boat arrived next afternoon bearing Chidley Bayard and his current delight, the proud Anne Bonny.

Anne looked like a legendary mermaid when carried from the sloop at the behest of her lover in the arms of a berry-black sailor, who took every attention to ensure her hem did not touch the water. The African held his mistress as if she were lighter than gossamer, ceremoniously placing her safely on the sand by the side of the master, careful that neither eye nor hand touch any inch of her shiny-shell skin. Bonny shook out her skirt and smiled a polite greeting at the sweating merchant who rushed over to assist them. I watched them shake hands and panicked as they turned in our direction. I grabbed Blackbeard's arm and said, "O nay! Anne Bonny . . ."

"Ah, that's the wench as sliced Maria Vargas as I recall," my husband mused. Then he added, "Bayard always had exquisite taste and no denying." He grinned ruefully at the young woman rapidly approaching our camp. I turned to make myself scarce but my husband took hold of my shoulder and held me in place. "Have no uneasiness, woman. I'll not permit any mischief." I stared gratefully into his raisin eyes and turned to face my enemy.

Now, I ain't joking when I say I never saw Annie look no finer than on that particular day. She was really quite lovely—and obviously very happy with her present situation. As we came into vision she asked a tentative question of the merchant, then the look of surprise on her face revealed that she recognized the legendary Terror of the Seas. Unfazed, she held out her hand and said, "Captain Blackbeard, I presume?"

Teach took her fingers in his and bowed as he replied, "Commodore Edward Teach at your service, ma'am." Then he shook hands with Bayard and slapped him on the shoulders as if they were old drinking mates.

Meanwhile, Anne's chilly eyes had wandered disapprovingly over to me. She gave me a cursory glance of disdain, looked away, but immediately turned back as my image registered. "Lola?" she gasped. "What . . . What are you doing here?"

"Hello, Annie," I mumbled.

"I thought you were still in Nassau. . . ."

"Nay, I'm—"

"She's with me," Blackbeard informed her. "May I present to you both—Mrs. Edward Teach." And I saw him stifle his amusement at the shock that drained Anne's slightly tanned cheek.

"She . . . You . . . Married?" she finally managed to spit out. We nodded simultaneously and held her narrowing stare.

Chidley Bayard, not remembering me, had no idea of our connection. He seemed anxious to be done with pirate trading and back on board the safety of his vessel. It obviously galled his sensibilities to be seen among the riffraff outside of Providence, but his merchant spy had located what Annie wanted. And so here they were. Bayard got down to business. He inquired, "I believe you have some cloth of gold, Commodore?"

"Aye," Teach said. He signaled Will Howard to bring down the bale. While we were waiting, the merchant babbled to fill the uneasy silence growing between us and when the material eventually arrived Anne and Bayard discussed its value behind the backs of their hands.

"What cost the roll?" Annie asked, smiling archly at the buccaneer.

"Ten doubloons," Blackbeard answered. And even I was taken aback at such a steep price. Anne caught her lover's collar and took him away from our hearing. I glanced anxiously at my husband but he kept a stony face and waited on their response.

"Five . . ." Annie offered. "And I'll not press my claim against your jade."

The captain smiled ever so slightly and asked, "And what claim might that be, Mistress . . . ?"

"Cormac," Annie replied in her most proper voice, "of the Black River Plantation in Charles Towne." She pointed at me and added, "This wench is indentured and owes me another three years."

"Be that so?" Blackbeard asked. I stood with my head down as they argued my fate. Then my husband gently opened my shirt and revealed the puckered scar above my breast left from Annie's attack. "So you are responsible for this I fancy?" His eyes held Annie's in a burning glare.

Bayard turned away in embarrassment but Anne maintained the captain's gaze and replied, "Aye. She's trouble that one is."

Blackbeard chuckled and said lowly, "Then I warrant you'll reward me for taking her off your hands." Anne waited to hear what came next. "Thus . . . if I let you have the cloth for *twelve* doubloons I reckon we'll have struck a mutual bargain."

"Twelve?" Annie exclaimed. "But you said ten. . . ."

"Ah, that was before you confessed to your temper, do you see!"

Bonny was now quite visibly furious. Her face was burning with indignation but she'd determined on having that cloth. "Pay him," she hissed to Bayard. She whispered something raunchy into his ear and he grew uncomfortable in his breeches. He quickly fished out his purse, proffered the extortionate fee, and signaled for his slave to carry the bolt to his craft. Annie swept off behind the servant huffing and scrunching the sand underfoot.

"The lady must want her frock real bad I'm thinking," Blackbeard mused to Bayard.

The toff looked up at the pirate and said, "My sister's invited us to the Governor's Ball. Anne wants to make an impression." Then he scurried off behind the rest of his party.

"Poor bastard's got his hands full with that queen." Teach laughed. "She'll create a storm there, I have no doubt!" Then he bit the coin to test the gold and licked his lips on the after-tang.

"Thanks," I said humbly.

"No matter," he said, laughing. "By all accounts, I fancy, you now belong to me." And he bent to kiss the sweaty beads that glittered on my forehead.

Of course, it was a while before we heard all about Annie's antics at the Governor's Mansion, but the story was later retold like this. Chidley Bayard's sister Kate was married to Bart Lawes, brother to Sir Nicholas Lawes, the governor of Jamaica. Sir Nicholas was throwing the grand ball that Annie wanted the cloth of gold frock for, but when she got to the party the other ladies pointedly snubbed Bayard's latest mistress. Now Annie could charm good as anyone, so she turned on her smile and tried to join in one of the animated conversations. Unfortunately, Kate Lawes was part of this particular clique. She gave Anne a withering look, then said spitefully, "Excuse me, I was talking to the *ladies*," as she turned back to the group with a superior lilt of one eyebrow.

Annie didn't move none, nor did she register any sense of insult. Instead she smiled even wider and said, "Then perhaps you would be so kind as to introduce me."

One of the other guests tittered at the wench's sass, then let out an embarrassed gasp when Kate Lawes responded, "I really do not think so, my dear. You are Chidley's new trollop—and hardly worth knowing. So pray, be a good strumpet and keep your distance."

She obviously expected the humiliated woman to wilt away—but she hadn't reckoned on Anne Bonny! Annie let her savor her moment of triumph, then as Kate renewed her conversation with her cronies she tapped her lightly on the shoulder.

A note of irritation froze on Kate's tongue as she spun round to hiss further insult but the moment she opened her lips Annie pulled back her arm and punched the mortified woman full in the mouth. The lady bent over and spat out two teeth in a foaming glob of blood. Then she screamed at the top of her high-pitched throat and the room erupted into chaos. "That'll keep you well away from me, you stuck-up sow!" Annie roared. And then a fence of jackets tore her from the ballroom.

Bayard flew after her cussing and moaning. He grabbed Annie by the arms and yanked her roughly to face his wrath. "What the hell . . ." he spluttered. "She is my sister!"

"Aye? Well she should learn better manners," Annie replied.

"But you knocked out her teeth. Her front teeth!" Bayard cried in disbelief. "What were you thinking?"

Annie wrestled herself free of his grasp. She pulled herself tall and said huffily, "She called me your harlot and told everyone to ignore me."

"But you *are* my mistress, Anne. What did you expect?"

"Expect?" Annie shouted. "I will tell you what I expect . . . the respect befitting my rank—inclusion in conversation—to be treated as an equal."

"Really?" Bayard mused. "You believe yourself to be *our* equal?" His smug face shook off an amazed sneer.

Annie ground her teeth in anger before spitting out, "If I am not considered good enough why did you bring me here?"

"Is that not obvious?" her lover said. He turned to go back and attend to his sister, leaving Annie uncertain of what to do next. She decided to follow him and see if she could mitigate the damage but before she'd taken two steps he whipped round and warded her off with his hands. "Not you!" he roared. "I cannot be seen with you in public again. You are a disgrace." And he charged off, taking his patronage with him. Annie slipped up to his room and packed her things, making sure she took all of the valuables she could find. Then she marched down to the harbor, ordered Bayard's captain to launch the boat for Nassau, and by the end of the week was back in Pierre's dress shop.

When we heard the tale, me and Blackbeard had a right good chuckle. "See, she did whip up a storm!" he laughed.

"Aye," I admitted, "you pegged her good and proper!"

Our convoy rested in Jamaica for about a week, until the tars had squandered all their plunder and thereby outspent their welcome. During that time Major Bonnet tried to exercise his leg much as the pain would permit but spent most of the day dozing on the sand or playing cards in the cool of the leaves. The angry wound was healing too slowly, and one day as I changed the dressing I felt myself being grazed by critical eyes. The watcher was a strong-limbed islander by the name of Zoola (sired by a swashbuckler to some old queen), who spoke with such a lyrical voice she sounded as if she were singing. She came to my shoulder, took the old soiled bandage from my hand and lifted it to her nose. Then she shook her head and lulled, "Man need pignut for that infection."

Ever ready to learn new recipes I replied, "Show me," and

rose to follow as she sauntered into the forest. I looked back at Captain Bonnet and promised, "I'll be back in a moment."

Just inside the edge of the trees Zoola pointed to a shrub that looked to me like mint. She plucked a handful of the serrated leaves and took them to a flat stone by the waterfall. She picked up a rock and ground the herb with a little water until the mixture resembled a gooey paste that she scooped up in both hands and carefully carried over to my patient. Then she lightly laid the mush over the entire sore and signaled for me to wrap the poultice in place. "This powerful magic against the poison," Zoola said. And she was right. The very next day when I took off the linen the wound was pink and calm, but when I made to repeat the same treatment Zoola introduced me to soursop instead, because now that the pus was drawn out we could apply this new infusion that worked better for ulcers and sores.

Zoola and I became mates. She helped me drain the yellow juice from aloe leaves into medicinal jars (which worked great for the worms that were plaguing the newcomers from the *Fancy*), and she showed me the wonderful coconut (whose oil could sooth burns and whose unripe juice helped heal the septic cock acquired in brothels). In return I gave her brimstone and vinegar to treat against lice, and showed her the tricks I'd learned to ward off babies. But what she really wanted was the white silk ribbon I used to tie back my hair. So before we left I clubbed her locks and wove it into the braid.

When the three sloops were fully loaded, the men voted to cruise the Atlantic seaboard where there was less chance of running into hurricanes. So we trolled the waters off Delaware down to Carolina, and although we took several small vessels with little resistance, the pickings were slimly disappointing. Blackbeard sensed his crew was growing tetchy—he had to find something worthy and grand. But before we could reach warmer water the skies dimmed sooty and threatened some impending storm. The men voted to ride out the wrath in a sheltered harbor so Blackbeard steered us to Topsail Inlet where a pretty white inn guarded the waters. We went ashore in the skiff, and were able to sail right up to the front deck and tie up on the porch pillar. The men who wanted to stay aboard ship did so but a large number chose to crowd into what they called the ordinary, bringing their hammocks to string up in the attic. Blackbeard had obviously been here before because he was instantly greeted by the landlord—a stooped-backed man called Robert Turner—who offered the sea villain his usual second-floor room. But when the thin face spotted me among the company it blanched wan enough to have seen a ghost. My husband introduced me as his wife with a mischievous wink, while I held out my hand to be properly recognized. I realized we must be somewhere in Carolina and, concerned how close we might be to Charles Towne, was relieved to discover we were in Beaufort, a good many leagues from where I was still considered a fugitive.

The White House stood on a hammock of land staring out to sea. Our room was at the front so I'd a fabulous view of the whipping wave caps that built like marching walls of water and spewed their vengeance onto the sandbars guarding the rim of the inlet. Now, I ain't never seen a house quite so nicely laid out, but something in the air crawled like a spider on the back of my neck and shivered me into a vague discomfort. Turner ushered Slouchy into his kitchen and I served out cheese, fruit, bread, and ale while we waited for the turkeys to finish roasting. The wind now assaulted the walls of the house, rattling the shutters and creaking the shingles. The moaning grew to a whiny wail, every now and then pierced by a harrowing shriek.

"Sounds like Francine's bitching again!" Gibbens chuckled from the fireplace.

"Enough!" Blackbeard warned. And the conversation instantly changed.

"Who's Francine?" I asked my husband. He looked down at the apple he was paring with his knife and mumbled, "None of your concern." Something in his tone warned to hush so I bit back my curiosity.

The men set up a game of cards and I went into the kitchen to see how the meat was progressing. I wandered to the fire and, absently turning the spit, asked Slouchy, "Do you know who Francine is?"

He glanced over his shoulder to ensure we were alone and whispered, "Best not to ask any questions." So it was only much later I discovered that she'd been Blackbeard's twelfth wife and had met a brutal end in this very house. See, when Teach had been a privateer he'd been captured by the enemy and held prisoner on a man-o'-war out of Calais for several months. He'd escaped in a bloodthirsty uprising, but the incident sparked a lifelong hatred of all things French, so whenever he found opportunity he'd specifically target Froggie vessels. Now, one time he captured a brig headed for Charles Towne with the captain's eighteen-year-old daughter on board. After dispatching with the rest of the crew he forced the young woman—Francine—to marry him. Apparently the poor girl was in so much shock she went along with the ceremony and mutely followed him up the steps of the White House for their wedding night. But once on the bed she refused to submit and kept her knees locked tightly together. I'm told Blackbeard was furious at the rejection and tried everything he could to gain her compliance. In the morning she was still a virgin and all she did was sob and moan at her plight. When next he tried to seduce her she bawled at the top of her lungs, which made her would-be lover so furious he finally tied her to the bed and had his brutish way, relishing the wavering pitch and depth of her screams. But after he'd taken his fill she wouldn't stop screaming. Blackbeard cut her bonds and dragged her by the hair all the way downstairs and into the back yard. He then, I was told, threw a noose over the big oak limb and hung the wretched woman until her voice fell limp as her neck. She's supposedly buried under that tree, and every night the moon fails to appear, her spirit roams in anguish. Now, I ain't sure that I believe in no ghosts—but I have to say there was a chilling noise that pierced the nighttime howling—and a clammy feeling hovering over the bed that I didn't much appreciate. So I was glad next day when the storm had blown itself quiet and we could once again set sail for the glowing Carribee Islands.

A few days into November found us off the coast of Martinique. Someone spotted a likely prize and the pirates slid into well-oiled action. Blackbeard stood by the quarterdeck rail and raised his glass. "A Guineaman, methinks, by the looks of it. . . . She's got mighty fine lines. What do you say, Mr. Howard? By thunder, I want her!"

The quartermaster looked through the tube and answered, "Spanish or French, I'd be thinking. Could be a slaver in from Africa. . . ."

Blackbeard shouted across to Hands and Richards, and as all were in agreement the ragtag navy set off after its prey. "Take a better look, shall we, gentlemen?" Night was fast approaching and the three sloops kept enough distance so as not to arouse suspicion. Teach decided to fly French colors to lull their prey into false security. "Let her think she's among friends," he mused. "See how close we can get."

Our convoy trailed the huge ship for a day and two full nights before one of the sharp-eyed tars was able to read her name, *La Concorde*. She was definitely French. And very fair game. So the three captains pulled up close together and determined their cunning ruse. "Break out the weapons!" Blackbeard cried. And the outlaws helped themselves to pistols and swords. "Prepare cannon!" And the order was relayed across all three decks. Teach turned to me and said, "Dress for battle, my little apothecary. And make haste for incoming wounded." I scurried to do my part even though my teeth were chattering. Our target was three times the size of us and I could see the glint of cannon in their gun ports. All the other vessels had submitted with barely a whimper—but even I knew—a ship this formidable would likely resist to the death.

Blackbeard returned from belowdecks looking like some dark apparition from Hades. He was wearing a strap stuffed with six loaded pistols, carried a sword in either hand, and had several deadly knives tucked about his person. His long black beard was braided with multicolored ribbons and pushed way behind his ears, and his hat had slow-burning cannon-fuses dipped in saltpeter that smoldered a halo of belching smoke. His face was blackened darker than Caesar's—and a more ferocious monster would be hard for any to envisage. "Run up our flag!" the commodore commanded. "Let them know that we're here, Mr. Dilly." The musician instantly took up his place at the mast and began beating a warlike tattoo on the goat-skin drum. We made our way toward the prize as it came down under steering-sail and carefully pulled up to her broadside so as not to expose ourselves to her guns.

"Cannon three—fire!" Teach commanded.

Morton yelled, "Fire in the hole!" and a boom rang out across the bow of the enemy.

Blackbeard took up his horn and shouted across to the French ship, "As you were, *mes chers*. And welcome to hell!"

When the French captain gave the order to retaliate, Teach clearly heard the instruction and so was able to avoid their shot by sheering off sufficiently to prevent any impact. Meanwhile, the other two sloops had crept up from the rear and were now in a good position to board fore and aft. For a moment the French officers seemed surprised that a sloop the size of ours would try to take them, so some bold sniper fired his musket, and the ball felled one of the rogues in our rigging. The unlucky tar dropped like an anchor to the deck and two mates dragged him over to where I sat crouching behind the ship's boats. I tied a strap around the top of his arm to arrest the bleeding, and then wiggled him under the lip of the longboat to keep him safe. A blast of grapeshot rang out and slashed our foresail, but fortunately only grazed the mast so the shower of splinters was slight. More whistling missiles seared through the air as our cannons responded to the clatter, and the awful shrieks of the wounded howled round the smoke-drenched deck.

Blackbeard's voice roared, "Get me to the fore, Mr. Howard. Bring us alongside the *Fancy*, if you will." The men seemed able to find their path through the coughing fury and our sloop swept quietly into position. "You take the command, Mr. Howard. I have some pressing business with these bastard Froggies. . . ." And through the belching fumes I saw Blackbeard and several of his men climbing ladders up the bow of the other vessel.

Now calculating on the superstitious nature of the enemy, the commodore had ordered a half dozen men to also blacken their faces. These ghastly apparitions appeared at the head of the ship like demons gliding through hellfire. The calculated effect worked beautifully—for the terrified Frenchmen were transfixed by the sudden appearance of diabolical creatures emerging through the white smoke of their bow guns. Before they came to their senses Blackbeard and his minions had swarmed the quarterdeck and the French captain's throat lay on the tip of the devil's sword.

"Quarter! Quarter!" the semiparalyzed captive cried. *"Mon Dieu! Pitié!"*

Israel Hands blew his whistle and the pirates spewed forth from every direction. Victory was ours.

Now, several of our crew got hurt in the fray. I'd a couple of shot wounds to deal with, multiple slashes that needed sewing, and one of the gunners from the *Revenge* lost his right hand. As patients were brought to my area I tried prioritizing according to injury, intent on aiding as many as possible. But more and more blood was oozing underfoot making the deck slippery as grease. Then, just as I bent over the stoic form of Ignatius Pell (who'd got a grizzly ragged thigh wound), I looked up just in time to see an escaped French soldier lifting his dagger to stab me. Without a thought I instinctively tore the knife from Pell's boot, and as the enemy dived for a forward thrust I brought my blade up level with his eye and pushed with all my heft. The soldier stared with terror at the hilt protruding from his face, before the knife slit through his senses and rendered them void. I think I must have struck his brain for something squished and gave way like butter, then the wetness seeped along the handle coating my wrist in slime. I knew he was mortally wounded. But I couldn't let go. I knew he was no longer a threat. But I couldn't help reveling in this strange oozing power. The amused boatswain rose on

his injured leg and gently pried my hand from the butt. "I . . .
I killed him!" I gasped. And the wave of sensation thrilled me
like bliss and I shuddered in absolute triumph. I stood there—
anointed in enemy gore—and realized I'd truly become a pirate.

For several moments I set still as rock, riveted by the dead body
at my feet. Then Major Bonnet hobbled up from belowdecks,
saw I was completely overwhelmed, and set about organizing
the chaos. Slouchy was already boiling tar and the carpenter was
sharpening the necessary knives and axes. The buccaneer who'd
lost his hand was taken belowdecks to the galley, and I flinched
at the godless scream when his stump was cauterized. Up above,
I clumsily plugged the bleeding gashes—another thigh, an arm,
and a difficult-to-sew hip—advising all patients to drink plenty
of rum for the pain. One man was shot in the shoulder. The bullet had passed right through but he'd lost all use of that arm. I
made him comfortable, trying not to think what we'd have to do
if the feeling didn't return. Another salt had been griped in the
gut. This poor soul wouldn't see morning so I gave him a huge
swig of laudanum to ease him along. And when I finally pushed
off the rim of the longboat, the fallen sailor was chattering in a
sweaty stupor. I think the tumble must have broken every bone
and all he could move were his lips and eyes. He looked wildly at
the sudden influx of light and grimaced when he saw my concern.

"Can you move?" I asked.

He tried—brought forth a dreadful moan in a vomit of
blood—and, realizing he was doomed, the battered soul begged
me to finish him off. "My pistol . . ." he stammered. "I beg
you. . . ." I tentatively removed the butt and cocked the pin. I
lifted a wavering arm to his temple. "Do it!" he pleaded. "Do . . ."

But a flood of panic froze my hand. I couldn't find the strength
to pull the trigger. Then a loud blast came from behind my

shoulder and I turned to see Captain Bonnet still holding a smutty gun. He looked at me. Nodded. Then turned smartly away.

Meanwhile, on the other side of the bulwarks the boarders were busily plundering their prize. Now, as it happened, *La Concorde* was a slaver in from Africa who'd unloaded some of her cargo in Grenada, and some in Martinique. But the vessel had been so ravaged by influenza, scurvy, and dysentery that the depleted crew was forced into quick surrender, and as only eighty-odd slaves were now left on board Captain Dosset decided to lower the flag the moment their deck was breeched. First, looters removed the gold dust and coinage straight to Will Howard's safekeeping, but everything else was left in place because Blackbeard had decided to keep this beauty as his flagship. Dosset and his officers wisely gave up their treasures in exchange for their freedom, so the pirates agreed to let them have the *Fancy* with enough beans to feed them to Martinique, and so all the French sailors squeezed on board. The slaver was rechristened *Queen Anne's Revenge* and lashed tightly to our remaining two sloops so the pirates could readily swing themselves across all three decks. And then the pent-up release of a ripe, rich prize sent the swashbucklers into a diabolical frenzy. The men drained every bottle of fine French brandy and the poor musicians were ordered to play tune upon tune with barely a break to savor a swig themselves. The major and I managed to make each patient comfortable, and when I finally washed up and changed out of my stained, caked clothes I scrambled over the gunwales and onto the throbbing prize.

Now I'd seen plenty debauchery in my former profession but, let me tell you, I ain't ever witnessed anything like the bacchanal that christened the *Queen Anne's Revenge*. For the rowdy revelers had organized themselves a warped mock trial to test the pitiful cargo crammed below. See, some tar had the not-so-kind notion that as they could only sell healthy slaves they should determine whom they wanted to keep on an individual basis. So the captives were hauled up on deck to be judged. Those who were obviously sick or frail were immediately thrown overboard and savagely devoured before our eyes by the begging mass of sharks who'd tailed the vessel from Africa. The strong, able-bodied men were split between the *Adventure* and the *Revenge*, where they'd be given the option of working for the sea villains or being sold on the block at a future destination. For the time being, however, they were locked in fresher holds so the areas could be sanitized. But the girls and young women—some so young they were barely walking—were casually given over to the ruffians to do with as each pleased.

There must have been twenty or thirty females saved from extermination only to find themselves brutalized time and again by all who took a fancy. And the vilest things were being done to these creatures—so foul, you could barely imagine. One pretty girl eventually tussled herself from the snoring, spent carcass of her oppressor and was so ashamed at her treatment she dashed to the side and dropped willingly into the foamy jaws of oblivion. Another proud female slipped the knife from her partner's sash and plunged it into her own chest. She didn't die instantly, though, as she'd hoped. And her disgruntled debaucher kicked her to the edge of the ship and huffed ripe curses as he tipped her over. The darkening deck was a mass of writhing naked flesh but there was no love or joy in this copulation—it was vicious, forceful, baser than base. And my heart went out to the youngsters for I knew such a torn reality would tip their worlds lopsided. I vividly recalled how it felt to be so used. I was angry . . . powerless . . . ashamed . . . emotionally spent. And then I saw my husband engaged with some terrified child. The girl was clawing frantically at Teach's buttocks and ferociously trying to wriggle herself free. But the harder she struggled the tighter his thrust until the flailing body fell silent. I ran over to see if she was still conscious as Blackbeard fumbled to button himself up. I muttered, "Did you kill her?"

The big man pushed her with his boot and her mouth emitted a tiny pop.

"By the powers, not I!" he cried. Then he yelled, "Gibbens! Come finish this off. I have pleasure in saying she's tender meat, and I'll warrant, much to your liking."

The air was electrified with lust and I'd sensed enough to make myself scarce. No female was safe this night. So I quietly spirited away and hid under a blanket alongside the wounded bodies in the sick bay. And I'm not sure to this day which sounded worse—the groans of the injured and smarting—or the yowls of the lecherous men.

In hindsight I'm able to think more evenly on Blackbeard—having now met my fill of all manner of marauders—and would (in his defense) argue that he was stronger and fairer than many a mangy sea dog because at least he knew the limits of violence. See, if you live in a brutal society where cruelty fuels sadism you've to be equally ruthless to protect yourself and your position. Yet it wasn't prize or power that drove Teach—he wanted to be remembered as the greatest buccaneer ever, which was his way of measuring success. Now, I ain't saying he didn't act rash in his youth like most whelps, but later he mastered self-control and wasn't any more violent than the other commanders. And when you compare his nautical treatment of prisoners to the punishments meted on land (hanging and drawing and quartering and pressing) I'd say he was far more gracious and civilized.

For at least you knew where you stood with the commodore—if you surrendered quickly he let you go, and if you lied or resisted you suffered his wrath. And his conduct with the Africans was really no different from anyone else who perceived the race as subservient, or assigned a different value to the lives of common slaves.

What made him such a terror then, you ask me, mister? I'd say it was circumstance. Blackbeard was living among sordid, raw creatures, with little enough prospects or education, who'd been dragged up to replicate animal behavior. These men were alienated from church and state, from family and society, so became desensitized and immune to bloodshed. You know, under the right circumstances, anyone can hurt or abuse or kill their fellows—as I myself discovered—and most of us don't ever question what we take to be society's rules. But these pirates wanted revenge on the world that had rejected them, and they refused to accept their unfair lot, determined that rather than giving in peacefully they'd make their mark in history and blast out with a bang.

Now, for many of our captives the freer life of pumping bilgewater and swabbing decks seemed preferable to the unknown drudgery on the other side of the auction block, so the majority quietly agreed to sign our articles and Blackbeard's navy swelled close to three hundred men. One by one the women got used up, and there wasn't nothing I could do to help a single soul because none of them spoke any English. Some died from their treatment. Some went crazy. But they all eventually ended up discarded like yesterday's food. We immediately headed for Bath Towne, where the commodore intended to sell the remaining slaves at public market. He'd apparently come to some business arrangement with Governor Eden to ensure that Carolina remained the lucrative safe-haven where such booty would find a rich welcome. I stayed quietly out of sight in the makeshift infirmary on board the *Revenge* and tried not to think what my husband was doing each night on his lascivious flagship.

Our arrival in Bath Towne caused quite a stir. We set up camp on Plum Point (where Blackbeard intended to retire and build a house), because it had one of the best views of the Pamlico Sound. On a clear day, across the bay at Archbell Point, the governor's vast plantation could be spotted. We sold our cargo, divvied the spoils, and helped the wounded find comfortable lodgings while the curious folk of Carolina afforded us no small degree of fame. Everywhere Blackbeard went people clamored to talk with him, as his well-oiled crew regaled the locals with tales of brave adventure. The whole town seemed to come to chattering life. Several young hopefuls tried to impress Teach enough to join the crew, not knowing his only interest lay in well-tested sea dogs. Meanwhile, I was happy to find a large apothecary store to restock my much-depleted chest because when my husband eventually returned to my bed in the drafty inn I was concerned he might have caught something nasty from his sour nights of debauchery.

Now, for some odd reason Ignatius Pell insisted on remaining aboard the *Revenge* to recuperate, so he sent out his orders through several of the tars assigned to the boatswain's station and twice a day I'd to take food and change his dressing. His wound was healing well, and as he wasn't hurt nearly as bad as some others, I didn't know why he wouldn't set foot in Bath Towne. So one day I thought to ask him. I sat on the floor rubbing ointment along the scar and looked up at the freckled face.

His tawny eyes shifted nervously as if he'd been staring while I carried out my task. I asked, "How come you're not with the major and the rest of your gang?"

He looked into the corner of the cabin and said, "I likes it here."

"But surely you'd be more comfortable in an ordinary?" I pressed.

That instant he lunged for my right breast and I suddenly understood why he savored my company. I pushed his squeezing hand away as he leered forward to kiss me. His face was screwed in a strange expression and he rasped, "I wants you . . . fair dues!" My response must have shown sufficient ignorance because he explained, "What belongs to Teach belongs to all of us I fancy." Now, I knew that the pirates shared their booty equally according to code, but I hadn't reckoned that would mean me as well. I was so taken aback I was speechless. "But I likes you a good deal more than the others. . . ." he confided. And this time when he touched my nipple I was so numb that I let him.

The boatswain rubbed my chest in little rough circles as I blubbered, "What others mean you, Mr. Pell?"

He cracked a dry snort and whispered, "Twelve, on my faith, by some reckoning."

"Twelve?" I gasped horrified. "Twelve what. . . ?"

"Wives," he cooed, trying to arouse my passions elsewhere. "Went and married all of them true enough."

"He's . . . twelve . . . mean you—I'm his *thirteenth* wife then?" My stomach lurched with his sickening grin.

"Aye—but here's the thing," he murmured into my hair. "If you please me, my service will be yours when the time comes."

"Service?" I echoed.

"Upon my life I'll vouch to keep you safe."

"From what?" I asked.

He sighed sadly, then let go of my breast for the top of my leg. As his hand crept closer to my inner thigh he mused, "Blackbeard . . ."

"He won't hurt me!" I protested.

"From his men . . ." he explained.

I didn't have no idea what he was insinuating so I asked him to speak out plainly. He responded by telling me the fate of some former Mrs. Teaches. Apparently, once the commodore had taken his fill of his woman he offered her up to the rest of the crew on some inescapable island where no questions were asked about who did what. And—rumor has it—none of these wenches were ever seen again.

"He means to abandon me likewise?" I asked incredulously.

Pell nodded, and then glued his whiskery mouth to my lips. "It's only on account of him needing an apothecary that you've gone and lasted this long," he explained.

I let him lower me onto the bed and fumble around in my linens. My mind was flipping cartwheels as I tried to make sense of this cruel information. "When will he . . . ?" I asked, responding automatically to the rubbing on my crotch.

"Soon," he said huskily. Then he stuck a sloppy tongue in my ear that was supposed to excite me. I let Ignatius Pell do his worst and after he'd taken his fun he squashed me tightly to his wiry frame. A little later he warned, "Now, don't you let on what we just done here. . . ."

"But," I exclaimed, "you said . . . !"

He gripped my ear and squashed it tightly in his clenched fist as he warned, "No telling what Blackbeard might do if he found out."

I scooted off the bunk and pulled my skirt down, growing

ever more confused and terrified by the moment. Pell gave a contented belch and found a comfortable position among the blankets. As he settled down to sleep he said, "See you on the morrow, my lovely."

And I finally realized that I'd just fallen foul of another pirate ruse—but that, unfortunately, was that.

12

A SUDDEN PLUNGE
IN THE SULLEN SWELL

1717–1718

Once the *Queen Anne's Revenge* had been cleaned out and refitted specific to our needs the convoy set sail for the Indies. The ship's cabin roof had been lowered to make the silhouette less visible on open water, and the bulwarks and gunwales raised for concealment and added protection. There were only fourteen cannons on-board when Blackbeard captured the vessel but now she boasted fresh-cut portals with twenty-two guns and enough full crews to man them. All of which kept Teach so very busy he didn't seem to notice Pell's promiscuous advances. I was now sharing the main flagship cabin alongside my husband but most evenings he drank and gambled with the men, occasionally joining me for a game of chess, and whenever he was otherwise engaged I found myself on my knees at the boatswain's behest in all the dank dark shadows where few ever ventured.

Our cruise went from success to further conquest as we

captured a low-loaded merchantman called the *Great Allen*. Now, this particular vessel sailed out of Boston (where the rash towns-folk had recently executed Bellamy's shipwrecked survivors) so Teach took particular pains to show the petrified crew the new face of buccaneer revenge. He boarded in his usual demonic attire and delivered a rousing speech that has since been oft quoted by those who quivered in its wind. Blackbeard roared loudly, "Gentlemen! Today is the day we avenge our Brethren for the suffering of all those mates so recently hanged. We defy the nobles for whom we once fought, since they have now decided that our services are no longer required! We built and stocked their rich, industrious colonies and now they want to reward us with the noose. So—we have a choice. We can dance the jig at the end of their ropes—or die as free and bold outlaws! Which is it to be, mates?" And the freebooters grunted throatily in favor of the latter. The commodore turned to the flinching prisoners and cried, "Say hello to the devil!" Then he chortled as his rogues stripped the captives of their most worldly possessions. But alongside a good haul of silver something flashy caught Blackbeard's eye and he stomped over to a handsome young officer sporting a square diamond ring. He grabbed the kneeling captive by the hair and stared ferociously into his clean-shaven visage. Then, apparently recognizing the man, the marauder spat between his eyes and drew his cutlass with a hiss. "Put out your arm if you would, Mr. Davies!" Teach demanded, indicating which one he meant with his weapon. The officer hesitantly pushed out his left arm until it was level with his shoulder. Without further warning Blackbeard gave a mighty swing and chopped the limb through the wrist, watching smugly as the hand rolled clear of the body. He strode over to the severed lump, picked up the grisly claw, rubbed the diamond ring on his jacket, and placed the trophy in his pocket. Then he dragged the wildly struggling Davies up the bulwarks and pushed the splaying officer over the side.

The other prisoners had no idea why this individual had been singled out but made sure to keep their horror mute so as not to be next in line. Now, as they didn't resist none, the commodore marooned the rest of the crew on a remote but visible island (leaving the two women aboard entirely unmolested because they chanced to be proper white ladies). The pirates then set fire to the vessel and drank raucously as they toasted goodbye to the sinking carcass. The crew of the merchantman seemed grateful to escape with only one casualty, knowing their cargo was fully insured against such calamity, and no doubt anxious to return to land with embellished tales of their clash with Satan. Indeed, soon as word of the *Great Allen*'s fate reached port the Royal Navy dispatched its finest man-o'-war to seek out the demon and his spawn.

Now, as it turned out, Blackbeard had recognized the murdered officer only by his distinctive diamond ring. It once belonged to a young woman in Charles Towne by the name of Lydia Rowling, a beauty who'd had the audacity to rebuff the pirate's lusty attentions. Of the three things that made my husband furious—disobedience—betrayal—and rejection—being spurned by a love interest apparently rated highest of high. So the buccaneer, pretending to respect her preference for a younger beau, graciously retired from pursuit leaving the sea clear for Davies. Truth be told he'd probably not given the couple no more thought until he spotted the officer wearing her ring and realized this new advantage. Later that night he wrapped the jeweled hand in a red velvet cloth and placed it inside a wooden chest. He planned to send it back to Charles Towne so Mistress Rowling would learn the fate of her beloved and the hefty price of having spurned Edward Teach. Some say that when she received the putrid gift the lovely woman grieved so hard she died of a broken heart. But whether that's true or not I can't rightly say.

Soon after that we suffered a sharp calamity. Our three vessels decided to split up in the Bay of Honduras and meet on the largest Cayman Island northwest of Jamaica, on the cocky assumption three crafts could plunder three times more loot. During the separation Lieutenant Richards tried for a slippery prize called the *Protestant Caesar*—a well-armed vessel commanded by Captain Wyer on its way to Belize to collect logwood, and currently stuffed with sugar and other supplies. Richards fired a warning across the bow, raised a painted version of the commodore's flag, and demanded Wyer's immediate surrender, threatening no quarter if the crew resisted. But the captain chose to retaliate and some well-aimed grapeshot smashed through the pirate's mainmast effectively disabling the craft. The *Protestant Caesar* swiftly made for port while the broken sloop was forced to bob toward Jamaica under oar. Fortunately though, the *Queen Anne's Revenge* had gone after a prize farther south, and having quickly taken a good supply of tanned leather, we were making our way toward Jamaica when we spotted the damaged *Adventure*. After Richards and crew climbed aboard the flagship the men voted to sink the broken boat and try for something swifter, because Blackbeard was determined to turn back after the *Protestant Caesar* so that Wyer couldn't never boast that he'd defeated one of our fleet. Now, give him his due, the commodore was such a skilled navigator he was able to place us on the exact trade route from Belize, and such was his focus he allowed several potential prizes to pass unchallenged until we spotted a likely replacement for the lost sloop. The men selected a large schooner that was duly renamed the new *Adventure* and its former captain—David Herriot—was pressed into joining the Brethren. Lieutenant Richards took command of the schooner, then quickly outfitted her with spare cannons transferred from the *Queen Anne's Revenge*. When all was ready, the replenished convoy waited on the unsuspecting Captain Wyer. Eventually, of course, the *Protestant Caesar* did make an appearance. But this time—when she spotted two pirate vessels and realized they were commanded by the infamous Blackbeard—her crew abandoned ship in the longboats and gave up their cargo without a fight. Teach let the mariners escape while his men ransacked for valuables and supplies, before the logwood on board was set ablaze and could be seen still smoking off our stern the following dawn.

Then somewhere out in the middle of dark water our flotilla was hailed by a passing buccaneer brig commanded by Captain Robert Deal. He'd once sailed with Charles Vane (but was now cruising on his own account) and as soon as he'd identified himself came aboard to drink with his old mates. Gossip was traded as news and we were amazed to learn that King George had decreed a royal pardon for all pirates who agreed to give up the sweet trade. Henry Jennings had apparently already surrendered to Governor Bennett in Bermuda, and rumor had it that Ben Hornigold was planning to sail to Jamaica for his reprieve. There was much excited chatter examining the advantage of such clemency—the general agreement being that as it wiped out all former crimes—and as the rogues were allowed to keep their ill-gotten blunt—one might as well go along with the charade as they could always return to the sea if honesty didn't work out. Blackbeard sat with a rueful grin on his face before announcing that next time he was in Carolina he'd think to ask Governor Eden for the papers, but when I asked if he was planning retirement he laughed so loud the echo made my ears throb.

In the meantime we continued past Jamaica to rendezvous with the *Revenge* on Grand Cayman Island before our convoy set sail for Providence. But then, one misty day before we arrived there, the authorities finally found us—and the instant we ran into their warship *Scarborough* we wily hunters transformed into cornered prey. This grim man-o'-war had thirty guns, a dedicated crew, and obviously felt able to tackle three drunken pirate ships so they sleekly moved into position and announced their intent to take us. Now their captain apparently expected we'd either try to flee or strike colors, but Blackbeard had no intention of running or surrendering so he ordered the guns to be loaded and weapons dispersed. He then maneuvered the *Queen Anne's Revenge* broadside, between the man-o'-war and his smaller vessels. "Show them our flag, Mr. Howard, if you please." The order to fire preceded the burst of cannon that flashed from the warship. I hunkered behind the boats on the quarterdeck, certain we'd never see Nassau again, and waited for my medicinal services to be called upon. Teach raised his horn and introduced himself as Satan before adding, "Pray well sinners! For the hour of your death is at hand. . . ." And the battle began.

This particular engagement was unlike any other I'd ever ever witnessed. We'd no intent to board so the aim was to shoot their ship to splinters whilst trying to avoid the same fate. Our volley was answered in kind, and before we knew it we were engaged in a running duel that seemed to go on and on and on. I didn't get no time to think when the wounded began staggering through the smarting smoke to the stern, and I rushed to pluck splinters and start binding wounds. Every time our craft took a hit I was bounced off my legs and as the deck grew bloody I shouted for someone to throw down sand so we'd not keep losing footing. And just when I thought we were done for, one of our missiles ripped through their bulkhead and tore a hole the size of a coconut. A cheer burst forth, and encouraged by this success, Philip Morton was able to gauge a kill-shot that leveled their mizzenmast on to the deck. The warship lurched and flailed, bounced wildly like a cork on running water, then before we could even reload our guns the craft had retreated into the mist and out of range.

"Will we pursue, Commodore?" the quartermaster panted.

"Nay, Mr. Howard. I reckon they'll not be plaguing us further."

Blackbeard knew that the disgrace of having to limp back defeated would be greater than any punishment he or his men could inflict. And I'll bet you ain't never heard this tale before because the Royal Navy don't like to boast of its losses. But I tell you—whatever the official version—that battle put a price on Blackbeard's head that many would thirst to win.

After that routing we decided it wiser to avoid Providence so we sailed through the Narrows past Cuba and never saw another sail for days. My surly husband began to grow bored. One drunken night he challenged his officers to a dare, shouting, "Come, let us make a hell of our own, and try how long we can bear it!" He ordered several pots to be filled with brimstone and placed at various points belowdecks. Then he and some other foolhardy men crawled into the hold, closed all hatches, set fire to the combustibles, and waited to see who could endure the stench longest. One by one the officers scrambled choking from the depth, gasping for air in a cloud of sulfurous fumes. Blackbeard was the last to leave and, proud that he was the best soul fitted for Hades, roared, "Damn you, you yellow-bellied sapsuckers! I'm a better man than all you milksops put together!" One of the spectators quipped,

"Looks like you've just come from the gallows!"—prompting the commodore to push back his sweaty locks, growl lowly, and suggest next time they try hanging themselves to see who could wear a noose the longest. . . . I found the whole episode childish but kept such thoughts strapped tight in my head. Outwardly, I congratulated my husband and further plumped his vanity.

One afternoon when Teach was busy mapping charts, Pell took me down belowdecks to a rank space where the buckets and brushes were stowed. He bent me over a pile of discarded sailcloth and quickly set to business, but before he'd finished a coarse rasp behind us announced that Garrat Gibbens had appeared, searching for pitch. "By the heavens . . ." he mused, "if it isn't the lovely Mrs. Teach rutting like a she-cat."

Pell came to conclusion and hurriedly fastened his breeches. He wiped his nose on a grimy sleeve and muttered, "Nice bit of rough, Gibby. And all yours—if you choose." Something unsaid also passed between the two boatswains and a silent tacit agreement slipped into place.

"As you were, darling. . . ." Gibbens commanded. And he took up the space just vacated by Pell. I cringed when I felt his calloused hands grip my hips and did my best to end him swiftly. He took great delight in yanking my long hair back until his mouth was able to suck on my neck, and as soon as we'd finished in one position he was charged up to go again. I began to worry that Blackbeard would miss me. And even more concerned what would happen if he found me.

When eventually I was allowed to leave I hurried to the main cabin. My husband was staring out the window but his countenance changed the moment I entered the room. Now I swear to God, that man could smell the sex on me. His nose quivered like a hunting dog's snout and his eyes narrowed to arrow slits. "Curse it! Where have you been?" he demanded to know. I blushed and stammered something feminine. He strode over to where I stood shivering and grasped my throat. The instant he saw the huge red marks something set in his eerie eyes— something cold as marble—something sharp as glass. "Whose doing is this, blast you!"

"The b . . . b . . . boatswain . . ." I stuttered between sobs.

"Pell or Gibbens?"

I turned my head to avoid the spittle flying from Teach's mouth and then nodded shamefully.

"God's death! Both of them?" he snorted. When I nodded again he pushed me onto the bed and made me confirm the culprits. After I'd finished confessing I waited with barely a breath for the strike on my sinful flesh. But he never raised a hand. Instead, he picked up his cutlass and blustered out of the cabin in search of his impudent mates.

Gibbens was busy on deck when Blackbeard's tetchy blade surprised the nape of his neck, drawing his instant attention. The boatswain was caught off-guard and fell back onto the planking in mock surrender. He knew why his commodore was there and joked, "By my blood, she's a lusty wench you've got there and no mistaking!" And perhaps believing that Blackbeard meant to share me soon enough he hoped his conspiratorial grin and stellar past service would alleviate any retribution for the taking of early liberties.

But the dark countenance the boatswain stared into gave no slack. "Lower your breeches, you base-souled bastard!" Teach commanded, while the rest of the deckhands crawled close to savor the entertainment. Gibbens instinctively reached for his dagger, then realizing his lack of advantage thought better of confrontation and carefully undid his codpiece, seeming more and more concerned at the commodore's temper. "And raise the shirt if you please. . . ." The boatswain's mouth gritted in a bold grimace (as if this were just another madman's test), exposing himself to the peck of eyes and ridicule. Blackbeard bent close to examine the nakedness, pushed the pirate's parts around with the hilt of his weapon and, seemingly satisfied with what he'd discovered there, he nodded that Gibbens could now dress. The sailor rolled on his knees to protect his vulnerability and decided it best to laugh off the undeclared joke. "Where's Pell?" Blackbeard roared. And the voices echoing down in the hull brought the other boatswain up from the galley.

"What's all the trouble, mateys?" Pell asked. He stopped short the moment he spotted Teach's drawn sword. "So 'tis your summons, Comm'dore?" he realized. Pell shot a panicked glance at Gibbens hoping for some clue to survival, but his partner merely winked, clucked his tongue, and grinned from one yellow fang across to the other brown stump. Gibbens was free and clear now. He could relax and enjoy the spectacle.

Blackbeard placed the tip of his cutlass on Pell's barely healed thigh and roared, "Strip to the knees, and don't make me have to cut you or I'll cleave your balls asunder!" The frightened man did as bid, his fingers fumbling to undo the buttons fast enough to save his future. But before he could lift his attention to further instruction the commodore had slit the front of the shirt, tearing it from the boatswain's pale frame. Teach walked slowly round the peeled man, taking full account of whatever it was he was looking for. "Jump to and get from my sight you miserable swine!" he bellowed. And he smacked the bare rump with the flat of his blade for emphasis. Next thing I knew my husband had thumped back down to the cabin. He slammed the door and demanded, "How many others have there been, you loose-legged slattern?"

I rubbed the tearstains on my cheeks and whispered, "None since we've been wed, sir . . ."

"Is that the truth of it?" He began to undress in a fury. "Then how, in the name of the devil, explain you this. . . ?" I stared in dismay at the small brown sores covering my husband's body. I'd seen these before on the *Argyll* and recognized the dreaded Great Pox.

All I could think to do was display my own body, which was clear of any blemishes—and then use the weight of my apothecary experience to push the blame to elsewhere. So I raised my shift to show a clear expanse of skin and murmured, "It . . . looks like . . . like Cupid's Disease. . . ." I gulped and continued, "Probably from those black women." I knew the sailors called this the French disease while in France they blamed the Italians. But the Puritans thought that it came from Africa and was spread by careless slavers. "I've no rash. . . . See?" I added, and dropped my clothing back in place.

"Can you treat it?" he asked quietly.

I nodded and spoke truthfully. "Sometimes it's cured and is no further bother . . ." but I added, "and sometimes it goes to the brain." I didn't know what else to say. A look of terror gilded the commodore's black eyes as he faced the depths of his own mortality. He swallowed hard, poured a good tankard of rum, then stood staring out of the windowpane into lone darkness.

Pell grabbed me by the arm the first time he caught me on deck and asked why Blackbeard was so incensed at our liaisons. I didn't betray his condition, but as I was frightened what my husband might do next I pleaded with the boatswain to keep his faith and protect me. He whispered urgently into my ear, "We've already set a course for Maine. . . ." I didn't have no idea what that meant so Pell briefly informed me that the Isle of Shoals was a popular dumping ground for the commodore's former wives. Apparently Teach would find some pretext to land on White Island and take the unwanted wife ashore in the skiff. Then he'd suggest she went exploring, and once she was out of sight he'd row back to ship and set sail without her, or invite the crew to form a disorderly queue for their share of her skin. I stared in utter dismay.

"What must I do?" I cried. I didn't want to be marooned.

"I believe you must plan on escape. . . ." I opened my mouth to ask something more but the boatswain squeezed my elbow and said, "Whatever you decide, share only with yourself. Trust no one, to be sure." And he staggered off across the deck to organize the sails. Next day Gibbens had been rowed across to the *Adventure* and Pell was back on the *Revenge*. I ain't sure that the Brethren voted on these changes but no salt dared challenge the commodore's orders when he slumped in such a rank temper.

Now, a little later, when other members of the superstitious crew also fell foul of the Pox, it was rumored to be a curse— the revenge of the slaughtered African women. So many officers succumbed to varying degrees of headache, malaise, and fever that Captain Bonnet assumed temporary command of the *Queen Anne's Revenge* while Blackbeard lay in a cantankerous stupor. The commodore suggested they sail for Carolina, and as my supply of mercury ran low the crew voted in favor of the apothecaries of Bath Towne. We planned to dock at Ocracoke (one of the deserted islands off the coast) where we could hide in safety, row over for medical assistance, and share out the plunder we hoped Governor Eden would transform into coin. But as more than thirty sailors had now turned poorly I ran dizzy trying to attend them all. Eventually I had the patients placed on our flagship deck—where any hands not on watch took turns giving water and cleaning up mess—while I went from cock to cock administering the brutal syringe. It was odd, though, that some were stricken with the reddish-pink rash while others developed the small brown sores, and no sooner was one batch of tars feeling better than another fresh outbreak burst forth. So I was really, really glad when we finally sighted the Outer Banks.

Blackbeard's strength returned by the time we made land. We hauled up in a sheltered creek where the ships could rest hidden from casual view. Will Howard transferred the saleable merchandise onto the *Adventure*, then Lieutenant Richards took the commodore, Caesar, and three other men to trade with Governor Eden, who was whispered to have a secret passage from shore to cellar to aid his nefarious smuggling activities—and who always paid promptly in gold. My husband promised to return with fresh supplies of medicine, flesh, and rum—and no one doubted his intent as he'd left behind his flagship.

The next day Teach reappeared laden down with supplies and wafting a paper he claimed was our pardon. He said Governor Eden had exonerated our entire fleet if we agreed to quietly disperse and go about honest business—so would the rogues agree to collect their pay and subtly melt into the Carolina countryside? Those patients still suffering looked forward to the comforts of land and were first to agree, and the two musicians were also eager to depart, confident that a fiddler and accordionist would always find gainful employment. But most of the old gang seemed reluctant to abandon their only homes and the newcomers appeared disoriented. We sat round a fire waiting for the quartermaster to start divvying up the booty when one of the fledgling salts was pushed forward of his group. He took off his cap and stood cautiously in front of the gathering before spluttering, "Begging your pardon, Comm'dore. . . . What're we reckoning to do in Bath Towne? I'm from London. . . ."

"Aye, I'm Glasgow!"

"Liverpool—we be. . . ."

The crowd chipped in their own information.

Teach stood up to acknowledge their query and was thoughtful for a few moments before responding, "Sweet merciful heaven—you're all free men! And verily rich to boot. I'll warrant there's many a pretty wench waiting ashore to wed with you." He stalked round the inside of the circle pointing at various tars as he continued explaining, "You, sir. Might you now have a mind to set up in business? Purchase a farm? Own a tavern?" Some of the more ambitious faces nodded with approval. "Or if the sea's in your veins—sign up legal?" Every eye was focused on his lips. "Well, forsooth, this is your chance!" He watched the quartermaster attributing the spoils into various hats. "Take your blunt and put it to good use. . . ." Then he paused before adding, "And for my part I'll keep my faith with the Brethren and promise you this. . . ." The company was stunningly silent as all ears prickled for the coming vow. "Any mate not content as a lubber may return to this very spot at midnight Good Friday. Watch for the signal fire." This seemed to settle the matter and the young spokesman nodded gratefully before disappearing into the crowd. Will Howard completed the payments, and boat by boat the newly retired pirates sailed off to their brighter tomorrows. But as the gathering thinned I noted none of the commodore's officers had taken the opportunity to leave. Major Bonnet sat with Ignatius Pell and Israel Hands; David Herriot was now fast friends with Lieutenant Richards and

Garrat Gibbens; and Caesar, Will Howard, and Philip Morton remained with Blackbeard, half a dozen faithful old sea dogs, and me. Some grand plan had been agreed that I didn't know about, for it seemed these chosen few were staying on Ocracoke to guard the ships. My husband took me roughly by the hand to our cabin on the *Queen Anne's Revenge* and deposited a collection of useless medicines on the table, informing me that mercury was in short supply around Bath Towne. I watched with bleary eyes as he collected his personal belongings and asked him if I should pack too. He shook his head, told me he'd heard of a surgeon who could cure the Pox, pushed the navigation charts safe under his bunk, and then left me to my fate. Of course I immediately realized my usefulness had ended—that I'd never see him again.

Now, if you've ever played Brag you might understand how I was feeling at this uncomfortable point. I'd to show the cards dealt from a previous hand without no shuffling—and fate had just upped the ante without my consent. My days were now numbered. But I remembered the cardinal rule—that you cannot see the blind man—so decided to play my hand blind. Now, my only options were to continue betting or to fold (and I'd played enough skillful games to know that you don't win big if you threw in or fail to bluff). Blackbeard held the better hand—but if I didn't fold out of turn—and never showed my cards to anybody—seeing my suits would cost him twice as much as any of the previous players. So I determined not to throw in my luck. . . . I'd play by my life and take the whole pot.

It was only much later I heard about my husband's antics in Bath Towne. He'd apparently decided to settle down and become a proper gentleman again, so began establishing himself with the locals and building the house on Plum Point. Seems he also started wooing Mary Ormond—a teenage debutant with education, breeding, and connections who would soon unsuspectingly agree to become his fourteenth wife. I'm sure she thought she'd be able to civilize her buccaneer prince, but I'm told that instead she actually met the fate that was destined for me. Of course, this is all hearsay and speculation. I only really knew what was happening on my island.

This early part of the year was unseasonably warm with just enough sunlight to camp on the beach, in preference to the hammocks on ship. But that first night I was so afraid for my safety (being alone and unprotected with all those sailors), I ensconced myself in the main cabin aboard the *Queen Anne's Revenge* and sealed the door tight with a chair wedged under the handle. I'd been given my share of the plunder along with everyone else—but only because they knew I'd never get to spend it. Now in the safety of the cabin I opened the sailcloth to see what I'd acquired . . . a cluster of gold and silver coins to add to the silver chalice still buried in my medicine chest. Quite a good haul, but not nearly enough for severance. I glanced out the cabin window to the men already starting to gamble by the fire and noted Slouchy, who'd appeared from nowhere, was busy preparing a pot of salmagundi. He'd sense enough to bury his riches, whereas the others who were addicted to dice—too lazy or overconfident—had opted to keep purses and hats at hand, and that would soon be their undoing. I drew a calming breath to clear my fuddle and then numbly forced my limbs into action.

First off I took the good whiskey Blackbeard had brought with the supplies, carefully removed the stopper, plucked the laudanum bottle from my chest and poured in enough to render a brown bear senseless. I shook the mixture vigorously, then waited for the cloudiness to fade. Next, I pulled the navigation sack from under the bunk and tipped the contents onto the floor—I needed a makeshift ditty bag to carry my possessions and this would suffice—but the rolled-up charts caught my attention so I carefully unwrapped the most recent to see if I could decipher where we were stationed and which direction I should run. I found the map to be a plundered French chart but recognized the words *Caroline* and *Virginie*—and when careful scrutiny showed *Charles Towne* too close for comfort I determined to head North for Virginia. I spotted *Okeken* (which I took to be Ocracoke) on a long, thin spit of land running almost the entire length of the colony and tried to memorize the dog-leg path I'd be taking. I wouldn't be needing no compass, though—there was only one way to go and that was forward. Now, I knew that sandbars shifted and split and didn't expect to get all the way on land without getting wet so I scrabbled about for useful items—rope, a sailor's knife, candles and tinderbox, hardtack, apples, and two buoyant jugs of water. I got my battle clothes organized (including my boots and cape) but decided I couldn't take the silver chalice or my chest so I stuffed the last of the figs into the sack. When all was ready I tidied myself up, picked up the whiskey, and sauntered out to the men at the fire.

As I approached I noticed they were engrossed in a game of dice but strangely enough there was no money in the pot. Instead, Slouchy was paying out faceup cards that already ranged from one to seven. The excitement hushed as I grew close and someone nudged Philip Morton (who happened to be holding the ace). The leer in their eyes told me what was going on— they were betting on who was to have me in which order. I feigned ignorance and said gaily, "Gentlemen! A gift from Governor Eden to welcome us to Carolina . . ." and before anyone raised suspicion I began pouring whiskey into their mugs. They downed the draft with annoying slowness but I kept refilling as each became empty, trying to dish out equal shares.

"Aren't you joining us?" Slouchy asked.

I smiled sweetly and said, "Aye. I'll go get my bowl and mug. . . ." Then I intentionally rolled my hips for their pleasure as I sashayed back to my cabin. I watched covertly through the window as the betting continued in my absence and everyone had their turn assured. But the opium didn't seem to be working any and I broke out in a panic. The only other temptation was a half-empty barrel of rum so I hurriedly ground up some dried valerian root and dropped it into the mixture to steep. Then, when I couldn't delay any longer without suspicion, I collected my mess kit and the rum and made my way back to the fire.

By now the men were busy eating. I casually put the rum on the ground, walked over to the cauldron, and scooped a ladle of pottage, and was pleased to see William Howard already helping himself from the barrel. Everyone was drinking heavily to celebrate the end of the cruise and I ate as slowly as possible, hoping on hope that the drugs would work before I'd to start giving out favors. Major Bonnet's eyes began to droop and I could see him trying to pinch his brows to stay alert. But Philip Morton was chipper as ever and I knew it wouldn't be long before they let me in on the dastardly plan.

Lieutenant Richards, I saw, had the deuce and when he couldn't wait no longer to get things rolling he shouted, "Morton—I'll be taking your turn if you don't shift your boozy arse!"

The gunner looked momentarily befuddled, then he wobbled to his feet and without further ceremony grabbed me by the arm and hissed, "Come away with me, wench."

I pretended I didn't know what was going on and allowed

the jack-tar to manhandle me some distance off to a patch of live oak trees. There was a sandy spot quite hidden from the others where he laid me down and immediately fell on top. He slobbered round my ear, muttering lusty oaths into my neck, all the while grinding his hips against mine. I played along with his enthusiasm and began undoing his codpiece. At first he seemed deliriously excited but as I fumbled into the necessary position his wood went suddenly limp and the rest of his body followed with a silent thump. The gunner lay unconscious on top of me and I panted to push myself free. I checked his deep-breathing chest and knew he'd definitely be out until morning. Good. I glanced around to make sure no one else was looking on, stealthily searched his pockets for the purse, and stuffed it deep in my cleavage. One down . . .

Now, I'd half expected the rest of the crew to follow us and watch—and it wasn't until I crept back to the fire I realized why they hadn't. Every single light was out. It seemed like my mickey had finally worked! But just to make sure this wasn't some trick, I clumsily tripped over Slouchy to see if he'd respond to my accidental kick. Nothing. I whisked off the major's hat with my skirt and got no reaction. And David Herriot didn't cease snoring even when I sifted sand in his wavering mouth. So one by one I frisked the dormant monsters and quietly stole their loot. I left Gibbens until the last though—and was sorely tempted to forfeit his gold because even in slumber he terrified. But then my greed got the better so I crept forward to where the buccaneer lay sprawled across a log and cautiously rooted around for his pouch. As I tugged against the pocket his eyes flicked open in a manic stare and his scabby hand reached up to counteract mine. But the rage in his eyes seemed to fizz to blankness, the squeezing grip fell useless, and with a mighty snort he rolled facedown into his blackest nightmare. I gave a hurried glance at the dying sun and realized I'd only about an hour of light left and needed to put as much distance as possible between us so ran quickly to the ship, slipped into my practical clothes, stuffed the coins into the waistband of my breeches, and left with the ditty bag over my shoulder and an unlit lantern in my hand. And I knew from the map I'd have to skirt round the marshes ahead so I set off by the grass-flecked shoreline alongside the patchy sunset.

The tide was ebbing, allowing me to squelch through the sucking mud, and I certainly preferred wading in wet boots to the potential venom of black swamp snakes coiled waiting farther inland. The moon rose enough to dapple the foam a lighter gray as I plodded my way up the edge of the Sound, and an hour or so later the boggy marsh set to firmer sand. By then I wished I were in Nassau (where my boots would have already started to dry) but I trekked on and on and on into darkness well aware that I'd passed the point of no return. Sometime before the witching hour I came to a bay that reflected the glistening moon in all her glory. The ripples resembled a writhing pond of mercury and everything was tranquil except for the slush of the sweeping sea. But I couldn't waste no time negotiating this obstacle so I carefully turned inland and assumed I was now heading east. Soon I came to an eerie woods full of shadow and untold rustling noises, but the thought of the terror I'd face if the groggy men caught up with me was more than enough motivation to screw up my fears and swallow them whole. So I stopped for a gulp of water, lit my lantern, and then picked my way through the forest of black, grasping limbs. I walked and walked until I could feel the blisters pop. Then I walked some more. Now, I didn't know if they'd come after me by land or water—but reckoning to be safer on the far banks where the open sea would give better warning I bumbled along in a jagged line—never too far from someplace I could hide. The sun rose pink then purple then gold, etching the sky in a moody slate of gray as the clouds rolled in to dim the horizon. This side of the island was a ribbon of beach, shells, and dunes, but wherever possible I scurried along under shadow of the trees. When I really couldn't stumble another step, and it was warm enough to believe the hunters were probably abroad, I began to look for a good place to rest away from sudden danger.

A flash of something in the trees sent shivers across my neck. And even though common sense told me it couldn't be one of the crewmen I instinctively dropped to the sand behind a hillock. As I peered into the gloom the light changed to shadow and was followed by a series of thuds that shifted like restless ghosts. Something puffed and whined—something surprising and wonderfully familiar—a mustang snuffling for fresh, sweet shoots. The silver flank was nudged away by a chestnut snout and I realized the horse was not alone. Had some scary hostile natives discovered me first? I lay panting with my chin flat on the dune, barely daring to lift an eye in case a painted face stared back. Then I heard a boatswain's whistle cut through the distance, a human shout from somewhere in the swamp, and a second whistle echo on the faroff shore. The pirates had apparently launched a sloop each side of the island and another band on foot—they were systematically hunting me down and I knew I'd have to move fast. So I opted for the lesser danger—I'd take my chances with the red skins.

Now, I ain't kidding when I tell you my heart was bumping fit to injure my chest as I moved stealthily toward the unknown shade. I couldn't see anyone else around but I'd heard that the Indians were cunning and brave so was alert for any type of movement above and below. Nothing. I exhaled my gratitude and moved toward the trees. The herd consisted of several wild ponies that scattered at my approach—but the dominant mare held her ground a little way off and stared me down with her ancient gaze. I drew a biscuit from my pack and approached her with the crumbs on a flat, extended palm, for she seemed less skittish than the younger fillies and perhaps was used to human contact. I noted she was a small, powerful gray with an unkempt black mane and tail covered in sandy dust. I estimated she'd be around ten years old but was fatter than I'd have expected from a diet of marsh grass. Someone who'd adopted her had apparently been feeding her corn (which immediately explained her easygoing temperament once she saw I wasn't no threat). I held her stare, silently willing her to accept my gift, and was pleased that she nibbled without the slightest nip or bite. I rubbed her forehead and removed a burr from her forelock, all the while whispering seductively into her ear. She stood calm as I petted her muzzle and moved her dappled neck as I scratched the itchy spots. But whether she'd let me ride her remained to be seen. Another whistle in the distance reminded me of my urgency so I stood on a broken tree stump, grasped a firm hold of her mane, and with my last push of strength managed to mount her back. She was the smallest mare I'd ever ridden so I decided to call her Betty—the gypsy word for *little*. She gave one quick shrug to see if I'd shift but I gripped my thighs and steered her toward the beach. I couldn't see any mast yet so decided it'd be safe to canter along the beach, and when the rest of the herd came out from the bracken to join us I prayed we'd be well concealed by the clouds of their hoof-spun dust. I didn't know whether a dozen galloping horses would seem suspicious or not—but there was no way I could walk anymore—and if I stayed on this spit of land I'd surely get nabbed.

Betty was a godsend, I have to say. She kept up pace a good hour or so, then dropped to a steady trot. At one point she turned inland and refused to stay on track so I'd no option except to give her head and trust she wasn't taking me to no Indian village. But she stepped nimbly through the brush and deposited me at a natural spring where me and the herd drank gratefully. I knew this sandbar must end at some point—where the restless sea had breached and reclaimed new passage—yet how accurate Blackbeard's map was I'd no real idea. I did note, though, that the wind blew mercifully in my favor. The sloops would have to tack to catch up . . . and I hoped upon hope that'd give me enough advantage. We trotted and cantered into late afternoon until the land dog-legged sharp north. I was initially tempted to hide in the lush, cool forest because I ached from ear to toe and had several times almost dropped into slumber, but some primitive strength urged me onward and common sense told me to follow its lead. So we took a quick break in the shade instead and walked the last long miles into evening. I reckoned the men would strike camp at sunset because they couldn't see nothing in the dark, and when the ponies grew fractious and tired I knew it was time to rest. Betty selected a small hidden clearing in a patch of scraggly trees where a narrow stream kept the grasses crisp. I shared the last of my apples and hardtack with my new companion while the rest of the ponies foraged their own meal. I waited until the horses settled and gently slipped a rope around Betty's neck, wrapping the other end round my own wrist so she'd still be close in the morning. Strangely enough she allowed this insult and seemed equally tolerant when I rested against her flank and fell into fitful repose. As soon as dawn broke we set off again and by noon stood staring at the edge of the world where the sea crashed through the gaping inlet.

I sat on Betty's back and stared in dismay. This was no tiny gap like on Teach's map—this was a huge gaping river I couldn't see across, with a crop of rocks and a suck of raging water. What should I do? I tried edging the pony down to the sea in the hope she'd swim me across. But she sniffed the danger, threw back her neck, and whined a definitive snort, pulling back from the tip and refusing to budge. Eventually I slid from her back and tried cajoling her down. All attempts were fruitless and I realized I must let her go. So I gave her a thankful pat, smacked her rump, and watched sadly as she led her herd back toward home. On the far horizon I saw hostile sail slowly gaining in size, and the billow of a schooner out at sea that might be headed this way. There was nothing for me to do now except plunge into the sullen swell—but to give me additional buoyancy I drank down the contents of my two water jugs, tightly replaced the stoppers, lashed a container to each arm, and hoped they'd keep me afloat when I grew too tired to swim. I stuffed my boots in the ditty bag, which I then tied on my back, threw my cloak in the water to look like I'd drowned and, with my stomach sat inside my throat, waded to where the rocks fell away to black water.

I pushed off and let the current sweep me up. And as I bobbed up from the first briny dunk I realized I'd made my choice now, and that was that.

13

GRIPPED BY FINGERS TEN

1718

The moment I soared to the surface I recognized my terrible mistake. Now, I ain't never known no water cold as that brink—it burned like a liquid ice and quite literally squeezed the gasp from my chest. My skin tingled with fire-sharp prickles and I could feel my heart trying to warm the half-frozen sludge, punching and wrestling and throbbing right up to my temples. I stared through salty eyes, trying to determine which way to swim, and set out in the opposite direction of the rocks. I thought if I thrashed my legs about I'd soon warm up—but this was no balmy Carribee—this was the raging Atlantic gnawing the edge of an untamed world. And instead of relaxing into a useful rhythm, my muscles drew tense and shivery. The closing sound of whistles and yells urged me on and I was glad I'd tied the jugs to my arms because they helped keep my head up when fatigue would have bid a sickly surrender. I kicked and spluttered and shuddered and spat, not really sure where headed now or why. But some push propelled me forward so I moved to its silent instruction like a sleepwalker. I'd no idea how long I'd been immersed but found myself bobbing inside the waves as my breathing gradually slowed to putters. The drumming in my skull grew fainter and dimmer and I swear I could see palm fronds peeking out of the pitching waves. I thought it'd be nice to taste coconut again . . . and wondered if I'd enough gold hidden in my breeches to buy one? The right jug loosed itself and wobbled from sight so I tussled to free the left jug and grasp it between both hands. Everything slid into grayness. My mind set chill as my body. I vaguely recall the swell of a boat, the spray of the oars, and a curse of amazement when ten steely fingers suddenly caught hold of my hair and hauled me up toward terrible blankness. As sense slipped away, my last hope was that they kill me quickly before my vicious husband returned.

My worst worry was that a thief like me would be keelhauled. I ain't never seen it done to any poor soul but I knew it was the punishment kept for the worst of all sinners. The pirates would strip me naked and tie me to the main yard with weights on my feet. They'd stuff an oil-soaked rag in my mouth, then drag me by rope under the hull of the boat from one slimy end to the other. The crusty barnacles would flay my flesh like razors. Then they'd laugh and do it again. Then again. Of course I'd likely not survive long—from drowning or shark bite or blood loss or fright or infection—and if I did I'd be horribly scarred, both outside and in. But even that would be preferable to what Blackbeard might drum up for trying to slip his noose. I shuddered, as much in panic as with cold.

Then my thoughts turned upward toward the fluttery light. I'd already endured so much—come so far—I couldn't believe it would end like this. I'd not been cast much luck before but I'd always made the best of it, and needed, now more than ever, to keep my thoughts buoyant and focused. It was hard sifting my foggy mind, though, when the darkness seemed cozy and lulled like a siren and beckoned me into its careless abandon. No—I didn't want to be remembered as Blackbeard's gypsy apothecary, or be forgotten as one of his nameless wives. I'd always been sharp at improvising, adapting to wind and change. So I wrestled to keep the air sucking in and out of bubbling nostrils and bit my juddering lips to still them from blabbing in terror.

Next thing I knew was the oily deck of a lurching craft. Something was weighing me down. At first I thought I'd been chained to the hold but the coarse rub of cloth on my chin suggested otherwise. I opened one tentative eye and scanned for foe. I couldn't see nothing except the slick planks beneath my cheek so I cautiously turned my head as slowly as able, and that's when I discovered I'd been wrapped in blankets and covered with tarpaulin. My arms and legs shook without restraint—and I obviously wasn't dead yet—but my limbs felt like limp lumps of clay and couldn't keep from quivering. I quietly pulled my knees to my chest and huddled inside myself for that last ounce of warmth. Where was I? This lilt underneath was too fierce for the *Queen Anne's Revenge*, and the near thrust of oars alongside the whip of close sail made me realize I wasn't on no familiar sloop. I thrust an ear up out of the makeshift cocoon and heard voices singing of a fine Sally Brown. The rocking took over my scanty thoughts and I pushed my head back in the blankets letting the awesome sea become mother.

I drifted in and out of comprehension unable, or unwilling,

to piece together what was happening. But it turns out I was rescued from the murk at the point when my flesh had gone blue. One of the local pilots, racing to guide the incoming schooner through the inlet, had spotted my floating head and ordered his African crewmen to dredge me for life. Then they turned their agile periauger into the wind and pulled alongside the larger vessel so the pilot could board and help navigate the treacherous shoals, and I was hoisted up like a bundle of sail and dumped in the schooner's longboat. This merchant vessel was out of Philadelphia heading for Bath Towne—but when the captain heard me muttering Blackbeard's dreaded name he decided to settle for Norfolk instead, to protect his valuable cargo.

Now, there was this plainly dressed lady on board, the wife of a Quaker pastor who turned out to be a minister herself, and she gently roused me from stupor. I never did know her name—she said to address her as Friend—but she nursed me until I could feed myself and she didn't ask no awkward questions. Fact is, I'd already decided to keep my gob shut tight. And the crew thought I'd been through enough to render me stupid so they treated me like the hapless village idiot. But by the time we reached Norfolk I'd the worse cough you'd ever, ever heard and although I could now stand for very short spells my body felt rampant with fever. The ministers took me to a house and arranged a bed, but were thoroughly dismayed when I insisted on sleeping in my old breeches. . . . I may well have lost something of my mind at that point yet was determined not to lose my loot as well. A few days later they left me in the care of this fellow Friend as they set out by wagon for Bath Towne.

The Virginia Quakers were an odd bunch—religious and deeply compassionate. They wore stark, drab clothes and spoke a funny way I ain't never heard done by others. After the Puritans had run their forefathers from Massachusetts they'd apparently scattered and moved farther south seeking sanctuary, complaining that the Pilgrim Fathers wanted religious freedom themselves without offering it to anyone else. Then William Penn set up Philadelphia, his harmonious experiment in liberty and democracy, and the Friends there prospered so well they wanted to spread their success to others. Their shopkeepers did away with haggling by naming a fair common price—they invented new drinks to wean folks off alcohol—and they didn't have no nasty bias against us gypsies. But the rest of the Virginian colonists were Anglican, and even after the Toleration Act stopped official persecutions the Children of the Light had not yet succeeded in freeing themselves of suspicion. They therefore formed a tight community that met for secret worship. I found all this out the day my sweats stopped and I could focus on my keeper, the sweet Lucretia.

Lucretia Fry was the widowed wife of a banker whose heart was big as her matronly chest. Her tired hair peeked in wayward strands from her starched, clean cap yet her gray eyes were calm and welcoming. I'd just finished gulping some delicate broth when she tenderly exclaimed, "Praise the Lord! Your fever has broke, my child." I shuffled into a comfortable position, immediately checking that my breeches were unmolested. She laid a cool hand to my forehead and pushed the matted curls from my eyes and I relaxed enough to turn and meet her gaze. Lucretia smiled and assured me, "You are among Friends here, and safe from danger." She'd been told I was found in the water and my ship had been wrecked by pirates. I didn't correct her any, but let her sing on in her drawling voice as she busied herself with my comfort. She brought me a rag to wash with and then set about trying to untangle my locks, all the while talking quietly and trying to set me at ease.

When eventually she paused to ask my name I thought for a moment and stuttered, "Mary . . . Mary Shane." I didn't want to tell her my real identity in case some buccaneer came a-hunting, or word got back to Charles Towne. Lucretia was one of those rare really good folks but I didn't know, yet, I could trust her.

"Can you remember what happened to your ship?" she asked. I shook my head and stared wildly into the corner of the room. She didn't press for answers but put her meaty arms round my neck and rocked me like a hammock. She whispered, "We need listen together for the Holy Spirit to hear what it is God wants done with you, poor child." I didn't have no idea what she was talking about but I let her hug me to and fro because she smelt of fresh-baked shortbread.

Over the following days I began to make myself useful around the house. Then one time when I was scraping carrots Lucretia looked me sharp in the face and asked, "Are you a Romany heretic, Mary?" I nodded my sin. But instead of the usual biting response the matron carefully took the knife from my grip and turned my chin in the cup of her other hand. She peered deeply into the depths of my skull as if searching for something precious and lulled, "Bless you, my dear. There is One—Jesus Christ—who can speak to your condition." I dropped my lashes in shame. "He gives guidance and power to those who open their hearts to Him."

At that point in time I could certainly use some of both so I mumbled, "How . . . ?"

She informed me that, "The mark of an authentic Christian is a changed life. Do you wish redemption, child?"

"Aye . . ." I replied. I'd sinned more than enough for one life. And from that moment on I became Lucretia's mission.

Now I ain't never been religious but I've got to say the Society of Friends lived as godly as any. Of course I didn't think much of their clothing—but they seemed happy enough without music or rum or gambling or groping or dancing. They found entertainment in the gospels. They found pleasure in hard, honest work. Their women were treated as equals because God's spirit rests in every soul. And they even accepted me. So I tried hard to connect with the Inner Light. I struggled to read the tiny print and recited the Psalms until they dropped from my tongue like a shanty. I waited in silence for revelation. I prayed and I watched what the others did. And then I prayed even harder.

Lucretia believed she'd a personal relationship with God. I wanted to have one too so I sat endless hours in the clammy hush but was never once moved to speak. I learned God is the spirit and Christ is that spirit made flesh, and that if I repented my abhorrent past I could turn to the Light and find hope. And I wanted so badly to be saved, I truly did. I knelt trembling before the word of God. But then when I learned that Christ will return to judge the resurrected—that some will go to Eternal Salvation and some to Eternal Damnation—that's when I realized my fate. I'd never get to see the Lord Jesus Christ because I was already wedded to Satan.

One day the town heard news fresh from the Indies. Captain Woodes Rogers had been appointed the governor of the Bahamas. He had decided to clean up Nassau and offered a full pardon to any buccaneer who surrendered before September. Now, many Colonial shopkeepers turned a blind eye to the piracy that stocked their cheap goods, preferring not to know from whence they were acquired. The Friends, however, could not condone theft or violence and wished that the law might rid the seas of these rogues. Everyone whispered how Governor

Eden protected the profitable outlaws, and moaned that as long as Carolina provided safe haven, the Virginia coastline would always be vulnerable. Something needed to be done. So the folks complained to James Blair first—he was the Bishop of London's man—but when their ships continued being ravaged the angry merchants turned to local justice and demanded immediate action. Blackbeard was denounced a public enemy and Governor Alexander Spotswood started collecting information to supply a warrant for arrest. Now, I ain't sure if it was just wishful thinking—but I got it in my head that this was my chance at salvation—that the Light was bidding me seek out Spotswood and give him the ammunition he so desperately required.

In the quiet of evening I explained to Lucretia how I'd started remembering my ordeal with the pirates and that I'd valuable information the governor needed to hear. At first she was rather skeptical, until I started to proffer specific information that no one could have gleaned from gossip. A flick of concern crossed her floury face but she nodded and said she'd see what could be arranged. So next evening at dusk I cleaned myself up and dressed neatly in the plain clothes donated, then we slipped to the harbor where one of the elders had arranged our passage up-river by barge. I'd spent every furtive moment that afternoon squeezing the coins from my tatty breeches and secreting them into the waistband of my dull brown skirt, before we set forth with a cold supper of ham, bread, and cheese to enjoy on our journey to Williamsburg.

I couldn't see much of the elder who acted as guide. He kept to the shadows, spoke very little, and seemed to communicate in whispers and grunts. Me and Lucretia ate propped up against some sacks of grain and then we huddled together beneath a grubby blanket wrapped round our woolen cloaks. By dawn we were on the grassy banks where our care was passed from one elder to another—a thin man who stood by a rickety trap and bid us move quickly in urgent hand gestures. We thanked the captain and our silent companion, then climbed aboard the smooth wooden seat of the cart.

Williamsburg unfurled slowly from the mist in the first promising glints of morning. Herders were guiding sheep to richer pasture, a farmer was running three piglets to market, and horses were laden with baskets, sacks, cages, bales, and bundles. We trotted down Palace Street to the most impressive mansion I'd ever ever seen, passing through a big stone gateway guarded on one side by a snarling lion, and on the other by a flourishing unicorn. The Governor's Palace rose three stories into the air and was flanked either edge with symmetrical buildings. The stately home glowed pink in the yawning sun and the panes of its gabled windows shimmered like rose-etched memory. The elder swept us up to the grand stone steps, helped us to clumsily dismount, doffed his hat in curt salutation, and left us at the base. Me and Lucretia gave each other a wary smile, then began climbing the teeth to the big black mouth. The door was wide open and bustling with people pressing in and out of the huge reception hall. I noticed the bayonet-tipped muskets decorating the walls and remembered someone mentioning Spotswood had been a colonel in Queen Anne's Army. Then a housemaid grabbed Lucretia by the elbow and steered us in the direction of the butler.

The governor's man looked us up and down to see what we were selling. Then he raised a puzzled eyebrow and finally met Lucretia's eye. "How may we assist you, ma'am?" he asked in a harassed tone.

"By the grace of Our Lord, we come from Norfolk to see Governor Spotswood."

"May I inquire as to the nature of your business, Mrs. . . . ?"

"Mrs. Jonah Fry . . ." she informed him. "And this is Mary Shane." Our names didn't ring any import so Lucretia continued, "This young woman has mercifully escaped the clutches of pirates and has important information which may be used in their apprehension."

The butler thought for an instant, then directed us up the staircase to the blue drawing room on the left. We were to be given an audience with the governor, when it pleased His Excellency to see us, so we sat through the long, dusty morning and into the afternoon. Folks came and went. Maids blustered in and out carrying jugs of refreshment for more honored guests, while white clerks and black servants furtively scurried off with papers and commands. Lucretia dozed for an hour or so, and then I took my own forty winks. Finally, when our stomachs were starting to grumble like thunder, a clerk appeared and told us to follow him into the chamber of power.

The governor sat behind a vast gold-leaf desk, spreading his girth in a well-padded mahogany chair. He was a formidable sight in his fancy gray wig, and peered lazily from two decadent eyelids set in a very long face with shiny high brow. His belly paunch stuffed the velvet waistcoat and balanced itself on his dazzling bright breeches, which he artfully adjusted for comfort as we entered the room. He wiped the back of his hand across his lips, then lifted his head to converse with the clerk. The younger man stood behind his chair and formally announced us as, "Two ladies from Norfolk, Your Excellency."

Lucretia bobbed a curtsey and began, "Thank you for seeing us, sir." His impatient hand signaled to get straight to business so she hurriedly explained, "The Good Lord has seen fit to save the life of this maiden that she may testify against the evil buccaneers who routed her ship and destroyed all other souls on board." This wasn't exactly what I'd told anyone—but in all fairness I hadn't said anything different either.

Spotswood beckoned me forward with his finger so I shuffled closer. "Sit down, child." He pointed to a damask chair in front of the desk and I quickly did as bid.

"Wait outside," he commanded of Lucretia. She gave me a glance of concern but was briskly escorted from the room. The clerk returned and mutely resumed his post.

"What is your name?" he inquired. I felt the seriousness of his stare but lied, "Mary Shane, sir."

"You are English . . . from London, if I am not mistaken?" I nodded

"Romany?" I stared at the fidgety hands in my lap and nodded again.

"I see," he muttered to himself. His languid eye suddenly widened and bore right into me as he continued, "And you say that your ship was attacked by pirates?"

I gnawed on my lower lip and murmured, "Aye, sir."

"Then explain to me what happened, if you please."

So off I went into my big, grand tale that began, "We had been at sea for ages. . . . I think we'd been blown off course because no one seemed to know where we were but we were supposed to be headed for Charles Towne. . . ."

"What was the name of your ship?" he interjected.

"Er . . ." I hesitated a tad too long before saying "The *Argyll*." He wrote down something with a fancy-plumed quill and told me to continue. "Well, we were short on water so the captain (I don't know his name) decided to make for land and someone said we could cut through the inlet ahead and take on fresh supplies. The master raised a signal flag and before long a sloop appeared that we thought was our pilot. But it turned out it was a pirate ship. And someone cried out it was Blackbeard. Then next thing I knew there was cannon and blood and smoke and fighting and everything turned upside down. Someone pushed me overboard and then I was drowning and everything turned black. But the real pilot boat found me floating unconscious and managed to bring me back to life." I was blushing, but hoped it would pass as relived excitement.

After a very uncomfortable pause the governor asked, "What made the crew think it was Blackbeard's ship?"

"It looked like the *Queen Anne's Revenge*, sir. It was flying his Jolly Roger."

The clever mouth smiled and said, "How do you know the name of Blackbeard's new ship? It bears no plaque—" I opened my mouth but nothing came out so I looked in panic at the clerk stood behind him. Spotswood pinned me with his glare and said carefully, "Are you his gypsy apothecary?" Now I was really scared. He'd heard of me! That meant he'd captured one of the crew and someone had spilled his guts. But there was nothing to be done except confess—and hope I could give him enough to save my own neck. The look on my face must have provided sufficient answer because he turned to the clerk and told him to send Lucretia home. . . . I'd apparently be staying at His Majesty's pleasure.

I spent the next two nights in the public gaol until the governor found time to examine me further. One of the four cells was packed with runaway slaves, manacled and chained to the bare walls until their owners arrived to claim them. Two airier rooms housed the town debtors, and I was pushed into a fourth dungeon containing a mad woman who wouldn't quit banging her head against the bricks. Soon as my eyes got accustomed to the murk I scanned each cell to see who'd given me away. No one I recognized. So when the keeper—John Redwood—brought my food I played the frightened maid and asked through chattering teeth whether there were any pirates here. Redwood informed me they'd recently caught two of Bonnet's crew, who'd quickly turned king's evidence, blaming Blackbeard for making them buccaneers when they'd formally been honest sailors.

"What happened to them?" I asked innocently.

"They were officially pardoned and sent on their way."

Ah! Now that he'd shown me my own escape-hole I smiled at the lonely jailer and cooed, "You're ever so brave in dealing with such demons!" He beamed back in pleasure and gave me an extra dollop of mush.

Next time I went before Governor Spotswood there were several other powdered gentlemen in attendance sat behind a long table. They placed me on an unpadded wooden chair and began by bluntly stating they'd no real interest in a foolish slip of a girl . . . it was Edward Teach they were after. So if I gave sufficient information to lead to his arrest—and if I agreed to appear as a witness for the prosecution—then I'd be pardoned and granted my freedom. They asked if I understood the terms of the agreement, I nodded, and the questioning began.

"State your full name."

"Lolomura Blaise, sirs."

"From whence?"

"London, sirs."

"Know you Captain Edward Teach who goes by the name of Blackbeard?"

"Aye, sirs."

"How are you so acquainted?"

I took a huge breath and whispered, "I'm his wife." Shock

registered on every chalky cheek and someone tried not to splutter. Governor Spotswood probed further clarification saying, "His *wife?*"

"Aye, Your Excellency. His thirteenth, far as I know." The room dissolved in outrage as the men began mumbling to each other. I caught snippets of *Thirteen?* and *She's barely more than a child!* before the governor brought them all to order. After the room hushed he continued, "He forced himself upon you, I take it? Pressed you into a bigamous wedlock?"

I nodded and looked shamefully down at the floor. Spotswood's voice softened a notch and he suggested, "We would like you to tell us everything. In your own good time . . ."

And so I span the grandest tale you've ever ever heard, liberally peppered with almost half-truths. I told them I'd been captured by an East End gang who forced me to steal, then got caught red-handed and transported for seven years' labor. That I ended up nursing in Charles Towne but fled from William Cormac's house when his daughter tried to kill me with a knife (I showed them the wiggly scar wound as proof). I stowed away to Nassau and worked for a dressmaker called Pierre, who one day told me to take a flag he'd made to the docks and there I met a terrifying pirate called Captain Teach. I didn't know much about buccaneers so I failed to recognize the infamous Blackbeard. He was about to eat and told me to join him and I obediently sat down because he hadn't paid me yet. The captain ordered me to drink a tankard of rumfustian, and not being used to hard liquor I quickly grew giddy and woozy. Next thing I knew we'd set to sea and I'd been kidnapped to become the next Mrs. Teach—I even thought we'd had a proper ceremony—but later discovered such marriages were illegal. When I found out that Blackbeard's wives didn't last very long I started doctoring to the crew members hurt in battle, intentionally making myself indispensable. But once Teach decided to make his base in Bath Towne I knew my usefulness was at an end and so I took the first chance to escape. I got far as I could up the barrier islands and in desperation jumped into the sea to try to swim the inlet, but I fainted during the crossing and was fished out by a pilot boat and taken to Norfolk to heal with the Quakers. But soon as I heard His Excellency was trying to capture those sea villains I begged to be brought here to tell where he's hiding so the mangy dog might pay for his crimes.

My monologue met with utter silence as the wigs absorbed my colorful plight. Then, as the sighs and exclamations faded, the governor began another series of questions that were carefully recorded by the clerk. "How long since you left Nassau?"

"A good six months, sirs."

"Hmmm! And in all that time you saw no earlier opportunity to escape?"

I raised panicked eyes to the table and blubbered, "We hid from a storm at an ordinary in Beaufort . . . but he'd already buried one of his wives there! And when we stopped in Jamaica it was at a pirate camp . . . so I wouldn't have found any safety." My eyes started drumming up tears that delivered the appropriate effect.

Spotswood changed tack with the general consent of the room. He asked, "What can you tell us of Blackbeard's navy?"

"Well—up to Christmas he'd three ships and several hundred men but they disbanded when Governor Eden pardoned them. They'll not sail again until Easter. . . ."

"Where will they rally?"

"Ocracoke. There'll be a bonfire signal at midnight Good Friday."

Eager glances shot between the faces at the table before some-one said, "It's over eighty miles of island. We'd need a precise location. . . ."

"Fetch me a chart and I'll show you," I promised, knowing exactly where the monster hid his lair.

Then they asked me to name as many buccaneers as I could recall and their roles onboard ship. I was quizzed about weapons—especially the cannons—but I couldn't tell much about poundage or shot. So I described the swords and pistols and axes and gave a rough estimation of how many. One of the men sought specifics about the layout of the *Queen Anne's Revenge* and another wanted to know the daily routine, both on ship and on land. I was pumped about Bath Towne—where Teach might lodge and with whom he acquainted. Much time was spent discussing the captain's relationship with Governor Eden, and the men were particularly pleased when I confirmed the smuggling tunnel that led to his cellars. I was grilled for hours and hours, given some water, and then questioned further. At the end of the morning I'd to confirm the information as mine and write my name at the bottom of a curly paper.

Spotswood added in afterthought, "Did you ever sign the pirate's articles?" I shook my head. There was, fortunately, no official record of my compliance. So he spoke quietly round the back of his hand with his companions and then announced, "I have commissioned your pardon and a letter ensuring safe pas-sage out of the Colonies. . . . *All* past crimes are hereby absolved." I curtsied gratefully and moved forward to take the documents. But Spotswood raised a hand in the air that stayed me and added, "I shall sign both *when* Edward Teach is apprehended." *Oh no!* "In the meantime, you will return to the public gaol and await our further instruction." The clerk steered me from the room as sticky tears of frustration spilled from under my lashes.

I resided in that stinking place for a good ten months, and if it hadn't been for my special relationship with the keeper I'd have likely been deranged as that other poor soul incarcerated alongside. By day I sat in the filthy straw and listened to her mindless babble—she'd apparently refused to marry the old man her father selected and was therefore being punished for her disobedience—but at night I accompanied John Redwood, who liked to play chess and dominoes as much as to romp on his comfortable cot. He ensured I was able to wash and keep warm, that I ate proper food, and earned extra treats. Of course I could have bought a much better deal with my hidden gold but I realized if I wanted to escape with my loot it was vital to keep it a secret. So I relied on charitable women for castoffs and bread, and on the lusty desires of my keeper for everything else. And I actually grew to quite like the mournful John Redwood.

Then one sweltering night in May we were awoken by urgent rapping at the gaol door. Redwood came back with a messenger from the governor bidding me ride to Palace immediately. Now, as it turned out, Blackbeard had done the unthinkable—he'd reformed his navy—blockaded the harbor at Charles Towne—and was holding the folks there to ransom. Spotswood wanted my input on how to stop him and urgently filled me in on recent events. He explained, "My spies watched the Ocracoke Inlet at Easter and your information was sound—there was a signal to rally there, answered by all the outlaws who had lewdly squandered their ill-gotten riches." My expression must have questioned why they'd not been apprehended then and there because the governor quickly added, "We had no jurisdiction until they entered Virginian waters—unfortunately they sailed south toward Cuba." And he didn't need to add . . . there was no one who'd readily volunteered to take on the mighty Blackbeard.

"How many?" I inquired.

"A good two hundred. The flagship accompanied by two smaller vessels."

"That'll be the *Revenge* and *Adventure*. . . ."

"Commanded by . . . ?"

"Major Bonnet—if he's recovered enough to take the *Revenge* back from Israel Hands—and probably Owen Richards." Spotswood was scribbling scratchy notes as I talked.

"They anchored off the bar at Charles Towne three nights ago," the governor continued, "and speedily captured a ship bound for England, a tobacco barge, two pinks, and a brigantine— while the remaining eight vessels at harbor dare not leave for fear of being likewise accosted." I nodded sympathetically. "Trade has been completely disrupted and the inhabitants are understandably terrified. They have just endured a long and desperate war with the local savages and now find themselves infested by sea-robbers." He looked me sharply in the face and added, "The Carolinians have appealed to us for any assistance we can provide."

"Couldn't the Royal Navy take them?" I ventured.

The governor moved uncomfortably and replied, "We have sent a request for His Majesty's assistance, but I fear it will arrive too late."

My mind was whirling—I didn't know what was going on in Teach's tertiary head. "What are his demands?" I asked.

A puzzled look waved Spotswood's pudgy lips as he confided, "Apparently he wants a medicine chest filled with all the laudanum and mercury the town has available."

Now I understood. I said in a quiet tone, "Many of the crew suffer the Great Pox. If the buccaneers intend to put to sea they'll need a good supply. . . ." It went without saying that Blackbeard himself was infected. And all other assumptions fell likewise silent beneath the governor's hastily donned wig.

"What would you advise the good folks at Charles Towne?" he asked.

"Give him the medicine. . . ."

"He will not make further demands for gold or some-such?" I didn't think so if he'd already taken that many wealthy prizes off the bar. "And he'll not later plunder the town once his demands are met?" Not if he wanted the colonists to accept him as a gentleman. Spotswood considered my own responses and then indicated to leave. As the messenger led me out, the governor asked, "Have you been kept fairly at the gaol?" I shrugged and looked at the floor. "I will send you some extra comfort," he promised. And thereafter I received a flagon of flat ale each day.

My cunning husband did as anticipated and left the folks of Charles Towne unmolested once they'd conceded to his demands. From there the pirates sailed north up the coast, with their holds stuffed full of valuables the commodore had no intention of sharing with that many others. So having previously given each outlaw a chance to leave amicably, he now resorted to wilier tactics. Six days later we heard the *Queen Anne's Revenge* had run aground and been lost. Now some said this was an act of the Lord—and others that fate had intervened—but Teach knew this coast like the curves of my body and wouldn't never get carelessly stranded. Far as I could tell he'd switched all of the goods from the sinking ship to Hands's sloop, took on board his favorite crew of forty, tricked Bonnet to go ashore on some fool's errand, then marooned the rest of the men on one of the sandbanks. He straight thereafter brazenly surrendered to the governor of Carolina and obtained all legal rights to the spoils on the *Queen Anne's Revenge* (claiming the ship was a lawful prize acquired from the Spaniards). The now-wealthy citizen publicly married Mary Ormond with all due pomp and ceremony, trying to ingratiate himself with the fine folk of Bath Towne, quite unaware that Spotswood was closing in.

But the restless demon inside Edward Teach couldn't settle and soon he was once again pillaging the easy local trade routes. Now, so long as Eden received his share he turned a deaf ear to complaint, so the desperate planters appealed to the authorities in Virginia for some much-needed assistance, and in August two men-of-wars finally arrived from England, and Spotswood was able to formally issue a warrant for Blackbeard's arrest.

But everything came to a head that fateful September. First off, the buccaneers held a weeklong debauch on Ocracoke to entertain other notable villains, including the brutal Charles Vane and his quartermaster, John Rackham. The fishermen listened to the raucous carousing that drifted into the sweetness of night—watched oars and sailcloth come and go ferrying women across to the bacchanal—heard boasts of gambling, drinking, and fighting alongside the clink of silver—and sweated the moment they'd be apprehended and have to surrender their catches. The townsfolk gazed in dismay at the crackling bonfires, growing increasingly worried the pirates might strike a permanent base here. Spotswood received so many pleas to dispatch the King's Navy he set about hiring two sloops able to navigate the shallow inlets and creeks. Command would be given to brave Lieutenant Maynard, an experienced and determined officer who was well-respected by his marines, while an expedition of soldiers under Captain Ellis Brand were dispatched on horseback to trap the sea villain if he headed back to land. Meanwhile, Stede Bonnet had resumed his former piratical career and was captured during a fierce battle on the Cape Fear River by Colonel William Rhett. Spotswood immediately rode to Charles Towne to interrogate the prisoner to make sure his men had the most current information available. The trap was tensing to be sprung.

On the seventeenth of November Blackbeard gave a blasé glance at Maynard's sloops approaching the *Adventure* on the evening tide, and promptly set to drinking with the local turtle-fishermen. He must have known the navy had come for him, but was also aware they'd not risk engagement until morning. Now I'm sure you've all heard stories of who did what on that infamous day but this is how it was told to me by them that ought to best know. See, Maynard announced himself at first light by hoisting the royal colors, and as soon as he came within hailing distance, Teach toasted him back with a glass of liquor swearing, "I'll give no quarter nor take any from you!" Now Maynard had to draw up real close because his sloops had no cannon, and soon as they came into range the pirates fired a broadside, seriously disabling the *Jane* and wounding many of her company. Maynard's own sloop, *Ranger*, was slightly battered, but the cunning lieutenant ordered all his men below so the deck would seem deserted. The buccaneers fired stinkpots that splayed out belching smog, but because the crew was in the hold the fumes had little effect. Then Blackbeard led the charge to board, and when dozens of marines wielding swords and firing pistols surprised them, the commodore finally realized he'd fallen into ambush. A furious battle ensued with casualties falling like deadweights, and when eventually the two leaders met face-to-face each fired off his pistol. Teach missed the naval officer's chest but took a hit in the shoulder from Maynard's gun—which merely enraged the burly swashbuckler, who promptly drew his cutlass and sliced the officer's sword in twain. Blackbeard moved in for the kill slash but before his blade could touch the lieutenant's neck a Scottish marine crept up behind and sliced the buccaneer's throat. The king's men set upon the falling rogue, piercing and stabbing until the demon lay still in a puddle of gore. And they tell me Teach took five bullets—had over twenty gashes—when they viciously sawed his skull from his torso. They then threw his carcass into the bloody water (where the headless corpse swam round and round the boat before sinking into legend) and suspended his dripping head from the bowsprit as proof that the monster was dead. The nine surviving pirates were immediately arrested and set in shackles. Maynard sailed straight to Bath Towne so his wounded men could seek medical attention, then he rounded up those unfortunates of Teach's crew who happened to be ashore at the time of battle. These villains would immediately be sent to trial in the high hopes they'd all meet the hangman. The victorious *Ranger* then took Blackbeard's rotting face—now tied to the mast of his own captured vessel—back to Virginia to a riotous hero's welcome. And I was summoned to Hampton to give my final witness. I have to confess, though, I don't recall seeing you among the rabble, mister—and I'm surprised that you remember seeing me.

The severed head bobbed from the mast of the pirate sloop like a grisly lantern. Every one was whispering, *Is it him?* Of course, as soon as I saw the profile I knew the truth. I nodded to Governor Spotswood, then quickly slipped off to wrestle my own dark conscience. Later, when the pardon was safe in my possession, I boarded a schooner bound for Providence. My mind kept replaying something I'd heard in the crowd—that, when asked if his wife had the whereabouts of his treasure, Blackbeard supposedly replied, "Nobody but himself and the devil knew where it was and the longest liver should take all."

Well, I'd managed to outwit every one of those damned demons, and had plundered my own share of the infamous booty. So that was the end of that.

14

CHEST ON CHEST OF SPANISH GOLD

1718-1719

The voyage to Nassau was all plain sailing and, as I was traveling legally for once, I'd plenty of time to stare into the night-dark depths and take stock of my new situation. I felt proud having finally tugged fate with my own pull, and wished now to be able to plot my own course. Spotswood had finally upheld his end, granting me full pardon, safe passage, and enough time to carry out the careful preparations I'd dreamed up those long hours festering in prison. I was going to renegotiate Pierre's kind offer to set up an apothecary at his shop, wishful that I might now become a proper respectable citizen, maybe even a surgeon or doctor to the less-discerning residents of Nassau. So I told John Redwood I'd been well-paid for my Judas service—to explain the appearance of sudden gold—and he helped me acquire the necessary tools.

First off, I invested in a large medicine pannier containing bottles of every shape and hue that boasted a fold-out shelf in the lid to secure the smaller vials. These I filled with cinchona tree bark, laudanum, mercury, oil of peppermint, extract of licorice, rosewater syrup, camphor, oil of turpentine, may apple, snakeroot, ginseng, witch hazel, olive oil, alum, chamomile, powdered rhubarb, and linseed oil. I bought a hardwood mortar and pestle, some brass hook-end balance scales and weights, and three dreaded mercury syringes. John managed to find an old naval surgeon's kit with most of the instruments still functional so now I'd also got spatulas, knives, pincers, and tiny saws (even though I didn't yet know how to use them). Most everything else I could find on Providence, that marvelous place I'd call home.

Now, you'll likely find this strange coming from a gypsy, but I never put no faith in prophecy, dreams, and omens. I think Grandmother Vadoma was the last with any real gift and although Ma pretended to read palms she didn't have no more skill at dukkering than I did. Of course, I'd heard tell that a cat dream spelled deceit, the hunting of wolves meant danger, magpies revealed that your lover wasn't interested, and talking to the devil told of harm already done, yet the significance of a dead spouse's floating head never once entered the discussion.

But Blackbeard was repeatedly stalking my sleep, his hollow eyes melting my back to the hammock as I writhed to wake in a froth of panting sweat. Night after night his dripping face appeared before me until I dreaded closing my lashes because I knew that he was waiting. One time his lips seemed to accuse me, mouthing in disbelief the single cry of *You?* And I flinched beneath the hostile spittle and tried to squirm to safety. My calm head chanted he couldn't no longer hurt me but my wild heart swung like a rope in a gale that I feared would break through my ribs in absolute dread. So all day long I'd think about my departed husband—trying to recall what it was that had attracted—trying to remember the parts that were human. Back then I believed that I'd married two intertwined beings—Captain Edward Teach the charmer (charismatic, seductive, learned, and cultured, who knew the seas like a preacher his Bible)—and Blackbeard the pirate (cruel, brittle, rapacious, and evil, who understood fear like Satan his minions). What was the line that connected, divided? How did transformation occur? I carefully analyzed all past events and came to this sharp revelation.

Inside of Edward Teach lurked a powerful demon. For the most part it slept in his groin, but every now and then it would lift a scaly paw and poke his humors to baser action. It demanded whiskey and rum and wine and sherry and gin and brandy and ale. And with every gulp its body would bloat and its terrible force grow stronger. You could tell, in retrospect, when the monster took hold for the shaggy face would set in an icy state that no sense couldn't never penetrate. The lips would thin to a steely grimace. The eyes would flare like two raw coals staring in untamed aggression. And as the unholy spirit swelled to the host's empty brain—the only words heeded thereafter would be the venomous hiss from its itchy taunts. The demon moved Teach like a vacuous puppet, lusting for blood and souls, and when sated would gradually slink back to slumber. Then the buccaneer king would belch or vomit and gradually fade into weariness that overcame his eyelids like a blanket of thick, warm wool. This much I'd ascertained—but on turning my mind to the rest of the crew I wondered how many others were possessed of similar spirits?

* * *

The Nassau I now found had changed. Most of the bucca- neers who'd accepted the king's pardon were still maintain- ing the pretense, at least in public, while those who'd flagrantly thumbed the offer had left for calmer waters. Then news arrived that Edward Teach was vanquished and that Stede Bonnet had just faced a cowardly execution in Charles Towne. I'm not sure which death shook the ears more—the chopping down of the invincible Blackbeard—or the slaughter of the well-connected gentleman pirate. For if the Royal Navy could bravely outmatch the outsider, and brutally punish the insider, what chance was left for the regular swashbuckler? The whole town was bathed in a subdued disquiet I ain't never seen the likes of before.

I hailed one of the unemployed tars at the dockside to cart my trunks to Pierre's dress shop, and on opening the door the first sight to greet my eager eyes was the back of James Bonny's head bent over a table with chisel and hammer. I paid the carrier and quickly dismissed him the moment I recognized that mop of sandy hair. "Jim!" I squealed.

The young man turned at the call, and when he saw it was me a delighted grin cracked his face. He turned to hug me crying, "Hey up, Lola! By the stars . . . where'd you spring from?"

And that's how Anne discovered my return—wrapped in the warm embrace of her recently reconciled husband. She stood in the doorway and snarled, "Put that trollop down, Jim. You don't know where she's been. . . ."

I blushed and mumbled, "Hello, Annie." Then I disengaged myself from the welcoming arms and asked, "Where's Pierre?" I realized at that point that Jim and Anne must be here together again so I wasn't sure I'd be able to stay and set up shop alongside.

Anne sniggered at the plainness of my clothes but the smile died somewhat when she spotted the well-stocked tools of my trade. "Do you intend staying?" she inquired. I nodded. "Then you'll find Pierre at his whorehouse." She smirked mischievously and added, "I'm sure you can remember the way."

"Leave your stuff here with me, lass," Jim offered. "I promise to keep it safe." And as everything was securely padlocked I smiled my gratitude and set off to see what other tacky surprises lay in wait.

Mary Gee was quite beside herself when she recognized me in the tavern. "You coming back to work, Lola?" she asked hopefully.

I gave her a quick squeeze and said vaguely, "I'm looking for Pierre. Have you seen him?"

Mary pointed to my old room upstairs and whispered, "He's entertaining a special mate. Be down before long, though, love. Come have a drink on me." She poured us each a tankard of ale and filled me in on events complaining that, "When Rogers arrived at the start of the year there must have been nigh on two thousand pirates in town . . . and now look at it!"

"So tell me about this new gov'nor," I interrupted.

Mary replied, "He looks like a leathery dog in a fancy brown wig." She thought for a brief while and elaborated, "Got a crooked nose and a dimpled chin . . . and I'm told was wounded in the Pacific, which is why he walks with a limp."

Now, apparently news of the governor's arrival preceded him so the outlaws had already determined who would accept the pardon and who would fail to comply. Charles Vane gave Rogers an audacious welcome in the harbor, setting alight a blazing prize that tried to ram the official's ship. Then the pirate fired a volley of defiance before escaping to sea under banner of King

Death. Rogers was, however, greeted cordially by the rest of the island, who gave him an unexpectedly loyal parade. The governor immediately set up a council of nonpirates to organize proceedings and entrusted them with the commission of *Piracy Expelled, Commerce Restored*. So first, they decided to rebuild the decaying fortifications—but as initial volunteers were sparse—and rumor came of a Spanish invasion—martial law soon forced every able muscle. Meanwhile, Benjamin Hornigold had turned pirate hunter and was dispatched to capture his old shipmates, with a special interest on the head of the saucy Captain Vane. Not a few weeks hence he'd rounded up some other motley outlaws ripe for hanging, and a sober air now clung to the strangely quiet streets. I listened to Mary's chatter and was secretly glad that order had arrived, for now I could set up a real apothecary and be protected by the law. It seemed like we'd all been awarded a rare second chance.

Pierre came downstairs as I sat devouring a ploughman's pasty. His high-pitched throat called out, "*Chérie!* You have managed to escape the monster!" I grinned and nodded. I wiped my nose on the back of my hand and said, "Aye—and more besides. . . ."

He put his powdered arm across my shoulder, glided onto the next chair, signaled for a glass of wine and then declared, "I want to know *everything!*" So I gave my friends a potted account of my adventures, ending in my decision to run a legitimate business.

After I'd finished speaking there was a lengthy gap before Mary broke the tension. She said, "You might have a problem, love. . . ."

I felt a waft of concern and asked, "How so?"

She looked across at Pierre and he explained gently, "The governor has brought with him the barber-surgeon and the apothecary. The doctor trained at the London Guild and is also a surgeon of the mouth." I went cold and felt suddenly redundant.

"What about midwives . . . babies?" I stuttered, grasping at straws.

Mary answered, "Most still go to Nanny, the local ju-ju woman."

My thoughts started swimming madly round my skull. I didn't want to work back at the inn but my options were shrinking even as we spoke. Finally, Pierre said thoughtfully, "We will set you up *secretly* at the back of the shop. . . ."

"But who'd be my customers?" I huffed.

"Those wishing to avoid awkward questions," Mary said.

"And pirates who care not for pardons . . ." Pierre added. "After all, are you not the wife of the most famous rogue? They will trust you." I reddened with shame and bit my bottom lip as if carefully considering the proposition.

"What about Annie and Jim?" I inquired. It looked like they were both firmly ensconced at the shop.

I learned that even before Chidley Bayard moved on to his next mistress Anne had returned feisty as ever, and she'd spent long enough with high society to bring back several popular patterns and novel ideas. With her endorsement, Pierre's reputation had grown throughout the Bahamas and gentlewomen came from far-off plantations to be fitted for special events. Some came out of curiosity (or spite) just to meet the young woman who'd stabbed Maria Vargas in combat, and knocked out Kate Lawes's hoity front teeth, but most made the trek for the chance to outshine others because Pierre never repeated the exact same dress twice. Meanwhile, Jim had returned from a profitable cruise that supposedly hauled up chest upon chest of Spanish gold—and although he was one of a huge band of rogues his share was enough to buy back Anne's temporary affection. So he did odd jobs at the shop and inn, and had whittled a niche carving peg legs and wooden arms for mates who'd been disabled. They were renting their former room, and if we could all get along amicably Pierre said he'd give back my old lodging but I'd have to pay full going rates. I shot my patron a beaming grin and rising from the chair said, "Thanks. It's good to be back."

Pierre stood up and kissed both my cheeks before looking me up and down and declaring, "*Merde!* Let's get you out of the hideous skirt!" I laughed and followed his buoyant steps along the dusty street.

Now, two things immediately struck me as odd. First off, Jim had so diminished in Anne's eyes I couldn't never imagine them ever getting back together regardless of how many gold doubloons he managed to acquire. And second, Jim's fortune seemed to wax and wane as if he were being paid piecemeal instead of having plundered one big score. And it didn't take me long to figure things out. I kept myself quietly engrossed setting up my apothecary in the background, watching and waiting for some obvious revelation. One day I needed a chisel to open a small tea chest and, thinking it'd be all right to borrow one of Jim's, I rummaged through his tool sack. At the bottom was a strange smoky bottle stuffed with some kind of herbs ground in dirt and sealed with the gut of an animal. Curious, I took it to the window to see the contents more clearly. Jim walked into view just as I'd got my eye squashed to the side of the curio. I smiled and asked interestedly, "What on earth is this?"

Jim flew to my arm and wrenched the jar from my grip. "Mind your own bloody business. . . ." His eyes flashed a mixture of fury and fear.

Thinking it might be a new form of opium I pressed for more information. "What's in the jar?" I whispered.

The blanched face spun round to ensure we were alone and then he said guiltily, "A love potion . . ."

Now I thought he was pulling my leg so I giggled, "Get away with you!"

But the earnest set of his mouth convinced me more than his tongue had. "Where'd you get it?" I quizzed.

"Nanny's village. It's powerful gris-gris . . . to win Annie back."

I was shocked that Jim would resort to such witchcraft—but even more surprised that it seemed to be working. I lusted to know more and wouldn't let him go until he'd told me who it came from. Apparently he'd paid the local priestesses a live cockerel, twelve eggs, and four candles for a jar of ground herbs mixed with grave dust and glass blessed by the goddess Yemaya. Jim believed that as long as he had this prize in his possession he'd also have Anne close by. I didn't know quite what to make of it all but realized that some supernatural force, other than the promise of dubious blunt, must be holding his marriage together.

Jim's booty was common gossip, but I was sure Annie didn't know where it was hid or she'd have already taken it and fled. She kept pressing her husband to buy her a horse and he said that he would as soon as the time was ripe, which to me suggested he couldn't yet afford it. I noted that any coins he fished up came straight out his pocket, and that the velvet pouch seemed better stuffed following his Friday afternoon strolls. Then a couple of weeks after Christmas I finally learned the source—it seems that Jim was spying on his former mates and reporting them to the governor—that for every recalcitrant buccaneer fingered, James Bonny was richly rewarded. Annie was there the night he let slip his secret and the disgust on her lips was enough to ward off a cobra. See, they'd just come back from a night of heavy drinking where Anne had overheard tell of a plot on the governor's life. But Jim was far too curious wanting to know minute details—who was implicated and said what—who had observed the conspiracy?

"What's it matter to you?" she pointedly asked him.

And then his drunk-loosed tongue foolishly answered, "Rogers will pay most handsomely for sound information as this."

We both stared at him, chins tightening with new comprehension. "Damn your bastard mouth, Jim Bonny!" Annie slapped him full across the face. "You worthless black-hearted coward . . ." She paced back and forth as Jim stood nursing his scalding cheek. "Your infernal gob will get us all killed. . . ." Glaring straight into his eyes she roared, "Now what's to be done?"

"I . . . I won't say anything to Rogers if you think it unwise. . . ." he apologized.

"But there's some folks around here desperate for a return to the old times."

"Aye, we might have to warn him," Annie said thoughtfully. "We'll decide on the morrow." With that she turned and retired to bed, and Jim followed meekly upstairs.

But by noon next day Mrs. Bonny had already been received by Governor Rogers and confided of the conspiracy. He instantly offered to pay for her loyalty but the cunning young woman just smiled, murmuring she trusted to be remembered in the future. The rogue ringleaders were promptly arrested and publicly flogged for their insolence in the market that following Thursday, but as they consisted of scum and dross, the governor gave no further thought to their thwarted plot.

I opened my apothecary on St. Valentine's Day and drew sporadic custom from sailors arriving in port needing treatment straight off the vessels. Word spread rapidly from tar to tar because I was cheaper than the overworked town surgeons, didn't ask nothing dangerous, and was accredited with special Romany powers that'd helped me escape Blackbeard's clutches. I'd heard that the survivors at Ocracoke and Bath Towne were being tried in the next few weeks—and when word came that they'd danced for the hangman I was ever so very relieved. Then whispers were murmured that one of the rogues had been unexpectedly reprieved . . . but no one knew who or why.

For the time being, though, Annie ran the dress shop with Pierre and Jim delivered the orders. I kept to myself as much as possible and we managed to muddle along amidst the sparking tension. Then one sad Tuesday Mary Gee collapsed on the floor of the tavern. I was gutted to learn that Pierre sent first for the barber-surgeon instead of me, who immediately checked her blood flow and pronounced her dead. She'd apparently been struck by apoplexy and there was nothing could be done except mourn. We had a whip-round for cobs among the regulars, managing to give her a decent send-off, and in the interim confusion Jim volunteered to run the bar. And—just like that—James Bonny suddenly discovered his niche in life. He slid behind the Silk Ship pumps easy as well-tarred caulking, and was an instant pull with the punters. Anne encouraged this new enterprise because it got him out of her way and Pierre was pleased to have a man in charge who wouldn't take advantage of the girls. It also didn't hurt Jim's covert work as governor's snitch—you'd be amazed what folks let slip when they get inside a tankard! In fact, the arrangement was so amenable that Annie set her eye on buying the place if she could persuade Pierre to sell it to them in installments. And as her usual good luck would have it, opportunity swept in sooner than expected.

See, Pierre had ordered some exclusive black velvet from Paris that arrived on a French merchantman bound for Martinique.

When the *Calais* docked he was invited aboard to collect his bolt and was dazzled by the beautiful array of rare silks, velvets, calicos, lace, and taffeta that filled the hold from floor to rafters. It was a dressmaker's heaven. And Pierre cast covetous eyes and an open purse at the captain, but was firmly informed that all of the other treasure was already accounted for. That afternoon he bemoaned his fate to me and Anne—and as he waxed on and on about the gorgeous creations cramming his imagination a glint of possibility lit the black of Annie's eyes. "If the captain won't sell, then let's plunder it and be damned!" she said. And it didn't take much for Pierre's yearning desire to count him in. By the time Jim returned with the previous night's takings, a crude, delicious plot was brewing—and before we were fully sensible to the consequences, we'd been drawn inside Annie's scheme.

Now, I ain't kidding when I confess I couldn't stop giggling at the thought of our makeshift crew—but I also knew that when pressed I could be bold as any Anne Bonny for I'd not been Blackbeard's partner for nothing. I explained in the cold voice of memory that fear and surprise were our greatest weapons, and that if we put together a clever enough plan we'd get everything we demanded without shedding a ruby of our own blood. So we decided to prey on the superstitious watch as the vessel lay moored in darkness. First off, we thought to attack tomorrow at midnight as the moon would be at its zenith, knowing this was the vessel's last stop before Martinique so most of the tars would be wenching ashore, leaving only a skeleton crew. Then Annie rubbed up the details for her brassy scenario. We were going to take an abandoned wreck from the dark side of the bay and create a scene from nightmare with some grisly pre-arranged props. We'd disguise one of Pierre's dressmaker dummies as a shipwrecked maiden, then splay the tattered sails, deck, and doll in copious amounts of turtle's blood. The boat would drift into view with Anne fixed in a gory tableaux holding an axe above the dummy as if to chop off her head. I'd be in the water, the unseen force pushing the boat along, while Pierre and Jim (disguised as blood-drenched cutthroats) would creep up the gangplank and take the deck . . . but *that's* where our plan fell short. Neither of these two were convincing enough, and we also required someone else waiting with horse and trap to remove the booty. We tossed several suggestions that fell into silence before Pierre announced, "We must have the real buccaneer if we wish to instill real terror!" Six pairs of eyes focused on his lips. "I have a friend who might be of great assistance. He sailed with Charles Vane . . . and is here to accept the pardon."

"Who?" Jim asked, far too quickly.

Pierre gave him a disdainful glare, tapped the side of his nose, and mimed the lacing of his own lips. "Someone who can be totally trusted," was all he would say.

"What share will he demand?" Anne asked.

Pierre chuckled to himself and said lowly, "I think he will settle for the jacket of the finest calico."

"And I want the black velvet," Annie stated.

They all looked then to me so I shrugged with no set prize in mind, confident they'd treat me right. Pierre, of course, wanted everything but was prepared to barter for the most gorgeous goodies.

Then Jim, having no use for material, asked if credit could be set against his purchase of the Silk Ship Inn? Pierre thought carefully for the longest time before finally agreeing that his labor would suffice as the first of their spit-pledged payments.

"Jimmy will drive the trap," Pierre decided. "My friend and I will clear the deck, and we will all assist with unloading. . . ." He looked squarely at Anne and added, "But make sure you wash off the blood before you touch any of my cloth!" And so it was agreed.

Later that evening me and Annie went down to the dark side of the dock to find a suitable floating craft among all the abandoned wrecks. We picked out a small sailboat with a battered mast and the remnants of tatty sail flopping over a heavily charred boom, making careful note of how to get back there in tomorrow's dark. Jim had purchased several turtles from the local catchers and left them upside down on the apothecary floor for our return, and before midnight every part of our despicable plan had been carefully arranged. Just as we were clearing up the debris Pierre arrived with our anonymous accomplice. He ensured the doors were bolted and the shutters drawn tight, then announced with a flourish, "*Mesdames*, may I present to you my good friend Captain Jacques Rackham. . . ."

I took one look at the stranger—noted the flare in Annie's nostrils—and felt some part of earth tilt and shift.

The captain removed his feathered hat and swept us both a gracious bow. I was pleased that he spoke first to me, saying, "Mrs. Teach, I'll be bound—I was last with your husband near Bath Towne. My condolences . . ."

And while I smiled nervously at his pulsing, lithe frame Anne stepped forward with an extended hand. "Pleased to meet you, Cap'n" she cooed, "I'm . . ."

". . . Absolutely ravishing!" he offered. "You must be the lovely Anne I've heard so much about."

Pierre clapped his mate on the arm and said, "Enough with the flirtation! We have business to discuss. . . ." Then he cracked open a bottle of his finest brandy and we sat scheming into the dawn.

So what can I tell you about Jack Rackham? He was handsome enough to be beautiful yet rugged enough to be tough—was definitely one for the ladies but I could tell Pierre was enamored of him too. His black locks clustered in those natural swirls that the wigmakers couldn't never imitate. His chin was speckled with stubble and his stunning blue eyes could undress you to the bone. He looked every inch the experienced lover—the sensual kind to seduce not ravish—and yet his playful smile didn't fool me, who could detect the dangerous cougar that lurked hidden in that tomcat's purr. Now, you've probably heard rumor that Calico Jack was more fancy than pirate but let me tell you—it wasn't no coward who ever made quartermaster—and it wasn't no whelp who'd deposed the vicious Charles Vane.

But don't worry none if you've had the wrong impression because unless you were there too, how could you know? History is such a precarious truth and subject to change in the wake of mythologizing. For the Jack Rackham I knew was not the broken drunk of tawdry gossip . . . well, not in those early days anyway.

Our plan went exactly to order. I can only imagine the amazement of the *Calais* watch when they spotted the ghoulish boat glistening out of nightmare, splashed with gleaming blood, an axe-wielding hellion poised ready to dismember the maiden corpse. The ghost craft appeared to glide without oar or sail, drifting closer and closer to the shivering souls on the merchantman. A scream of panic burst from the darkness and one of the French crewmen burst into prayer mumbling, *"Notre Père qui es aux cieux . . ."*

Meantime, Jack and Pierre stormed the gangplank and had

their pistols raised point-blank range at four terrified sailors, shaking their heads in disbelief and still unable to take their eyes off the demonic scene ahead. The raiders, with powdered faces and hands, had skillfully drawn charcoal features that made them look like ghouls gamboling in outsized clothing. The youngest French tar screeched like a virgin. The other three were too confused to offer a resistance. Jack savagely gagged and tied up the prisoners while Pierre spoke harshly in their native language demanding the keys to the hold. Within minutes I managed to propel the craft alongside, then Anne snapped into action rowing round the stern toward the dock. Soon as Jim tied her off she washed her arms clean and scrambled aboard to help Jack and Pierre haul the cloth up on deck, as I hurriedly donned dry clothes. Then me and Jim ran the goods down the plank and threw them into the wagon. It was swift and exhilarating. It was daring and mad. Pierre also stole their good wine—he swore the best in the world came from France—and Jack took all of their nautical charts, which was force of habit for a sea dog. The whole operation was concluded within the hour so we dropped Jim back at the Silk Ship to avoid any suspicion falling in our direction. We soon lost Pierre in the thrill of his heavenly cloth but not before he'd opened one of the vintage bottles to toast our success. Jack washed the muck off his face, then came and entertained us ladies. A little later on he asked me if I'd heard the newly arrived news from Virginia. When I shrugged my face he leaned over and warned, "Israel Hands was reprieved at the final hour and, I've heard tell, is gunning for you to exact revenge. . . ."

I blanched and swallowed the rest of my wine with a gulp. But wanting to return the favor, I waited for Anne to move off and refill the cups, then whispered, "And you needs be wary of that wench—she's poison." Rackham flashed me a knowing smile and winked. I guess some fools just never listen. As we drank and chatted, the rush of excitement died away and I eventually dragged myself off to slumber—leaving Annie and Jack to forge the desperate bond that only the noose would sever.

Now I knew the very next morning that Anne Bonny had fallen for this pretty marauder who later boasted he'd taken her the same way he looted ships, "No time wasted, straight up alongside, every gun brought to play, and the prize boarded." By the end of the week she'd made Jim move into Mary's old room at the tavern and promptly took to flashing her new swashbuckler in public. Rackham swore to honor the king's pardon and then set about impressing his mistress with the shiny blunt she so delightfully helped him dispose of. And I was shocked by the change that came over this stony jade—I think for the first time, ever, she truly was in love. Gone were the spiteful snarls and the bored, angry huffing, the looks of disdain and the snide snippy under-breath comments. Instead we were treated to the long, glazed mooning, incessant bland chatter and constant keen smiles. I ain't kidding when I tell you this, Annie's face would physically glisten whenever Jack came anywhere near, her bosom would sheen with excitement, and she laughed so quick and so often I grew worried she'd wear out her throat. Of course, I don't know how Jack felt about his new lady but they both seemed to crave each other's approval. She devoured the glamour and excitement. And he seemed to savor the abandon and willing and dare. So I generally left them both to it and went about my own matters. Meanwhile, Jim was doing a roaring trade at the Silk Ship trying to work off his debt and frustration, and wisely steering well clear of his wife and her beau.

Two nights after we'd taken the *Calais* I walked back from the tavern unaccompanied and soon as I stepped through the doorway an ironlike hand shot across my mouth and twisted my neck as if wringing a chicken. I couldn't see or think or breathe but I managed to tear my mouth free and scream with all my guts. The rough arms pushed me violently across the room and kicked my stomach as I lay vibrating on the floor. A spark struck the tallow of a candle and in an instant I was staring at the weasel face of Israel Hands. He pulled up a chair and pinned me in place by stamping his boot on my hair. Then he showed off his only front tooth and snarled, "You always was trouble, you pox-riddled doxy." The passion in his venom made me gasp. "Thought you could take all that booty and not pay the piper, eh?" He slid out a knife and the candlelight licked its sleek edges. I realized that he'd got a bandage round his leg, and from the pose he adopted it looked like he'd perhaps lost a kneecap. But before I could spot any other weakness he was dragging me toward him by my locks like a fisherman hauling in nets. I slid involuntarily closer and closer, clamping my hand to my roots to protect the scalp. When my skull hit the chair leg the yanking ceased, but then I felt the knife cut a nick in my throat with the promise it would slice me a new smile. "Where's my blunt, bitch?"

I was moments away from an open vein and desperate to bide more time. I squealed, "In the box! The box . . ."

The blade grew sticky and I could feel my own juice sliding down my cleavage. Keeping my head speared on the tip of his weapon he wound my hair tight as it would go and tugged us both on our feet. I immediately turned, felt my head catch fire, and kicked him hard as I could in the shattered knee. He grunted in pain, and the moment there was slack I turned and pushed him backward against the chair. The pair of us fell into a wrestle of confusion but when I heard the weapon clatter to the floor I tussled to loose my locks from his grasp. The pirate seemed momentarily stunned but his fingers were groping to recover the knife. Then he sprang like a squirrel, twisting me over the base of the chair, his arm across my shoulders pinning me to the wooden seat. Hands whipped free his cord belt and bound my bleeding neck to the spokes. I now knelt at his mercy. "Where's this box then, darling?"

"In . . . in back. Under the table."

I watched from my disoriented viewpoint as he lit a lantern and hobbled through to the apothecary, making a futile attempt to release the rope at my throat. I heard curses and bumps as he bumbled around, and then the eventual rattle of the chest where I kept my wealth. "By the devil . . . locked!" he roared. I heard him stumping back. He needed the key I kept hidden on my person or it would take all night to saw through that padlock. Hands slid the chest onto the seat by my face and he grunted, "Open it." But I sensed that the instant I did he would kill me anyway. The light of the lantern cast a netherworld glow on the buccaneer's livid face. He pressed so close I could smell the rancid tooth and hear the hiss of anger rattling deep in the throat. "Open it, harlot!" To drive his point home the intruder pressed my left hand to the top of the box, splayed my palm flat, and sawed through the knuckle of my smallest finger with several brutal tugs of the blade. I screamed and then started shaking. He moved the knife to the next finger . . . knowing I'd never find future employment if I couldn't hold syringes or cocks. "Open it—or I'll cut 'em off one by one to your thumbs and then eat 'em up before you!" My wavering fingers rooted around in my bodice for the leather thong. As soon as it came into view Hands raised the knife and slit the key free.

By this point I was bloody and dizzy, the pain like a throbbing sting kicking inside of my temple so that I didn't really see what happened next. All I recall is a charging roar, a flush of light, and Pierre with the largest smoothing-iron flying through murky air. He hit Israel Hands so hard that a dull crack was followed by a bubbly groan and the pirate fell stunned to the floor.

"*Merde alors!* Who is this?" Pierre cried.

"Blackbeard's master, Israel Hands," I stuttered. "He . . . He came to kill me."

Pierre patted the top of my head, and then he picked up the splattered blade and cut my neck free. "Is he dead?" I asked hopefully.

Pierre pushed him gingerly with his foot and noted the gash to his skull. "*Non,*" he announced. "We will have to keep him docile."

I pushed myself slowly to my feet and staggered to the apothecary. After I'd bandaged my mangled stump and wrapped a neckerchief round my raw throat, I returned with enough laudanum to send Master Hands to his captain. Pierre suggested we make him look drunk, stuff him aboard the next craft bound for Europe, and hope he drowned in his vomit or met some otherwise lethal disaster. And to imply that he'd induced his own sorry state we carefully cleaned up his hair and covered the wound with an old beret. Then we doused his face with brandy, left the empty bottle in his waistcoat, and propped him up between us as we dragged him down to the docks.

A naval ship was preparing to leave on the tide. I shouted to the watch in my best doxy voice, "Ahoy, lads! I've brought you this from the Silk Ship—I think he's one of yours!"

At a time when press gangs would settle for anything no one questioned but that he was one of their own. "Bring him aboard, sweetheart." Pierre and I manhandled him onto the deck and dropped him against a water barrel. "Has he paid you yet?" some kind soul asked.

I pouted with my sore hand in my pocket and said, " 'Course not. Why do you think I'm here?" while Pierre mimed the role of disgruntled panderer, pacing and prodding and cursing.

One of the officers felt in Hands's pockets and said, "Sorry, love. You're out of luck."

"Story of my life . . ." I quipped as Pierre's stiff arm yanked me away.

Now, as it turned out, that ship was bound for England. And we hadn't actually killed Israel Hands. But the blow to his brain had rendered him stupid and—last I heard—he was begging the streets of London as a beaming fool.

So the remnants of Blackbeard's crew wouldn't be messing with me any further—and that was that.

15

———— ❧ ————

DARED THE KNIFE
AND TOOK THE BLADE

1719–1721

After our successful pillage of the *Calais* Anne took to piracy like a dog to a bitch's backside, snuffling for every opportunity, even though we almost got found out. See, the French captain lodged a formal complaint with Governor Rogers and when he mentioned the haul was of lavish cloth—and that the demons had spoken his native tongue—eyes naturally turned to Pierre. So almost a week later the governor escorted the captain and the four eyewitnesses to the dress shop. Pierre was bent over the bolt of black velvet, cutting out something for Annie. I was in the apothecary so I quickly locked away all telltale signs, then stood eavesdropping in the hallway. The captain strode over to the worktable and pointed to a cockerel-shape carved in the knob at the end of the velvet roll. He gave a confident snort before announcing, "Look! The coq of Gaul!"

Rogers bent over to examine the brand mark and asked, "Where did you get this cloth?"

Pierre acted suitably outraged and spluttered, "From the captain himself . . . I have the purchase note. . . ." He rummaged through the pullout draw. "Voilà!"

Rogers glanced at the document and stiffly nodded as Pierre began cussing his countrymen in French, waving at the other bolts stacked on the shelves and inviting them to check. Of course, all the prize cloth was carefully hidden throughout Pierre's other numerous establishments so no other cockerel rolls were unearthed, but in the midst of all the commotion Anne came down from her room alerted by the noise. The crewmen, however, did not recognize the actress without her gory makeup—but the governor knew well enough who she was and changed his tone when he saw her.

"Mrs. Bonny!" he exclaimed. "Pardon the intrusion but we are looking for merchandise recently stolen from the *Calais* by a cunning band of pirates."

"Really?" Anne asked innocently. "And why are you looking here?"

"The freebooters were French. They stole valuable materials and vintage wine."

"And whom, pray, is under suspicion?" she inquired in her best-polished voice.

Everyone looked toward the dressmaker.

"Oh, surely not Pierre!" Annie giggled. She moved over to the men and whispered behind her hand, "Does he look like a buccaneer to you?" She flopped her wrist in a mocking gesture for emphasis.

"Where were you six nights hence?" the captain asked the accused.

"He was with me," Anne announced, "at the Silk Ship Inn. My husband is landlord there and can verify what I say."

"At what hour did you leave?" the governor wanted to know.

"Friday? That was the night our assistant got bitten. . . ." She paused as if trying to remember all the details. "She had left to come home around midnight and swears—bless her heart—a ghost ship floated toward her across the bay. Now she's a wee bit simple and sensitive to such omens, and in the shock of it all swooned in a dead faint and lay unconscious on the ground. She came round to find a huge rat sat gnawing on her finger! Can you imagine?" Annie shuddered at the image. The men looked uncertainly at each other.

"Then what happened?" prompted Rogers.

"Pierre and I were playing checkers when the poor wench staggered back to the inn, eyes wide with terror and gibbering. So of course we immediately abandoned our game, brought her back here, and attended the wound. But it took hours to calm her down."

"So Monsieur Bouspeut was with you the whole evening?" Annie nodded. "And where is this assistant?" he demanded.

"Lola! Come here!" Annie yelled. I waited a minute and then appeared before them. "Show them your finger," she ordered. I obediently lifted my left hand to reveal the injured stump. The captain looked over at Rogers for guidance.

The governor nodded toward Anne and said, "I know this woman to be honest and trust her account." The Frenchmen conferred with each other, apologized for the misunderstanding, and left even more disoriented than when they'd arrived. I knew that having savored the wonderful tang of rash bravado, Mrs. Bonny would be needing that rush again soon.

At this point I'd have to say Jack and Anne were truly in love.

And Jim was pissed. Knowing Jim wanted to pay off his debt to Pierre, Rackham made an honorable divorce-by-purchase offer to buy Anne's freedom. The men had all but agreed on the price when the furious woman appeared on her own account and refused to be sold like an animal. Now, Jim was even more pissed—having neither wife nor money—and vowed to teach the adulteress some measure of respect. Meanwhile, Rackham was making quick raids against the Spanish—because his lover's expensive tastes were rapidly depleting his savings—sailing with various privateer captains in search of easy pickings. I could tell whenever Jack was back, though, because Anne's room would stay locked for days. And I knew that it was serious because she wasn't messing round with no one else.

Now Rackham had acquired the moniker "Calico Jack" because while other swashbucklers reveled in flaunting the forbidden fabrics of the nobler ranks (satins and silks and velvets), he preferred the Calcutta cottons fashioned for him by Pierre. Originally born in Bristol, he now worked out of Cuba, where it was rumored he had several women and a makeshift family of very good friends. I have to say in his defense that he was generous with money, cheery and popular, if at times a little lazy. But I could tell beneath all that flamboyance he was ruthless, just like his woman. See, last year Jack was Captain Vane's quartermaster but took command of their brigantine after Vane refused to engage with a French man-o'-war. Rackham accused Vane of cowardice so the crew voted to oust their former leader, and as the ensuing cruise was very profitable without the unnecessary cruelties so often accompanying Vane, Jack was readily confirmed the new captain until he took the pardon and switched to legal privateering.

On one of his visits Jack brought along George Fetherston.

George had toffee-rich eyes set in a rather determined face, and although he wasn't flashy like Rackham I found him quite entertaining. He was a big-boned man with slightly receding hair, a jovial, deep laugh, and a joke for every occasion. But what I liked best was his voice—he sang like a thoroughbred gypsy and was always the first to start off the shanties. When I told him I'd once been a dancer he kept asking me to demonstrate this step or that, and soon I'd revived the magic that I'd tried to suppress in my blood. See, ever since I'd lost my finger I thought men would find me repulsive—deformed—that I'd no chance of finding a partner. I was still lithe and nimble, with bigger breasts and shapelier calves, but at that silly age when just a crooked tooth could make all the sweet seem useless. But George made me feel the most special on earth, and for that I will always be grateful. We slid into a comfortable groove, and he ensured that I'd always got a steady supply of patients before that wondrous summer so abruptly ended, when James Bonny decided to have his revenge.

Of course, Jim waited until Rackham was absent before storming into Pierre's shop, grabbing Anne by the wrist, clicking a flintlock at her ribcage, and forcing her to appear before Woodes Rogers to answer a formal charge of adultery. The cuckolded husband was careful not to implicate himself in any nefarious doings as he lodged his self-righteous complaint against Calico Jack Rackham. The governor, while mindful of Annie's favor, agreed that a moral example needed to be set, so he ordered Mrs. Bonny to receive a dozen lashes in the marketplace after the coming Sunday service. Anne was so livid that her face turned scarlet—and if Jim saw the rage of her scowl his stomach must have tied in a monkey fist. For today was only Tuesday. . . . Who knew what Annie might do?

I didn't have to wait to find out. First off, she told me something else I hadn't known about Blackbeard. In the days before Teach fell out with Captain Jennings he'd built a watchtower on a hill outside of town with panoramic views of the waters. At the base his crew erected their tents and here, apparently, Blackbeard used to conduct business. She and Jack had walked there one day—and agreed that if ever she were in trouble when he was at sea she would light a bonfire on the peak. We set off to spark that signal, knowing there was a good chance it'd be spotted because we knew the privateers' favorite haunts. So we fed the snaking flames long into the night until sooty and hungry and weary. And as we sat staring past the crackling sparks Annie looked over at me and asked curtly, "Why are you helping me?"

I was stunned. I really couldn't answer. Perhaps because I was used to doing as she ordered? Or because I still owed her some years from my life? What is it that makes the kicked puppy return to its master knowing the welcome will spurn only further abuse? If anything, I guess it was habit—borne on the wind of an attachment my tongue couldn't never have named. I needed Annie's acceptance, and the more she withheld that approval the hungrier my craving became. She had some strange power over me, but why that worked so effectively I just didn't know. Maybe she was stronger and cleverer? Or did I submit in preference to remaining invisible? It seemed that any sense of self came refracted from my mistress . . . and I thought to have escaped that bind . . . but some things never change.

I shrugged my shoulders at Anne's strange question and stared at her ruby eyes burning in the firelight. "What's your plan then?" I asked.

"Devil be damned if I take their thrashing . . ." she hissed.

"If Rogers wants to mess with me I'll hit him where it hurts hardest!"

"In the crotch?" I assumed naively.

"In the pocket!" was her retort. Then she rapidly explained the scheme that had simmered to boiling. When Rackham returned they'd steal a sloop and go cruising together between here and Cuba. They'd specifically target vessels bound for Nassau and hold the whole of the island to ransom. As she grew more excited she gabbled that I could come too as surgeon (if I wanted to be with George—who would surely prefer to sail under his friend's flag), yet we'd have to pretend to be men when fighting or the victims wouldn't be scared. We'd need at least another eight or so hands, but once word got round that Rackham was looking, there'd be plenty of privateers who'd willingly recant their pardons. And they'd be crew enough who'd sail with women when they realized the hidden advantages. She planned to strike on Saturday—if Jack wasn't back then we'd sail out to meet him—and my job was to make Rackham's new flag, a skull above two crossed cutlasses. Annie seemed to have it all worked out and I wondered how long she'd been brewing this scheme.

By Wednesday morning the smoke at the watchtower had dwindled away to a single gray rope. I set to work on the flag, but Pierre ensured that Anne paid full for the cloth while fussing and flapping continually in the background. He said he would help with whatever was going down but didn't want to know the specifics. I wondered why he was so agitated, and thought perhaps he felt slighted having not been invited to join. But I didn't know how to broach the subject without giving away any secrets, and Annie hadn't once mentioned bringing him along. Meantime, she was busying recruiting among the drunks as they rolled from the sand into consciousness. Anne avoided those who frequented Jim's bar and those who'd never been outlaws, and stumbled upon one of Vane's old mates who agreed to stand vote as quartermaster. Assuming my consent, she bid them all meet up together in the apothecary Saturday noon, and if half of those approached showed willing we'd have enough to take down a sloop.

Thursday, after I'd finished my sewing, I was sent to market for fresh supplies. Pierre eventually agreed to get the rum and ale so we wouldn't need to go through Jim, and Annie worked down her list for everything else. In the afternoon we tried out our male disguises, packed personal trunks, and ensured we'd plenty of suitable medicines. Pierre brought over new barrels for water and under cover of darkness we filled these using buckets at the well. This work was thoroughly exhausting and by early evening we were fatigued enough for bed. I'd just slipped into a deep warm sleep when the sound of creaking footsteps crashed my senses. I raised my head to listen more clearly, and heard Anne's delighted cry to welcome Jack home. And suddenly it seemed like this crazy scheme might actually work—now someone who knew what they were doing was at the helm. I snorted my relief and rolled back into carefree surrender.

Friday morning was a whirl of comings and goings, whispering and plotting, checking and sorting and storing, but now that Jack was back, me and Pierre had lost all usefulness. That same day the pair took a walk on the sand to pick out a likely target— they were going after a sloop called *William*, which they'd turn into the *Revenge*. But while they were gone Pierre came purposefully into the apothecary, pulled up a chair, and asked me to sit down alongside. I could see something was bothering him.

"Lola, *ma chérie*," he said in a solemn tone, "do you intend going back like the dog to the vomit?" It hadn't really occurred to me I had a choice. So I nodded dumbly. Pierre looked at me with the saddest expression and quietly swore some French oath under his breath. He took both of my hands in his grasp, stared into my wavering eyes, and asked, "And how do you think all this . . . this . . . madness will end?" I hadn't thought. Not that far, anyway. So I looked away from his gaze. "It will end badly. . . ." he predicted. "Very very badly." Letting go with one hand he made a sign that indicated a noose around the neck. "Think of the great buccaneers—Kidd and Blackbeard and Vane and all the others—and then think of Anne and little Lola. Ahhh! My heart grows heavy from the worry. I have not slept well since the governor came to the shop. We were *this* close to being caught," he said, holding up two fingers a half inch apart. ". . . This close." His cheeks wobbled in frightful memory.

"Annie wants me to go," was all I could think to respond. "And George . . ." I started to say, but then thought better and stopped my tongue.

"George Fetherston?" he asked in dismay. "And what is this man to you?"

"I . . . I'm not sure yet," I answered. I nibbled my bottom lip in despair. Why was Pierre upsetting our plans? And why was he asking me questions I couldn't answer? "He's kind to me," I muttered. "I know that he likes me."

My friend patted my hands and explained, "Many men out there find you attractive. You deserve better than this . . . this inferior pirate."

I looked down at my mangled finger and turned to stare at the floor. Pierre followed my sight and realized how vanity had lowered all feeling of self-worth, so he squeezed my palms and said gently, "You do not have to go because you are told to. And why give your loyalty to Anne who cares nothing for you?"

"But she's my . . ." I tried to argue.

"She cares nothing," he repeated. "And this George will forget you the moment he sees another skirt." He paused for emphasis and then added, "I tell you this as the good friend—take care of your own life." I heard the words coming from his mouth but I couldn't accept their meaning. Something was obviously gnawing away at the Frenchman's thoughts. He finally let go of my hands and sat back on his chair looking at me with one arm flung over the back rail. "It is my deep regret that I said nothing to save you before. . . ."

"Before?" I mumbled. "When?"

"When you came with that terrible man from Blackbeard's ship." He reddened with anger, or embarrassment, and continued, "I was the coward not to warn you. I should have forbidden it!" He put his hand to his brow and pushed back his hair.

"Will Howard?" I asked. Then I gave a brief chuckle and said, "He was the best of the lot!" But I could see the regret on my friend's screwed-up brow. "It's not your fault, Pierre. I hold you no blame."

"Thank you, *chérie*," he whispered. I could see he was drowning in accountability but I hoped I'd put him at ease.

"So you think it's more dangerous now to get caught?" I asked. And recalling the flippant remarks I'd heard bandied around the inn, said boldly, "But who's to say we won't be granted another pardon?"

He held my eyes and said pointedly, "*Non.* I am sure there will be no more pardons. And I do not believe *you* should go."

"But they need a surgeon. . . ." I argued.

"And when they do not require nursing how do you think the men will use the women? You will not have Blackbeard's protection this voyage. . . ." And I started to see the cruise through masculine eyes. "I am frightened for you," he confessed. "I have the bad feeling . . . here . . . in my bones." He pointed to his chest and I was overwhelmed by his passionate concern. Pierre scratched his chin and then continued in his own unique manner by asking, "Lola—does the fish know that she is wet?"

"What?" I exclaimed. I didn't have no clue what he meant.

"The fish . . . she knows only the water around her, n'est-ce pas? You are the fish, Lola." I looked at him with a puzzled frown. He continued, "But there is another way through the water, where you do not have to ride the same wave as everyone else. You can swim. You can be like the salmon and move against the tide."

I've thought about that for the longest time ever after. Pierre was right. I didn't just have to accept what came at me—I could fight to burn my own trail instead of bobbing along on gray waters. I was young. I was healthy. I had experience and skills that few others possessed. I *could* make it on my own! So I sniffed back the wetness collecting at the base of my nose and whispered, "Thanks, Pierre. I . . ." But before I needed to embarrass myself further a customer came into the shop, and my friend left quietly to attend them.

Throughout the rest of that long afternoon I thought about how to break the news to Annie. I worked out a logical argument and then practiced saying the words out loud, over and over until I could remember the choicest sequence. Then I watched my face in the mirror-glass as my lips gave the same earnest speech to my own reflection. And finally I began repacking the medical supplies to ensure Jack's crew would have enough to last them to Cuba. But I worked myself up into a guilt-ridden frenzy before the lovers returned from the docks because this decision was the hardest I'd ever ever made, and although one-half of me wanted to cast myself loose, the other half wasn't sure I'd have guts enough to do it. Soon as they came back, Pierre herded them through to the apothecary, and after the dressmaker had locked the store he stood to watch my performance from the doorway. The glowing pair had obviously been drinking and were lusting for each other's flesh, so Anne appeared to listen with half attention and Jack kept trying to nuzzle his cheek on her chest. Pierre raised an eyebrow prompting me to begin and I launched straight into my monologue, never stopping to draw breath. When I ended with, "So I won't be coming with you," Jack finally raised his eyes long enough to look at me while Annie merely shrugged her shoulders and said, "Suit yourself." She squeezed Jack's buttocks and murmured something low. And as she led him away with a giggle he looked back over his shoulder and beamed like a moonstruck fool. Pierre raised his hands in silent applause and poured me a much welcomed glass of brandy. After all that worry I felt as if a dreadful weight had been lifted—like I'd shaken off some melancholy ballast that kept my soul from dancing.

Now, it turns out that same afternoon Anne had been aboard the *William* as the guest of Captain Francis Crane, who fancied he had just bought himself the finest doxy in Nassau. While she'd been entertaining the captain, Jack (under guise of eager procurer) had been casually spying on the crew from the waiting rowboat. Anne discovered that the *William* was planning to sail on Sunday's high tide so she promised to return on the morrow with a send-off the captain wouldn't never forget.

On Saturday morning Jack borrowed Pierre's wagon and packed up everything they'd be taking with them. The crew began arriving just after noon, and by early evening the formalities had been decided and the plan explained. Naturally there was much debate about taking a woman—but when they realized the whole scheme hinged on Anne's feminine wiles—and that she and Jack were financing the operation—they agreed to hold negative tongues until after the raid. If Annie performed well she'd be voted in. And if she failed, well, none would be going a-cruising anyway. The men agreed on Rackham as captain, Fetherston as master, and Corner for second-in-command and their quartermaster. I acted as scribe as they drew up articles and one by one they signed their marks—John Davis, John Howell, Patrick Carty, Thomas Earl, James Dobbin and Noah Hardwood. Jack knew the waters to Cuba so he agreed to navigate, and Anne would organize the galley. They joked she could act as powder monkey in battle—little knowing she'd fight more ruthlessly than their best. But when George asked if I'd be coming too I shook my head, said I'd help them to capture the sloop, though, and mumbled that I'd decided to stay in Nassau.

Now I'd once told Rackham about my escape on Ocracoke and he'd listened enough to remember that laudanum could take out the stoutest of stomachs. So he bought three vintage bottles of wine from Pierre and bid me carefully steam off the seals to doctor these in a similar fashion. I did such a good job he insisted on paying me for my part in their enterprise, cleverly persuading me to go aboard the *William* as Annie's friend—I'd carry the wine—and that way we could smuggle a pistol in the basket alongside the knives in our boots. Anne would get Captain Crane drunk, while I distracted the other tars, and soon as they were incapable, the pirates would take the deck. Pierre reluctantly agreed to wait with the trap until all the goods were safely stowed, then he and I would depart as the sloop hauled anchor. High tide was at three o'clock and the time was now two hours to midnight.

Jack took his crew and assembled them in various shadows along the docks. We'd shared a cold-meat supper with plenty of rum, enough to stir up the courage, then Pierre drove us to the beach and temporarily retired from view. The boatswain whistled us aboard with two fingers while Jack rowed back to the shore and began silently ferrying his men out to the anchored craft. The buccaneers secured themselves in the ropes, just out of view of the deck, balling for action like tigers about to maul. Annie went into Crane's cabin with one bottle of wine and left me to distribute the rest to the others. I saw several jack-tars milling around at first but after Corner's shadow slipped stealthily on deck, one by one they began sinking into darkness. I ended up dancing for three keen suitors and had to keep moving, as an excuse not to drink too much of the tainted wine. One of the sailors finally undid his breeches to boast of the treat he had waiting in store and waved his wood about, urging me to kiss it. Suddenly a strangled gurgle tore from deep belowdecks. I panicked, fumbled for the loaded flintlock in the basket, and stood waving the pistol at the three woozy men. "Kiss my arse, you mangy bastard! On your knees—all of you—if you value your life!" Three sets of pupils burst in comprehension. But no one moved. Then a cold flush of realization dribbled down my spine—I had only *one* bullet. They would know that.

Yet before their wavering minds could press any advantage Annie appeared by my side sprayed in the captain's blood, stabbing the air with a dripping knife and daring the next foolish challenge. I heard Jack's low signal, then the splash of bodies tossed overboard, and realized through a descending fog that the men on deck were now ours. We'd taken the *William!* Jack whispered urgent orders and Dobbin was dispatched to row over the stores. Everyone helped bring them aboard, and I waited anxiously to be taken ashore while suppressing the nauseous gurgling in my stomach. But as soon as the longboat was empty the new captain signaled it hauled up on deck. Corner barked orders, ropes started creaking, and I realized the sloop was edging into the tide. "Hey!" I said to George. "I need to get off. . . ."

He laughed, shook his head, and said, "Cap'n Jack's orders!" So I stumbled down to the cabin to reason with Anne, but she wasn't there.

Crane's butchered body was, though—draped awkwardly half on the bunk and half on the floor—the blood from his mangled throat congealing underneath him. Annie must have hacked numerous blows to fell the beast for telltale holes were pitted about his groin and chest, and I'd seen enough swashbuckler work to note an amateur hand at play. I heaved in disgust and brought up most of the supper I'd earlier enjoyed. But the opium had already leeched in my blood and I knew if it overpowered my will I'd be stuck in another long nightmare. The cabin had a water cask so I steadily gulped down as much as my gut would hold, and then opened the window to let out the smell. Without further thought I pushed a trunk to the opening and wiggled myself in the gap. The water was probably six feet below but I thought if I slid down the stern I could ease in like an alligator. So I crawled, hand over hand down the wood, and when I felt the water embrace me I kicked off and headed for shore. No one heard my plop. No one missed my presence. I struck out with long, determined strokes, praying against hope that Pierre would wait. He did. I felt the grab of my dress as he struggled to haul me in, then the joggle of horse hooves wobbling me home, then the hot milk he spooned in my mouth to warm me. I awoke around noon in a chair by the fire with a head aching so hard I thought I'd been hit by a boom. "Did they make it?" was the first thought that came into clarity.

Pierre gave a serious nod and said, *"Oui."* I exhaled loudly and realized that I too was finally free.

*   *   *

You've no doubt heard the rest of the legend—how they bloodied the seas for more than a year—how coincidence sent them Mary Reed—how Captain Barnet captured them drunk? But that's for the telling of another day or other tongues. As for me . . . I try to think kindly of Annie. Rackham's body was put in the gibbet after execution and strung from the rocks at the Cay that now bears his name. I heard Anne was pregnant and pleaded her belly at trial, but I don't think she ever hanged . . . she just fell off the edge of our world and into future folklore. It's rumored her father secured a release and married her off to a Carolina planter, but whether that's true or not I shan't say. Jim Bonny, as it happened, tattled one too many times and last year was found with his throat slit out back. So Pierre resumed former ownership of the Silk Ship and I help out when it's busy.

There is something about me, ain't there? You noticed the moment your eyes grew used to the dingy light of the tavern. And you came here, like everyone who struts these worn boards, for tattle of Anne Bonny and pirates. Well, I trust your curiosity has been sated as much as my thirst, Mr. Defoe. Or should I address you as Captain Johnson? But, pray, sir, take pains that your published account contains nary a mention of Lolomura Blaise. . . .

And I really can't tell you too much more now. So that—as they say—is that.

ACKNOWLEDGMENTS

Thank you to all the family and friends, press-ganged aboard the pirate life, who have accompanied my many escapades: Heather Unwin was there when I first found inspiration in Nassau—Steve and Symon Perriman sailed alongside to Jamaica, Hispaniola, the Spanish Main, and the Carolinas—Tricia Clark, my mate in Beaufort, also signed on for the Mansfield Plantation trip—Valerae Hurley explored Charleston with me—Michel and Bryan Faliero gave their kind Southern hospitality—Sarah Green and Eunice Brezicki shared their expertise at the Latta Plantation—Matt and Karen Clauss enabled the voodoo experience in New Orleans— and David Banks and Patty Cardillo were part of the gang bound for Mexico.

My gratitude goes to Scottish and maritime historian Dr. Eric J. Graham for casting his well-seasoned salty eye over the technical details of the book. Any remaining errors are, of course, entirely mine. Also to the following folks, who have aided in the research process: Kathryn Green at the Mansfield Plantation in South Carolina—Gilles and Betty Cloutier for their offer of assistance at the Hammock House in Beaufort—and the friendly staff at the Beaufort Historic Site, Beaufort Maritime Museum, and the Latta Plantation. Thanks also to Matthew Godwin of the Crowe Law Firm for his legal advice in Beaufort.

Finally, a very special acknowledgment to my chief crew members: Symon Perriman at Microsoft—for all manner of computer assistance; Vangie Schlesinger—for her keen reading and foreign language skills; Ann Collette at the Helen Rees Agency—my wonderfully efficient and supportive advocate; and Emily Rapoport at Berkley—whose fine editorial advice helped me navigate the dark waters of publication.

It's been a mighty fine adventure sailing with you all!

Printed in the United States
by Baker & Taylor Publisher Services